Enjoy Reading

Marilou Gompf

2008

THE CARMELO DIARIES

THE CARMELO DIARIES

A California Saga

Marilou Tomblin

iUniverse, Inc.
New York Lincoln Shanghai

The Carmelo Diaries
A California Saga

iUniverse, Inc.

For information address:
iUniverse, Inc.
2021 Pine Lake Road, Suite 100
Lincoln, NE 68512
www.iuniverse.com

While the geography, locations, and name of historic people are authentic, the stories and characters in this novel are fiction.
Any similarity to persons, living or dead, is coincidental.
Cover Photo by Tommy Tomblin

ISBN: 0-595-29062-0

Printed in the United States of America

Dedicated to María Rael Nowell, whose Spanish family ancestors came to New Mexico in 1692 and whose father, Juan Bautista Real, was my Spanish professor at Stanford University. María read this novel and complimented the parts that tell about Spanish colonial life and the influence it had on her own life. She was a beautiful, talented, professional storyteller, and a totally kind person as well as a lifelong friend.

Acknowledgments

I wish to express my appreciation to my patient husband, Tommy, who shares my passion for the Central California coastal country where we live. A special recognition goes to my neighbors and friends of thirty years, Dorothy and Sidney Kay. They read every metamorphosis of this novel and gave me good advice. I wish to thank my very dear friends, Ione K. Miller and Patricia M. Scott, who read some of the first versions of the novel and gave me suggestions. I am pleased that my daughter, Laurie Rockstad, and sons, Doug Dyer, and Glenn Tomblin, encouraged me to go forward with the publication of the novel.

I wish to acknowledge my professional editor, Roberta J Buland, West Hartford, Connecticut, who taught me to consult English grammar and composition books so that I could relearn the art of punctuation. I also want to thank Marilynn Forrest, Fairbanks Alaska, who so loved my characters that she helped me bring them to life.

I appreciate the prodigious quantity of preserved adobes and public buildings from the Mexican era that exist in Monterey and San Benito counties. Many can be visited almost every day of the year, and others are opened on special occasions for touring. The Missions San Cárlos de Borromeo and San Juan Bautista have been restored and are open for daily mass. I enjoyed reading books about California in the Harrison Memorial Library of Carmel, and I am thankful that I own a collection of some sixty books and pamphlets about California lore and history. My thanks as well to the rarely acknowledged native population who lived within small tribal groups in California and who subsisted off the land. I wrote the historical part of this book from a woman's point of view, because women were a vital part of the early civilization here, and yet they are so rarely mentioned in any list of pioneers.

I salute all who were born in California and those who have come and stayed to participate and live in this land of reality and mystique. This book is written for you.

PROLOGUE

▼

The principal characters of this novel are fictitious; however, the buildings and geographical locations exist even now, in the twenty-first century. Many of the public buildings and private homes described in the novel can be visited in Monterey, San Benito counties, and in San Francisco. Several historic personages are depicted, such as Thomas and Rachel Larkin, Mariano Guadelupe Vallejo, John C. Frémont, John A. Sutter, John Rogers Cooper and Encarnacion Vallejo de Cooper, and several Mexican governors of California.

El Rancho del Rio Carmelo, a figment of my imagination, is formed from parcels of formerly unoccupied Mexican land grants in the tidal basin and headlands of the Carmel River. The ranch in the story occupied both sides of the Carmel River and much of the land on the south side of the Carmel River that flows from the east, through mountainous countryside to the Pacific Ocean. Vast herds of cattle grazed on either side of the river and on the low foothills of the Santa Lucia Mountains. My husband and I have a home, located between the foothills and the shore of Carmel Bay, and we are privileged to know all the seasons and weather vagaries of the region. This land is the true inspiration of the novel.

The name, California was inspired by a sixteenth century Spanish romance novel, in which Queen *Calafia,* ruled over a mythical island with that name. It was first bestowed on the peninsula of Baja California. When Captain Juan Rodríguez Cabrillo made a voyage north from Mexico in 1542, he discovered what is now San Diego Harbor, and he named this land, Alta California. Captain Cabrillo sailed in search of gold and a fabled northern waterway; however, this became a disastrous journey with many delays of sailing dates due to strong winter storms. Cabrillo died before his ships returned to Mexico.

Alta California was not visited again until 1602, when Captain Sebastían Vizcaíno reached San Diego Harbor. His ship sailed north until they reached a river near the coastal mountains of what is now called central California. This was on the feast day of Santa Lucia, and Vizcaíno named the mountain range after the saint. The river was named *Carmelo* in honor of the Carmelite friars, who accompanied the expedition. I thank Captain Vizcaíno for his enthusiastic descriptions of the central coast of California as it encouraged more voyages of discovery.

Alta California was not colonized until 1769 when Spain thought this venture would strengthen their rights to the territories north of Baja California. Gaspar de Portolá led a land expedition from Loreto, Mexico to Alta California. By plan, Father Junípero Serra with a small group of Franciscan friars arrived from Mexico by ship and proceeded on land to establish Christian missions. Without the influence of these sea captains, soldiers, missionaries, and men and women who made Alta California their home, this story would never have been fabricated.

CHAPTER 1

▼

January 26, 2000. Pebble Beach, California.

A sudden cacophony of shrill sounds startled the sleepy desk attendant at The Retreat, a five-star hotel near the famous Pebble Beach golf links. He recognized the intrusive blasts as belonging to a burglar alarm. Knowing that they emanated from one of the shops in the vicinity, he called the Monterey County Sheriff. Two officers arrived at the hotel and followed the noise to the door of a glass-walled gazebo that housed The Old Booktique. The store had been trashed, and it seemed that a burglary had occurred. The owner was called and summoned to the scene.

It was five AM when Rita and Mike Minetti received a shocking telephone call. It was a summons to the bookshop. After they dressed quickly, Rita put a warm jumpsuit on their small daughter, Carmelita, and Mike drove them slowly from their home in Carmel to Pebble Beach. The fog was thick and the lace lichen hanging from the oaks added to the surreal atmosphere of the Del Monte Forest in the early morning. Relieved to have Mike driving, Rita nervously patted the hand of her little girl, who was almost asleep in her car seat. Rita saw shadowy figures moving inside The Old Booktique, and headlights of the patrol cars cast an eerie glow through the fog. She shivered.

After they parked, Mike quickly walked toward an approaching officer, while Rita and Carmelita followed along. As they drew closer, they saw the shop in disarray. Books were thrown about everywhere, and chairs were overturned. Mike picked up Carmelita while Rita approached a woman officer of uncertain age, who said, "I'm Officer Jenkins. May I see your identification, please?"

"I'm the owner of The Old Booktiques, Rita replied while she unzipped the inner compartment of a large leather bag and handed a driver's license to the officer. "We have a good security system. The safe has a separate alarm."

"The building alarm was deactivated, and it was the one on your safe that went off. You may look around, but do not touch anything. We need to go over every inch for fingerprints."

Rita went directly to the mahogany bar. There she saw the small refrigerator was disconnected and shoved out from the wall. The safe behind it was open and seemed empty. Soon she was on her hands and knees.

"*The Carmelo Diaries*," she gasped. "They were in the safe, and now they are gone. They are the original ones and are very valuable."

"And who knows that?" The officer asked.

"Several people," Rita sighed.

"Family?"

"Yes. I inherited those diaries from my grandmother, Clara Torelli."

Officer Jenkins had an aura of bland professionalism, and in a tone of boredom she said, "So?"

"*The Carmelo Diaries* were written in Spanish by Clarita de Segovia. She was born near here almost two hundred years ago."

As the officer did not seem to be paying much attention to what Rita said, Mike, who had been observing and listening while holding on to Carmelita, walked up to Rita and gently touched her shoulder.

"The *Diaries* are very valuable. They are the only known diaries written in Spanish by a woman of that era. My wife has an offer to do a TV documentary based on the story told by *The Diaries.*"

"We appreciate your information, Mr. Minetti," said another officer who had joined the group. "However, we have our procedures. We'll let you know what we want from you. Right now you'd better go home and have some breakfast. We'll let you know when you can come back to your shop."

"I run a business here. I have orders to fill today," Rita protested.

"We're sealing the building. No one can be here except our personnel."

Daylight was approaching as the Minetti family walked back to the car. They felt exhausted and somewhat disoriented, as if they had been up all night. A third sheriff's car arrived and a tall, lean officer alighted and strided up to Mike.

"I am Captain Lewis. When I arrived, one of my officers told me your wife said someone in the family could have taken *The Diaries*. Give us names of people in your family whom we might need to interview."

"I don't think that Rita said quite that. She merely answered a question about who would know the value of *The Diaries*. She comes from a large family. There were over a hundred invited to her grandmother's ninetieth birthday party."

"When did her grandmother die?"

"Two years ago."

"Are there any family feuds?"

Rita entered the conversation again. "My little girl is an ninth generation Californian. There are so many in our family that we barely know each other."

Captain Lewis looked Rita up and down. Mike did not fail to notice. "Is there anyone you suspect?" The captain continued.

Mike stepped back a little and gave the officer an overt appraisal.

"My child needs to go home for breakfast. Let us know when we can return to the shop," Rita said. Mike held Carmelita's hand, and they all walked back to the car.

When Carmelita was buckled in, she gave her mother a penetrating look. "Why did we have to go to your store?" Carmelita had talked in sentences since she was two years old.

"The sheriff woke us up and told us to meet him at The Old Booktique."

"It was messy," she said with authority

"Yes, it was. We're almost home now and we will eat," Rita assured her.

Carmelita tugged at her knitted blue cap, and out tumbled her soft tawny hair that had a reddish cast in the early morning sunlight. Her mahogany eyes gleamed, and her cheeks were a rosy glow. "Can I have pancakes?"

Rita patted her small hand. "Maybe."

"I'll cook some pancakes," Mike announced as soon as they arrived at their home, which was located on a high bluff above the town. "Mommy needs to go to her office and work until we call her for breakfast."

"Daddy, I need you to help me put my animals in the ark." Carmelita answered in definite tones.

"I'll help you get started, Mike said as he sat on the floor with Carmelita. "Then I'm going to mix up the pancakes."

Rita went upstairs to her office. While sitting at her desk, she immediately noticed that something was missing. "Mike," she called downstairs. "Can you come up to my office, right now?"

As soon as she saw him, she said, "I think someone was sitting at my desk this morning. I feel like Goldilocks in the three bears story. Maybe someone was looking through this pile of papers. Was it you?"

"I wouldn't dare move anything in here," he laughed and he drew her close to him. "Just look the room over, but don't touch anything. If you really think someone has been here, we'll call the Carmel police and have them check for fingerprints."

"Oh, Mike, this is awful of me," Rita sighed. "I shouldn't think the worst. Don't call the police. I don't want them in our house right now. It wouldn't be good for Carmelita."

Mike looked at the troubled face of his wife. She was not her usual self. Her face was often animated when she laughed at his jokes, and she liked to toss her auburn hair in excitement. He was fifteen years older than she, and he always marveled at her enthusiasm and optimism. Now she was serious. "Were the Spanish diaries in that safe?" he asked as he gently rubbed her shoulders and neck. Rita was still seated at her desk.

"Yes, the ones Clarita de Segovia started in 1827. She wrote on vellum."

"I remember now. She started writing in a journal when she was fifteen and was forced to marry a complete stranger. Aunt Clara used to tell us the story," Mike said.

"Clarita continued to write about her life even after she became the wife of Felipe Vargas and lived on his ranch near the Mission San Juan Bautista."

"How many diaries are there?" Mike looked at her and noticed the downturn of her face and continued. "Were they all together?"

"There were three early diaries that have always been called *The Carmelo Diaries* by the family. They were written in Spanish. Grandmother Clara told me there were important differences between the photocopy that she gave me and the Spanish originals."

"A translation is not an exact copy. Maybe there are differences in wording," Mike commented.

"Clara also alluded to the lost Vargas family jewels. At the time I did not ask her what she meant. I think I should start reading all the diaries right away. That includes the journals where her granddaughter tells of Clarita's later life in San Francisco.

"Why weren't all the diaries together?"

"All the diaries were together until last week. I took *The Carmelo Dairies* to the shop, because I wanted to show them to Dave Goldman."

Mike looked puzzled. "Ah," he intoned. "He's the guy who might make a docudrama about early California." Mike put his arm around Rita and gave her a kiss. She relaxed a little. "Who do you think would want *The Diaries*?"

"Lots of people" Rita admitted. Grandmother Clara told Claritia's story to many people in her last years."

"Why don't you have a photocopy of *The Carmelo Diaries*?"

"It is almost impossible to Xerox those old diary pages. They are too fragile. Mr. Goldman is planning to see me next week when he comes to watch the Pro-Am Golf Tournament Pebble Beach. I was going to show the books to him."

"So this Dave Goldman knows about *The Diaries*?"

"Yes. A friend of our family, Shana Tyrone, had often heard Clara tell her stories. She is mildly interested in using the story in the diaries for a TV drama. When I told her I wanted to do something with *The Diaries* right now, she told me about Dave Goldman, and I contacted him."

"Do you think your grandmother wanted you to sell *The Diaries*?"

"I think she had plans for *The Diaries*, but it was too late in her life. She definitely wanted me to do something with them. She was always trying to make things happen. You know, Mike, she always wanted us to get married."

"Probably."

"She often reminded me that you were a cousin only by marriage."

"When did she tell you that?"

"Oh, I don't remember. I never liked the way she manipulated the lives of my parents. At the time that my father wanted a divorce, she made it impossible, mostly by loaning him money."

Mike was not listening to the story about Rita's family. "So exactly when did she tell you to marry me?" He asked.

"Remember about five years ago when I told her that you had driven me home from the Shore Club on that really stormy night?"

"Yes, I remember it well," Mike smiled.

"That's when she told me to think about marrying you."

"And what did you answer?"

Rita gave a knowing glance. "I told Grandmother that you were just a good friend who would give anybody a lift to their home on a rainy night."

Mike laughed. "I told you she was a smart lady. After Gloria died, Clara called to tell me she didn't want me stepping out with any of the ladies who asked me to take them to the Commodore's Ball. Then she told me to make sure that I dropped into your new shop. After that conversation I was always thinking up ways to ask you out. I was concerned about the difference in our ages."

"I thought it was peculiar that you were one of the first persons to come into my shop and buy a book?"

"Now you know that my favorite reading is the sports section of the paper." They both laughed. "Do you remember how we met?" Mike said.

"Yes, at a family wedding."

"I think I fell in love with you then."

"I knew you were married, and I thought it was your family duty to dance with me. I was excited about dancing in the grand ballroom of the Fairmont Hotel."

"I was captivated with you because you were just in love with life."

"I was told you were one of my new cousins by marriage. I remember you were very nice to me and told me that I looked pretty. You rascal."

"Where's Carmelita?"

"She's playing in her room."

"Do you think she might take a nap?"

"We were all up pretty early. I'll put her in her bed with her favorite bear."

"I'll see you in our bedroom," Mike whispered. "I hope she'll take a long nap."

CHAPTER 2

▼

This is the copy of the first pages of *The Carmelo Diaries*. It begins with a preface written by Grandmother Clara.

"The Carmelo Diaries were written in Spanish with an educated, flourishing penmanship. Clarita Isabel de Segovia was taught to read and write by her mother, María Isabel, a native of Spain, who had been sent to California because her family feared that Napoleon's soldiers would invade Castile. The first Diary was written on thick vellum pages that were sewn into a cowhide leather cover. The wording in the translation sometimes sounds awkward and it includes some of Clarita's Spanish words. The explanation of the Spanish words in common usage in early Alta California can be found in the glossary."

"June 15, 1827. Tomorrow is my wedding day. It is the day that every woman expects to be the happiest in her life. I think it will be my worst. This is the reason I am writing this book of days. Very few people in Monterey can read. It is for my grandchildren to read.

"Yes, I have received bolts of silk from a ship moored in the bay. My husband-to-be gave me a brooch of pearls and other jewelry when our banns were read in church. After the wedding mass at the Mission San Cárlos, we will ride to Monterey in a triumphal procession, and Papa will provide for a large *fiesta* and three nights of dancing, but I will be miserable. I do not know Don Felipe. I have only seen him once, and he is almost the age of my father. He is not even from Spain. He is from Mexico and a good friend of governor José María Echeandía.

Since Alta California is no longer under the protection of Spain, Papa says I will be safer when I am the Doña of the Vargas *hacienda*. I told him that I did not want to marry yet. I am fifteen and can easily wait a year for another suitor. Papa was furious with me and has kept me in a room on the upper floor. He has put guards at the door every night and only my stepmother, Esperanza, is allowed to bring me food and to take me out for a walk in the courtyard.

"I have cried each day. Yesterday I rode with Papa on his horse to the mission for a blessing before the marriage. When I stepped inside the chapel, it took a minute before my eyes adjusted to the darkness. Then I saw Don Felipe's brother, Diego, come out of the shadows, and when I started to kneel and pray, he knelt at my side and started whispering. 'You will be a beautiful bride, Clarita Isabel. Never fear that my brother is so old. I will see that you are with child in your first year of marriage. My wife is barren, but I know that I can give you children.'

"I was terrified. He was telling me that he would make me commit a mortal sin as soon as I was married. I already knew that Don Diego was a man to avoid. It has been told that he has his way with the Indian girls of his ranch.

"'My saintly mother taught me to be faithful in marriage,' I whispered.

"'*Ma Paloma*,' he said softly. Then he took my hand, held it tightly, and he caressed my hand.' You do not understand that you need a strong man like me to protect you.' He kissed my hand and left quickly.

"After the year of 1822 many things became different in Alta California, and I do not understand much about it. First, the flag of Spain was lowered at the *Presidio*, and Papa said that Alta California was the object of suspicion in Mexico. It is well-known that the Fathers of Saint Francis are loyal to Spain. There has been talk about closing the missions and giving their lands to the new governors that Mexico sends to us. Papa says his Rancho Carmelo was a grant from the king of Spain and that he might lose it. During this time my sweet mother died and I am left without her presence, although I pray to her every day. Papa sent my brother, Estéban, to Spain. He will study to be a priest.

"Three years ago, I rescued a young man from the sea. He calls himself 'O'Farol, El Yanqui.' He had nowhere to live, so he came to live and work at our ranch. I was happy to be his friend as I was lonely after my mother died. I helped him learn to speak our language. He stayed at our ranch three years, but Papa sent him away because he asked me to dance at the wedding of our cousin, Consuelo. Soon after, Papa told me I must marry, and that Don Felipe had asked for my hand. We were invited to a grand *fiesta* at his hacienda. It is almost a day's ride from here. It was then that he presented me a beautiful pair of dancing shoes that had just come from the ship in the estuary. He spoke only a few words to me. When I talked to Papa about my fears, he told me that the best marriages were the ones that were arranged. He was not acquainted with my mother until after the marriage ceremony. When I returned home, I told him that I did not want to marry anyone. I said I wanted to go to Spain and be a nun. Papa said it was too late for that, and he became very angry. Esperanza told me that I had the good fortune to marry a rich man and that I could help our family because Don Felipe has the ear of the Mexican governor. That was the first time that I knew the lands of Rancho Carmelo were tied to the future of the Mission San Cárlos.

"Once more I told Papa that I wanted to be a sister of the church, and it was then he led me to a room upstairs that had once been a storehouse and told me that it would be my bedroom until I married. I do not believe that he knows that the brother of Don Felipe has plans for my life as soon as I am a member of the Vargas family.

"I have heard nothing from O'*Farol* since he was told to leave, but Cousin Consuelo tells me that she has seen him in Monterey. He works for a man named Cooper, who was a sea captain but now sells things from the ships' stores to the people of Monterey. Soon this man is going to marry Encarnacion Vallejo. Earlier this year he was baptized as Juan Bautista Rogers Cooper in the San Cárlos Chapel at the *Presidio*. He needs to be of the Catholic faith to marry Encarnacion Vallejo, who is eighteen and comes from an important family of Alta California. She will be able to live in Monterey, but I must go to the hills of the Gavilán and live with Don Felipe on his ranch.

"It is evening. I am now writing by the light of a candle. I want to record all that has happened. This afternoon after *siesta*, Esperanza came to escort me to my bedroom downstairs. There stood a huge leather trunk and another one was nearby. I knelt at my altar by the bed and asked the Blessed Virgin for guidance. Esperanza brought in all the gifts that arrived from my husband-to-be. We carefully packed the six dresses, the six *rebozos*, the six *mantillas*, the six beaded jackets, and the six pairs of satin slippers. Then we packed the bed linens that had been saved from the chests of my mother. I was given the black dress that I am to wear at confession tomorrow before the wedding mass. I am worried about what I will tell Father Pedro. I wanted to ask Esperanza about this, but she had only a simple wedding to Papa, and she did not go through these formalities. You see, her mother was an Indian neophyte at the mission, and although her father was a Spanish soldier at the *Presidio*, she has never been a part of the Monterey social life. Esperanza has always lived on Rancho Carmelo and has been a part of our life here. When I wanted to tell her about O'*Farol*, *El Yanqui*, she told me that since he is no longer at the ranch, Papa has forbidden us to say his name. I know that I have sinned in my heart, because I love *O'Farol*, and yet I have decided not to tell Father Pedro about it. Until today, I thought that the marriage to Don Felipe was the worst thing that could happen to me, but now the threat of Don Diego worries me more.

"I cannot tell my confessor about Don Diego, because I cannot put my fears into the right words to make him understand. After my prayers were said to the Blessed Mother, I promised her that I would be a good wife. As soon as I said these words, I saw the candle grow brighter and I knew she heard me. I found a little cross that belonged to my mother. It was under the lace cloth that I use on my altar. Now I can wear it at my wedding and it will help me to remember that the Blessed Virgin wants me to be a good wife to my husband. I hope he will stay beside me every night so that I can have a baby as soon as possible. Then Don Diego will stay away.

"I can talk to no one. I will keep this little book with my prayer books and it will be safe. My mother wrote the prayers for me and that is how she taught me to read. Tomorrow I will ride in the grand wedding procession. I will wear my mother's dress with pride and do all that is required of me by the family and the church. Esperanza tells me to bring honor to both families. Only God knows what is in the future.

"August 1, 1827. Don Felipe left this morning for Monterey. He went with several of the *vaqueros* and a *carreta* loaded with hides and beef. It takes all day to ride to Monterey. He might stay a week. You see, Governor Echeandía has arrived, and my husband says he must spend time with him every day for a week. The governors of Alta California usually live in Monterey at the *Presidio,* but this governor does not like our climate. He wants to live farther south where it is warmer. Don Felipe has been kind to me, and he likes me to be near him at night. He told me that he would find a place for us to live in Monterey if the governor wants his services for the remainder of the summer. I would like that because I could see my friends and, most of all, Consuelo. Encarnacion will be married soon and I would like to attend the festivities. There will be a general *fandango* for everyone in the town. I wonder if *Yanqui O'Farol* will be there. I will not dance with anyone except my husband. I don't think Papa will attend the wedding. He likes to stay at Rancho Carmelo.

"My husband, Don Felipe, is very formal. He calls me Doña Clarita. When we are alone he calls me *Encantadora* and *Amapola* and tells me to call him *Querido.* These special names are the part of our marriage that I like. It is like a secret little game because no one else knows about it. I do not think it unusual that I call my husband Don Felipe in public. When we are alone he shows me affection and tells me stories of when he was a boy in Mexico City. Don Diego will meet him in Monterey so I shall not fear that he will visit me here at the ranch. Most of the time I am told to stay in our bedroom and make lace. I can walk around the large walled *patio* of our *hacienda*. I would like to ride my horse, but I am not allowed to do that. All the land around this *rancho* looks much the same. It is different at Rancho Carmelo. Our ranch has pastures stretching to the sea, and our lands pass through the valley of the Rio Carmelo. I have explored most of it with my horse and my Indian handmaid who is a daughter of one of the Indian neophytes. At Rancho Rincón, I do not go out or have anybody to walk with me. I have only a maid to bring me water and take care of my needs. She keeps her eyes lowered and rarely says a word.

"I am learning to preside at our dining table when we have guests. I do not have much else to do, because Doña Eulalia, my husband's sister, takes care of the household. She has never married and does not talk very much to me. When I'm with her, I feel like a stranger and that is why I like the evenings best. After dinner when we do not have company Don Felipe and I retire early. When the candles are blown out, we share the bed and he becomes a handsome young man. I was afraid of him when we first met. He looked rough and stern. Now, he talks to me softly, and he is very gentle.

"Consuelo is the wife of Captain Manuel García. She says that many of the soldiers are rough with their wives, but Don Felipe touches me with soft hands. Life is all so different now that I can hardly remember all that happened the day we married. There were three days of *fiesta* and on the third day, Don Felipe brought me here to this ranch, which is called Rincón del Gavilán. I have been here ever since. I am praying that I will be with child soon.

"A week has passed. When Don Felipe returned, I was able to tell him that we will have a child. He gave me a beautiful fan that he bought from the last ship that came to port from China. It is black with decorations of mother-of-pearl. I am going to take it with me when we go to Monterey tomorrow. We will stay with my godparents, who are the parents of Consuelo. Together we will attend the festivities for Encarnacion's wedding. There will be a *baile* for special guests, and then everyone will celebrate at the big *fandango*. They even invited the officers of the French ship in port.

"September 24, 1827. After the reception at the courtyard of the Vallejos there was a small gathering of the families who know each other. There was dancing, and I was able to wear one of my new pairs of shoes. Don Felipe wanted me to wear the red ones with the red silk skirt he gave to me. He dances well, but when he became tired he found Don Diego to dance with me. That man is no different than he was on the cruel day before my wedding. I like to be told I am pretty, but he tells me in a way that makes me feel ashamed. He promised that he would come to see us when Don Felipe goes to the south with the Governor. This sent shivers through my body, and I decided to plead with my husband to take me with him to the South. I cannot go by horseback with the men, but we can take a boat to Santa Bárbara and avoid the dusty hard journey.

"On the next day during the town celebration of the wedding, I sat with the married ladies on the benches in the shade of trees in the courtyard near the Custom House. Consuelo and my godmother sat next to me. I felt at ease and we laughed behind our fans at many of the antics of the townspeople. Then I looked up and saw *O'Farol* standing in front of us.

"'I came to pay my compliments on your marriage, Señora Vargas,' he said speaking our language in his flat sounding way. He is younger than most of the foreigners, and he is very tall. Although he has become tan by the sun, he has pale skin. His short red beard matches the color of his hair. I was glad that I had my fan, because I could hide my emotions. I do not remember much of what I said except that I introduced him to my godmother. Later she told me that Captain Cooper calls him Señor Guillermo.

"I wanted to look at *O'Farol*, but when I raised my head, I saw his very blue eyes, and I felt a rush of deep unhappiness. I remembered that I had rescued him from the sea and that I had taught him many of the Spanish words he knows. I remembered how I would ride with him along the banks of the river. It was by the river that he held my hand and told me that he wanted to stay in California.

"Suddenly, I was no longer happy to be in Monterey, I asked Don Felipe if we could visit my father. He made the arrangements, and after the wedding *fiesta*, we made a journey over the hill to the South and to the lands near the Mission San Cárlos and arrived at my beloved Rancho Carmelo. We were able to stay with my father and Esperanza for three weeks. I attended mass at Mission San Cárlos and visited the grave of my mother. Papa talked alone with Don Felipe. The next evening, the men were guests of the Fathers for a dinner at the Mission. There is a rumor that Governor Echeandía has been ordered from Mexico to close the Missions and give their lands to the neophytes. The governor must appoint managers for the mission, and some of the mission lands will be given to a few favored families. Foreigners will now need papers from their governments if they wish to stay in Alta California. Those who have been born in Spain may be sent back to Spain. Papa talks of going back to Castile if his *rancho* is taken away from him.

"I remembered the days at Rancho Carmelo when I was younger. Then there was singing by my mother and playing of the guitar by my brother. We had little dances with each other if we had guests. When *O'Farol* lived at the ranch, he was sometimes invited to do a gig. He told us it was a dance of Ireland, the country of his parents. I know now that my brother will never come back. After we said our farewells to Papa and returned to Rancho Rincón, I had a cold empty place in my stomach.

"Don Felipe likes to give me presents, and today he gave me a lovely bracelet made of stones from Mexico. He seems happy about the coming of our child and talks about a baptismal *fiesta*. Governor Echeandía will move his place of habitation to San Diego. Don Felipe must certainly leave Rancho Rincón next month. When he told me he needed to go to San Diego with the governor, I cried and asked to go with him. I told him I could not live without him. This is true because I am really afraid to stay here if he goes away. He promised to find us passage on a boat that will take us to Santa Bárbara. There are wild Indians who might attack, and it is a journey too difficult for a woman with child to travel by horseback. Our trunks can go with us on the boat. When we reach Santa Bárbara, I will stay with the de la Guerra family while Don Felipe accompanies the governor to the South."

CHAPTER 3

▼

January 26, 2000 Carmel, California

The telephone rang with an insistence that sounded like someone using a doorknocker, and yet Mike and Rita were slow to awaken. From the next room Carmelita began to stir and Mike went to her. He soon brought her downstairs while Rita prepared a morning snack, which they ate and they planned their day. Mike owned the Golden Views Realty Company, and his work hours varied. Today, he had an important appointment with a business friend and client.

"You and Carmelita just stay here today," he cautioned Rita. "Find your inventory records for The Old Booktique on our home computer. Write something for the record of how you acquired *The Diaries* and tell a little of their history. Don't talk to anyone about what has happened. If the sheriff phones, don't say anything about the unusual appearance of your office. There will be plenty of time for that. Just close the door to the office."

"But I want to go over to the shop. I know I can't go in, but I want to tell customers that we'll be closed all day," Rita protested.

"Trust me, Babe," Mike said as he ran his hand through her bouncy hair. "We don't know what's going on, so it's best to lay low. Of course, you need to change any appointments you have with customers today."

Rita smiled at his wanting to take care of her. She had been on her own for a long time before getting married, so she was used to making her own decisions and being independent. Even though she trusted Mike's judgment, his expression of concern was still new to her.

"That's, OK, for today," she laughed. "But you must realize that you don't know everything about this complicated family you married into."

"Perhaps not. But do be careful. You can call your clients from here"

"I suppose I could. See you later, darling," she smiled.

Rita phoned her clients. Then she went to Carmelita's room. Rita looked at her little girl's reddish golden ringlets, which always needed careful combing. Rita loved being with her, and she moved a little wooden train around the tracks while she watched Carmelita place the wooden people at the station. She wished her Grandmother Clara could see Carmelita now.

"*The Diaries* are valuable," Clara had told Rita "I know of no other descriptions of early California written in Spanish by a woman. At that time, many of the *Californios* could not write anything except their signature."

Rita's grandmother told her stories about their family like a lecturer. She made explanations. "Our family always considered learning to be important. My mother had several tutors and various instructors in music and the arts. Then she caught the eye of one of the richest men in San Francisco, and she was married at eighteen to Gustavus Schaeffer. They both were determined that their two children would attend one of the great new universities in California."

Rita always quipped, "And so we began a family rivalry because you went to Stanford University, and your brother went to the University of California at Berkeley."

When Clara told the stories, she would often read from *The Diaries*. First, she carefully took the books, wrapped in a silk shawl, and read aloud from them. Because she would translate the story as she read, the words came out differently each time. Clara also read from several small satin bound diaries that belonged to her Grandmother Isabel. These stories, written in English, told more about Clarita's life and the world in San Francisco in the 1880s. Clara also read from letters written about the San Francisco earthquake when her parents' mansion on Nob Hill was severely damaged. At the time of the earthquake, the Schaeffers were vacationing at their farm near Menlo Park, about thirty miles south of San Francisco. They lived there until another home could be built in San Francisco.

Both Rita and her brother, Charles, had always known about *The Carmelo Diaries*. Clara had promised *The Diaries* would be passed on to them. This fact started Rita thinking about the possibility that her brother had a part in the burglary. There had been a serious quarrel a few years before their grandmother died. Clara always insisted that her daughter, Anita, refuse to divorce Rex. By the time Rita was in high school, she realized her parents were not happy. It was really Clara who had wanted Anita to stay married to Rex

Atherton. Clara made her wishes apparent by every scheme that money and ingenuity could provide. Rex Atherton II was a country club golfer who spent money easily and was always in need of more. Clara had social ambitions. Although she was proud of her Spanish heritage, she wanted Anita to marry into a socially prominent San Francisco family. She let it be known to his parents that she would support Anita and Rex, when they were married. Rex enjoyed the wealth of Anita's newly widowed mother, and it could have been a happy arrangement if he had more discreet about his attentions to other women. Neither Anita nor Clara acknowledged that his frequent golfing trips were unusual, and by the time Rita was five, the Atherton family was living at Stonecrest, Clara's mansion on Carmel Bay. Rita remembered that when Daddy Rex came home with presents and stories of celebrities and famous places, her mother would be happy, and yet it only lasted a few weeks. Soon he avoided family dinners, and he would go off on another golfing trip.

Clara enrolled Charles in a local prep school, and then he went away to college. When Rita was of high school age she became a boarding student at The Santa Lucia School in Monterey. One of her dorm friends said she knew Daddy Rex like a father. Rita tried to pretend that she knew all about this living arrangement. She was furious with her father and the fact that someone else saw more of him than she did. She was angry that both Clara and Anita had lied to her.

When she asked Charles about it, he just laughed at her. "I wondered when you would figure it all out. Dad likes to live the life of a bachelor, but he doesn't have the money to do that. So he lives with various ladies. He's a smart guy. He always picks the rich ones."

"Will our parents get a divorce?" Rita remembered asking Charles.

"No, they are both happy the way it is. Dad can come back to Mother any time he wants. Then he has a fling with some gal, and he goes to Bebe's house in Palm Springs. Mother likes her little social circle here. It's the only life she knows. Mother is so boring. She doesn't know how to happy. Don't be like her," Charles advised. "Wise up and live your life, girl."

That was long ago, Charles was in college and they still talked to each other. The four years difference in their ages meant they seldom saw each other except at Christmas when Grandmother Clara had her series of fabulous parties that ended with The Stonecrest Cotillion, a tradition for a well selected guest list of guests from San Francisco and Pebble Beach.

About eight years ago, Rex told the family he was moving to Hawaii so he could golf in a warmer climate. Clara gave him enough money to live on, provided there was no divorce. While there, Rex met Cindy, a beautiful bathing suit model, and after a few months, he wanted to marry her. When he asked Anita for a divorce, Charles agreed with his dad. Clara immediately flew to Hawaii, and taking Rita with her, she made sure that Rita was in the room when she explained to Rex that she would not tolerate a divorce in the family. She arranged a trust for Rex that would provide a steady income for him, and the money would revert to Rita if he should ever get a divorce or remarry.

The thoughts of all this were going around in Rita's head while she played with Carmelita on the floor. She felt guilty for being an accomplice with Clara. Her grandmother provided the only real stability in her life. When Clara sent Rita to France to study at the Sorbonne, Charles accused Rita of selling out to her. Rex was never able to marry Cindy and in time, Rex asked Bebe to come to Hawaii to live with him.

After Charles and Missy Howard were married, and the social conventions of their wedding were observed, Rita had no more communication with her father. Charles and Missy lived in Napa County where he worked for his uncles at The Torelli Wine Cellars. Then Charles bought his own vineyards. The estrangement in the family began at Clara's funeral. The will was read in the mahogany paneled library of Stonecrest. Charles chose to sit across the room with the Torelli cousins. Rita, Mike, and Anita sat by the bay windows near Clara's lawyer. All the heirs were given equal amounts of money and securities. Anita inherited Stonecrest and all the furnishings. Clara's jewelry was given to the granddaughters. Rita inherited *The Carmelo Diaries* and an extensive collection of her grandmother's rare books and first editions. Charles left Stonecrest immediately after the reading of the will. That was the last time she had seen him or heard from him.

Rita wanted to forget much of this past. "Let's go out to play," she said to Carmelita and she dressed her daughter in a warm down parka with a hood. The phone rang. "This is Captain Lewis from the county sheriff's office. We would like you to meet us at The Old Booktique. We have some things we want to go over with you," he said.

"I can meet you later when my husband comes back," Rita answered.

"You are sole owner of the shop. We need only you, and I can drive you there," he said as he hung up.

Rita called Mike and left a message with his secretary, she took Carmelita to her play area in the garden. As soon as she saw the sheriff's car enter the cul de sac on the street where they lived, she extracted Carmelita from the swing and sang "Old MacDonald's Farm" while she carried her into the house. "Daddy's coming home early, and he wants us to get ready to go 'bye bye' with him."

"Bye, bye," Carmelita repeated, and Rita remembered she had always thought she would not let her child use baby talk. She laughed at herself. When the doorbell rang, Rita was already on the phone and talking to Mike.

"What's up, Babe?" he asked.

"Mike, they want me to answer questions at the shop. They just now called me, and the officer is ringing our doorbell right now."

"Tell them we'll meet them at the shop. I'm on my way home now."

"We'll have to take Carmelita." Rita stopped. "Oops," she breathed while the bell kept ringing. Carmelita went with her to the door and she peeked through the gauzy curtains that covered the glass. "Bye, Dear," Rita finished on the phone to Mike.

"It's Captain Lewis of the County Sheriff's Department," a voice called.

"Mommy has some business. Do you want to play in your room while Mommy talks?" Rita whispered to her daughter.

"I want Mommy," was Carmelita's reply.

"My little girl is upset," she called out while stalling for time.

"Ma'am, It's very hard to hear you."

"What do you want?" Rita called loudly.

"I would like to take you to your shop so we can check over some things together," she heard.

"My husband will be here any minute, and we'll meet you there."

"I really don't see…" Captain Lewis began as Mike pulled into the driveway. Soon the men began to talk, and Rita went inside to pack a snack for Carmelita and change from jeans into tailored black slacks.

The sheriff's car drove off, and when Mike came in he kissed both Carmelita and Rita. Carmelita was their only child. He had two sons who were students at the University of California at Davis and Sonoma State. They got along well enough but he didn't see much of them. This was his family now. There was a closeness here that he had always wanted.

"What did he say to you, hon?" he asked Rita.

"I guess he just wants to ask me some questions but I'm afraid I'll say something wrong. I want you to calm me down."

"First, we didn't do anything wrong and you haven't done anything wrong. We don't need to be on the defensive or it will seem that we really have something to hide. But we'd better get going now. We can discuss it on the way."

Rita began to talk as soon as they were at the end of the street. "Mike, I guess I'm hurt and mad at the same time. It's so invasive. I don't like to suspect anybody, and yet they are going to ask me for names of people who know about the value of *The Diaries*. I wonder if the person who did this will retaliate."

They were now stopping at the security gates at the Carmel entrance to Pebble Beach. The driver in front of them must have been a tourist, because he was paying admission and asking the gate clerk questions about the map he was examining. The delay gave the Minettis more time to talk

As soon they arrived and stopped in the parking circle near the shop, Captain Lewis came over and without formalities began asking questions. "Who else knows about *The Diaries*, Mrs. Minetti?"

"Well, Tessa, of course. She's one of my oldest friends, and she has keys to the shop. She wouldn't need to break in, so we can rule her out. Then there's Dave Goldman from the Histrodrama TV channel. I've told him about *The Diaries*. I have an appointment with him at the shop next week. There's also Shana Tyrone from MTG studios. She has talked to me about doing a fictional script or a special about nineteenth century California. She wants it to be a woman's story and portray different ethnic points of view. She was excited when I told her that my Spanish ancestor had a half sister whose mother was from a native California Indian tribe. I think I told a lot of people about my diaries because I thought it would be good publicity for the shop."

"There seems to be somebody out there who wants to get their hands on those books," Mike said.

"I want to check on something before we enter the shop," Captain Lewis said as he went to his car.

Mike whispered to Rita, "I'm curious to see what else has been taken from the shop."

"It could be any number of popular favorites. I have several autographed copies of Steinbeck and Nabakov. Even an autographed first edition of Tom Clancy's first novel, *The Hunt for Red October* brings a good price." She sighed. "I guess I'm ready to go into the shop if they'll let me."

"If they want to ask about your family, what are you prepared to tell them now, dear?" Mike asked quietly.

"I don't suspect anyone. I want the police to do what they do best. I don't want to be the one to point a finger at anybody. Particularly the family."

"They'll find out that you and your father and brother don't talk to each other. They'll find out that everyone's a little jealous of you because they think you inherited more of the goodies. If asked, you need to be candid. Don't be emotional. Just state the facts. You and your mother lived with your Grandmother Clara for many years. You were the grandchild who knew her the best.

Tell it like it is. If asked you can tell them that she promised to will you many of her books and *The Carmelo* Diaries. It's as plain as that. Give them names of all her grandchildren, if you want to."

"Is it any of their business?"

"If they're going to solve the case it is. This isn't like one of your arguments with your girlfriends. This is a serious situation."

"Oh, Mike, you can be so fair and square to everyone. I don't want to be emotional, so please, don't talk to me like I'm a child."

When she looked at Mike she could see that he was hurt, and she knew he did not like to argue. He became exceptionally quiet and said nothing.

She put her fingers on his sleeve and softly stroked his arm. "You're not mad at me, are you?"

"No," he laughed. "And you know why."

"You clown. You'll see that I can be calm and collected when that policeman confronts me. He'll pay attention to what I say."

"That's because you look so sexy," he laughed.

"Mike, you think you're being funny, but that attitude will really make me feel self conscious."

"Honey, I'm the one who really knows all about you. It's not just your pretty face peering out from that tawny red hair, but it's what you do to the clothes you wear that looks so great."

"That's not true. I've had nothing but the barest of courtesy from the sheriff."

"Just be yourself, honey. We do want to cooperate. We need to find out who is behind all this so we can get on with our life." He gave her a kiss.

She lowered her voice to talk to Mike. "I don't plan to say anything about the papers in my office at home."

The sheriff motioned for them to follow him as he walked toward the gazebo.

"May we come in now?" Rita inquired as she stood waiting.

"Yes, but I want to talk to you, alone," he added and closing the door, he flipped the door sign to "Closed."

Mike noticed the sign and although he said nothing, his displeasure was evident by his scornful look. Rita glanced around at the disarray in the shop and shook her head. Looking outside, she could see Mike trying to amuse Carmelita. "I want to sit down," she said motioning toward a large antique carved Chinese desk that had been in the library at Stonecrest, and she pulled up two Chippendale armchairs. Then she folded her hands and waited expectantly.

"Mrs. Minetti, don't you find it strange your shop alarm didn't go off? It was deactivated, and the one to the safe was tripped Do you know any reason for this?"

"Maybe they didn't know that the safe had an alarm also. They might have been in a hurry."

"I want to know who has the code to the door and not to the safe? Just a list of names, please."

"Is this required?" she asked earnestly.

"If you don't tell me it could be considered withholding evidence," he replied sternly. She thought he enjoyed seeing her nervous.

"Tessa, my friend and assistant, Mike, my husband, and Marquita, the lady who cleans. They all have the combination to enter the shop but not the safe."

"What about window washers or other cleaning services?"

"No one else has the entry door combination. The shop is really quite small. We do a great deal of mail order business. We specialize in personal service to our clients. We track down rare books."

"Who has access to the safe then?"

"Just me. I think Mike could find the combination in our business records, but he has never used it," she added and wondered if she was being too chatty.

"How soon can you come up with a dollar estimate of what is missing?" Captain Lewis asked

Rita stood up and knelt down to inspect the mess on the lower shelves of the bookcases. "I need some time to make my inventory of what is missing. Are you through dusting for prints?"

"My men have taken care of that," he said with a tone of authority, and then in a more relaxed tone he continued. "You seem pretty young to be in the business of old books. And you say you own the shop?"

Rita sat down and looked at him quizzically. She said nothing.

"I mean ladies your age usually go in for owning spas, beauty shops, gift stores, and that sort of thing."

"I like history. I have a master's degree in history," she said sharply. Again she had the feeling that she was defending herself in a situation where she wanted answers.

"Everything was removed from the safe. Did you have the contents itemized?" he continued.

"Of course," she answered tersely and felt miffed that she was being questioned on what she considered were her business methods.

"You mentioned *The Carmelo Diaries*. They are valuable?"

"They are insured, but recently they have become more valuable," she volunteered. She leaned forward. He liked the casual look of her V-neck sweater with the smart tailored slacks. She was more relaxed.

"More valuable? But why?"

"They are one of a kind. They are history. There are two parties interested in them. One wants to do a documentary and the other has suggested a miniseries based on the contents of *The Diaries.*"

"So give me a ballpark figure. How much money? I mean the taking price and not the asking." He looked as if he enjoyed this new phase of questioning.

"Sir, they are not for sale. Never have been."

"On whose authority?"

"Mine," she said fiercely as she shook her head with conviction and looked him in the eye. He was intrigued with her. She had an unusual yet pleasing look with high cheekbones that seemed to glisten from time to time, and she had intelligent eyes. Her skin was like a pearl, and she wore very little makeup. Her most striking feature was her abundant auburn hair. He realized that he enjoyed asking her questions.

"You'll need to explain that."

"Why?" she said defiantly, and he liked her even better.

He glanced at the paper he had in his hand. "Let's see. It says here 'Owner of The Old Booktique-Clarita Atherton.' I take it you use your maiden name. Are you the sole owner?"

"Is that important?" She answered in a challenging voice.

"Why, yes, because if you have a silent partner, for example, their interests and motives might be different than yours."

She looked at him thoughtfully. "In theory that is true. If there were others there might be disagreements about *The Carmelo Diaries*, but I am the sole owner."

"What does your husband think about your business?" he continued as he looked out the window at Mike who was entertaining Carmelita with a game.

"I had the business before we were married, and we agree on its importance," she shot back quickly.

"So tell me about *The Carmelo Diaries*,"

"They were willed to me by my grandmother, Clara Torelli."

"Did she write them?"

"Oh no, they go back much farther. There are several diaries. including the ones written by Clarita's granddaughter, Isabel Alonso Shaw. However, the really valuable diaries are the ones written in Spanish by my first ancestor to be born in

California. She was born in 1812 on a ranch near the mouth of the Carmel River." Rita became animated in the explanation.

"Do *The Diaries* have a sentimental value for you?"

"I grew up hearing my grandmother translate them as she read to us. She told me that *The Diaries* were particularly rare because not many Spanish ladies kept diaries, although this was a custom with New England women."

Captain Lewis gave her his full attention. He liked the way her brown eyes softened to liquid tenderness when she spoke of her grandmother. "Did the film-maker want to buy *The Diaries*?"

"Yes, at first, but when I told him I could furnish him with other information and also family stories, he said he wanted to include me in the project."

"How did the filmmaker know about them? Did you advertise?"

"He first heard about *The Diaries* from Shana Tyrone, who had met Clara several years ago. My grandmother was the family's greatest storyteller. She would often talk to people in The Lounge at The Retreat. She would order a bottle of Dom Perignon and she would always drink just one glass herself, and invite a few others to share the bottle.

"Then many people knew about *The Diaries*?"

Rita realized that the captain wanted more information and was leading her into more conversation about her family. She motioned to Mike and he came inside with Carmelita. "It's getting cold out there. We'll go to the back of the shop," he said.

"So Grandmother Clara told many people, Captain Lewis said "And have you known your husband a long time, Mrs. Minetti? He seems a bit older than you." Rita was now incensed, but she did not want to let Mike know, so she kept her voice low.

"I've known him all my life. The next thing you're going to ask me will be about our dog or my mother, right?"

"If I think it is relevant, I will. We've got to cover it all. Then we'll track down all leads. We'll get an expert to tell us about the market for old books, and we'll arrange to interview the people most able to profit from the theft. There's always the angle that *The Diaries* were taken to keep you from having them. Maybe the filmmakers wanted to make up their own story, and they hired someone to get rid of *The Diaries*. Ah?" his voice trailed off.

"All this upsets me," Rita announced "Almost as much now as when I first saw the mess this morning. We'll be up all night checking the prices of the missing books."

"I suggest that you change the entry code to the shop right away," Captain Lewis said as he assumed a fatherly tone. He handed her his business card. "This is where you can reach me."

"Thank you," Rita said as she glanced at the name of Timothy Lewis.

"Call me tomorrow if you find out anything or if you can think of anything new. I'll call you tomorrow afternoon. Above all, you must not worry. I know police work seems tedious, but it's our job and our questions are necessary." He knew that he would enjoy this case.

When Captain Lewis left, Rita quickly began to make a mental estimate of what was taken. Mike was annoyed with what he had seen of Captain Lewis from a distance. There was nothing at the bookshop to amuse Carmelita and she was cranky. "I think you'd better call Mrs. Russell and have her take Carmelita home for supper. Then I'll help you with the cataloging," he said to Rita.

After Carmelita left with Mrs. Russell, Rita felt free to express her emotions. "I still feel unsettled and need to do this work, Mike. Could you go over to the Sanderling Room and bring back some of their Wild West Chili? We can talk a little while we eat it, and then we'll get down to business here."

"What did you tell him?" Mike quickly asked.

"Most of the questions seemed routine, but at the end, I thought they were too personal. He said all his questions were necessary. He seemed a little nicer towards the end when he told me to change the entry code to the store, and said he would call tomorrow to keep me posted. What do you think?"

"I think he likes to talk to you. Just as I told you." Mike laughed, now that he was certain that Rita was relaxed.

"When we finish putting books back in their places, let's go home."

"Sure thing. We both have busy lives."

"Mine is even busier now. I need to read my copies of *The Diaries*. I have not read them for several years. I'll start tomorrow."

"Don't you think you'll get the originals back?"

"Whatever happens, I wish I could compare them. Grandmother Clara once explained to me the difference between the English copies and the Spanish original. The copies are only a translation. She also told me that only the original diary had a list of all the Vargas family jewels. I never asked her what she meant by those words. Perhaps this has something to do with their disappearance."

"Then let's get going," said Mike as he picked up books from the floor and placed them on the largest table. "We'll put the place in order, and you and Tessa can handle the business tomorrow."

They returned to their home in two hours.

CHAPTER 4

▼

Clarita's diary continues.

October 1827

"I have been contented since Don Felipe said he would take me with him to Santa Bárbara. I hear the word *político* day and night. The governor is living in San Diego most of the time, and he often visits a group of *Californios* living in Santa Bárbara. The family de la Guerra y Noriega is the most influential in this area.

"I asked Don Felipe to allow me to visit Papa before we departed for the South. I traveled in a *carreta* while Don Felipe and his riders accompanied us. During the time we were at Rancho Carmelo I attended mass almost every day at the Mission San Cárlos. Life at our *hacienda* is simple compared to the strict manners at Rancho Rincón. Papa's household has easy ways. Esperanza continued the traditions of my mother. Large clay pots planted with flowers fill the *patio*. In the evenings, the children of the workers are invited to come and sing for us. It is autumn and the best time in the year to enjoy the outdoors.

"After Don Felipe left, Esperanza and I had picnics on the beach where the river meets the sea. We took my little sister, Dulcera, and our maids. I asked Esperanza if I should talk to a doctor in Santa Bárbara. She looked at me with surprise and said I was young and it would be easy to have a child. She always lived at Rancho Carmelo with her mother who was from the tribe of Indians who live up the River Carmelo. Her father was a soldier at the *Presidio,* and he was killed. She told me that Papa is troubled now. He fears the new government in Mexico will take his land away.

"The next night, after a good meal and while sitting in our *patio,* I told Papa I was worried about his health and asked him if it were true that the government of Mexico wanted to take the lands away from the missions. He nodded his head. He talked with me as we did in the old days. He is happy that he will be a grandfather. He said it gave him something to live for and he promised to give a grand *fiesta* at Rancho Carmelo after the baptism of our child.

"Papa told me that our ranch was a grant from the King of Spain. This included grazing rights on the lands of Mission San Cárlos. He came to Alta California in 1798 when Father Lasuen was the Padre Prefect of Mission San Cárlos. Governor Borica was reluctant to give out many land grants. In 1800 it was different. The Russians were arriving in the North, and Spain wanted Monterey to be a stronger settlement. Men of good character were allowed to use the lands near the mission, and Papa was given grazing rights in cooperation with the mission fathers. Papa was given a *carta* that listed his rights to the land. Father Lasuen signed the paper. The boundaries of Rancho Carmelo are marked with the San José Creek to the South and the hills where the sycamores begin in the North. Governor Arrillaga agreed that Rancho Carmelo could be established. because it would be important to the defense of the whole area. Papa asked me to tell this story to my husband. I must explain to Don Felipe that the Spanish *Californios* want to live as they are. It would not be right for new people to take over their land.

"I am writing this in my diary because I might forget the words of Papa. He told me that at the time I was born, the Spanish government wanted to break up the mission lands because they wanted to give land to new settlers. Then Spain needed gold to pay for their debts of war, and they decided the missions should pay for the military support of Monterey. They asked the Padre Prefect to make the mission more profitable. Papa helped the mission sell their hides to ships from England, France, and Russia in the best way possible. There are secret places in the coves behind the rocks at Punta de Los Lobos. He sent his *vaqueros* there to sell the hides. With the help of Papa, the Mission San Cárlos paid for the protection and the defense of all of Monterey.

"Papa now fears the new laws from Mexico City will make it easy to deport all foreigners from California. The laws are aimed mostly at the mission fathers. Padre Prefect, Sarría, has refused to take an oath of loyalty to Mexico, and he has been arrested. Governor Echeandía will not deport him, but Padre Sarría cannot leave the Mission San Cárlos to carry out his duties of visitations of the other missions. Papa worries about what will happen to our ranch if the mission fathers are forced to leave.

"Although I was angry when Papa confined me to an upstairs storeroom before the wedding, I understand how he worries about what will happen to our family in California. If I have a son, I shall insist that Bernardo is one of his names. I told this to Papa. I also told him since my husband is a friend of the governor, I will try to save Rancho Carmelo from the government of Mexico when it plans to give away the mission lands and our grazing rights.

"I have the sweet feeling of knowing that Papa loves and trusts me. When I embrace him, he seems very frail, and I wanted to stay at Carmelo so I could be of help, but I know my duty to my husband and I know I shall have a son to carry on our traditions."

There were no entries in the diaries concerning the voyage to Santa Bárbara. It would have been interesting to read Clarita's description of the coastline. Grandmother Clara said the true importance of the diaries of Clarita was the story it told about the women in Alta California in the nineteenth century.

"October 1827. Santa Bárbara. I have not written all these weeks because I was ill most of the time on the boat. Don Felipe and I had time to talk, and he assures me he will do what he can do to protect the Rancho Carmelo. If my father is deported to Spain, I will have first claim on the ranch.

"I felt active as soon as we put foot on the land, and soon we were escorted to the *hacienda* of José de la Guerra y Noriega. It is the home of the parents of Teresa Hartnell, who lives in Monterey. She is also visiting in Santa Bárbara while her husband is in South America on business. After we all rested, Don Felipe rode off to San Diego with many of the governor's men. I stay with the family of Don José until my husband returns. Doña María de las Angustias de la Guerra y Noriega is about my age, and she seems to enjoy talking to me. I was introduced to her in Monterey when she visited her sister, Teresa. In a few days I felt a part of the family circle. I learned some useful things about my health. Doña Teresa Hartnell has a young child whose name is Guillermo Antonio.

"Santa Bárbara is as lively as Monterey. We talk of weddings, baptisms and also of their troubles with the new government in Mexico City. Don José de la Guerra y Noriega has been selected to represent Alta California and will leave soon for Mexico City. I surely hope that the governor will not ask my husband to serve in Mexico City. Although it is a great honor for my husband, I am still afraid of what Don Diego might do to me.

"Late November 1827. We are at sea, and I have time to write. Doña María gave me some precious ink to take back with me. She thinks it is good that I am writing about my voyage. I need something to do while Don Felipe is sleeping in the afternoons. We are sailing back to Monterey. I have been looking at the sea creatures as we pass them in the ocean. This time I am enjoying myself because I am not sick. Don Felipe is tired from his travels to see Governor Echeandía in San Diego. He says that the governor wants to make San Diego the capital of Alta California.

"During the first day at sea, I asked Don Felipe questions about the governor, and he told me he is a kind man, but sometimes he is in poor health. The governor thinks the weather is too cold in the North. I told Don Felipe that the governor is not at all popular with the *hijos del pais* of Monterey. They like him a little better now, because he gave some authority back to Don Mariano Estrada and took sides against Captain Miguel Gonzalez who arrested Don Mariano. Don Felipe was surprised that I knew about the problem. I explained that in the community of Monterey I have many friends, and most of them live inside the *Presidio*. What else did I say? I told him I was still worried that Papa would lose his ranch if the governor gives orders to break up the property of the missions. Don Felipe told me that Papa should keep a small house in Monterey and find out for himself what is going on. He said that the Mexican government plans to divide some of the early Spanish land grants. Governor Echeandía will then give out new land grants as a reward for service to the Republic of Mexico. I am learning about people called *deputados,* who are going to be chosen for a meeting where they will talk about our problems.

"Today I decided to use the words 'my husband.' When we talk together, he says I should not be so formal. As I approach motherhood, I am talking to my husband about many things. I tell him what the *Californios* think about the Mexican governor. The young men of the Vallejo family, Mariano Vallejo and Juan Bautista Alvarado, whose mother was Joséfa Vallejo, are men who will be important in Alta California. I want to help both my husband and my friends. He tells me not to worry about Rancho Carmelo, because Rancho Rincón de Gavilán is my home, and he will see that our children will own that land. He does not yet understand I feel an obligation to the de Segovia family. I write my name according to Spanish custom, Clarita Isabel Vargas y Segovia, and since my brother is a priest and cannot inherit the ranch, I should have claim to Rancho Carmelo. It is a beautiful place with gentle meadows that slope to the sea. It has good land for running cattle.

"My husband tells me that he may need to go South before the birth of our child. I pleaded with him until he said that I could visit Rancho Carmelo if he leaves. Esperanza will take good care of me there. I have not told him why I fear to stay at Rancho Rincón when he is absent. He would not understand, but I know the truth about Don Diego.

"I thought I would look like a fat old woman by this time, but I have not had an appetite, and I look no different. I can hide myself under the lovely new skirts that were made for me in Santa Bárbara. My husband bought beautiful silks from the last boat that came into port. He also gave me a blue silk shawl with red embroidery from China and a new lace *rebozo* to put around my head. He wants to be proud of me when we greet our family and friends during the fiestas of *Navidad*. Now that I am married, I can wear my hair piled high and held with one of the tortoise combs he has given me. Don Felipe has arranged for us to live in a house in Monterey when he helps the governor.

"Late December 1827. During *Las Posadas*, we entertained our friends in the *patio* of our little house in Monterey. We attended mass at the Royal Presidio Chapel. It is part of the original *presidio* and is the only place of worship in Monterey. During *Las Posadas,* we walked to many of the houses of our friends, and they served refreshments, mostly hot chocolate and special sweets. I remember last year at Rancho Carmelo when there was much singing and playing of guitars during this season. Esperanza continues all the Spanish customs of my mother, and we gathered all the children of the neophytes to hear the music and eat special food. We let the children act out the journey of María and José when they were looking for shelter before the birth of the Christ Child. *La Natividad* is an especially happy time for the children.

"I did not know that my life would change so much in one year. Last year I lived at Rancho Carmelo. I saw O'*Farol* every day. He organized the *rodeos* and was always building something. He found time to go riding with me up and down the trail by the river. Sometimes we went to the headlands to watch the waves in the ocean. He told me to call him Guillermo. Papa included him in our celebrations of holy days. At that time, I thought that my life would always be at Rancho Carmelo. Perhaps it is good that I did not know how soon I would be living far away and with strangers.

"February 1828. The governor is still in Santa Bárbara where he went in December, and he has summoned Don Felipe. I am safe at my beloved Rancho Carmelo, and I can play happy simple games with Dulcera, my little sister, while Esperanza is busy with her many duties around the *hacienda*. She will have another child this year. Life is happy here. The only thing of sadness is my loss of Guillermo. When I am here, I think of him all the time.

"I shall always remember the morning I found him. It was at a time when I rode my horse every day, and I rode everywhere by myself. I often rode my horse to the mouth of the Bay of River Carmelo. On that special day I saw something thrashing out to sea and something else close to shore. I have seen the sea wolves nearby, but what I saw on this day was different. Also I heard cries of a human. It was low tide, and I could ride out a little distance. What I saw in the sea was a person. I could also hear yelling. I dropped down from my horse and entered the surf. I was glad that my brother had taught me to swim, and that I had been in the surf before. It was a rather calm day, and I was able to reach the creature, who was trying to swim although he was exhausted. I stretched out my arm and pulled him to shore. It turned out to be a young man with bright red hair and torn clothes. When I dragged him onto the sand, I turned him on his side, and he coughed water. He was breathing hard and gasping, and I could see he was exhausted. He said nothing and quickly went to sleep. While he slept, I tethered my horse to a small tree and after taking off my wet under skirt, I put it on a bush to dry. I did not dare leave him. After some time, he awoke and looked very confused. We were both silent When he finally spoke, he used strange words that did not make any sense. He pointed to himself and said something that sounded like *feria* He added something else that sounded like the blowing of wind. I had never heard words like that. Finally I used sign language, as I do with the Indians, and I made him understand that I would take him to my home.

"That is how O'*Farol* came to live at Rancho Carmelo. I was twelve, and I think he was sixteen. He looks different than the *Californios*. He has eyes of deep blue and a pale skin. My mother had blue eyes, and I like blue eyes. He is good at doing things with his hands, so Papa soon found work for him to do. We did not know where he came from for a long time. Later when he learned some Spanish, and I learned a little English, I understood that his parents had died, and at first he lived with an aunt. Then he was put on a boat that sailed from Boston. He learned to be a carpenter. Life on the boat was hard. They beat him and almost starved him, and I do not think they were good Christians. The ship dropped anchor near Punta de los Lobos in hopes of selling some of their goods without paying tax at the customhouse of Monterey. He took a small boat and rowed toward the shore. He did not know the water was very rough. I loved him from the first moment I saw him, but not in the way my husband expects me to love him.

"Guillermo is a good carpenter. Rancho Carmelo is a long distance from Monterey, and we always needed men to help us. Papa seemed to like him, and he liked him more when he learned our language. His true name is Will O'Farrell. Padre Juan called him Guillermo, and everyone else said O'*Farol* or *El Yanqui*. He went to mass with us at the mission, but he did not eat with us.

"At the time I pulled him from the sea, I was grieving for my mother who died from a fever He helped me understand that she would always love me. He told me that his parents died of the plague. They came to the land of the *Yanquis* from a place faraway He knew what it was like to be lonely, and he liked living on our ranch. He always seemed to be building something, and he was very good at making leather ropes. I am telling all this to explain why I was very surprised that Papa was angry when we danced together at Consuelo's wedding *fiesta*. I did not know that Don Felipe had already asked for my hand in marriage. There is much inside me that wants to see Guillermo again. I think he is a good man.

"Before I left Rancho Rincón, Don Diego stopped me when I was walking through our garden. He told me that being with child made me even more beautiful. I do not believe him, and I know that all he wants to do is to touch me. Doña Eulalia, the sister of Don Felipe, is not someone I trust, so I have said nothing to her about the actions of Don Diego. I light a candle every day by the altar of Our Lady of the Angels, and I express my gratitude that I am here at Carmelo It is a time of year for family gatherings. We have had rain almost every day, and the hills are green with new grass so we keep the cattle close by. I hope Papa and I can talk more about the things I have learned about the governor. Papa is a proud man, and he needs to be careful that he does not talk so much about being Spanish. His best friends are the mission fathers, and they are Spanish.

"Don Felipe says we need to be friends with the new government in Mexico, so we can keep our ranches. It is just a matter of time, and the missions will be told to let the Indians go their own way. The mission lands with all their cattle will be given to other people. The Indians are supposed to be given small plots of land, but most people think they will not know how to use the land and they will go back to living in their former ways. Don Felipe expects to keep his land. Perhaps the governor will grant him some of the mission lands. My husband tells me that Papa should not be friendly with the mission fathers. He does not know Papa."

CHAPTER 5

▼

January 27, 2000

Rita awoke before anyone else on the morning after the burglary. She went downstairs to the kitchen where the family ate most meals. It was situated in a large alcove by a bay window that looked onto a small garden bounded by a low fence of Carmel stone. The garden faced east, and instead of the usual Monterey pine trees, the lawn was surrounded by a grove of tall eucalyptus. This allowed Rita to enjoy the sunrise as she looked out the window every morning. After she brewed a pot of tea, she sipped the warm invigorating liquid, and drew circles with a pen on a blank piece of paper. Starting to write whatever came into her mind, she was confounded by conflicting ideas and emotions.

She began to remember the tales her grandmother told about their ancestors and the vast Rancho Carmelo that bordered the Carmel River. When Rita was a child, the people in those stories seemed very real to her. Even now she thought she could see them marching in a parade. When she was young, she accompanied her grandmother to the annual Adobe Day Celebration. Almost all of the historic adobe buildings, public or private, were opened to the public on that special day, and the guides were dressed in clothing of the nineteenth century. Clara also took her to the yearly parade and commemoration of the founding of Monterey in 1770. Rita remembered the riders who wore black hats with broad brims, embroidered satin vests, and colorful red sashes at the waists. Their horses were thoroughbred and bedecked with gleaming silver trappings on the Spanish saddles. The spectacle was very traditional, and Clara told her it was authentic.

When Rita was a little girl, she dressed up in old, yellowed silk gowns and lace Spanish shawls that her grandmother kept in a large leather chest in the upstairs trunk room. Loving the stories of early California, she imagined herself to be the young Clarita of olden times. This was part of her childhood.

Rival emotions were present today. The loss of *The Carmelo Diaries* was very personal to Rita. She now knew that her grandmother's translations of *The Diaries* could be different in meaning than the original journals of Clarita, and she wanted to compare her copies with the Spanish originals. Then she could decide if her grandmother had used too much of her imagination in the narrative. Rita wanted to be accurate and familiar with all the diaries before her meeting with Dave Goldman.

When Mike came down for breakfast, Rita told Mike about her apprehensions. "I feel the weight of too many things. I don't want to disrupt the routine we have set up for Carmelita. She must not know that I am upset about the burglary. I need to supply Captain Lewis the information he wants and give him the inventory immediately and I want to reopen my shop right away. Are you concerned about the motive for the burglary? It makes me feel vulnerable." She paused to look at Mike.

"Don't worry about Carmelita. The burglary is the problem to attack," Mike answered. "Right now it seems like a mountain to climb. But you've got me to help you."

"I told you once that I used to go through periods of melancholy. I desperately wanted to be part of a family where the daddy and mommy were together and where they all hugged and loved one another. Now that I have you and Carmelita, I am sometimes afraid it will all be taken away."

"That's not going to happen," said Mike emphatically.

"Maybe all this is just an emotional reaction, "Rita said aloud, trying to convince herself the truth of what she said. She didn't want to discuss her suspicions with Mike or Captain Lewis. "I need to move on," she told Mike as he helped her by making fresh orange juice.

"Do you really want to collaborate with that producer of TV historical dramas? Do you want to sell the story of Clarita that is found in *The Diaries?*" Mike asked.

"Yes." Said Rita with real energy. "With the extra money from this project, I can employ someone to manage the shop and I'll oversee the buying end. Then, I can spend more time with Carmelita, and maybe we can have another child."

Mike finished making the juice quickly, and putting his arms around her, he said, "I like that idea. Do whatever you need to do about the shop today, hon. I'll take care of the Kido, and I'll even make my famous spaghetti for dinner tonight."

"You must be reading my mind again, darling," she laughed and kissed him as he sat down at the table. She ground the beans for his morning cup of coffee and made an omelet for breakfast.

"I think I'll tell Tessa to take the day off".

"Close the shop another day," Mike encouraged.

"Good idea," Rita said with relief.

Mike looked at her with delight. She looked her best without any makeup. He remembered the first time he had seen her in his bathrobe in the morning. She had come over to his house to tell him that she could not go with him to the Bahamas. The weather had become vicious and somehow he had convinced her to spend the night with him. She had agreed if he would find her a bathrobe to use in the morning. He now looked at her with a smug little smile and she caught his mood. "What are you smirking about?" she said with a little laugh.

"I just thought about the first morning I ever saw you in my bathrobe."

"And what a ratty old terry cloth thing it was."

"I don't remember you complaining then," he chuckled.

"But I've bought you better ones since." She paused to listen. "I hear Carmelita. I'll bring her down. After breakfast, she's all yours. I'm going to take you up on your offer to take care of her," she said and went upstairs to her daughter. When they both came down, Rita seemed quite serious. "Was Marquita here yesterday? I'm in such a fog, I can't remember anything."

"Hon, you always tell her to come to clean up when she has the time. She might have come while we were out."

Rita did not answer and continued making the breakfast. Soon after the meal, Mike took Carmelita with him to do errands. As soon as Rita was alone, she quickly went upstairs and entered her office. She used her zoom lens camera to take pictures of the room and continued taking pictures in the small adjoining bathroom and the file closet. On a notepad she wrote several descriptions. The phone rang. She was reluctant to answer it, but thought it might be about something important.

"Good morning, it's Captain Lewis," she heard. "I wondered if you came up with anything you forgot to tell me yesterday."

"You said you'd call in the afternoon," she answered. "I decided to close the Booktique today because I have so much to do."

"I'd like to pick up your information as soon as possible, and I also want you to give me a list of the members of your family who might have some interest in

The Diaries. Since it is a family story, it's their story, too." he said as if he were telling her something new.

"Then call me at the shop around three o'clock and don't call me until then," she answered quickly. "I need time to work."

"I'll have some new ideas for you," he promised and hung up.

Rita called Tessa. "Hi, pal," she said casually. "How about another day off. I can't get myself organized for customers. I have to prepare an inventory for the police and do some work in the shop."

"I want to help you."

"I think it will be better if I do things here for awhile, but you can come to the shop in the afternoon. Mike's an angel, and he's taking care of Carmelita today."

With that accomplished, she turned on her computer and found the inventory statements for the police. She printed a few copies, and then she began looking around the room. Something was missing. It was not something that would be significant to anyone else but to Rita it was apparent. Rita kept a collection of figures and animals on the windowsill above her desk. As her eyes traveled, she remembered the occasions when she had acquired each one. There was a standing statue of a crystal Lalique cat, a gift from her grandmother. Beside it was a woven strawberry basket from France, a rock with holes from the beach in front of Stonecrest, a little silk elephant that Mike had given her, and a silver baby rattle from Tiffany's. She noticed the absence of a little carved upright bear. It was a special remnant of the past. Although she occasionally added something to the sill, she had never taken any object away. She reasoned that Marquita could have straightened and moved things around. She looked around the room. Although there were clusters of other sentimental things, she could not see the little bear.

Rita looked into the file closet and it seemed to be as usual. The office had once been her bedroom. When she and Mike married, they added a master bedroom for themselves, and this room became her office. There was also a small bathroom, a relic of the 1930s, with no windows, a freestanding washbowl, and a toilet. Rita had painted it yellow, added a big, lighted mirror and wicker shelves with yellow towels. When Rita inspected the room today, she noticed that the hand towels and soap had been used. Everything else was in place. Now she was certain that some uninvited person had been in this part of their house and that it had happened yesterday. Why?

"I'm not going to let this distract me," Rita said out loud to no one, and sitting at her desk, she read some pages of her copy of the translated *Carmelo Diaries*. The wording seemed a little awkward in spots, and yet the ethos of the writer remained.

Rita's ancestor, Clarita, was childlike and yet mature when she was fifteen. Clarita accepted tradition, and yet she did not understand the unsuitability of her attachment to Will O'Farrell. Rita stopped at Clarita's words, "I do not know my true feelings."

When Mike and Carmelita returned home, Mike found Rita in the office, and Rita asked him, "Do you think it was unusual that Clarita wrote about her feelings in the diary?"

"Why do you want to know?" he asked.

"Maybe to prove to myself that I need the original diaries. If I had the old Spanish diaries, I might know more about Clarita. I could compare her Spanish words with the English words in the translation. I could check to see if Clarita wrote the words *sentimiento* or *emocíon* in the original diary."

"When was the diary written?"

"1827. That's the same era as Jane Austen's novels. Austen wrote stories about a small sheltered domestic world. I personally think that Clarita would write about feelings. When Clara read the story aloud, she often added her own anecdotes or comments. She always included a few Spanish words to give flavor. Clara referred to the governor either as Governor Echeandía or Don José María. It was interchangeable. Clara emphasized that it was important that Don Felipe Vargas was a close friend of the governor. Clara explained that Clarita hoped the governor would help the Segovias keep their ranch. The inheritance of property was important to her."

"Go back to reading. You'll probably come up with the answers. Carmelita and I have our own things to do."

CHAPTER 6

▼

April 1828

"The governor has been in San Diego, and he called his *diputados* to a meeting. We have heard no news from any of them. The *diputados* from Monterey made the long journey to the South because they wanted to tell the governor that all should meet in Monterey, which is the true capital of Alta California. It has rained so much this year that travel was difficult.

"When my husband returned, he told me about the argument between the governor and Juan Bautista Alvarado, who was the secretary of the *diputados*. The governor told him that as *comandante general* he could live where he could do the most good for all in Alta California. Then the *diputados* replied that they had a right to meet at the true capital. Echeandía did not object to this and told them to return to Monterey, but he blamed Don Juan Bautista because the protest was in his writing. My husband told me that Don Juan Bautista takes too much to drink and then he becomes disrespectful. He even pushed the governor into a corner and pretended to have a dagger. Although they parted as friends, my husband fears that there will be more trouble from this *Californio*. Since my time for becoming a mother is near, I do not have much to do here at Rancho Rincón. I have become more interested in everything my husband tells me about the governor and what is going on. He sometimes listens to what I tell him. I explained that I have known Juan Bautista all my life. We are almost the same age. I think it would be good for everyone to hear what he tells of the incident.

"Our bedroom is now beautiful. I have been able to train a young girl to arrange our bed with the linens and pillows of my dowry. The sheets are embroidered with edges of lace. My husband bought me a polished wooden chest and a blue silk scarf from China and I have made my own altar to the Blessed Virgin. On top of the chest I have placed a silver cross that my mother gave me and I put fresh flowers on the altar everyday. We also have a round table that I have covered with a velvet cloth, and my husband and I drink our morning chocolate there. This bedroom is our very special place and where I stay when he is busy talking to people.

"I did not know that I would have so much to do when our child was born. It will soon be my saint's day, and this is the first I have written about the most important event of my life. Now that it is over it all seems like a dream. I cannot remember the details. I gave birth to a boy. We named him Felipe Bernardo after his father and grandfather. We call him Ardo. Papa was so happy that he rode from Rancho Carmelo to see us the next day. Then he gave the child a gold coin and he presented me with a family ring that had belonged to my mother. Esperanza arrived in an oxcart as her child is coming soon. The *carreta* was made comfortable with many blankets. She is wise in the ways of a mother. She brought a young girl to help me and brought one for herself. Papa will ride beside the *carreta* when they go home.

"The governor has been living in Monterey since May, and now we are planning to entertain him. My husband promises me that I can help plan a *fiesta*. I would like to have music and dancing on the evening of my saint's day. It is warm and fragrant in this valley during the summer. I told Don Felipe that it would be good for all of us if the governor could enjoy himself at our ranch for several days. We could have riding contests, races and bull baiting. We should invite Juan Bautista Alvarado and his cousin, Mariano Vallejo, the acting commander of the Monterey troops, my cousin Consuelo and her husband, Miguel, from the *Presidio,* and of course her parents who are my god parents. I know José Castro enjoys every *fandango.* The Hartnells may be able to come. Since my visit with the de la Guerra family in Santa Bárbara, Teresa and I have much to talk about. I told Don Felipe that it would be good to invite a merchant family such as José and Prudencia Amesti. Prudencia is the elder sister of Mariano and also a cousin of Juan Bautista. Then we should invite Captain Cooper and Encarnacion. She is quiet although she talks to me when we sit in the garden together. Above all we want to show the governor that life is *simpático* in Monterey and we are all like one big family. If the governor finds this land a pleasant place to live maybe he will want to stay in Monterey longer. I can truly say that my husband is so proud to have a son that he listens to me. My prayers have been answered. I know that Don Diego will come to our special fiesta; however, I have learned to avoid him. I surround myself with my friends at all times. I never let myself be alone.

"I must describe my Ardo. He has much curly dark hair and his soft gray eyes are becoming a deeper color. He has rosy cheeks. He seems very strong and he does not cry much. Papa says he looks like my brother when he was a baby. Papa brought a little crib and we put it in our bedroom. I am near him during the night. I am glad he was born in the summer time because he will grow strong. My baby is a hungry child and Esperanza told me to eat well. That is easy to do when it is summer as there is much good food in our garden. At this *rancho* they make a soft cheese that I like, and we have four women to make *tortillas*. Although we do not have large herds of cattle at Rancho Rincón, we have enough to supply us with the beef we need and for making soap and candles. Doña Eulalia has been the housekeeper for Don Felipe ever since his young wife died many years ago in Mexico. She does not talk to me very often, so it is hard to learn to be the mistress of this ranch. But I must succeed.

"September 1828. Soon I will not be able to write until I find more paper and ink. I shall ask my husband to send the Hartnells some of our most tender meat from the young heifers, and I shall write a note to Don Guillermo Hartnell asking him for some writing materials. Teresa says her husband is planning a school some day and he has paper and ink. He is a generous man. Poor Don Guillermo. The governor has ordered strict rules about trade with other countries. This is not good because it is said that he owes many debts.

"My husband says that the *Californios* have not been paying enough taxes to the government of Mexico for all the things we buy from the ships that come to Monterey. The governor must bring order to Alta California and so he is strict about what boats come into port. They must unload everything at the customhouse for inspection and payment of taxes. Then they will take it all back to the ship where we go to buy what we want. My husband said that the *Yanqui* traders have not been paying enough tax. I listen and say nothing but I know how hard it is for the ranches to sell their hides. This was one of the ways that *O'Farol* helped us at Rancho Carmelo. He found buyers for our hides and for the hides of the mission. I think that is how he met Captain Cooper who is a merchant and a *Yanqui*.

"The governor is strict about passports for foreigners. There seem to be more foreigners arriving every year and most are Americans. All must apply for permits to stay here or to travel or to marry. I wonder if O*'Farol* has a permit. Consuelo says she sees him when she goes to the Cooper store and sometimes at mass. He smiles and tips his hat but only says, '*Bueños Días.*' I am sure he must be speaking our language quite well by now. Perhaps I shall see him when we stay in Monterey in the house that my husband has had built for us. It is made of adobe and painted white like all the others in Monterey. It is very simple and has only a *sala* and two other rooms. There is land all around the house so we can add a vegetable garden and have a place for cooking and a place for my maids to sleep. I want to plan our meals and direct the activities of the maids. In this way I will escape Doña Eulalia and can learn to manage a household. When we stay in town I will be able to talk to friends and Consuelo who has two children.

"Our *fandango* was well attended. I enjoyed wearing the new dress that my godmother had made for me. It has a red silk skirt and a beautiful black lace top.

"Although I had heard that the governor is not popular in Monterey, he seemed charming and he danced with all the ladies. He has not been as strict as we feared. He wants to be friendly and he listens to my husband. I think it will soon be time to talk to him about Papa and our ranch. We need to have a friendly governor who will approve of the boundaries of Rancho Carmelo and register the land grant in Mexico City. Although Papa is considered a Spaniard, I was born in Alta California and I can have rights to the land. Father Sarría here is *comisario prefecto* of all the missions and he has been in California since before I was born. He can swear to my birth and parentage.

"Of course the missions are under investigation by Mexico City. The government there wants to take over the missions and use the land. They will give the mission lands to men who are loyal to their government. Even my husband is worried that this might change our way of life.

"October 1828. Monterey. There is so much of interest here. Don Felipe, Ardo, and I are staying in our Monterey house. He has arranged for a porch to be built so we can sit out and enjoy the fine fall weather. The outside door leads into a room where my husband has a table and some chairs, and he can greet visitors and messengers from the governor. There is much talk here about the foreign boats that come into port. My husband helps the governor enforce the taxes and because of that he is not so popular. "This is the news of the day. There are some Americans who have been granted entry to Alta California. They were given permits to travel from mission to mission. They took a boat called the *Franklin* and escaped with it from our harbor. Then they refused to pay the rightful taxes. The crew shouted bad words to the Mexican flag. We sent cannonballs after the ship, but it did not stop. Who knows where the boat will go? What I do not learn from my husband, I find out from Consuelo who lives near the house of the governor inside the *Presidio*. Since I go to mass at the church every day I also hear the news from other friends. One Sunday when Don Felipe and I were at mass, I saw *O'Farol*. He has grown a beard and looks older. I do not know my true feelings. I wanted to see *O'Farol* and now I have seen him I am full of questions. I did not think it would make me as sad as I feel now."

CHAPTER 7

▼

January 27, 2000

The doorbell rang and pushed Rita out of the nineteenth century. She had been considering the words used in the modern translation of the original Spanish diaries. If she had these *Diaries* now, she could compare the text to what she was now reading. Glancing toward the porch and seeing Tessa, Rita ran down the stairs to welcome her friend of many years.

Tessa was someone she really wanted to see. They had known each other since their high school days at Santa Lucia School. Tessa worked out daily at the gym to keep a trim figure, since she had a tendency to be plump. She wore her dark curly hair short and often varied her hairstyle. She always flashed a ready smile of friendliness. Although she had none of Rita's striking good looks, there was an earthy enthusiasm about her that everybody liked. She had been divorced two years ago and had moved back to Carmel when Rita offered her a job at The Old Booktique.

"You have a degree in English and I need someone compatible to work with me," Rita told her. "You may think you don't like business, but you'll like it at my store. We'll do well together."

Tessa put down the bouquet of tulips that she brought and hugged Rita. "I'm sorry about all this, hon. I don't need the day off. Let's go over and make the Booktique ready for customers. I know you have appointments tomorrow. It will be good for you to get back to work."

"I guess so. I'm sort of in a state of shock. I'm glad you came just now, because I'm not getting anything done here."

Tessa took the flowers and found a vase in the pantry. After arranging them casually she set the vase on the table in the breakfast nook.

The phone rang. Rita let the machine take the message.

"Mrs. Minetti, this is Captain Lewis," it began. "A very important development has come up. Please call me. Use Extension 431."

"I didn't think the police would be so involved. When my mother had a burglary last year, they said it didn't warrant a detective," Tessa said.

"Captain Lewis seems really interested. Mike keeps kidding me about him."

"Call him back and hear what he has to tell you."

"I'd rather talk to you. Nobody else knows how valuable some of those books are. When we go back to the store, you can call some of the rare and antique bookstores around here and in San Francisco. Find out if some of our titles have turned up. I'll go upstairs and get my list," Rita finished.

"You said the safe was opened. Was everything gone?"

"All gone, including *The Carmelo Diaries*. I didn't really know that I had such an emotional attachment. I feel disconnected from something that was part of my life."

"Oh, you of the oldest California families. I wasn't even born here," Tessa laughed.

"No, you were born in Paris when your father was number two at the embassy there."

They laughed in an easy camaraderie. "I'll be at the shop in a little while," Rita assured her, and she gave her the list of the missing inventory.

After Tessa left, Rita called Captain Lewis and was told that he was out and that she could leave a message. The phone rang in about five minutes.

"This is Timothy Lewis. You know, Captain Lewis. What's up?"

"I'm returning your call. Also I wanted to tell you that I finished the inventory of missing editions," Rita answered.

"I called to tell you of the interesting new developments. I hope we can meet at your shop. Make it at four o'clock."

"I'll probably be there by noon and we can talk at four if you think it is so important."

"I want your reaction to something."

"Can't you just tell me?"

"No, I want to show you something."

"I'll stay at the store until four. Anything else?"

"You never can tell," he said.

Rita went up to her office and e-mailed a letter to Dave Goldman telling him about the burglary. She asked him to confirm the date and time for the meeting the next week.

Then she called UPS and rescheduled the deliveries of a special boxed and autographed set of Carl Sandburg's *Abraham Lincoln: The War Years* and an autographed first edition of Lawrence Durrell's *Alexandrine Quartet.*

When Mike and Carmelita came home about eleven, Rita told Mike about the call from Captain Lewis." He intimated that there was something new that he discovered. I'll get Marquita to stay here at the house with Carmelita. I intend to go to The Booktique and stay all afternoon. Captain Lewis will drop by about four," she explained.

"I told you that he likes you. Can I be there, too?" Mike asked teasingly.

"Of course, Darling, "Rita laughed and after she settled Carmelita with her toys, she filled Mike in on more of the details of the morning.

"Tessa will be with me this afternoon. Can I still count on you to make your special marinara sauce?"

Mike nodded and looked at the sports page again while Rita quickly showered and dressed in black leather pants and an aqua blue turtleneck sweater. She gave lunch to Carmelita and left.

As soon as Rita arrived at her reserved parking area, she saw two panel trucks and television equipment being set up in front of her store. A young hyperactive woman, dressed in a black knit suit with a very short skirt, pushed a microphone close to Rita's mouth and said, "Does anybody want to shut down your business, Miss Atherton?"

"I don't understand why you are here," Rita replied.

She kept on walking and soon saw the door of the shop slightly ajar. She hoped Tessa was inside the shop. When she looked across the lawn toward the resort hotel, she saw a cameraman from the local TV station photographing the circle of specialty shops where her bookshop was located. Tourists were standing around looking at the scene and hoping that some recognizable celebrity would soon appear.

"Your shop was been broken into," the TV station newswoman called out as she followed Rita.

"That's hardly news," Rita snapped.

"A burglary in such a secure area as this. I think that is news," said the reporter from *The Peninsula Sentinel.*

By this time, Captain Lewis had arrived. Quickly crossing the lawn, he came up beside her, and walked with her to the door of the shop.

"Don't say anything, Mrs. Minetti. It will just compromise the case."

"Has something new happened?" Rita asked him.

"The local TV station decided to make something of it," he replied. "Is that your assistant," he pointed toward Tessa.

"Yes, that is Mrs. De Mont. She's helping me get ready for business tomorrow. Is this what you called me about this morning?"

"Yes, I had a tip that reporters were going to be roaming around out here this afternoon."

"Why are they here?"

"*The Peninsula Sentinel* received a phone call this morning from the Amicus Shelter Thrift Shop in San Francisco. They had been given some valuable eighteenth century books this morning. A homeless lady who eats breakfast there brought the books in. She said she found them in a paper shopping bag that had been tossed into a garbage bin. One of the books had an inventory marker from your store."

"Did the reporters call the police?" Rita asked with interest.

"No, but our office received the call from Amicus because your store is located in our county's jurisdiction."

"Have the reporters been into the shop?"

"No, Mrs. De Mont would not let them in. She did the right thing. By the way, did you bring the inventory?" When Rita nodded, he went on, "Let's get inside." He escorted her quickly through the door.

Rita looked outside and saw that the reporters and the cameramen were still milling around outside. "How long are those people going to be here?" she addressed Captain Lewis.

"Probably until they get some kind of a story."

"I'm not going to tell them anything," Rita said emphatically.

"You may have done so already."

"I don't think so. Why is this so important to them?" Rita frowned.

"It depends on what else they have for the news, today," he said trying to change the subject. At the same time he was enjoying all her facial expressions.

"Let's sit down here," Rita said as she pointed to the chairs at a broad table half filled with books. "Do you want me to go over the inventory with you?" and she handed him a manila folder.

"Yes it is always helpful when you cooperate," he said rather sternly. Then with a softer voice, he added, "and I will personally do every thing I can to help you."

Rita acknowledged his change of attitude. "Thank you," she replied.

"Why do you think your store was burglarized?" he queried.

"Someone wanted *The Carmelo Diaries*."

"Then why was the place trashed?"

Rita shook her hair, put her hands behind her neck, and took a deep breath. "I'll have to make my own assessments about that."

"Someone might be trying to harass you. I think you are holding something back. Give me the names of a few people to question."

"I don't want to give you any names until I am certain."

"That's not the way we work. If I think you are withholding evidence, I could order you to do any number of things. But then, I think you want results as much as I do." He smiled as if he thought he was complimenting her.

"This whole thing has disrupted my life. I have started to read a translation of *The Diaries,* and I am even more convinced that the original Spanish books are more valuable than I thought. I don't want to involve innocent people."

"Are you always this trusting? I think this burglary is one of mean intention." The captain settled into his chair.

Rita wanted to answer without showing emotion. "I have yet to take another careful look around the shop today. I also want to talk to Tessa."

"Oh, here is the deputy who is going to take some pictures. By the way, Mrs. Minetti, you really need a first class safe. The one you have is just a fancy lock box. Have you ever thought of using a TV surveillance monitor?"

"I suppose I should do both those things. One thing is for sure. I'm not going to leave the shop until that TV crew outside leaves the area. So please give them that statement, and tell them not to bother me anymore."

"Are you always accustomed to giving orders to everybody?" he laughed.

Rita had a sharp repartee on the tip of her tongue, but instead she said, "I am being businesslike and honest."

"I appreciate your position, Mrs. Minetti. I will allow you a little more time to come up with names while we finish our inspection, and I will deal with the press."

Rita wanted to make the shop ready for tomorrow. She hoped to take a careful look at her desk but not under the watchful eye of Captain Lewis, who in spite of his bland appearance often exhibited an aggressive manner.

"Excuse me, but I am going to talk to Tessa." Rita paused a moment. "I don't think you've been introduced to her." Captain Lewis remained sitting and looked at her with a benign and somewhat calculated informality."

"Yes, I would like to be introduced to her. She is the next person I need to question. Everyone must be interviewed. Even your husband."

While Rita walked toward Tessa's computer station, Captain Lewis arose and caught up with her. Tessa observed their arrival and smiled pleasantly as she pushed herself away from the computer screen.

"Tessa De Mont, this is Captain Lewis of the Investigative Division of the Sheriff's Department," Rita initiated at once.

He nodded with interest, and they shook hands. "Do you have a minute right now for me to ask you some questions?"

Rita left them quickly and sat down at her own desk. She experienced a feeling of apprehension. She had not looked into her desk last night. She opened the center drawer and saw paper clips, a calculator, some Post-it notes, a book of stamps, and a blank memo pad. She was sure that other office conveniences, such as her appointment calendar and personal address book were in the desk drawer. It seemed different to her now

A strong wind came up, and Rita looked out to see the cypress trees blowing in an easterly direction away from the ocean. She rose and recognized Mike making his way through the obstacle course of the press and their equipment. In his business, Mike was accustomed to dealing with all kinds of people, and she imagined that he was saying the right things without alienating anyone. She stood up and went to where Tessa was working at her computer. Captain Lewis was talking with his photographer.

"I'm baffled," Rita began as she pulled up a chair beside her friend.

"By the Captain?"

"No, by the turn of events today."

"It's just the way they have to investigate," Tessa said casually.

"No, I mean my desk."

"It looks OK. Pretty neat and clean. I didn't see it yesterday."

"It doesn't look like it did before the burglary?

"Oh, that's crazy. You're upset. You probably forgot how you left it."

"No. It seems as if someone changed things inside my middle drawer."

"That's pretty weird."

"What was your desk like when you came in?"

"It was neat. But I knew you and Mike had straightened things up."

"I didn't touch your desk. I never do that."

"Rita, you are letting all this bother you too much. You really haven't been yourself since those Hollywood people first contacted you about using your diaries."

"Maybe they're responsible for all this? They think *The Carmelo Diaries* are valuable."

"I told Captain Lewis I didn't have any ideas who might want to break into our little shop." Tessa offered.

"No matter what happens, we're going to open for business tomorrow. Did you take any important phone calls before I arrived?"

When Tessa shook her head, Rita went to greet Mike.

"Do you think we'll make the eleven o'clock news tonight, Babe?"

"If they get a story. What did you tell them?"

"I told them a joke," he said and gave her a little kiss. "They want to make the most of what happened here."

Captain Lewis walked over to them. "I think we're just about through here. Please think about what other information you can give me, Mrs. Minetti?" he said and looked very much like an inspector.

"You have my inventory to look over. It might be everything you need." She said with finality. She wanted to say nothing more to the police.

When Mike went over to talk to Tessa, Captain Lewis assumed his tone of confidentiality and said, "I have great hopes that we can put together the pieces to this puzzle."

Captain Lewis wanted to solve the case, but not too soon. He had moved to Monterey from Idaho two years ago. As yet, he had not spent much time in the environment of Pebble Beach golf course and The Retreat. Rita, Mike, and now Tessa interested him, so he really wanted to stretch out the investigation.

"I'm sure you'll have more questions to ask," Rita finally said and kept hoping he would leave soon.

"That's the spirit. We can help each other."

"Then take care of the press out there," she said and they shook hands. She wanted to close the shop as soon as the police left.

Captain Lewis spoke a few words to Tessa and walked out, while from inside, Rita and Mike watched the activity on the lawn in front of The Old Booktiques. Captain Lewis enjoyed talking to the enthusiastic young reporter and both were posturing to impress the other.

"They seem like young dogs chasing their tails," she said to Mike as he gave her a friendly pat.

"He looks like he just graduated from the latest class of police public relations school," she continued.

"Don't be so hard on him. You're just jealous now that he's giving all his attention to that cute young reporter," Mike kidded.

"I'm not jealous of anybody," Rita said glumly. She was annoyed that the outside television crew was lingering in front of her shop. "I think that the good Captain will try all sorts of ways to make himself look good to the world while he's investigating this case."

"That's his job, hon. For God's sake," Mike admonished.

"He says he's going to interrogate you, Mike. So be careful."

"OK, I'll tell them that I arranged the whole thing as a joke." When he saw her lower her shoulders in exasperation, he quickly said, "Rita, you don't have anything to hide. Tell him whatever you want to. Just don't take what he says to you personally."

"Well all this is very personal to me. I'll tell you more about that later," she said mysteriously.

The police and the press left quickly when their roles were played out. Rita watched them taking one last panoramic photograph of her shop and the surrounding buildings. The Old Booktiques was not much larger than a garden gazebo, but it was located in the center of the shopping circle. She wondered if they would really see it all on a TV broadcast.

Tessa soon left and Mike and Rita returned to their home where they settled into their domestic roles. While Mike cooked the marinara sauce, Rita gave Carmelita some dinner and the phone rang.

"Are you watching the six o'clock news, dear?" her mother, Anita exploded breathlessly.

"Not tonight, Mother. We were late getting home and we are in the process of making dinner."

"It's about your store. Turn it on at once and call me back when it's over," she said without further conversation.

Rita did just that. "Mike, now can you see why I didn't want to say much to Captain Lewis? I think he's media happy. I also think he's intrigued with the Pebble Beach mystique and all that," Rita said brandishing the hand grater as she talked. She had turned on a thirteen-inch television set that was installed for kitchen viewing. The screen showed the Retreat, the spacious round of lawn in front of the shopping circle, and Captain Lewis in front of The Old Booktique. The flamingo glow of the recent sunset completed the setting.

"We really don't know much more now than when we first arrived at the burglary scene," finished Captain Lewis.

Instantly a crisp voice took over. "This is Kitchie Glaser. We'll have more to tell you about this daring burglary right in front of The Retreat. Tune us in at eleven o'clock," she said.

Soon the station switched to Tom Brokaw who was commenting on what the Vice President said that was contradictory to what the President said at his press conference. The phone rang, and Rita's mother started the conversation in the middle of a sentence.

"I think so, don't you?" and then she proceeded with a reply. "Why didn't they show you? Was it awful, dear? I would have thought that you would be in the interview. The reporters may visit you tomorrow. Be sure you wear your turquoise blue sweater. It does so much for your hair. It's your best feature you know."

"Mother, I'm not even planning to talk to them."

"It would be wonderful publicity for your little shop."

"The people who buy antique books aren't influenced by a burglary or a TV interview."

"Well you know best. You always do," she said with a lazy laugh and sigh. "By the way, guess who came to see me yesterday?"

"I can't."

"No, I don't think you could. It was Charlie."

"What Charlie?"

"Your brother. My son."

"What did he want?'

"He didn't want anything. Don't be bitter. I detect bitterness in your voice, dear. Charlie is at The Retreat at that prestigious conference for California Winemakers. It's an honor to be invited to attend and he was even asked to speak."

"I'm happy for him. I'm happy that he was chosen."

"You don't sound it, dear."

"Mother, it's been an impossible day. And, yes, it was an awful mess. All my business was interrupted. Police were all over the place yesterday and it was the same thing this afternoon. We are still making dinner, and Carmelita is very hungry."

"I'll hang up then, but do call back. I want to tell you what Charles said."

"Later then, dear," Rita promised as they both said goodbye.

CHAPTER 8

▼

January 1829

"The season of *Navidad* was different this year because we traveled between the *casita* in Monterey and Rancho Rincón. We always took Ardo with us, and everyone praised his good looks. When I was in Monterey, I rarely left the *casita*. Life is so pleasant within the adobe walls that surround our courtyard. That is where we eat many of our meals, and we have benches where we sometimes sit beneath the sloping tile roof that gives us shade. Since there has not been much rain, we can entertain visitors on the porch.

"The Blessed Virgin has answered our prayers, and I am with another child. When a boat came in from China, Don Felipe inspected the cargo at the Customs House, and the next day he went out to the ship to buy a necklace of pearls for me. He hopes for another son. Of course, but I am hoping for a daughter so that I can name her María Isabel after my mother. Perhaps my state of health is the reason for my laziness, but I do not wish to entertain much at this time, and I am content to sit and play with Ardo. He laughs when birds fly into our garden, and he looks at his hands when I sit him up on the pillows next to me on our beautiful bed.

"Now that my husband has a son who is born in Alta California, he is more favorable to the *Californio* point of view, and he tells me he thinks the governor is too hard on us. He says the actions of the *diputacion* are really the wishes of the governor and not that of the *diputados*. Don Cárlos Carrillo wants to have a boat built for local trade to sail up and down the coast, but Don José María Echeandía is delaying it because he says Don Cárlos must wait for a special permit from Mexico. We could understand this if it was a man from England or a *Yanqui* who wanted to build a boat, but Don Cárlos is from an established family who lives to the South of Monterey.

"My friends in Santa Bárbara told me about the troubles of the Carrillo family. Doña Josefa, daughter of Joaquin Carrillo, is about my age and wants to marry an American sailor in his late twenties. Last year he sent her a written promise of marriage. She accepted him with the blessings of her parents, but the couple cannot marry until he becomes a Mexican citizen and is baptized with a Spanish name. My husband tells me that the governor also courted Doña Josefa. Therefore he is slow to grant the papers that are necessary for the marriage. It is said that the *Yanqui* is tall, handsome, and cheerful. It is a true love story, and I hope they will be able to marry.

"April 1829. My husband went south with the governor to San Diego. I am now at Rancho Rincón de Gavalán, and I wish I were closer to the sea. There is always something new to me here. At Rancho Rincón even the trees are different. The house here is surrounded with pine trees and groves of sycamores surround the fields. They have cactus in the courtyard to keep out stray animals The *hacienda* where I grew up is built on a hill, and I could always see the blue ocean from the upper floor. I used to ride my horse to the beach almost every day. We had many herds of cattle, I liked to watch the little calves follow their mothers and then grow strong on their own. Our *casita* in Monterey is near the estuary and when I am in the courtyard, I can hear the sound of waves and of the seals barking. Here I can only hear the lonely sound of the wind through a valley."

At this point the first diary ends. Clarita continued her journal in another book, covered with California cowhide the pages of vellum were sewn to the cover with thread made of cowhide sinews.

"May 1829. Much sorrow has come to my life. The mother of Consuelo, who is a cousin of my mother, has died. She is my *madrina,* and I wanted to go to the visitation held for her in Monterey. Also I wanted to attend the funeral, but there was no one here to take me. When I went to mass at Mission San Juan Bautista with Doña Eulalia, I lit candles for Doña Loretta, and I gave Father Salvador a gold coin so that he will say prayers for her soul during the next month. Consuelo's brother, Don Tiburcio, brought me this book that I am writing in now. He also gave me a garnet rosary from Spain. My godmother wanted me to have these things.

"Ardo is so lively that it tires me to play with him. I always take a *siesta* when he takes his long nap. The weather is warm here and I like to doze in the shade of the oak trees. Don Felipe has arranged for a hammock filled with pillows for my comfort and that is where I rest with Ardo close by in the *patio*.

"What I write now will be difficult for me to tell. My husband must be told the whole story when he returns. On a pleasant day last week, I was taking a *siesta* as usual. I did not know that anyone else was around when I felt the breath of a person. Someone was near me. It was Don Diego. He put his hand on my mouth while he whispered that soon he would be my master. When I stood up, he pulled me towards him, and when I tried to scream, he put his mouth on mine. I bit him and turned over the hammock in order to escape. I started to run and called for my maid to take care of Ardo, who was awake and crying. I tripped over my skirts on the rocky path, and turning my ankle I fell on my face. I suppose Don Diego went to the house and told them I had fallen, because soon, two maids appeared and when they saw blood on my face, one went for water from the well at the end of the garden.

"The next day, I suddenly had the pains of birthing, and our child was born two months before her time. She lived only a day. She was too small to survive. Father Salvador came from the mission, and this precious child was baptized as María Isabel in the last moments of her life. I know she is with my mother and the Blessed Virgin in heaven, and for that I am thankful. I already miss her very much. I do not know what Don Diego said to anyone. I know it will not be the truth. I am writing about it here so that it will be known if I should die. I vow that I will never let Don Diego have his way with me, and that I will have the courage to tell my husband what happened, even though he may not believe me. I asked the majordomo to send a rider with a message to Papa and to Consuelo about little María Isabel. I instructed Consuelo to give the deputy governor at the *presidio* a packet from me with instructions to dispatch a rider to my husband who is with the governor. I am a little weak but I am no longer frightened because I have made a vow to protect myself.

"Doña Eulalia has not said unkind words to me since the death of María Isabel. She does not dare tell me I am lazy. Consuelo visited us and stayed with us several days. We went by *carreta* to Mission San Juan Bautista, and we had prayers said for María Isabel. I have learned to love this mission. A *Yanqui* sailor painted the main altar and the *reredos*. It took him many years. When I attend mass, I listen to the Indian choir and feel a special holiness.

"Consuelo told me that Henry Fitch and Doña Josefa were to be secretly married after he was formally baptized Enrique Domingo Fitch at the *presidio* chapel in San Diego. Domingo Carrillo, an uncle, was to be the godfather. At the last minute, Don Domingo refused to take part and forbade the marriage by the order of governor Echeandía. They could not marry. The *padre* quietly told Don Enrique that there were other places that they could be married. They could go to a place where the laws are not as strict as in Alta California. One of the persons present at the intended ceremony was Captain Barry from the ship on which Don Enrique sailed. It is said that Doña Josefa spoke up and said, 'Why don't you carry me off, Don Enrique,' Captain Barry quietly agreed with the arrangement. That night Don Pío Pico, a cousin of Josefa, took her on his horse to where the ship was anchored, and before daylight their ship was on its way. There is no news of the ship or the lovers; however, the ship due in the ports of Lima and Valparaiso some time this summer. This is the first good fortune I have heard.

"Both Consuelo and I hope the couple can remain married, although we know that father Domingo and some of the other fathers will be displeased. The governor is furious. I have heard nothing of it from my husband. I do not know what he will say, since he is such a good friend of the governor. Also he does not like *Yanquis* and does not approve of them marrying the *Californio* ladies. He will probably tell me that the Carrillo family has been shamed. Don Enrique and Doña Josefa have many problems to overcome if they want to come back to Alta California as a married couple, and yet I am sure they are very happy to be together now.

"There is some good news. Consuelo was left sixteen Spanish gold doubloons by her mother. Although her husband, Miguel, is a lieutenant at the *Presidio*, they have only three rooms for themselves. This is too small for their growing family. Now they can live in a house outside the walls of the *Presidio*. Miguel has found someone who owns such a house of adobe on a good plot of land. This man received the house from the governor, and now he lives on the ranch he owns near the Bay of Monterey. He accepted the offer of gold doubloons.

"Consuelo also told me that she talked to *O'Farol*. He offered his sympathy on the passing of her mother. He said Doña Loreta was a noble lady. Consuelo told me that he speaks Spanish now, although his red hair betrays him as a *Yanqui*. Then, she told me her mother found him helpful in finding the clothes that she needed. Consuelo said she advised him to go in business for himself, but he told her that this is impossible because he is not a Mexican citizen. Consuelo said that the governor might deport him. She said her mother told him to save any silver or gold that he receives, because money sometimes speaks more than the word of a gentleman.

"I laughed at this statement, because Consuelo always said that she does not think *O'Farol* is a gentleman. Today I answered her. 'Your mother told me he was an honest man and can be a citizen when he gets his papers of Mexican citizenship.'

"During this conversation I felt myself turn cold, and then my face felt warm. I was afraid I would say something wrong to Consuelo, but she chattered on and on. 'I think he wanted to marry you, my dear cousin but that was impossible. You were already promised.'

"I said nothing to this statement. I had never told Consuelo much about O'Farol except that I had rescued him from the ocean, and that he helped Papa at the ranch.

"June 1829. Since the early death of our daughter, my husband has been kind, and yet he seems to be in another land. I hope he does not want to go back to Mexico, because I do not want to be so far away from my family. He told me the governor has many enemies here and at the Monterey *Presidio*. Only the officers that came with him from Mexico get paid. The other soldiers might revolt. It is not really the fault of Don José María because he has been sent so little money from Mexico City. The government tells him to take hides and beef from the missions. My husband has been acquainted with Don José for many years. He says he is not a bad man, but not the right person to be a governor of Alta California at this time. The government has changed many times in Mexico. And even Don Felipe does not know who is in charge now.

"Alta California has many kinds of people, and Mexico does not understand how different we all are. There are the Spanish people who were born here. Then there are people from Mexico who have been sent here for different reasons. Next, we have the Indians, who have been trained by the Fathers, and there are Indians, who are savage and go back and forth to the hills. Finally, there are the *Yanquis,* who want to make their homes here, and lately there are other *Yanquis,* who dress in leather clothes and who have come from across the lands to the east and who have come to hunt wild animals. They are very different from the ones who have come by ship. Everyone wants the army to defend us and keep the coast free from pirates and the Russians. Yet nothing is sent to pay the soldiers. They don't even have good clothes. The missions and the mission fathers have supplied the *presidio* with food for the last ten years but the mission fathers do not want to help any more. The government of Mexico wants to close the missions and give their lands away. They say the governor will soon choose a man who will distribute small plots to the Indians and give out the remainder of the mission property to friends.

"July 1829. Don Felipe decided that Ardo and I should move to Monterey again. While we are living in our *casita,* he will have some Indians make adobe bricks and tiles, and he will use people from our ranch to build the house with this adobe. We will add on a room for Ardo and add another outside room that will be our kitchen. Our maids will sleep there. We will also have a storehouse. While there is no rain it is a good time to make adobe bricks. We will be more comfortable this winter.

"Ardo is already walking. I will find a maid who can follow him around and keep him safe. Now that we entertain dinner guests, I have much more to do. Whenever a ship comes to port, the important people of the town have the officers to dinner, and we are expected to have an occasional party when the governor comes to town. My husband wants me to visit with ladies and make lace. I do not know if it is possible. This custom is becoming forgotten. Very few ladies here know about the old customs now that my godmother is gone. Doña Loreta was important to us all, and no one has taken her place. Consuelo is too busy with her children to arrange social functions. They are now living in their new house outside the walls of the *Presidio*. This is good for them, because her husband is not with the soldiers who want to revolt. Miguel wants to be friendly with the governor and hopes that some day he may be given ranch land of his own. At the present time Consuleo and I can walk along a path to visit each other. She now has another baby.

"Near the end of summer, Papa told Esperanza to prepare a feast to celebrate the anniversary of our marriage. Don Felipe brought the governor, and there were many other important men of the town. Papa told me that the governor said he was going to give out land to *Californios*, and that he would see that Papa's claim for Rancho Carmelo was sent to Mexico. Consuelo and family attended the *fiesta*. Afterwards we took our children on a *merienda* beside the river. Her boys watched the gathering of the cattle, and they were amused with the tricks of the *vaqueros* on their horses. We took blankets to spread out under the trees, and after the children rested, we told stories, picked flowers and counted the clouds. A wind swept up the river valley, and then we used the blankets to keep the children warm while we slowly made our way back in the *carretas*. All this gave me a sense of happiness, and I forgot about Don Diego and his words. If my husband must leave for a long time, I will ask him to allow me to bring Ardo here while he is gone. I want Ardo to know about this beautiful place near the shore and the ocean. I want him to learn to ride here under the watchful eye of his grandfather.

"November 1829. We are in Monterey. During the time we were at Rancho Carmelo, I found that there has been a real plot to revolt against the governor. When I went to the house of Captain Cooper for a party, I heard a story that was whispered by the sister of Encarnacion. At that time no one knew the details. It seems there is a convict who has been sent here from Mexico for his crimes. His name is Joaquin Solís, and he tried to get the soldiers to take over the *Presidio* in Monterey while the governor was in the South. Then a few nights ago, some soldiers at the *Presidio* tried to take over the governor's headquarters. They also decided to break into the house of Mariano Vallejo. He will be leaving Monterey, because he has been assigned to a post in the San Francisco Company and will no longer be in command at the *Presidio* here. Juan Bautista Alvarado and José Casto went to visit Mariano here before he left, and soldiers from the *Presidio* crashed in a door. Mariano, Juan B and José were dragged off and were put into a jail. This was the beginning of serious protest against the governor. This seems strange, because Mariano, Juan Bautista, and José are not the ones who are against the soldiers, and they even signed statements saying that the men needed to be given their due pay. When my husband heard about the break in, he was very angry. He sent a message to Joaquin Solís and demanded that he come to Monterey immediately to explain the situation. This man told my husband that he wanted to prevent further problems among revolting soldiers, but Don Felipe knew that Señor Solis was plotting against governor Echeandía. A plan for the future of the soldiers was written up and a meeting was called. The *Yanquis*, Señor Cooper and Hartnell and some others were invited, and my husband said they signed the petition. They also want a different governor and one that is chosen by local men. My poor husband was very sad because he knew that all these men were against his friend the governor, who is still in San Diego. He dispatched a rider to tell him to come to Monterey.

"My husband tells me that the *Yanquis* want things to be peaceful so they can continue to sell their goods to us. He thinks that Señor Solís wants power and is trying to spread a revolt to all California. Don Felipe has not slept well since this happened. He is not very kind to me and has not given me any presents since María Isabel died. I have stayed close to Ardo and have not walked outside the courtyard, although Señor Solís has gone to San Francisco to get more troops to help him.

"Now is the season of *Las Posadas*. Monterey is quiet. I want to go to Rancho Carmelo with Ardo. I want to be safe and observe the holy days without having soldiers around us. I must go to confession, because I need to ask forgiveness for my selfishness. Don Felipe was angry because of my request, and we will stay here in Monterey.

"January 1830. Don Felipe did not feel well in December and only went to mass the night before *Navidad*. Miguel escorted Ardo and me to the festivities at their house. Ardo is happy to be with the children of Consuelo and Miguel, and we are safe when we are with their family. Señor Solís gathered an army in the north, and they marched south from Monterey to meet the governor and his army. I am now able to go to church without the jeering of his soldiers.

"Don Felipe does not sleep well and says very little to me. Governor Echeandía used men from San Diego and Santa Bárbara. He gained a victory over the men of Solís, so I think Solis and his men went to Mexico. Don Felipe told me very little about it and has not told me whether we will stay in Monterey.

"At this time we cannot go outside because there is so much rain. The mud runs everywhere around the house. We stay in our bedroom most of the time, and I make up games to play with Ardo. We sing, and I teach him little verses to say. I teach him to say prayers by my bedside altar. I am happy with Ardo, so this is a pleasure. I wonder what the coming year will bring to us."

CHAPTER 9

▼

January 27, 2000 in the evening

Mike told Carmelita a bedtime story after dinner, and Rita tucked her into bed. Then she called Anita.

"Sorry, but it took a little longer than I thought. I wanted to put Carmelita to bed before I sat down to talk," Rita said to her mother.

"Oh, I understand, dear. And I'm very pleased that you turned out to be such a good mother. I wouldn't have asked you to call if I didn't have something to tell you."

"About Charlie?"

"Well, yes. First, he told me what I already knew. He said that he and Missy had been living separately and that she had the girls right now. He said that Missy wanted a divorce, and as part of the procedure, they went together to a marriage therapist. Charlie said it was helpful to both of them. It surprised me that Charlie said he now realizes what a bad example Rex has been all these years. You know what I mean, dear. Your father was always running around all over the country. Now Charlie sympathizes with me. I never thought I'd hear him say that. The therapist told him that it was very important for a girl to have an attentive father and now he understands you better."

"He brought me into it?"

"Of course, dear. He sees how important family is. Anyway, he wants to be a better father to his daughters, and he and Missy are beginning to talk over their problems without blaming each other."

"Is that what you wanted to tell me?"

"Oh no. That is just the beginning. He said when he finishes the seminar at The Retreat, he wants to see us again. I invited him to stay at Stonecrest a few days. He accepted. He has been developing his own prestige wine label, you know. He needs financing and now he realizes the importance of his Torelli connections. He said when he and Missy listed their assets, he realized he was not willing to give Missy any share of his new designer wine business, and then he really dropped a bomb," Anita paused.

"Am I to guess?"

"He said he and Missy were learning about creative ways they could understand each other and live together. They decided to stay married for the sake of their daughters, and Missy is willing to put her own money into the Val du Soleil venture. Together they can make that business a top contender for prizes in the boutique wine category. He wants to talk over his new ideas with me?" Anita paused momentarily and before Rita could reply, she continued, "I think Missy would be good at putting on a charity wine auction. They are very popular now. Don't you think so? Oh, yes, and I want you and Mike to come for dinner, tomorrow night. You will, won't you?"

"We will, Mother." Rita answered knowing it was better to agree quickly with the inevitable.

"And be sure and wear something bright. I like that grape colored knit suit that looks so good on you figure. Nothing black," and she hung up.

Rita mulled over the news and was relived that Anita ended the conversation quickly. She found Mike in the den.

"That was Mother," she started. "Remember she said she'd call me back? She really had something to tell me. It took me by surprise. Charlie is at The Retreat attending a conference, and he paid her a visit."

"What did he want?"

"Those were my very thoughts."

"Is your mother eager to be friends with Charlie now? Charlie turned against your mother, too."

Rita summarized Anita's conversation. "He even told her he realizes how important the Torelli name is to the wine industry of California."

"You mean he's not putting down Italians now?"

"Not this month."

"He wants to see us. Mother has invited us to dinner."

"No."

"Mother doesn't ask us to dinner very often."

"That's just it. After the first overture from Charles, she is again sitting in the audience and clapping for him."

"Having dinner with Mother and Charlie won't influence us. We know what a jerk he is. So obsessively selfish. I'm sure the therapist knows this already. She probably told him to mend his fences everywhere."

"Why would we want to go to dinner with him after what he said and did at your grandmother's funeral?"

"I want to go. It's for my own reasons, and I'm not caving in. I have a theory about something, and this might bring me closer to an answer. It is something I want to discuss with you. But not yet."

"OK, but you have to promise to tell me before we go to that dinner."

"I'll tell you soon."

"Let's talk about something else. Do you realize that the big Pro Am Tournament is next week?"

"Oh God, I forgot. The place will be crawling with people."

"Don't you have an appointment with that guy from Hollywood? Maybe he's coming up to watch the golf?"

"I think he is, but I don't know for sure. Did I tell you that I started reading Clara's translation of *The Diaries* today?"

"I think so. Tell me what you think of them."

"I still find the story fascinating. I want to add the stories about Clarita's later life. Clarita's granddaughter, Isabel, wrote several notebooks that tell about Clarita's years in San Francisco. She lived a long time in that city and knew a great many people, including mayors, business tycoons, and *Californio* families. This would be a good addition."

"Then, you better just do it," Mike agreed and he gave her a quick kiss.

"Right now. I think it's going to storm, and all I want to do is go to sleep," Rita sighed, and both she and Mike retired early.

Rita slept soundly through wind and rain. When she awoke at six and heard the soft patter of rain on the roof, she knew it was a morning to stay indoors and be cozy. She talked herself out of a fast neighborhood walk and reluctantly climbed onto a stationary bicycle they had installed in "the X room." She was being needlessly hard on herself about a few stubborn pounds. While she peddled, she thought about her project. She was now reading the second diary that covered the years from 1829 to 1836. Juan Bautista Alvarado was governor of Alta California. She decided to use some letters that Clarita had written to Consuelo during those years. She had found all of them in her safe in the upstairs office.

When Rita finished her exercises, she made a fire in the family room and began to prepare their breakfast. A cat had walked across the patio making the automatic lights illuminate the garden, and she could see that it would be a gray rainy day. It was a good morning for an old-fashioned oatmeal breakfast and maybe she would treat Mike to a pink grapefruit with a dash of liqueur. Somehow the gloomy weather inspired her to pay extra attention to their food.

Mike soon came in from picking up the local newspaper on the front porch. His dark hair had become curly in the misty humidity. "I hope your getting up so early doesn't become a habit," he gave a little sigh "I like to wake up and have you beside me."

"I like that, too," she said mimicking his tone, "but I didn't want to disturb your beauty sleep. Have a cup of coffee while we talk a little."

"What kind of a day do you expect?" he asked earnestly.

"Challenging. I would love a nice normal day with eccentric and knowledgeable collectors coming into the shop, but I think the day will be filled with talk about the missing inventory."

"Don't focus on the burglary," Mike said. "Do what you need to do at the shop. Let Tessa do the rest. As far as the saga you want to tell, I don't think you really need the original diaries, right now. Concentrate on the story line. Have you thought of using some of Clara's stories?"

"Oh, very definitely. But I want it to be authentic. I'm worried that the copies might not be an accurate translation. I want the Spanish originals. I want those diaries returned," she told him

"Don't make a fuss about what you don't have, Babe." He told her.

"You're right."

"Were you surprised that Charles made contact with your mother?"

"In a way yes, and yet I'm not really surprised," she answered emphatically. "Charlie is always hopping on the bandwagon with whatever side of the family seems to be best for him at the moment. He used to butter up Grandmother Atherton when Daddy Rex was ungenerous with him. Then she would invite him to her house at Tahoe or to her San Francisco apartment. She would give him a weekend of fun with speed boats and water skiing or let him have anything he wanted to buy at the stores."

"Do you think he has an ulterior motive now?"

"Of course. He always does."

"Then why humor him by going to your mother's for dinner?"

"I don't know if it's a good thing or not, but I want to go to watch Charlie's reaction to a few things that will be said."

"Then you really do have something up your sleeve," Mike followed.

"I'm in a state of puzzlement."

"I wasn't surprised to hear about Charles and Missy having marriage problems," Mike said pensively. "It's that crucial time in their lives when they both might want to be doing something else."

"I don't think they are that reflective. Neither of them have much patience. Missy might become bored when she's living in the vineyards. It's good she'll be involved in the business in some way."

"When did they first move there?"

"When the girls were ready to go to Holy Name School. Charles had already started his own vineyard and was driving back and forth to San Francisco every few days. Missy agreed to move to the ranch, because she didn't want the girls to board at school. If she personally drives them to school and supervises all their recreation, she feels in control. She likes to feel important and busy. Charles told Mother that the house is 'very Provence' with all the fabrics coming straight from Avignon and the furniture copied from a picture of the rooms at the Mas de les Roches in the Luberon. The garden is probably all sunflowers and lavender."

"You really are a bitchy little sister," Mike commented laughingly.

"It's my role, and I've learned it well."

"I still want you to tell me what motivates you to attend the dinner party."

"You'll be the first to know," she said and hurried upstairs to Carmelita's room. "Is that a promise?" Mike called after her and no more was said as they both had a busy morning.

Rita went to The Old Booktique as soon as Marquita arrived to take care of Carmelita. The store was ready for customers, and Tessa was busy arranging a reschedule of all the appointments that had been cancelled. Rita made several telephone calls to clients, and answered questions about the burglary as best she could.

Captain Lewis telephoned. He informed Rita that the first part of the police inspection was complete. Then he said, "We haven't talked to your Mr. Goldman. His secretary said he couldn't be reached. He was in an all day conference. Have you been able to talk to him?"

"Frankly, I haven't tried," Rita said. "I've been awfully busy, and I thought maybe he would call me. We were in the process of setting up an appointment for next week. He's coming up to watch the tournament."

"Let me know when you talk to him," Lewis replied, and he hung up quickly in is characteristic way of never saying goodbye.

Tessa greeted customers while Rita was on the phone and the morning passed. They looked out toward the golf course and could see no golf play. The rain was intermittent and unpredictable, and the sky told them this weather would continue. The Old Booktique was no longer newsworthy for the local TV station, so the roving reporters were now focusing on hoopla for the upcoming golf classic. Rita knew their stories would read, "Will the games be rained out this year as in the past? Will Tiger Woods make a new record? What celebrities have the most chance to be scratched?"

The Old Booktique was no longer in the spotlight, but Rita was uneasy about her brother's reappearance, and she was worried that she had not received a communication from Dave Goldman. She still hoped to give him a preliminary proposal next week. By two o'clock she gave up trying to get through her agenda. She left the shop for Tessa to handle and went home. Since Carmelita was still napping, she continued reading her copy of *The Carmelo Dairies*.

Mike came home early, and after he took Carmelita for a splashy walk in the light rain, he was ready to talk to Rita about her day.

"My head is filled with Spanish names and quaint colonial customs. Those early *Californios* were not a part of the world at that time. They lived in a time warp. Their politics and military skirmishes seemed like antics in a comic opera. There were only about a thousand people in all of Alta California in 1828. That doesn't include the Indians.

"No pollution anyway," Mike laughed.

"It was feudal." Rita explained. "Everything revolved around their ranches, which were vast stretches of land. They had large families and used the Indians to do all the manual labor. The women were devoutly religious, and they only socialized with their own kind of people. The Spanish didn't even seem to know much about the Russians at Fort Ross above San Francisco Bay."

"Remember this is just from the point of view of your Clarita," Mike commented.

"I think that was pretty true for most California ladies of that time. They lived a conventional life." Rita patted the booklet she was reading. "This translation is useful, but I'd like to have the original ones. More than at any other time, I need those diaries."

"Let's give it some time," he answered. "The police have just started their investigation. Now let's go and make dinner together."

CHAPTER   10

▼

March 1830

"We are living in Monterey. I have two delights. Ardo grows well, and Consuelo and I are escorted to church by one of the soldiers at the *Presidio*. I have much to pray for and so do all the ladies in Monterey. There is violence surrounding us and we want to raise our children in peace.

"There are great differences in opinion about who should be governor, and sometimes the men fight with each other about this. Many of the *Californios* want more land, and the easiest way to this is to take it away from the missions. This will be a decision of the governor.

"When we go to church, we walk to the house where Encarnacion Cooper lives, and we all go together. Encarnacion brings her baby, Anita, with her. She told us that she expects another child in the autumn. Encarnacion and I were married in the same summer, and I wish I could give birth to another child, but my prayers have not been answered. I do not seem to please my husband as when we were first married. He is never home and spends all his time with the governor, who goes back and forth to the south. Don José María has made some friends in Monterey, because he has distributed some land to *Californios*. He also gave some land to a few *Yanquis*. They must swear to support Mexico. However, no one is certain to keep anything if a new governor is appointed. Some of the people in Monterey say that a new governor will come soon.

"Estrella, the youngest sister of Consuelo, lives with Consuelo and Miguel. A soldier in the regiment is courting her. His family name is Estudillo, and his family lives on a ranch between Santa Bárbara and Santa Buenaventura. The family came from Mexico with Governor Echeandía. Although they are not Castilian, the family is from Spain. Narciso has a beautiful voice, and whenever he is able, he comes to sing at the window of Consuelo's house. Of course, Consuelo will not let her sister walk with him unless she can find a chaperone to accompany them. Narciso always talks with her after mass on Sundays. They plan to announce their banns after Easter. Since Papa is the godfather of Estrella, and her parents are in heaven, I think he will give a *fiesta* for her at Rancho Carmelo.

"October 1830. We have heard that Manuelo Victoria has been appointed to be the new governor, and my husband was angry when he returned home from his rides with Don José María. I dare not talk to him, except to do his bidding. I try hard to please him in hopes that we can have another child. Perhaps the festivities after the wedding of Estrella will bring happiness to us all, and my husband will love me again.

"Encarnacion gave birth to a son, Juan Bautista Guillermo, and her husband became a Mexican citizen. He can now be recognized as a landowner. Estrella became a bride at the *Presidio* church, and the next day almost all the town made a caravan over the hill to the Mission San Cárlos for another blessing and then enjoyed food and dancing at Rancho Carmelo. It is with a heavy heart that I must say that Don Felipe stayed away from the *fiesta* and I believe he was at Rancho Rincón. He is drinking *aguardiente* and it makes him wild. Then he sleeps.

"The wedding gave all of our people in Monterey a chance to have a happy time. First there was a *fandango* in town for everyone. I wanted to wear new shoes, but Don Felipe was not at home when the last *Yanqui* ship came into port, so I wore the satin ones he gave me before our wedding. I wore a lovely lace blouse. Then I saw *O'Farol,* and we talked just as if we were talking together at Rancho Carmelo in the old days. He knows Estrella, and although he decided not to go to Rancho Carmelo for the *fiesta*, he joined in the festivities of Monterey. He speaks our language very well now. He said he is going to buy cattle for Captain Cooper and then build some ranch buildings for him. This is something that he learned how to do at Rancho Carmelo. He is going to follow the example of Captain Cooper and stay away from any political matters. He thinks that the *politicos* are going to be always fighting as long as Mexico is so unsettled. He also thinks that Governor Echeandía will be replaced soon. He said that my husband should tend to his ranch and remove himself from what is happening. He was very serious and the tone of his voice was kind and gentle when he said, 'Doña Clarita, life is going to change in Monterey, so you must to change with it.'

"After the wedding *fiesta*, I remained a few weeks at Rancho Carmelo. Ardo likes to ride with a *vaquero* who Papa trusts. He puts Ardo on the saddle of a gentle horse, and then Papa lets him hold the reins while they both ride around the corral. My husband left for Monerey after the wedding, and I returned with the family of the Garcías. Many of us travel together in our *carretas* on the journey from Monterey to the distant *ranchos*. It is never wise to travel alone. During the time I visited Rancho Carmelo, I did not want to tell Papa about the many absences of my husband. It would make him sad. Papa has never taken a part in the government in Monterey, and he does not understand the action of the *politicos*. He often asks me why the younger *Californios* like Mariano Vallejo and his cousin, Don Juan Alvarado, want to go to meetings and plan to change the laws. I love the old ways, but since we are no longer part of Spain, we need to support our own people who live in Monterey. The government of Mexico does not really understand life in Alta California.

"We hear about changes in government in Mexico every time a ship comes into port. Now we hear that a new governor has been appointed, and it is said that he is a friend of the missionaries. We have also heard that he is a cruel man who will treat the people here like they are bad children or worse. Of course, all the *Californios* want to own a ranch, but this new Governor Victoria is against any parceling out of land and cattle that belong to the missions. Since he is a soldier of Mexico, he judges everyone's actions according to the interests of Mexico. There is a Mexican law that exiles all Spaniards, and the new governor will use this law against those who were born in Spain. Papa is worried. He could go to the Sandwich Islands. There are many ships from Monterey that come and go from that place. Spain is too far away for an old man to travel. Also he needs Esperanza to be with him and it would be easier for them to live in those islands than in Spain. Of course, it will not be good for Ardo and for me, because we love to visit Rancho Carmelo and my family.

"February 1831. Since it is the season of *Las Posadas*, my husband has been kinder to me. My husband was ill during that time. We did not stay in Monterey, and we went to Rancho Rincón where we can entertain. We attended mass as a family at the Mission San Juan Bautista. The music at this mission is said to be the most beautiful in all of Alta California. Padre Tapis has worked with the neophyte choir at this mission ever since he retired as *presidente* of the missions.

"The hills are tinged with light snow, and everywhere I look the land is barren. Many trees here at Rancho Rincon lose their leaves. I like the winter quietness.

"Our friend José María Echeandía tried to do much at the end of his term of being governor, and he called for a meeting of the *diputados* in Monterey so that there would be no new rebellions and the townspeople could be safe. However, when Don Felipe and I went to Monterey, we found that Don Manuel Victoria had arrived in Monterey. He had taken over the authority of Governor. He was sent from Mexico. He immediately announced that the missions were to remain as they had always been, and that he announced many punishments for all that had happened in the last few years under Governor Echeandía.

"The new governor is going to stir up much trouble because he will not let the elected *hijos del pais* have their meeting of the *diputados*. My lifelong friend, Mariano Vallejo, Antonio Osio and others, are going to make a formal complaint to Mexico. They are risking being put in jail, but they are young men and do not have wives to look after. Don Antonio Osio was married to Dolores Arguello, who was born in Yerba Bueña on San Francisco Bay. I did not know her, but I am sad that she died at childbirth a few years after they came to Monterey.

We are in seclusion because my husband is ill and no longer involved in politics. I do not think we will suffer from the harsh methods of the new governor, because we live so quietly. Governor Victoria favors the death penalty for many small problems. Everyone was shocked that an Indian boy was shot for stealing a few buttons. Our former governor was a person to look the other way in lesser offenses. We are not prepared for such a violent man, who is proud of being severe and harsh. They say he ordered Don José María to leave Alta California, but we think he is staying somewhere in the south while he gathers loyal men who will help him against General Victoria. Don Felipe talks of taking some of his *vaqueros* and riding to Santa Bárbara and talking to his friends there. Since he is weak in body, I do not think he will. Unfortunately for me, Don Diego arrived from his ranch near the Pajaro River, and he is staying here, so that he can be company with my husband. I am trying to keep out of his way, and since I am a good rider I am teaching Ardo what I learned at Rancho Carmelo.

"It is important for a man to be an excellent horseman. He must know more than the art of riding. He must know the ways of horses and respect them. The art of Spanish riding comes from a long tradition. Ardo will learn to rope and run cattle when he is older. At this time, I want to fill him with the pride of his ancestors, who won battles against Saracens and freed Spain from their rule. Ardo uses my saddle, which is just a small version of our *Janeta* saddle and is square and strongly made. It was designed so that a rider can stand in his stirrups and ride. The warriors in early times could easily hold a lance and sword for fighting. I let Ardo hold the pummel, and he has a small coil of rope there. He must practice holding the reins in his left hand while he rides in the arena that is found beyond the house and courtyard. Don Felipe takes great pleasure in knowing about his progress, and he is looking forward to feeling well and then he will walk to the corral to watch his son.

"September 1831. The weather is hot in this valley, but there is always an afternoon wind that sings a song. Some say it sounds like moaning, and that is why the reverend fathers named the mission to the south of us for Our Lady of Sorrows—*Nuestra Señora de la Soledad*. Ardo is already three years old and has never been sick, which is a good thing, as we are far from a mission father and there is not a doctor in Monterey at this time. Don Felipe does not take much interest in what is going on anywhere, although Don Diego brings news of the foul doings of Governor Victoria. When Mariano was sent to San Diego last year because of the soldiers revolt, he met Francisca Benicia Carrillo, daughter of Juan Joaquin Carrillo. Although I know he already had a *novia*, he and Francisca fell in love at a beautiful *fiesta*. They have made plans for marriage in the future. When Mariano came to Monterey the last time, Consuelo learned that Governor Victoria neglected to send their marriage petition to Mexico. Since an officer cannot marry without permission from Mexico City, they will need to wait for it to arrive by the next boat. Meanwhile Mariano has been meeting with the other Californios with surnames such as Alvarado, Castro, Osio, and Ortega. They are trying to force the governor to call up the *diputados*. Consuelo says she has heard that the governor does not intend to call an assembly, so I do not know what poor Mariano Vallejo and his Francisca will do.

"Everyone knows what happened to another Señorita Carrillo, who eloped and married Enrique Fitch in Valparaiso. They could not even marry in Mexico. When they returned to Alta California the next year, Señor Fitch was placed under arrest, and Doña Josefa was sent to the house of Captain Cooper to live. After many appeals to Governor Echeandía, Doña Josefa and son were allowed to go south by boat to be near her husband, who was imprisoned in San Gabriel. The couple were asked questions in a church court and although their actions were proven honest, the church considered the marriage void. They needed to remarry. Señor Fitch would have done this, except that his son would then be without legal parents. It was finally decided that although the marriage was not legal, it was not considered null. None of us understand all this and think it has to do with laws of our church. Both Josefa and Don Enrique were released from their exiles, and the following Sunday, they took the sacraments that were supposed to precede their marriage. They were able to hear high mass on three festival days. And they were ordered to recite together one-third of the rosary of the holy virgin for thirty days. Also Señor Fitch must give a bell of at least fifty pounds to the church in Los Angeles. This is what happens when someone marries without observing the church's rules.

"I hear about the personal problems of our *Californios,* because Consuelo talks to her husband about these things. However, she has heard that Governor Victoria wants revenge against the *Californios,* which include Captain Vallejo, some of the Carrillos, and José María Padrés, who is a leader of the opposition. The governor has ordered these men to leave Alta California There are many others who have felt his wrath. Only the mission fathers think of him as a good governor. Consuelo says the *Californios* in the south will probably start a revolt.

"My husband is sad he cannot be by the side of the governor who needs him. He has asked Don Diego go south to be with Echeandía and to represent the family. I am glad he will leave. I do not like his sudden appearances. When he comes to Rancho Rincón to talk to my husband, I see as I turn the corner of the patio or go to the room of Ardo.

"Yesterday Don Diego encountered me. 'It will not be much longer, *ma paloma,*' he said. This could mean anything except that he pressed his hand against my cheek, and then he brushed his fingers lightly over the top of my head. I quickly slipped into the room of Ardo and started praying at the little altar that I made for us there. I pray that I can always escape from Don Diego.

"March 1832. My life has been quiet here at Rancho Rincón. I take care of my husband by putting cold cloths on his head when he is too warm, and I cover him with another shawl when he is suddenly cold. I read to him when he wants to hear the beautiful words of prayer from the books of my mother. Sometimes he tells about his life when he was a young man. I wish I could have known him at that time. He told me that he loved to dance and ride fast horses. He told me that he likes music from the guitar, and I promised him that I would teach Ardo to play the guitar. When we go to Monterey, we can find someone to teach him. I go to the kitchen building every day to see that the porridge of cornmeal is made for him. I make certain that they cook the daily soup of beef and vegetables. On his good mornings, he likes to sit in a chair by the window, and at that time the two of us drink our warm chocolate from special silver cups that were wedding presents. He tells me of all the beautiful clothes he will buy for me when we return to Monterey. I tell him that I like it here at the ranch and do not need the fancy clothes to wear. I truly feel contentment here.

"I receive letters from Consuelo by a trusted *vaquero.* She tells me of all the bitterness and unrest between groups of *Californios* as well as foreigners. We give the rider something to eat. Then he rides back to Monterey with my letter to Consuelo. She is lonely for her husband who has accompanied Governor Victoria to the lands in the south. The governor wants to restore order in Alta California, and he took the Monterey regiment with him. He left his secretary, Captain Zamorano, in command of Monterey. Later Captain Pacheco joined Governor Victoria, although they did not expect much fighting. When Captain Pacheco reached Santa Bárbara, Señor de la Guerra warned him about the anger of the *Californios* in Los Angeles. However, Captain Pacheco had orders to march, and the two forces of *Californios* met a few leagues from Los Angeles in the direction of the Cahuenga. Captain García tried to keep his men in order, but someone said sharp words, and poor Captain Pacheco was killed as well as José María Avila on the other side. Governor Victoria, himself, was wounded and taken to the Mission San Gabriel to be tended by a man who knew about medicine. The battle was over, and Governor Victoria asked to be returned to Mexico. He wanted to be far away from the people of our land. Consuelo was grateful for her husband's safe return. She gave a string of pearls to the statue of the Blessed Virgin in the chapel. I am thankful for the return of the men, although, it means Don Diego will be retuning to Monterey. Again, I will have fears of what he will do and say when he comes to see my husband."

CHAPTER 11

▼

"It is the year of 1832. Who is the governor? We do not know. There is even talk about having a governor who will make his headquarters in the south—this would probably be Don Pío Pico. At the same time, we would have a governor in the north. Don Pío even took the oath of office for the position when the council met in the *Pueblo de Los* Angeles. When all the men of the council met in Los Angeles, there was a change and they decided to take back José María Echeandía as governor of all Alta California. Don Pío gallantly declined any office and said he really wanted to go back to living on his ranch. Captain Zamorano, who was a friend of Governor Victoria, really wanted the position of governor. He appealed to all the foreigners in Monterey, and he had them sign a roll of names of men who would defend us if the soldiers from the south should march into our lands. The foreigners elected Don Guillermo Hartnell as their leader. He is the husband of Teresa de la Guerra. Is not all this a strange mixture?

"Here at Rancho Rincón, we hear about these things long after they have happened. That is why I do not know who is the governor or if he lives in the North or in the South. As much as I want to see Consuleo and let Ardo play with her children, I have grown to like the quietness here, where I serve my husband and devote myself to his health. Our life has a sweet rhythm, and I feel part of it.

"One of the fathers from Mission San Juan Bautista brought us a lovely small guitar, and he stayed with us several days and showed Ardo ways to play it. It is an answer to my prayer. Now we shall have music. Father Mateo is such a pleasant guest, and his words bring comfort to my husband. Don Felipe and I talked about Father Mateo, and we asked him to come once a week. He can give Ardo music lessons, and he can talk to Don Felipe about spiritual matters. Even Doña Eulalia smiles when the good father eats the noon meal with us. She now has a reason to arrange for special foods, and with summer coming, we can add all the vegetables that are now growing in our garden. Father Mateo told us that there are two priests in the Sandwich Islands. They have lived there for five years. They were sent from France to start a Catholic mission, but the Protestant missionaries already living there want them to leave. They are Jesuit priests, and do not have a connection with the mission fathers here. When I told Father Mateo that Papa was thinking about going to the Sandwich Islands, he said it would not be good for him. He said if the French priests are forced to leave, there would be no one there to give him religious comfort, and no one to give him last rites when he dies. I agreed with Father Matteo that Papa needed the church at this time in his life.

"I received a message from Consuelo that we are to have a new governor from Mexico, and he will arrive soon. No one knows who it will be. I am hoping he will be a wise and fair man, and we can go to him and apply for a grant for the land from the government of Mexico. When I go to see Papa I will ask him if he has a good drawing of the boundaries of our lands. Since I cannot leave my husband for more than a day, I hope that Papa and Esperanza can visit us here.

"September 1832. Ardo celebrated his fourth birthday this summer with a small *fiesta* in our courtyard. We had most of the celebration in the evening when the sun went down. We make sturdy candles on this ranch, and we use them to light up the entire courtyard. I gathered up the children of the *vaqueros* and taught them a little song. Then I taught them how to form a circle around Ardo and sing to him. Consuelo and her children came to our ranch. Papa and Esperanza arrived and brought my little sisters, Dulcera and Felicia. Father Matteo brought some of the neophytes who play musical instruments. They played the violin, guitar, and also the drums. We women wore our best silk skirts and satin shoes and lace blouses. I dressed Don Felipe in his best velvet pantaloons, and he wore white stockings. Most of all he enjoyed wearing his best brocade waistcoat. We carried him out to the courtyard and he enjoyed all the festivities. Ardo wore a little velvet suit that I made for him. Don Felipe presented him with a glorious red silk sash, and we wound it around his waist three times. He also gave him a deep blue velvet cloak with silver trimmings, and Ardo can wear it when he is older. It was a happy time for everyone, and even Don Diego and his sickly wife, Catalina, came and clapped at all the entertainment. The party continued for two days, and all the guests stayed for a week.

"Papa and Esperanza came a week before the *fiesta,* and they brought us spices, molasses, grapes, and the cheese they make at the ranch. The new food tastes most delicious. Summer is indeed a time to enjoy the food of our gardens, and we fed all our family and friends many meals. This was a time for us to learn about the new governor, who has set sail for our shores. His name is José Figueroa. He is a seasoned army man and will bring us ten new Fathers who are Franciscans of the *Collegio de Nuestra Señora de Guadeloupe de Zacateca.* They will be in charge of the Mission San Cárlos and the missions in the north. This will be a welcome return of order for the citizens of Monterey.

"When Papa visited us he brought us a letter from my brother, Esteban, in Spain. It took over a year to arrive. He has been ordained and sent to Madrid to work for a bishop. He writes that he heard that there have been many revolutions in Mexico City. He thinks that Papa will be safe enough in Alta California. Papa is an elderly man who has caused no trouble. He advised Papa not to attempt a long sea journey to Spain. He told Papa to find someone young and strong to manage the ranch. Above all, he wants Papa to go to the new governor and ask for a land grant to be recorded in my name. Papa agreed with all that Esteban wrote us.

"November 1832. There is now a gentleman who lives in Monterey who knows about healing and medicines. In the winter, Rancho Rincón is lonely and cold, and my husband decided that we should live in our house in Monterey. Then he can talk to the man who heals. I will arrange for more *caritas* to be built, and then we can take Don Felipe and our clothes to town. Ardo and I will ride into Monterey with some of our *vaqueros* so we can make everything ready for him.

"Early December 1832. There is not much time for me to write. My days have been filled with the moving of my husband. I used almost every person at our ranch to make *la casita* comfortable for him. It may be a long time before we return to the ranch, so we must take almost everything. The only items left behind were the large bed and altar in our bedroom.

"Later December 1832. We are installed in our adobe house in Monterey. The thick walls keep it warm. At first, my husband was in good spirits, but it took most of his energy to make the move to Monterey. The only time I am not near him is when I walk to the house of Consuelo and we attend the earliest morning mass. Encarnation Cooper sometimes goes with us. It is important to her that she goes to church every day. She has so much to do at her home. Her father, the old sergeant, died and now her mother and two sisters, María de Jesus and Rosalia, live with them. I think there is also a niece and they are always taking in some of the children of her sister, Josefa, who died. Also living with them is the half brother of Captain Cooper, a Señor Larkin, who arrived earlier this year from Boston by the way of the Sandwich Islands. He brought a lady with him who is a recent widow. They plan to marry, but Encarnation says Señor Larkin is determined to remain a citizen of the land of the Yanquis and to not become a Catholic. They may need to go to the Sandwich Islands to be married. The Coopers are always generous with their hospitality. Captain Cooper was the guardian for Josefa Carrillo Fitch during their difficulties. The Coopers can always find a place for one more person. I think they will soon need a larger house. I know that the Captain has acquired several pieces of land to the north and the south of here. Consuelo says that *O'Farol* has been building adobes and corrals for Captain Cooper.

"January 1833. I am thankful to the Blessed Virgin that we had the *fiesta* for Aldo last summer. Don Felipe has not been out of his bed since we arrived in Monterey. Ardo goes to play at the house of Consuelo, and we keep it quiet at our house so my husband can sleep. When Ardo and I walked home yesterday, we stopped to see the Coopers. We noticed a gathering of people outside the house, and we learned that a boat had been sighted in the morning, and now we are all certain that it is the one that is bringing the new governor. What excitement. We went to tell Consuelo. After we made sure that Don Felipe was well attended, Ardo and I walked to the estuary. Captain García and his men stood at attention near the landing place. They wore faded uniforms, which were old and mended. Many people from Monterey were gathering. With the new governor came his brother, Captain Francisco Figueroa, another captain and some lieutenants, an officer for the customhouse, a surgeon, Manuel Alva, about thirty soldiers, and several Zacatecan friars. It was a splendid parade that embarked. The new governor made a speech to reassure us that he had come to restore order and he had our interests in his heart. All of Monterey felt the warmth of his message.

"I was surprised when I saw *O'Farol* making his way toward us. After greeting Consuelo and me with formality and good manners, he stooped over to talk to Ardo. He asked about my husband and my father. I asked him about his work, and he told me he was building for Captain Cooper. He said he really wants to be on a ranch, because he likes working with the *vaqueros* and the animals. I told him that Papa had been advised to stay in Alta California although he is not a Mexican citizen. It is easy to talk to *O'Farol*, and I suddenly told him that when my husband regained his health we were all going to live at Rancho Carmelo. I do not know why I said these words, as I do not think it will come to pass. Then I told *O'Farol* that we need someone who will work with the *vaqueros* at Rancho

Carmelo. I wanted to see if he really was interested in coming to our ranch. We do need a strong man. My husband can no longer ride a horse or direct the activities at Rancho Rincón. Later, I felt ashamed of myself for talking so much. I expect to do penance for that.

"As we stood and watched the governor and all the soldiers leave the boat landing, a cold winter breeze came across the bay. I had dressed myself for the warmth of the mid day sun. Now, I shivered as the cold wind increased. *O'Farol* took off his jacket and put it on my shoulders. He then took the hand of Ardo and escorted us back to the cluster of houses that lay between the *Presidio* and the customhouse. I do not know where he left his horse, but he walked us to our adobe house and opened the gate of our white picket fence. He smiled a broad grin and said "*Adios, Señora Vargas*", and he tipped his hat to Ardo. My heart was filled with emotions. There are many uncertainties in my life. At this moment I feel safer because our new governor has arrived."

CHAPTER 12

▼

January 28, 2000

On Friday night, Mrs. Russell, who lived next door, stayed at the Minetti home with Carmelita, who had a cold. Rita and Mike made the short drive from Carmel to the most impressive house on Stillwater Cove. Stonecrest was discreetly hidden by a long driveway lined with cypress trees and was guarded by a European-style wrought-iron fence, punctuated with spear pointed finials. Rita knew the combination to the electric gates at the entry, and they quickly entered the driveway, passing through the misty light of lanterns along the way. Mike had suggested they arrive early at Stonecrest in the hope that there would be an opportunity to talk to Rita's mother alone. However, when the door opened, it was Charles who welcomed them into the entry rotunda. He greeted them with the formal affection of a non-tactile embrace, and he immediately launched into an explanation of the names of the wines he had brought. These were prominently displayed on a nineteenth century Mahogany sideboard that had once belonged to Grandmother Clara.

After this brief greeting, Charles showed Rita and Mike the wine bottles, and he began to talk. "My Chardonnay grapes were grown on a little strip of property in the Carneros area," he began. "It's the premium vineyard land of all the North Bay"' he said in a carefully articulated voice. "I was lucky to get the land, and I know I paid too much for it, but my friend, Rollo, from prep school days wanted to sell it. I think he needed the money." Charles paused briefly to gauge their reaction, and then he continued. "I named it *Del Oro-Carneros*. In this business

- 79 -

you have to be careful that you don't use any other vintner's wine name. It's very crisp for a '97, but soon it will develop more body. You are knowledgeable about wines, I know," he added as he looked at them carefully.

Rita and Mike listened politely as Charles proceeded to tell them about every bottle. There was a Modo Primo, Anderson Valley wine from 1996 and a Gewürztraminer 1997 that Charles said was as good as the one that won the silver medal at the last competition of the American Wine Society. "I've picked out my absolute best Merlot to serve with dinner," he confided. "But you know how Mother is. She wants to serve Dom Perignon '85. She still has a few bottles from that year."

Charles ushered them into the room the family called The Library. It contained three walls of books, and the fourth wall was a floor to ceiling window that looked out onto the lawn, which sloped down to a small boat landing and Stillwater Cove. The Library was a warm and informal room. Clara Torelli loved books so much that she had purposely omitted building a fireplace on the off chance that a blazing disaster could occur.

"Hello darlings," Anita said as she entered the room and embraced Rita and Mike with a show of family camaraderie. She had changed her hair color again. Now she was a chestnut brunette. She wore a long, deep blue velvet skirt with a simple white blouse that had ruffles at the neck and sleeves. She had undergone facial surgery last year, and her general appearance was much younger than a woman in her early seventies.

"I am sorry your dear child is ill," she said to Rita. "But there will be many more times when she can be part of our little family parties." Rita nodded and looked over at Mike. "Charles, dear, have you told them that it was The International Wine Conference that you attended," Anita chattered nervously.

"Oh I just barely began," he said with a chuckle. "First, I'll call for Alma to bring in the champagne, and we'll have a toast to our dear Clara Torelli. You remember her, don't you, Mike?"

"Sure do. You know, she was Aunt Clara to me."

"Of course. We're kissing cousins, aren't we," Charles continued. When Alma brought in the silver ice bucket stand, he skillfully uncorked the Dom Perignon '85 and poured a little into a glass that she held. After an approving taste from Charles, she served the others. Roberto, Alma's husband, brought in a tray of hot hors d'oeuvres and small glass plates. Soon Alma passed miniature linen napkins. Alma and Roberto, who had worked for Clara Torelli, stayed on to be with Anita after her mother died. They knew everything about managing Stonecrest.

"We are going to toast to Mother. She is responsible for inviting us all here, and she is sharing Grandmother Clara's favorite beverage with us," Charles said.

"To Mother," Rita said quickly and gave Anita a pat on the shoulder. Everyone sipped.

Charles continued with his explanations. "I just attended a wine conference where the attendance was strictly by invitation and for vintners of the premium vineyards of the world. This is a group who specializes in limited production wines. We even had a blind tasting. Sometimes they are called, handmade wines," he said with a laugh.

"In the best sense of the word, you know." Anita commented and smiled at Charles with the satisfaction of a mother whose child had just won a blue ribbon at the fair.

"There were men who came from the upper Rhône and from Burgundy and the finest chateaus of the Bordeaux region. A few came from the Loire Valley. Then there were some very knowledgeable Germans from the Moselle valley. One turned out to be a father of one of Darcy's classmates at Holy Name. He spoke perfect English with a slight southern accent. I also met three interesting Australians, who were associated with a winery I visited fifteen years ago. Remember when I took a trip there and went out to Adelaide in South Australia? The people in that region are of German heritage. Their families started the first vineyards as soon as they immigrated to Australia in the last century." Charlie informed them.

They finished the bottle while Charles told them about a Japanese sommelier who wrote for the *Wall Street Journal*. "He was the only one from that profession who was invited to the conference," Charles went on. "They have their own organizations, you know. They like to act very important. They think of us growers as farmers."

Charles laughed with an extra staccato that Rita had heard before. She was not listening attentively to him, because she was assessing his demeanor. He was dressed casually and yet expensively in an azure blue cashmere turtleneck sweater and deep gray Armani slacks. The sweater emphasized his intense blue eyes. His abundant hair was still brown. Some of his features favored his English ancestors, although he had an olive skin. He looked trim and in good form tonight. Rita noticed his nails were manicured. Probably done at the Spa at the Retreat, she thought. Later she told Mike, "I have brown eyes, auburn hair and a fair skin. We've never looked like a brother and sister. People are always surprised to find we are related."

Alma announced dinner, and Charles continued talking while he took Anita's arm, and they walked from the library through the long entrance hall into the dining room. It was the one room in the house that Clara liked to show off. She thought of it as the centerpiece of her home. Clara and Leonardo Torelli had moved to Pebble Beach on the Monterey peninsula in 1955. They built Stonecrest to please themselves. They called it a country house because they both came from San Francisco, where they lived in a large apartment in a landmark building on the top of Nob Hill. After they built Stonecrest, they lived at Stonecrest most of the time and considered it to be the family homestead. Above all, Leo wanted a spacious dining room, large enough for Torelli style family dinners. Anita Torelli and Rex Atherton II were married at Stonecrest in 1960. Clara made Stonecrest her permanent home after Leo died in 1961, and she continued entertaining the Torelli family.

Tonight, Anita had placed one of her Chinese Chippendale tables near the carved stone fireplace in the dining room. She wanted to create an intimate dinner atmosphere, so she omitted a floral centerpiece and placed a small bud vase with a deep velvety red rose at each setting. She used her ivory porcelain China with a thick gold band on the rim, and used service plates with hand painted and embossed, colorful peacocks

"Mike, you sit on my good side," Anita smiled. Everyone knew she was a little hard of hearing. "Rita, dear, you sit on the other side and Charles," she paused, "I'm putting you right across from me so I can feast my eyes on you. It has been so long. Since it is a wintry night, I am starting us with a simple artichoke bisque. Do you want to serve a wine with it, or can we wait and have it with the salad course?" she said to Charles.

Charles leaned over to Mike. "How's it going, Old Boy. I hear real estate is really booming here now. I took some walks around The Retreat and saw several new houses going up. They must have leveled the old ones. There's a vacant lot near Stoncrest that will cost fifteen million before they even start building, eh?"

"At least," Mike replied "And when..."

Charles interrupted, "And your business, Sis. You do have the best location of all the Pebble Beach shops, you know. Everyone can see it as they come out of the hotel."

"I like the spot, but of course I don't depend on walk-in business."

"Mother told me that you sometimes get people from The Retreat like film stars and maybe a Hollywood producer."

"I do get interesting people and that's," she started to say.

Before she could answer, Charles rambled on, "I had to take a peek in the kitchen, Mother. I wanted to find out what you were serving. I brought both my Carneros Chardonnay and the special vintage Cabernet Sauvignon." He looked around. "Just in case you served lamb, I also brought a great bottle for that. It's a Merlot, a special blend of Cabernet Sauvignon and a little Cabernet Franc added. Grif Mastersen gave it to me. Since you are having chicken, I'll leave the special Merlot here for you to have some other time, Mother. Then you can impress your Pebble Beach friends with it."

Anita softly interrupted. "Oh dear, I don't entertain that much."

Charles went on. "You should, sweet lady," he went on. "And be sure to invite a man friend who knows wines. He'll appreciate your choice of vintages."

Anita smiled happily, and she patted Rita's arm. "I'm glad you wore the lovely lilac sweater, dear. It shows off the beautiful color of your hair. And that black skirt is just the right length. Don't let yourself get frumpy just because you had a baby. I do so wish Carmelita could have come, but you and Mike are such good and wise parents to keep her in. You two are always watching out for her welfare." She spoke a little louder. "Did you ever think your sister would really get married, Charles? Next time we toast, we must lift the glass to Michael who made all this come true."

Charles murmured something and arose to go out to the kitchen. He returned with Alma, bearing a tray that held three styles of glasses for the wines that would accompany the ensuing courses. Charles again did the honors of uncorking a much, described bottle. He chose a simple Baccarat wine glass of medium height for the Sauvignon Blanc and, after tasting the wine, he announced, "It will be perfect with this simple salad of mixed lettuces, as it has a hint of grassiness." When all their glasses had been served, he continued, "Swish the liquid around a little. You can truly see the lovely color. It is a treasure I can say this quite honestly, since it's not my wine. It's one from the Torelli cousins." He paused, "And here's to Mike. We're glad you are on board."

"I won't drink much of it, dear," Anita said warily. "Not because it isn't wonderful, but I must tell you I'm not one to be interested in the nuances of wines. A good shot of Talisker Scotch is really my favorite drink."

"Dad is the same. Maybe it's the way of your generation. Ours is more into wine, you know. But Mother, wine is in your genes. You are a Torelli, you know. They are getting to be the one name that's known everywhere, even in France, now."

Anita smiled. "My mother and father always served wine. However, they didn't talk about the different kinds as people do today. Rex introduced me to good Scotch Whiskey, and I have liked it all these years."

"By the way, Mike, have you been selling lands for vineyards in Monterey County?" Charles said. He had finished his salad quickly.

"No, not really. That's a specialty all its own. We sell quite a bit of commercial property but not ranches."

"You should consider it. It's not too late. Buy some yourself and you'll be able to sell it long before your child goes to college. Then your wife won't have to work."

"I like my work, Charlie. I like owning The Old Booktique."

"Yes, but there's only so many old books that you can get interested in selling. And then when your kid starts taking lessons in everything, you'll really know what it's like to be busy. You'll be a soccer mom." Charles paused to finish his wine. "A girl, isn't it? Then there will be ballet lessons, riding lessons, and Girl Scouts. That's how Missy has spent her last five years."

Will it never end? Rita thought. Between Charles and Anita it was a pas de deux of compliments. Then there was tedious wine conversation interspersed with a few verbal arrows, which she hoped she had diverted. She had questions she wanted to ask him, but she realized it was hardly worth starting a sentence, because Charles was determined to dominate the conversation.

"Are you going to visit any Monterey County wineries?" Rita said instead.

"We were guests at a vertical tasting at The Vineyard of the Pinnacles, which is considered the best. I may go to some other wineries later if I can get away from my vineyard again."

After they finished the salad, Alma brought fresh popovers and Roberto followed, proudly carried in a large silver platter of sautéed squab, glazed, new potatoes, tiny carrots and small, poached crabapples. It was a winter menu that Alma and Roberto had learned to prepare for Clara Torelli. Anita followed her mother's traditions that included a formality of service. She soon began to relax, and she sipped the wine that Charles had just poured.

"You can see that I changed my mind and served a red wine," he said. "Merlot is perfect for this dish, because it isn't always the meat on which one puts a focus. It is often the sauce or whatever compliments the meat."

"The Merlot is wonderful, Charles, but I think we've talked about wine long enough. I want to ask Rita about her burglary," Anita said as she turned toward her daughter. "Have you heard anything more from Captain Lewis, dear?" She paused as if wondering what she would say. "Did you know he interviewed me?

He was very much nicer than I expected. You know how those detectives are when you see them on television. No manners at all."

"I didn't hear from Captain Lewis today, Mother. We're not his only case, and since no one was injured and there was relatively little damage he's probably given our case to the deputy."

"Oh no, that's not what he told me. He said he would be taking a personal interest in the case, and he would be involved and…"

"Pardon me, Mother. I was so enthused about the wine that I forgot to ask Rita about the burglary. What is this all about? What did they take?" Charles put in.

"Some rare books with autographs. Ambrose Bierce, John Dos Passos, Zane Gray and others that only an English major would love."

"Mother said that *The Carmelo Diaries* were taken. Why would anyone want them? I always thought I'd borrow them someday, so I could have them photo-copied for the girls. Especially Darcy. She's quite a student, you know. Of course, she would need to have a translation made for the Spanish ones. French is her language. She's taken French since kindergarten."

"Frankly, I'm puzzled," Rita answered. "There are many reasons why someone would steal *The Diaries*. Of course, since they were in a safe, it could be assumed they were valuable." She paused. "Captain Lewis has his own theories," she added.

"Oh?" said Charles and then he turned to Mike. "What do you make of all this?"

"I haven't actually talked to the captain. I'm just trying to help Rita. Right after it happened, we had a lot of cleaning up to do at the shop. To get the place ready to reopen, you know."

Anita put her small narrow hand on Mike's arm. "That's what I mean. Mike is so great to have around. You don't know how lucky you are, dear, she said to Rita.

"Oh, yes, I do." Rita said brightly, and although she had been alert and cautious in her answers, her face relaxed as she smiled at Mike. "He's the best."

Alma quietly cleared the plates and Roberto carried in the tray of small silver compote dishes with pale lemon, apricot and raspberry sorbets. In addition, there were little brandy glasses and two bottles of *eau-de-vie*.

"I thought of using one of Mother's recipes and having *Tiramisu,* but I know everyone is on a semi-diet. You'll notice the scoops are very small."

"You have thought of everything. A perfect hostess," Charles complimented.

As Roberto started to put down the liquor glasses, Anita held up her hand. "I've decided we should go into the study and have a nightcap and demitasse, Roberto. It's much cozier," she added to Rita.

"Mother, we really should be going. I hate to leave such good company, but Carmelita is croupy and might be difficult for the babysitter."

"Oh, I was having such a good time. The evening is young, but if you say so then I suppose you have to go," Anita pouted.

"We really do, Mother."

After Roberto left, they talked a little about next week's tournament, and as they all walked toward the entryway, Charles slipped his arm around Rita's waist and said, "It's been good seeing you, Sis. By the way, I happened to see a friend of yours the other day. He collects rare wines and was up to visit our famous valley. He's a producer of special TV shows. He gave me his card, but I don't have it, and I've forgotten his name. Maybe you could refresh my memory."

"You might mean Dave Goldman. I guess he collects many things."

"Antique cars, too," Charles agreed. "He must be loaded. Anyway you and I have a lot to talk about, Sis. We should get together more often."

"Mother enjoys seeing us."

"Maybe eventually, she'll see things differently about Dad. Although I don't think it makes much difference now. He and Bebe understand each other. He's at a senior masters amateur golf tournament right now, and he took Miss Maui with him as a roommate. Bebe flew to Aspen to ski. She said to meet an old beau."

"Then maybe it's better to leave well enough alone."

"You should really see Dad. He wants to see you and your baby."

"Maybe some day," Rita said with a little sigh.

After familial goodbyes, Mike and Rita were soon on their way home. They were barely in the car when she said, "I don't think I could have stood the conversation for one more minute."

"It was better when he didn't talk to us," Mike agreed. "His wife is divorcing him, you say. Maybe she just wanted a turn to talk." They were nearing the edge of Pebble Beach by the Carmel gate. "Hey, you said you'd tell me something if we went to your mother's house for dinner. Is it about their divorce?"

Rita did not know if it was a good time to tell Mike what she had discovered in her home office. She knew Mike. He usually saw all sides to an issue and was not one to suspect people. He would want facts, not hunches.

"Some of it concerned their divorce, but there are some other issues."

"Frankly I'm too tired for a discussion now."

"I know what you mean. "I'm glad we never had many dinners with Charlie. You might not have married me," she laughed.

"I would have abducted you. I would have sold everything and gone to South America with you."

"What about a year in Tuscany right now? Carmelita is a good age to take anywhere we want to go."

"Sounds good to me."

"Un-huh," she murmured and patted him. "I hope Carmelita is asleep and not as ill as I said she was. I'm in the mood just to cuddle up in bed with you and make love on this chilly winter night."

"I thought you'd never ask," he said. "I know all about how to keep my lady warm.

CHAPTER 13

▼

March 1833

"The arrival of Governor José Figueroa brings me great hope. On my morning walks to mass with Consuelo and Encarnacion, I hear what is going on in Monterey. We also talk about faraway places where Captain Cooper has been. Captain Zamorano has resumed his duties as secretary. They say that the new governor has pledged that he will learn all about Alta California. He now knows the names of Carrillo, de la Guerra y Noriega, Pico, Bandini, and many other families that are important from Santa Bárbara to San Diego. He understands the viewpoints of the *Californios* and knows that no matter what Mexico wants, he cannot accomplish it unless he has the cooperation of the people who live here. He does not want to favor one side or the other, and everyone agrees that he can be a person who can talk to all the people.

"Governor Figueroa made a clean start by granting pardons to all who have taken part in the many arguments and rebellions during the last year or so. All the townspeople liked this because it is hard to raise our children when there is fighting going on in the streets. We can go to the ships and buy material for our dresses. Encarnacion says that Captain Cooper is pleased when he can provide well for all those who live under his roof.

"As feeble as my husband has become, he likes me to tell him what I find out when we walk to mass every morning. It makes me listen even more intently, and sometimes while I am kneeling in prayer, I find myself thinking about how I can make this interesting for him. Then I must ask the forgiveness of our Blessed

Mother. I must always remember that I am in church to say my prayers. I pray for the health of my husband, and I pray that Don Diego will only see me as a sister. He now keeps a small adobe house in Monterey and comes from his ranch once a week to see my husband. I dread every visit. I leave when he arrives, even when it rains. I take Ardo and go to visit Consuelo or Encarncion. Ardo likes to play with all the children.

"There is always something going on at the house of the Coopers. Once in awhile I see Señor Larkin. He looks like some of the other *Yanquis*, very pale and not a man of the outdoors. He wears the clothes that one does for a funeral, that is, a black coat, high collar, and black tie at the throat. *O'Farol* is not like them at all. He wears the clothes of a *Californio*, leather pants and loose shirt. His face, although fair, has the look of a man who is touched by the sun. He resembles a *ranchero* and his slender frame and height give him grace. However, when he goes to mass on Sunday, he wears a silk shirt and bright vest or a red sash, and if it is cold he wears a dark *serape*. Outside, he always wears a brimmed hat, sometimes of leather. He takes it off when he greets us or when he enters the church. I think he is a true gentleman.

"They say that Señor Larkin is good at figures and has helped Captain Cooper with his business. He was a storekeeper when he lived in the *Yanqui* country near Boston. Although he is a half-brother of Captain Cooper, Consuelo and I think he is a man who will go forth on his own very soon. We hope that he and his lady will bring a store to our community. Encarnacion sometimes does not tell us much, and we do not ask her questions. She is such a sweet quiet lady, and this may be the reason she can manage such a large household of different people of different ages. I sometimes want to pray that I can become like her, but Mother taught me that it is a sin to want to be someone else. We must always be ourselves and use our time to improve ourselves and help others.

"Some days there is a feeling of spring in the air. General Figueroa has indeed brought order to Monterey. I hope the rest of Alta California will understand what he has done. The entire town of about thirty families and the soldiers at the *presidio* are looking forward to a *fandango*. Already there have been small dances at the homes of the Munrás, the Estradas, and the Coopers. Consuelo says there will be a Governor's Ball when the next important foreign ship arrives. All the ship's officers will be invited and they will bring us news from everywhere in the world. A party is a good way to attract ships to our coast. The officers and men of the ship always attend our *fandangos*. I wonder what it is like to be at sea for so many days. Consuelo is having Doña Elena Gonzales, widow of a soldier, to make a new dress for her to wear at the ball. It has a wide skirt that will swirl when she dances. It is made of a beautiful red silk. I wish I could go to the ball, but Don Felipe is not well enough to attend. Being with many people would surely be too tiring for him. We now have the best of all the workers from Rancho Rincón to help us in Monterey. They live down near the shore and come to our adobe everyday. Ramon, the brother of Esperanza, tells them what to do.

"I have three young maidens to cook and watch Ardo when he plays. There are many dangers here in Monterey that we did not have at the ranch. If Ardo strays from the courtyard, he could get hurt. Horses run quite freely on the muddy paths that lead from adobe to adobe. I do not entertain, but I am learning things about what is expected of me by watching Consuelo. Since I have been here, I have learned much about managing the maids who cook I can telling them how to prepare the meat that the men bring to us from our ranch. I have even taught the maids how to make hot chocolate. It is the one pleasure that my husband enjoys every day. We still keep the ritual of our ranch mornings as we sit together and slowly drink the sweet warm liquid. It is the time of day he says I am his *Querida, and* we talk about Ardo who comes to see him every afternoon. Sometimes Ardo plays the guitar for him. At other times we just talk.

"June 1833. Don Felipe remains in poor health, but as long as he is quiet and not excited, he seems to enjoy living in Monterey. He wants to live long enough to watch Ardo grow tall and show the world that he is a good horseman. My poor husband does not seem to be helped by the visits of Don Diego. His hands shake, and he seems to look smaller after he leaves. I do not know what his brother says to him, because they talk so quietly at the end of the *sala*.

"The ball for the governor was a great success. My husband insisted that we attend for an hour or so. He said that he wanted to show the other gentlemen of the capital that he was still an important figure in Monterey, and he gave me a beautiful pair of earrings and a necklace to wear. He said he was planning to give them to me when I had another child. He said I had pleased him with my devotion and he wanted my face to shine in beauty when I wore the bright jewels to the ball. It did not matter to me that I did not have a new dress, because I wore the one that had been made for me when we had the party for Ardo last summer. Consuelo was magnificent in her new dress, and she cut a pretty figure as she danced around the room with her husband, who is considered an important man, a senior officer at the *Presidio*. The youngest Vallejo girl danced in a spirited way. She threw down a hat, and one of the Rodriguez young men was appointed to pick it up. He finally found the lady who owned the hat, and they danced together. Everyone in the room clapped to the lively music. We were familiar with the tunes. Consuelo said the music and dancing went on for many hours after we left. The men who played the musical instruments agreed to take turns playing music all night. Governor Figueroa and the officers of the ship, *General Jackson*, were full of praise and took their turns dancing with the ladies. Perhaps a romance may begin between some of them, because our young ladies like to marry the *Yanquis*.

"I will stop here and tell about the single most important problem that our new governor has before him. It is about the missions, the mission lands, the Indians, and the fathers of the mission who want to keep everything as it has been. During the time that my husband was active and checking on the cargo that came to the customs house, I heard much from him about this problem. It was something that Governor Echeandía tried to solve, but he did not do so. Many *Californios* thought that the missions should be left as the mission fathers had started them. This is true of Cárlos Carrillo, who was a delegate to the congress in Mexico. When he was in Mexico City, he told them how the missions had supported the soldiers and the *presidio* for many years. He thought that this system had saved us from being taken over by the Russians or some other foreign power. There are others who think the fathers have been against the republic of Mexico and say that the mission keeps the Indians as children instead of helping them to be free men and women. Señors Pico, Vallejo, and Osio even go so far to say that the fathers have been cruel to the Indians by using a whip to insure obedience. Don Mariano is *comandante* of the *Presidio* at San Francisco Bay, where there is a small village called Yerba Buena. Don Mariano said that his soldiers and the garrison had not received supplies and food so they could live. He asked Governor Figueroa to fix a certain amount of supplies to be furnished by the missions of the Monterey and San Francisco districts. A change is needed.

"There is already a law about the missions giving some of their lands to the neophytes, so they can rise from their low state. My husband tells me that the law was sent from Spain about the time I was born, but it was never obeyed. The missionaries were to be spiritual advisors only. This law has been ignored all these years. Of course, I have seen much more of the neophytes than many of the people in Monterey who have always lived in town. Esperanza's mother and family have lived in and near Mission San Cárlos for many years. Her mother was an Indian neophyte. Her father was a corporal at the *Presidio*, but he died from a sickness when his children were young. That is when their family came to our ranch to live. Esperanza has been part of our family for much of my life. She has her own kind of goodness. It is well that we had the services of Ramon, her brother. He also helps me here in Monterey.

"Summer 1833. We are going to stay in town rather than live at Rancho Rincón. Don Felipe goes out no more. I try to get him away from the large chair with pillows that he likes to sit in all day. With the help of Ramon, we sometimes walk together around the garden that is now in bloom. I have coaxed the growth of a pink rosebush I planted here last winter. It grows wild on the ranch and seems to like our climate. I hope to have many vines growing against the wall on the far side of the *patio*.

"Consuelo tells me that the governor has given orders to go farther than any other governor towards freeing the Indians from their attachment to the Mission San Cárlos. This is what the government in Mexico told him to do. It is a task that needs a careful leader. The governor must give some of the mission lands to those Indians who know how to use it and yet keep some of the land for the use of the mission and its school. The governor made a journey to the south, and he visited the missions there. Captain García accompanied him on the trip, but he quickly rode back to Monterey, because he was needed to at the *Presidio*. The governor thinks that there are very few Indians who are ready to work their own land. Left to themselves they might even go back to their old ways and leave Monterey to live in the hills and valley lands. This process of liberation will take much of the governor's time, for each mission has its own Indians and its own methods. A majordomo must be appointed for each mission. The fathers of the mission are concerned about the souls of the Indians and what will happen to them when they are not living within the walls of the mission. The Indians are supposed to form a *pueblo*, but Consuelo says her husband does not think the Indians will be able to do that. He fears they will be at the mercy of greedy people, or that they will run away as the fathers of the mission predict. When I go to the house of the Coopers there is much discussion of what will happen and Don Juan Bautista Cooper, as he is now called, has been heard to say that many *Californios* will apply for the use of the mission lands.

"Papa and Esperanza have come over the hill and are living in Monterey for the summer. I told Papa that Don Juan Bautista Cooper has employed *O'Farol* for several years and that he measures the ranches of many *Californios*. I reminded him that Esteban wanted him to register our ranch with the government. I asked him to use *O'Farol* to measure the lands of Rancho Carmelo. I told him that he could draw a design to present to the governor. He answered he heard that *O'Farol* was a hardworking young man, and he told me he would talk to Captain García about this. Then he wrote a simple letter expressing his wishes, and he gave his permission to chart the Rancho Carmelo. The ranch must be recorded this summer while we are all *simpático*.

"We learned that Cristina Delgado, who had been a Mission Indian and is now a widow, was given a ranch of many *varas*. It is located near the mouth of the Salinas River. As soon as Captain García came to call on my husband, I asked him about a meeting with the governor concerning Rancho Carmelo. The captain said he would ask Papa to use *O'Farol* to do the measurements on our ranch. *O'Farol* is good at this work. I have not seen *O'Farol* to talk to him about it again, but I know he can make good drawings of Rancho Carmelo. A long time ago when we took our horses to the mouth of the River Carmelo, he drew many pictures for me in the wet sand.

"October 1833. Papa has come to Monterey to meet the governor. *O'Farol* produced a *carta* of good quality and he brought from the ranch a branding iron with the 'C' and the backwards 'R'. The ranch uses this sign to identify the cattle. Papa dressed in his best pantaloons of dark blue velvet and a deep red velvet waistcoat that Captain García had purchased when the brig *Leonidas* last came into port. Papa was presented to Governor Figueroa, and he gave him his written claim to the lands that he has used since his arrival in Alta California when Mexico was ruled by Spain. Papa told me of the kindness of Don José Figueroa. He enjoyed the attention of a man such as this. The governor listened to his stories of those earlier times. The governor invited Papa to have dinner with him on the following night. Since our petition was made under such good conditions, we all have great hopes that the land will belong to our family. This is very important since Don Diego has hinted that he will inherit Rancho Rincón."

CHAPTER 14

▼

Rita had dreams all night. Maybe it was because she was not sleeping soundly. At two AM, she noticed that Mike was also awake.

"I dreamt that you and Charles were fencing against each other. You know, like you were in an old Zorro movie," she said to him.

He murmured, "Maybe it was all those different wines and the rich food." And then he was back asleep.

Rita continued waking up, and she dozed restlessly. She was dreaming about the first Clarita back in 1833. After Rita reread the old diary, she began musing about the life that Clarita lived in early Monterey. Those were supposed to be the halcyon years of old time California, and yet to the people who lived in that era, the times were filled with uncertainties, duties, and challenges. This was true even for those who did very little manual labor and could occasionally purchase luxuries. Her next dream was about another burglary. She dreamed that she had entered her bookstore, and all the furniture and bookshelves were gone. The space had been turned into a flower shop. This was disturbing to Rita because it was more real. She went downstairs to finish her sleep on the sofa. When she awoke she had a feeling of disappointment. She had been in another dream in which she was a little girl, and Charlie had just taken her cat and sold it to a friend. When she awoke this time, she sat up and blinking, she shook her head. Clearing her thoughts, she went upstairs to check on Carmelita.

Although it was only 5:30, Carmelita was standing and bouncing up and down in her crib and saying, "I want up, Mommy. I want Mommy. Play, play."

Rita picked her up and hugged her. Carmelita felt cool and was without a fever. "Baby, baby, I'm so glad you feel O.K."

"I'm no baby," Carmelita said emphatically. "Big girl. Big girl."

"Of course you are," Rita said encouragingly, and after dressing her in play clothes, they went downstairs. She would not let the burglary consume her. Rita had finished giving Carmelita her breakfast when Mike appeared.

"So this is where I find my girls," he greeted them.

Carmelita slid off her junior chair and ran to him. "Play, play," she intoned.

Mike put down his cup of coffee and went to the storage room for the big toy box containing a wooden train. He set up the tracks for her, and she busied herself by handing him wooden pieces. "I know it's Saturday, but I've got a meeting this morning with volunteers who will do the scoring at next week's tournament," he said to Rita.

"Oh, I almost forgot the AT&T tournament is coming up. There's just too much happening, Mike. And I'm still worried about how I will fit it all in."

"Take a deep breath, hon. Maybe you shouldn't go to the shop today. Play with Carmelita. The weather should be pretty good for a change. Take her to Dennis the Menace Park. She likes the slides."

"I think I will stay home. Whatever I do, I am going to keep her with me all day," Rita replied to Mike's suggestion.

"By the way, what was it that you promised to tell me last night? You still need to tell me your reason for going to Anita's for dinner."

"I wanted to see what was going on with Charlie."

"That whole charade seemed like it was for Charlie's ego. Anita certainly knows that you two don't waste any affection on each other."

"Underneath it all there is probably some love between us, but we're not like you and your brothers. You cuff and play like half grown-puppies, and then you go off, arm in arm together somewhere."

"We do that because we like to be with each other. We like physical contact, and it's fun for us."

"That is amazing," Rita marveled.

"I didn't catch any underlying friendliness between you people last night. Everyone seemed to be playing a part."

"You're right. We were all jockeying for a position."

"Your Mother was striving to be like your grandmother. You were on the defensive, and Charles was explaining everything to us."

"Well, now you've just trashed my family. I took you along to help me out, you turkey," she said.

They both laughed. "I know he's patronizing all of us. At first I took it a little personally, because he assumed I didn't know what goes into the making of a wine. Truth is, I wasn't one of rich kids of Napa. We lived in the vineyard," Mike stopped as if he was thinking about what he just said. "Then I realized that when Charles is talking, it doesn't make any difference to him who is the audience. When he asks me a question, he doesn't care whether he hears my answer."

"Then I don't have to explain him to you."

"No, but I'm still puzzled about why he made his appearance. I think he was really courting your mother. Incidentally, she entertains very well. She underestimates her abilities as a hostess."

"I'll tell her that you complimented her."

"Not with that tone, Babe. And she really does need approval, and from you. More than you think. You're everything she wanted to be. Moreover, I can put up with Charlie being pompous and self-important, but I don't like it when he tries to put you down. He knows that you and Anita have been close in the last few years, and he wants to be in on the action."

"He always wants to be top dog."

"I think there's more."

"Can you believe there was a time that I really worshipped him? He was my big brother."

"When did you change?"

Rita suddenly remembered her dream about Charles and the cat.

"I didn't have a cat," she said.

"What?"

"I had a dream last night. In the dream, Charles sold my cat to a friend." She hesitated. "Sold it," She repeated. "Of course I didn't have a cat. But when I was ten, he did sell my new puppy. He was a little Dalmatian, named 'Spot.' I never thought I would see him again. A year later I saw my puppy at a friend's house. He had grown some, and he had a different name, but we both recognized each other."

Mike crossed the room and put his arm around her. "You've got me now, and Charles is not going to charm me or buy me or change my mind."

"Mike, somehow, I think Charles has something to do with what has happened in the last few days?"

"With the burglary?"

"Well, not exactly, but there's something else I didn't tell you about."

"Ah, ha," he exclaimed exuberantly. "At last, I'm getting to the secret."

"It's not a secret. It has to do with something I noticed when we came back to the house after the burglary."

"You think Charles hired somebody to do a job for him?"

"I don't know, and that's why I don't want to talk about it, even to you. I think I'm closer to the answer."

"Why?"

"I think someone was in my home office, while we were at The Old Booktique the morning of the burglary. Whoever it was wanted me to know it."

"Babe, this is serious. Do you think Charles was here?"

"I still don't know. I just may be paranoid, you know." She paused as if to apologize for her suspicion. "I think someone deliberately left some clues for me."

"And you think it was Charles?"

"I have reasons. He knows my habits."

"And what habit would it be?"

"I am sentimental about objects and put them on my shelves and window-sills."

"Like a shell from Maui or an empty bottle of Chanel perfume that belonged to your grandmother." Mike laughed.

"Laugh all you want. And I thought you would. The little wooden bear is missing. Charlie gave it to me a long time ago I think he wanted me to know he was in my office."

"My God, why didn't you tell me?

"I wasn't sure of how to tell you. I didn't have any reason to suspect Charles until Mother told me that he was staying at The Retreat in Pebble Beach. Then I began to be suspicious."

"Did you learn anything last night?"

"Yes."

"Is that all you're going to say?"

"It all sounds so circumstantial. And I am still puzzled. I think he entered our house and took the little bear, because he's trying to rattle me. He wants to bother me, and he wants me to suspect something."

"Babe, I don't think you or anyone is that important to Charles. I don't think he would go out of his way to harass you."

"You may be right. However, I did find out something last night. He told me that he met someone I knew, and it turned out to be Dave Goldman from LA. I haven't said much to you, but for the last two days, I've been trying to reach Dave and I haven't had any luck. I really need to set up an appointment for this coming week. I think Charlie has talked to him and is trying to make a deal with him that involves a TV show and California stories. Whether or not he had anything to do with the burglary, I'm sure that Charlie wants to get into the act."

"Maybe he promised him *The Carmelo Diaries,*" Mike joined in.

"I believe I contacted Dave first. I also told him I had other diaries and letters. And he said that is what he wanted for his project. He wanted something authentic."

"I didn't realize you had already done so much toward selling the idea. So you think Charlie could want to get into the action? Why?"

"That's partly the reason I wanted to see him last night. There could be quite a lot of money involved if the project is carried out at the level the studios proposed. I think Charlie could be short of money right now, and particularly if Missy wants a generous settlement from him. I know that he has never been one to miss out on a lucrative deal. I also think he wants to keep me from selling the story to Dave."

"What do you think we should do? Mike asked.

"That's what I wanted you to tell me."

"Look, you really haven't lost anything yet. You have only begun the negotiations. Just be patient for a few days and see how it plays out."

"I feel better now that I have talked to you. Or do you think I'm being paranoid?

"Trust your gut feelings when it comes to your brother. And it's good to be prepared for anything."

The phone rang.

"If it's for me, tell them I'm on my way. I really need to get going, hon. Ultimately it's your decision. Remember it's your show, Babe. I'm sure it will turn out OK." Mike told her as he left the room and the ringing phone continued its insistent demands until Rita answered.

CHAPTER 15

▼

"This is the last day of the year 1833, and I have not the heart or spirit to write. For the sake of my son, this must be recorded.

"At present, we are living at the home of Consuelo and Miguel Garcia. They are very good to me. However, I know we cannot stay here long. Already, they need more rooms for all their children, and Consuelo will soon have another child. At least, I am able to help her at this time. Since we moved to Monterey, I learned how to direct the maids in household matters. After the baby of the Garcías is born, and I am certain that my dear friend is healthy, Ardo and I will surely live at Rancho Carmelo with Papa and Esperanza. I will be very careful, and we will travel only in the presence of Captain García and military escorts.

"Because of Ardo, I have kept my thoughts filled with hope. When I attend daily mass, I think only of the good that I can do for my family. I do not dare to think of the darker parts in my life. I will remember that my husband was a good man, and I will write a letter to Ardo that he will open later. It will tell him about his father and Jalisco, Mexico, where he lived when he was young. Ardo will want to know these stories when he gets older. I also want him to know what a devoted father he had. I will tell Ardo that his father was proud of him. Now I can record what I remember of the last six weeks.

"The autumn sun was warm, and with the help of Ramon, we were able to carry Don Felipe out to the garden when the weather was fair. Don Diego insisted on seeing my husband every day. I told Ramon to remain within my view of him so that Don Diego would never find me alone. Because the government of Mexico has officially told the Mission San Cárlos to give the Christian Indians the plot of land that was promised to them, Ramon will surely be one of those to receive his own place to live and farm. It will be good for him, but then I will be without his services. Oh my, I must continue to tell what happened later.

"Don Felipe had just eaten. We had invited Don Diego to take a simple mid-day meal with us, and we ate on a small table that was brought into his room. I had just nodded to Bonita to bring us some fruit, when my husband looked at me with pain and terror and said, 'Bring me the *padre.*'

"Don Diego commanded, 'Send Ramon to the San Cárlos Church and request a *padre,*' and he carried my husband to the bed. Then he shouted at me, 'Leave, woman.'

"When I did not obey, he picked me up and carried me to Ardo's room. I was kicking and screaming, and he called for one of the male Indians in the garden.

"'She is a wicked woman,' he shouted. 'Her husband is dying, and she must be kept away from him. She will cast an evil spell on him.' He threw me on the floor, bolted the door from the outside and left. He told Pedro to sit beside the door and to keep me inside.

"I heard his boots scrape the hard dirt floor outside the room. Then I heard his footsteps again, and he opened the door. I picked up a chair and was ready to throw it at him if he came closer.

"'I have decided to punish you for biting me when you lived at Rancho Rincón,' he said. 'You are a beast.' He smiled in a frightening way, and as I started forward with the chair, he drew his sword and pointed it toward me. 'My brother will die very soon, perhaps tonight.' He paused and looked me in the eye. 'He has written a will and has given me all his property. That means the ranch, the Monterey adobe, and his chest of gold coins. I am to take care of his son, Felipe Bernardo. I will see that he is educated. Perhaps in Mexico.'

"I gasped, but did not put down the chair. I started to scream, and he came a little closer.

"'You can live here or at my ranch and you can be my mistress. If you please me, I will treat you well. My wife is dying, and it will happen soon. Even though I plan to remarry, I will keep you as my mistress, because I will show you how to please me.' He laughed.

"I cannot write any more about this. His words were ugly, and he is truly a demon. I would gladly kill myself to escape from this man, but I must be wise to protect Ardo. I continued to hold the chair in front of me and did not yield to him. Before long, we heard Ramon arriving in the courtyard with the *Padre.* Don Diego took a small statue from the altar in the room and threw it at me. I could not avoid being hit by it. My first thought was to hold the chair and protect myself from him. Although I felt warm blood running down my arm, I did not dare to take any attention away from my defense. He left in a rage, slamming the door, and I heard him give orders to the Indian who guarded the door.

"I crouched in the shadows away from the window and listened for sounds and voices. My only goal was to escape Don Diego and to find Ardo. I knew that we must leave this house. I did not allow myself to think how impossible that would be. I prayed to the Holy Mother, as I knew of no other help. My heart was beating very fast, and I forced myself to sit and breathe slowly. Quietly I began to make plans.

"I realized when my husband died, someone would ask for me. It is expected that a wife attend her husband's funeral, and I decided that I would escape with Ardo to the house of Consuelo and Miguel. Don Diego would not dare to go there to menace me. I knew I must take another course of action after the birth of their child. I was filled with anger and sadness at the same time.

"Then I heard voices near the door. Night comes quickly in the winter, and I decided to keep quiet in the dark until I knew who was entering the room. I could hear Ardo's voice, and when the door was opened, I saw Ramon holding a candle for him. 'We must find clothes for you,' I heard Ramon say to Ardo.

"After they entered the room and closed the door, they were surprised to see me. I spoke to them quietly. I told them I was bleeding from the sharp edge of a silver statue Don Diego hurled at me. I told them Don Diego wanted to make me a prisoner.

"Ramon said he would take us to the house of the Garcías. 'You cannot take anything with you. We must leave at once.' He blew out the candle, and the three of us quickly ran through a little garden where the dirt is soft and reached a path by the side of the house. Ramon found a horse that strayed near the path and as soon as I mounted, he gave Ardo to me. He found another horse and followed us.

"We quickly sped into the night, and within a short time, we were standing on the porch of my dear friends. I knew my mother and godmother in heaven would help us. It is wrong for a wife to run away from a dying husband, but I was frightened for our safety.

"I told Ramon not to leave me until it was certain that the Garcías would give me shelter. Then, I made him promise to go back to Rancho Carmelo and tell my father what happened. I know if Don Diego thinks Ramon has helped us, he will have him punished with a whip or even something worse. I realized it was possible that no one would believe Ramon, so I told him to find Esperanza first. I took off the cross that I always wore around my neck, and placed it in his hands. 'Tell Esperanza to take this to Don Bernardo.' At that time, Miguelito García came to the door, and Ardo and I were welcomed into the house. Ramon took my horse and rode swiftly away into the black night.

"Don Felipe died soon. Captain García told the governor that it was important for me to be with my own family. At this time, I was sad that I was more worried about what would happen to Ardo and me. The events leading up to the day of his death were like a pile of heavy sand. I asked the Holy Mother to forgive me. I am still doing penance for neglecting my husband the night of his death, and when I receive my personal belongings and my leather chest, I will find some gold coins to give to Padre José María de la Real at the Mission San Cárlos. He needs help in these uncertain times.

"Don Diego arranged the funeral, which was held at the chapel of the San Cárlos Church in the *Presidio*. Governor Figueroa, Secretary Captain Zamorano, Captain García and his immediate officers attended. The Cooper family, the Munras family, Don José Estrada, Señor Larkin, and several new Americans also were present. Don Juan Bautista Alvarado is in the south and Don Mariano Vallejo is living in the north. They were not present. Ardo and I sat with the García family, which included the Captain, Consuelo, and all the children. Two Indian maidens brought woven rugs for our comfort. Doña Eulalia was kneeling with Don Diego in the front row.

"Although we brought nothing with us to the home of the Garcías, Consuelo had many black dresses that I could chose to wear, and she had clothes for Ardo since her son, Miguelito, had outgrown the little black pants and jacket that he wore to the funeral of his grandmother. I kept a black veil over my face so that I would not see any of the people directly.

"Afterwards, Captain García accompanied me to the home of the governor where the will was read. My husband asked to be buried at Rancho Rincón in front of the altar in the little chapel by the side of the *hacienda*. It was true that he had bequeathed the ranch with the animals and the Monterey adobe to his brother. It was also true that Don Diego was appointed to be the protector of Felipe Bernardo and to provide for his schooling. It was a short document, written with flourishes and the only writing of my husband that I could recognize was a feeble *rubrica* at the bottom of the page. I was full of sorrow.

"Captain García explained that he would accompany me to Rancho Rincón for the burial, and then he would send his servants to carry our clothes and belongings to his house. Don Diego began to protest, but the governor intervened and said that Ardo and I should stay with the Garcías throughout the winter, if we desired to do so. I did not speak, and I stayed very close to Miguel. I had told him about the actions of Don Diego, and he had seen the deep cut on my arm. Captain García told the governor that I would be a great comfort to his wife when he left for the north to help Don Mariano quell an Indian uprising.

"I must note here that the governor has more important problems to solve. There is the matter of Indian unrest everywhere in Alta California. There is also a problem with José María Híjar, who was told by the government of Mexico to bring new people to Alta California. The governor needs to visit the people of the south, the de la Guerras, Carrillos and the Picos, and he must visit the missions San Gabriel and San Luis Rey. It is fortunate that the governor listens to the *Californios,* and he likes and trusts Captain García The governor does not make hasty decisions of his own. This quality of understanding makes the governor popular. He is sympathetic to the Indians and he wants to help them.

"Now that I have no home, it has become important that the governor gives our family the title to Rancho Carmelo. I hope to persuade the governor that Rancho Carmelo is where my family has lived for many years. I do not want to say that it was a concession from the King of Spain. I am praying for guidance during the coming year."

There were no diary pages written for a few years. Clarita had much to say later about what happened during that time. Her granddaughter, Isabel, wrote about these times in her blue satin notebooks. She wrote in English, and the books helped Rita understand this portion of Clarita's life.

CHAPTER 16

▼

"Mrs. Minetti, this is Captain Lewis," Rita heard as she picked up the phone.

"I thought I'd hear from you soon," she replied in monosyllables

"This is an interesting case, because some little pieces have fallen into place, and yet it doesn't seem to be near the solution. Have you heard from your Mr. Goldman?"

"No, and that is as much of a mystery to me as anything else," Rita answered.

"Will you be at your shop today?"

"I'll be in and out. Tessa will be there all day, as we usually have browsers that come in on Saturdays. I've promised to be with my little girl, and I'll have her with me today."

"You haven't been contacted by anyone else?" Things are just the same with you, eh?"

"That's just about it. We've been catching up with pre-orders at the shop," Rita continued in a matter-of-fact voice.

"I've talked with your mother," Captain Lewis said abruptly.

"Yes, she mentioned it. She said you were much nicer than she expected. She probably was thinking of some of the tough city cops she's seen on television."

"Did she tell you what she said to me?"

"Not really. And I don't know what questions you asked her. We were invited to Stonecrest for dinner, and the conversation meandered from subject to subject."

"She was very interested in the burglary. She said she had been left out of all the excitement, and she wanted me to fill her in." He paused. "She was well aware of the importance of *The Carmelo Dairies.* In fact, she didn't seem to care or know much about your other valuable books."

"*The Diaries* are always brought up in our family conversations."

"You didn't tell me that your brother was in town," Captain Lewis said with a tone of calculated concern.

"He was attending a conference held at The Retreat."

"Your mother said I might want to talk to him. I understand he drove back to his ranch, but might be around next week. Will you see him then?"

"Maybe. We see a great many friends during the AT&T tournament."

"Sounds like you don't talk to him very much?"

"If you have a younger sister, I bet you don't talk to her much either. There isn't a lot we have to talk about together," she said.

"Well, ma'am, I only have brothers," he quickly put in. "You did see him though. When he was here?" He said almost offhandedly.

"My mother probably told you that she invited both of us to dinner. We mostly talked about the wine conference he had just attended. He is very enthused about his wines. He grows the grapes on his own land, and he employs a good winemaker."

"Your mother didn't know anything about your offers from Hollywood."

"It's not exactly Hollywood." Rita answered a little exasperated. "I'm waiting to hear from Mr. Goldman about a special production. We are still in the planning stages of a television special or a possible miniseries."

"Are you negotiating yet?"

"I gave Mr. Goldman a description of the story. I told him I had diaries written by the first Clarita who was about to be married at the age of fifteen to a man she did not know. He was interested when I told him about the rest of her life. It spanned all of the nineteenth century."

"I think this Mr. Goldman is someone we need to interview. When did you last try to talk to him?"

"I've called several times and left messages. He hasn't returned any of my calls. I have other things to deal with," she said emphatically.

"I'm going to find him. Then we will know the nature of his interest in your story. I am busy, too. There's only so much time we can spend on your case."

"Have you found out any more about the other items on my inventory?" Rita said in an effort to change the subject.

"Frankly no. There seems to be several incidents of burglary around here. If you read yesterday's local paper, you probably saw that a Cormorant Lodge guest lost several thousand dollars worth of jewelry. Someone claims that the jewelry was taken from the room. Also the largest gourmet market in Carmel was burglarized. Many cases of vintage wine and champagne were taken from the locked cabinets in the tasting cellar. I am working on providing extra security for the tournament next week, so I do need your concentrated cooperation now. Maybe I'll drop by your shop this afternoon to see what you come up with. Do you serve tea to your special customers?"

"No, but it's a good idea. After you contact Mr. Goldman would you please let me know? I think it's strange that I haven't heard from him."

"When do you think it would be a good time to talk to your brother? Did he have any weekend plans? Will he be staying with your mother when he comes back next week? Should I call him at his home?"

Rita thought it was a contrived string of questions to catch her off guard. She could not wait to tell Mike about the conversation. "What a fishing expedition," she could hear him say. She continued to be wary of what she said to Captain Lewis.

"Just follow whatever procedure you use in all your other interviews. I'm sure you'll find Charlie very cooperative," she said casually.

"Remember, I hope to see you this afternoon," he told her and concluded the call.

Rita quickly dressed Carmelita for outside play and left the house for Monterey. It was a crisp winter morning illuminated by the bright rays of direct sunlight. The air was so clear that when she looked ahead every pine needle cluster seemed to be etched against the blue sky. As they drove down the hill from Carmel on Highway One, they could see for miles ahead. Monterey Bay stretched before them like a shining deep blue sapphire, and Rita caught a glimpse of a U.S. Navy vessel moored near the Coast Guard Wharf. When they left the freeway, they drove on streets with names like Munras, Figueroa, and Alvarado. These are names of people in *The Carmelo Diaries.*

Rita drove past the San Cárlos Catholic Cemetery where her ancestors were buried. Crossing a little bridge, they entered Dennis the Menace Park that delighted everyone with its colorful activity apparatus for children. It was situated on what seemed like an island facing Lake El Estero that surrounded it. Usually there were people in kayaks passing by on the lake, and it was home to numerous waterfowl that lived in the rushes near the shore. Adults liked to go there with their children.

After Rita parked the car and escorted Carmelita to her favorite small merry-go-round, she stood to admire the view of the sparkling water and saw a collection of boat masts near Fisherman's Wharf and the Custom House Plaza.

The shoreline across from the park had been cleared of buildings and was truly a window to Monterey Bay. She knew that *el estero* meant the estuary in Spanish, and she thought of how the tall sailing ships must have looked as they entered the channel back those many years ago. What a sight it must have been when José Figueroa came sailing in from his lengthy voyage. There was a large crowd wanting to see the long awaited new governor. She was looking at the same bay that was so important to the life of the early colony. Father Junipero Serra held the first outdoor masses near this location. Soon he realized that he needed to change his plans and build his mission away from the *Presidio* and its soldiers. He found a place five miles southwest that was on a hill above Carmel Bay and the Pacific Ocean. This site was near a fertile valley and the Carmel River, and it was better situated for his undertaking. It was in this little valley that the *hacienda* of Rancho Carmelo was situated.

Carmelita ran from place to place, and then she called to her mother, "I want to Swing Swing."

"I liked swings when I was a little girl." She told Carmelita. "I had a big swing set on one of the lawns of Stonecrest" Rita lifted her into a seat that could be buckled and gently pushed her high into the air. Occasionally, she gave the swing a little push. She was still thinking about all the unanswered questions. She came up with several scenarios that would explain what had happened at the shop, but why she hadn't heard from Mr. Goldman? Was Charlie somehow involved in the theft and why? Would Captain Lewis keep bugging her?

Until two days ago, she thought she was living the perfect life. In her past Rita had led a life of more intrigue. She had once traveled to Vienna to spend the weekend with a U.S. senator. She had accompanied one of the world famous golf pros on a tour of Europe. and in both cases she played hide-and-seek with the press. She had settled down in a life that she had really wanted all the time. She had a husband whom she truly loved and an exuberant small daughter. "Hold tight, Carmelita." She called as she noticed her daughter holding on with just one hand. Then looking toward the edge of the park, she saw someone coming towards them.

Captain Lewis, dressed in a new blue warm up suit, walked across the bridge in great strides. "I thought I might find you here. I've talked to your Mr. Goldman.

"Do you want to know what he said?"

"Do you always ask so many questions?" Rita said as she gave Carmelita a more vigorous push than she expected.

"Mommy Mommy—I'm flying," she yelled happily.

"That's my business," he said looking at her approvingly and admiring how precisely she filled the jeans she wore. She was well covered up by an oversized thick white sweater, but as she moved forward and backwards with the motion of the swing, the silhouette was appealing as if she had choreographed the scene.

"If you're not going to tell me, why did you come out here?" She stopped and laughed, as she looked at him in his polyester outfit. "To gloat?"

"Of course not. Don't you remember the last thing you said to me? I was to tell you when I talked to Dave Goldman? And you wanted to know what he said," Lewis replied.

"I didn't think you'd track me down today just to tell me that. You told me that you might come by the shop this afternoon."

"I was able to find Goldman." And he added. "It was easy."

Rita, not knowing what to do next, kept on swinging Carmelita.

"He said he'd be coming up to the tournament next week. I told him he wasn't under oath or anything like that, but that you mentioned his name in regards to a historical drama based on *The Carmelo Diaries*. I asked him to tell me what he planned to do with your story."

"And, I bet he laughed," Rita interjected

"You're right. He said he never talked business with someone like me while he was considering a new project. He said he read about the missing *Carmelo Diaries* in the paper and thought your phone calls were about that."

"I guess that means he is interested, anyway." Rita managed to say.

"You might say so," Lewis said casually. "Now it's your turn to let me know when you hear from him."

"And what else?"

"That's all."

"I don't believe it," she said frowning and shaking her head.

"You must have a reason to say that," he said warily.

"Not anything in particular except that my husband told me to take plenty of time with any business offer. I'm in no rush. Originally I planned to read Mr. Goldman some pages from Clarita's leather diary. I also planned to take him for a drive by the Carmel Mission and some of the Monterey adobes. I thought it would put him in a receptive mood."

"I've been around here over a year and I haven't seen any adobes. We could do that right now. You could be my guide."

"No way." she said emphatically. "This is my day with Carmelita. You just go over to the Larkin House on Pacific Street, buy a ticket, and you'll have a guide who will tell you what there is to know."

"So you recommend it," he said as if trying to extend the conversation.

"Most heartily. The historic adobes are all close by," she said, hoping he would leave right away.

"I'll keep in touch. I think Mr. Goldman has some connection with the missing books," he finished and walked toward the edge of the park.

Soon after that, Rita and Carmelita went to a little Italian grocery store on the hill above the oldest historic part of town. She bought thin little bread sticks, a kind of Italian meatballs, and Mozzarella, Provolone, and Gorgonzola cheeses. When they told her that the cannelloni was filled with veal and spinach, she decided to buy that for their dinner. The pasta was homemade, and the cannelloni was displayed like prize jewels in a case. After she bought some warm ravioli, she took Carmelita to El Estero Lake and they ate their lunch. Carmelita took some of the stale bread they had brought and threw bread to the gulls and pigeons. It was an active morning, and Carmelita was tired and ready for a nap when they returned home.

Rita called the shop at two o'clock. "Tessa, I can't make it in this afternoon. I'm going to stay here with Carmelita,"

"I've been busy every minute," Tessa announced quickly. "Captain Lewis called to say he would be over later. Rita, I just can't handle so much."

"Just close The Booktique early and come over here. We can talk about what needs to be done at the shop next week, and we won't be interrupted. I've picked up some wonderful Italian goodies for dinner. Stay and share it with us." Rita suggested. "And we'll taste the bottle of Merlot that Charlie gave me."

"You're on. I'll close at three, no matter what. Besides I have something else to discuss with you."

Tessa was sitting in Rita's kitchen promptly at ten after three. Rita started to make coffee for her, and noticing Carmelita's flushed cheeks, she said, "Maybe I shouldn't have taken her out to play this morning, but it was such a beautiful day and I wanted to let her have some fresh air."

"She probably has a little sunburn, Rita. But don't fret about it, I really don't need coffee."

"With all that has gone on at the store I wanted to talk to you about next week. You know it's going to be the AT&T Tournament. We might have to play it by ear next week. With all those parties and golf people milling around it won't be a week for our kind of customers. I'm just going to be relaxed about expectations."

"I want to talk about next week with you anyway," Tessa said as she nervously put the individual tea packets in and out of the tea basket that Rita had placed on the table. "I want to leave town."

Rita was dividing her attention between Carmelita and Tessa. "OK, pal. Do you have a new boyfriend?"

"Well sort of," Tessa stammered. "I just want to take a couple of days off next week," she said very fast as if it would sound better that way.

"What days? I do need you some of the days."

"I don't know, but this is really important."

"I hope it's a great boy friend. Can you tell me who it is?" Rita said, and when she saw Tessa's frightened face, she reached with her free hand to pat her friend. "But I hope it's that British golfer who was at The Retreat last month. He was a pretty neat guy."

"It's more important than that. This might change my life."

"Then you'd better go do your thing."

"You're such a good pal. I hope I can tell you about it soon," Tessa said in a voice that concluded the topic of conversation.

The afternoon had become gray, and looking across the yard Rita could see that the puffy clouds were gone, and the sky was darkening early.

"When Mike comes home, I'll have him make a fire. You can stay and we'll have a cozy dinner, just the three of us. Did I tell you that Mother had us to dinner with Charlie?"

"Did he talk about his divorce?"

"Not much. He was so full of his wine conference the rest of us didn't have a chance to say much. Mother hung on to his every word. She seemed to forgotten that Charlie told her she was the fault of their bad marriage."

Tessa looked as if she were going to say something, and began arranging the tea bags again. "I'll have a glass of wine, but I shouldn't stay for dinner. He's going to call me, she said quietly.

"When you find out your plans, tell me what days you want off?"

"I'll be at the shop on Monday, That, I know," she promised.

"Did Captain Lewis drop by before you left?" Rita asked.

"For just a few minutes."

When Carmelita began playing with the wooden train, Rita poured them both a glass of wine. She looked at hers and swished it around a little. "Charlie says this wine is special. It is unfiltered and aged twenty-two months in French Oak. I don't know exactly what that means, but it costs sixty dollars a bottle, and they only make a hundred cases. I guess we'd better be impressed."

Tessa looked into the glass and giving a sniff, she tasted it. "Lovely, lovely," she said thoughtfully.

"I'll give you something to hold you 'til dinner," Rita said, and set a plate of cheeses and some crackers on the table. "Good, there's Mike," she said happily. To Rita, all the perplexities of the day faded away as he entered the room and lifted Carmelita to his shoulders.

"It's good to be here, he exclaimed. "There's going to be a big storm coming in, and I feel like a sailor returning to the port." He put Carmelita down and kissed Rita. "Hi Tessa," he said as he sat on the floor by Carmelita.

"Hi, Mike."

"Did you have a picnic today, dolly?" he asked Carmelita.

"I fed ducks, Daddy," she said smiling. "I want to play games now."

"Give Mike a glass of that expensive Merlot before we drink it all up," Tessa suggested. "I better leave my favorite little family before it starts blowing too hard."

"If you'll stay, I'll hustle up the dinner right now," Rita offered.

"No, I really need to go," Tessa said as she started putting on the coat she had draped over the chair. "I'll see you Monday morning."

Mike accepted the glass of wine that Rita brought him, and settled into his familiar pattern of playing with Carmelita before dinner.

"How was your day? Did you go to the park?" he said turning toward Rita.

"We had a great time. Captain Snoop even found us there and said he wanted to tell me about his talk with Dave Goldman. I'll fill you in later. Did it all go well at the luncheon?"

"Routine. I would rather be out doors playing with you girls. Tessa looks like she's lost a little weight. How is she?"

Rita looked at Mike's sympathetic face and became thoughtful as she was trying to appraise Tessa's mood. "She's beginning to look trim again. I think she's in love with some guy." Rita answered. "I'd like to see her wear some new clothes. Maybe a sexy low cut blouse. Gee, I sound like Mother," Rita laughed. "Anyway she wants a couple of days off next week. She wouldn't tell me much, but she implied she was going to meet someone special in The City."

"That's good for her, but won't you need her at the shop?"

"Yes, but she's my friend. I want her to be happy and in love. I think I'll treat her to a facial one of these days. I think she needs a boost right now. I really hope something good works out with this guy. She's such a pushover for a heart break."

"Hon," Mike interrupted. "You can't make her over, body and soul. She's got a lot of love to give, but she needs to find someone to appreciate her as she is. She's sweet and needing affection and ready to give it."

"Look who's Mr. Analyst now," Rita laughed. "Are you ready for your Italian supper yet?"

"Always ready for food," he laughed. "Although I need to get myself to the weight room tomorrow. I've done too much sitting lately."

"You look wonderful since we got married. You were too skinny before that great event. Of course, we both need to keep up with our health regimes. Why don't you go over to the gym at the Shore Club right now? I'll stay here with Carmelita. She's not quite over her croupy cough."

Mike finished his glass of Merlot, and put a soft piece of melted provolone cheese on a round of toast. "What else did Captain Lewis want?"

"Remember when you left and the telephone was ringing. Well, he was calling to talk over the case, and he asked me if I had talked to Mr. Goldman"

"You didn't tell him about Charles or what we talked about, did you?" Mike immediately responded.

"No, but he made a point to tell me that he had talked to Mother. I thought I'd better tell him that we all had dinner together. And sure enough, Mother had already told him about the dinner. Then he asked me where he could find Charlie."

"Damn it all," Mike exclaimed. "He'll find out that we're not the best of friends."

"Oh, I think I handled that pretty well. I told him to try calling Charlie at his home in Napa this weekend. Captain Lewis wanted to meet me at the shop. I told him that I was spending some time with Carmelita at the park." She paused. I might as well tell you. He showed up at Dennis the Menace Park. Would you believe it? I was swinging Carmelita when he came up."

"Aha, I win my bet. I told you he had the hots for you."

"Oh, Mike, don't be silly. He's just a snoopy busybody. Why else would anyone choose that profession? Anyway he told me that Mr. Goldman read about the burglary in the paper, and he also told him that he was coming to the tournament next week. Captain Sleuth asked him his plans for using *The Carmelo Diaries,* and it seems that Mr. Goldman brushed off that question like it was a gnat. After that I got rid of him and Carmelita and I went to Tony's Market to buy things for dinner."

"Speaking of dinner. When will it be ready?"

"Pretty soon. I'm glad we can stay home tonight. It's really going to blow."

"Maybe it'll be like our first real evening together, Mike agreed.
"Even better," she answered.

CHAPTER 17

▼

January 30, 2000 Carmel

A typical Pacific coastal storm consumed the Sunday. Trees fell during the night, and most residents on the Monterey peninsula were without power. Rita called her mother to make sure that Roberto had started the generator at Stonecrest. "This might go on for quite a spell," Rita told her.

"The generator is working, and we are warm. I'm glad I had our party before the storm, aren't you? I think it went well and I really liked what you wore." Anita said in one breath.

Rita finished the conversation quickly. After Mike took blankets and a card table and made a tent for Carmelita to play at camping, he settled down with the sport section of the Sunday paper.

"I need to find out about Clarita's life after 1833," Rita told him.

"Use what your grandmother told you."

"No, I want to be accurate. I'm going to read a packet of letters written by Consuelo and Clarita." Rita told him, and going upstairs to her office, she sat in a comfortable chair and read the letters which were quite fragile and the ink was somewhat faded, but the copy that Grandmother Clara translated into English was legible.

March 1834

"Consuelo, *la simpatiquísima,*

"I am sending you this letter by way of my most trusted messenger, Ramon Marcos. When you send a letter to me, do not give it to anyone else but Ramon.

"I greet you with love and want to thank you again for protecting me after the death of my husband. At the present time, I am safe here, and I am helping take care of Papa. Esperanza tends the household and takes care of Papa. I read to him and tell him stories.

"Ardo plays the guitar for him after supper in the evening. Papa enjoys whatever Ardo does. Now that the rains are almost over, he takes great joy in watching how well Ardo rides. I embroidered Ardo a shirt, and he wears a small pair of leather *chaparreras* that were made especially for him. He looks like a real horseman with his gauntlet gloves and quirt. The *vaqueros* have taught him how to use their *riatas*. He will be ready to take part in a *rodeo* before many years have passed. I have been teaching Ardo to read. You should see my little group of pupils that include Ardo and my little sisters. When the weather becomes really warm, we shall move from the porch to a corner of the courtyard under the leafy trees. On days of good weather, I long to ride to the mouth of the valley where the river meets the ocean, but I do not dare go beyond the gates alone.

"I fear that Don Diego will send someone to capture me and make me a prisoner. Eventually he will be able to claim Ardo. It pains me much that the Last Will and Testament of my husband makes his brother the guardian of Ardo. It says that he is to provide me a home, but as I told you in strict confidence, Don Diego says I must be completely subject to him. The night my husband died, he kept me captive in a room with a guard at the door. And it was then that he told me of his desire for my body. He said I was to live my life in service to him in whatever way he wished. I do not want to tell you this, but I must ask you a favor. If I am seized and taken to the house of Don Diego, I want you to show this letter to your husband. Tell him to ask the governor for my freedom. I have been with no man except my husband, and I wish to live with the family of my father. I swear by our mothers and the Blessed Virgin that what I have said is true.

"Keep this letter with your jewelry. I hope that you will not need to show it to anyone. With my deepest affection for you and your family,

"Clarita Isabel Vargas y Segovia"

"April 1834" Dear friend and cousin, Consuelo,

"You have wondered why Ardo and I left the funeral of my husband so quickly and how we found our way to your house. On that day, it was *O'Farol* who found me in the corner of the church by the statue of the Blessed Virgin. Ardo was clinging to my skirts. *O'Farol* told me I was in grave danger at that moment, and he said he had arranged for my escape. He told Father Juan that I had taken ill and that he would escort us to the house of Captain García and his family. Then he put a bright-colored serape over my shoulders, a broad brim hat on my head and told me to follow him quickly. Picking up Ardo, he tucked him under his cape, slipped out of church and into a side alley near the wall. I followed like a shadow. We crept through the small room where Father Juan had a bed, and we ducked into the house of the governor and then into the barracks. Guillermo arranged for our flight by giving a soldier a gold piece and he had two horses waiting for us. We arrived at your house before anyone else. All of you were with the casket in the church courtyard. We huddled near the hearth in the kitchen house, and then Guillermo gave Ardo a piece of honeycomb and bolted the door. He told me to hide under the serape until it was dark, and he promised to stay with us for a while. He sang a song to Ardo about knights and castles. The Blessed Mother was with us, because Ardo did not cry, and the soft singing put him to sleep. I thought *O'Farol* had helped us because I had once saved his life when he was trying to swim to shore. Now, I know that *O'Farol* has always loved me. When he rescued Ardo and me, he quietly told me that he loved me and would always protect me. Last week he came to Rancho Carmelo and brought us news that the governor will grant us the land of our ranch if it is measured again. Papa gave him permission to do this, and he talked to him as if there were no years of separation between them.

"*O'Farol* works for Señor Larkin, so he will ask his permission to return to Rancho Carmelo and stay for several days. He will take some *vaqueros* with him and ride to all the points of boundaries and then make the maps we need. Señor Larkin sells foodstuffs and cloth, and I asked *O'Farol* what work he did for Señor Larkin. He told me that he is building a sawmill for Señor Larkin. He directs the laborers in the building of a grand house for him. *O'Farol* enjoys working with his hands, and no other gentleman can be found in Alta California who will do this. It is very necessary work, and I admire him for this. He says that when he and Señor Larkin are by themselves, they talk in English. Don Tomás often gives him advice. Of course, I know that Don Tomás married the *Yanqui* lady, Raquel, on board a *Yanqui* ship in the Santa Bárbara harbor. Señor Larkin does not wish to become a Mexican citizen; however, he told *O'Farol* it might be wise for him to become a Mexican citizen. Then he could own land and build himself a house someday.

"I must stop writing as Papa and I are going to ride to the mission. He wants to talk to the new *padre* in charge. He is a priest from Zacateca by the name of José María del Refugio Sagrado Suarez del Real. We all know that Mission San Cárlos is to be part of the Mexican plan that takes away the mission lands from the mission fathers. Father José wants to slaughter much of the cattle before this is done. As you know, the mission cattle have often grazed on the lands of Rancho Carmelo. Many of the neophytes have already left the mission, so our *vaqueros* will be needed to slaughter the cattle and tan the hides, which are mission property. Someone we do not know will be appointed *comisionado* of the mission lands and property in the future.

"Please write to me, but remember to give the letter only to Ramon.

I send greetings to all your family and especially to my new little godson, Luis.

"Your loyal and devoted friend,

"Clarita Isabel Vargas y Segovia."

Consuelo's reply
"August 1834 Dear Cousin, Clarita,

"Today I am thinking of our mothers. They were cousins who came from Castile. They did not know each other until they met on board the sailing vessel that took them to Mexico. They became friends during the long voyage to Mexico and when they joined other ladies on a boat bound for Monterey, they became like sisters. Their families had arranged their marriages to men from Castile. It was during the second time that Don José Arrillaga was governor. What a different life they lived. It was a land that was very strange to them. Also they were far away from their families. At least they knew one another. I was fortunate that I married a man that I had met and liked, although Papa arranged the marriage. Life has been good for us, and we will soon live on the ranch that our governor has granted us. It is located near the Pajaro River where the birds are very large. It is in the direction of Rancho Rincón. Oh, that you could live there. We would be only a few leagues apart.

"I know that living on a ranch will be different for me. There is always much that happens in Monterey now that we have such a fine governor. Monterey is where we have our friends, and therefore we will keep our adobe house in town. We want to attend the *fandangos* and baptisms of our friends. At the ranch, I will have a room built for each child, and I will have an Indian maiden to take care of each one.

"My dear friend, I can tell you now that I will have another child before the end of the year. My life at the ranch will be filled with our children. We will attend mass at the Mission San Juan Bautista that will supply us with all the Indians we need. I will continue to teach Domingo how to read and write as our mothers taught us. I will also teach Dolores to read and write, as well as how to embroider and make lace. It pains me that Encarnacion Cooper cannot write letters to me. She signs her name with such beautiful strokes of the pen.

"The governor is putting in force the Mexican law that says the missions must be turned over to the government, and my husband and the *Presidio* troops are staying close to the governor at present. The governor wants the change to be gradual and he wants to protect the people here, in case there are outbreaks of violence. When it becomes more peaceful, Miguel plans to buy cattle, and we will live on our ranch all year round.

"The wife of Don Diego died. The funeral services were at the Mission San Juan Bautista where they attended mass. Miguel was present at the funeral in his official capacity, but I can tell you that Miguel and Diego do not like one another. I did not attend the service, as I was not feeling well. At that time I did not know about the coming of our next child.

"I hope that soon you will have the approval from the governor for the grant deed to Rancho Carmelo. Kiss my godson for me.

"I remain your devoted friend, Consuelo Merced García y Avila".

Rita searched for another letter from Consuelo. The only one she could find was incomplete. There were only two pages of that letter, and it seemed to be written after the previous letter of August 1834. This letter begins at the top of the second page with no hint as to what preceded it.

"I love the warm summer days at our Rancho Laguna y Cañada. We often take *carretas* filled with blankets and children, and we go to the river for a *merienda*. Miguel is occupied with showing his men how to build a house. He also uses carpenters from the mission San Juan Bautista. Miguel wants to build at least two rooms for our first shelter. Later on, we will use these for bedrooms and we will build the rest of the *hacienda*. The Indians from the mission have been taught to make tiles, and the summer is the best time for making them. In all, we have about fifty people working for us now. We have several *tortilla* makers, and other women who cook outdoors to feed everyone. You wrote that the Mission San Cárlos is losing the neophytes. It is the same at Mission San Juan Bautista. I do not know, but wonder if some of the land promised to us will come from the lands of the mission. Miguel says he has not ridden around the entirety of our ranch. He warns me that some of the land is swampy and near the ocean, but we grow vegetables and plant trees near where we live. Our ranch extends many leagues." *The next pages of a letter from Consuelo were written from Monterey.*

"The *Yanquis* continue to arrive, and Monterey has become a place of great activity. The boats from the Sandwich Islands come often, and they bring us things that are useful. The store of Señor Larkin is the most important place in town. One can trade hides or otter pelts for shawls, shoes, woolen blankets, tools and dishes from the country of China. Of course, coins will buy spices, ribbons, and ornaments to dress our hair. I can take Domingo and Dolores and walk to the store. It is much easier for us to go to the store rather than going out to sea in those little open boats.

"I have not seen *O'Farol*, although I hear that Señor Larkin speaks well of him, and I also hear that he has been introduced to the governor. He now wears velvet pantaloons and white stockings and a fancy bolero when he is invited to a *fandango*. Some of us wonder when he will try to court one of our ladies.

"Encarnacion tells me that her husband has sold some of their house and properties in Monterey to a *Yanqui* by the name of Jones. Her husband will use the money to buy other properties.

"You asked me to tell you about what is happening. I have written what I know. The appointment of majordomos to take over the missions is the talk of all the gentlemen, but unless Miguel tells me something in particular, I do not know what is going on with the governor. Miguel says that Governor Figueroa is good for all the *Californios*. They will receive land grants and acquire more land where they can live with the Indian neophytes who will do the heavy labor.

"I am sad that you must stay at Rancho Carmelo and cannot visit me in Monterey. I do not think that Don Diego will be a threat to you. I hear that when his mourning period has passed, he will court the youngest Vallejo girl.

"I understand how important it is for you to do your duty by your father. My prayers will be said for your father's health.

"Your devoted friend, Consuelo Merced García y Avila."

CHAPTER 18

▼

Rita found the letters to be heavy reading. She grew drowsy and went downstairs where she found Carmelita asleep on her pallet and Mike stretched out and dozing by the fire. She succumbed to the monotonous patter of the rain on the roof and went to sleep on the couch. All of them slept until Rita heard a knock on the door. Mike and Carmelita continued to sleep. The knocking seemed to be at the back door so she hurried through the kitchen to answer it.

"Rita, Rita," called Tessa through the closed door. "I'm sorry to bother you like this, but your telephone isn't working. Most of the phones in Carmel are dead."

"I bet the power lines are down everywhere. Look the light still won't go on," Rita said as she ushered Tessa inside.

"You should see Pebble Beach and the Del Monte Forest," Tessa exclaimed breathlessly. "Several of the roads are closed, and water is pouring onto the Seventeen Mile Drive in umpteen rivulets."

"You know, I telephoned Mother a little while ago. Something must have happened since then."

"Mine still works, so it just depends," Tessa explained taking off her plastic rain cape that she put over a chair. "I passed The Retreat on my way here. I don't think they'll be able to play the practice rounds tomorrow. All those white tents look so bedraggled and forlorn. A lot of canvas is flapping in the wind, too."

"This year they have put up more hospitality tents than ever before," Rita commented. "Serves them right. They take a beautiful golf course and the most spectacular scenery in the world and make it all look tacky. Even the Shore Club parking lot has been turned over to hot dogs and souvenirs."

"Which leads me to why I came. If it keeps up like this, I don't think you'll be very busy for the next few days. I told you I could be at The Booktique tomorrow morning, but I can't. In fact I'm on my way to San Francisco right now."

"In all this rain?" Rita was surprised.

"Oh, it won't be bad. At least there won't be much traffic. Once I get onto 101, it's a straight shot."

"Does this have to do with your mysterious friend?"

"Of course. Or else I'd be sitting beside the fire at home."

"It sounds like you two are pretty serious. At least you aren't waiting around for a phone call. Still, I hate to see you start out now. Can I make you a cup of coffee or give you an Italian meatball sandwich?"

"No, I'm too excited to eat," she said, and it seemed to Rita that Tessa looked even prettier than the day before.

"Well, give me a call if you are going to be gone more than a few days. The storm's not supposed to last. I'm that kind of a boss, you know." Tessa looked so serious that Rita added, "Really, pal, I just want to know how you are getting along."

"Right now I'm flying on wings of love," Tessa laughed as she started to pull on her boots. "Rita, you'll be the first to know anything."

"Did he say something wonderful?" Rita said changing her own mood.

"Oh, yes, "said Tessa, stopping to close her eyes and smile in a satisfied way. "He always sounds wonderful."

"Can't he come down here?"

"No, because he wants to see me right away. And he said it in a very intimate way. He's staying in San Francisco, because he has some power breakfast meeting in the morning. He told me that tonight is the best time for us to be together," she said with emphasis.

"Sounds romantic," Rita added.

"Oh, it is. And those were his words. And he used that fantastic word 'Us' like he's never used it with me before. He said, 'we're going to do something just for us.'"

"You're flying so high I still think I'd better give you something to eat and have you calm down a little. It's raining pretty hard."

"He says the storm's passed up there. I'll be all right. Honest."

Rita remembered her friend from the days when they were teenagers. Tessa was excitable and eager today, almost as she used to be in those other times. The last two years of disappointment and divorce seemed to be wiped away, and now Tessa was her enthusiastic self again.

"I'm really really happy for you, and I'm glad our phone isn't working. I wouldn't want to miss seeing you like this."

Tessa had tied a scarf around her head and was ready to leave. "I'm glad I saw you, too," she said as she threw her arms around Rita and hugged her.

Both Mike and Carmelita had been roused by the voices in the kitchen, and when Rita went back into the living room, Mike asked her what all the excitement was about.

"Tessa couldn't get us on the phone. I guess the lines are all down around here. Anyway, her guy called, and she's on her way to San Francisco to be with him. She came by to tell me what the storm had done in Pebble Beach, and said she won't be in the store tomorrow."

"I thought I heard her voice. You say she's really excited?"

"This guy must have said something very important. Anyway she's finally forgotten about her divorce, and she's on to a new life. I was asleep when she knocked at the front door, so she went around to the back."

"Let's all get dressed and go out. We'll find some place open for lunch," Mike said. "I'm starving."

Winter weather in coastal California is capricious, and the storm had spent itself by early afternoon. Although the sun shone with intense brightness, the wind was crisp and cold. The Minettis ate at a casual style restaurant located at Lover's Point in Pacific Grove. From the second tier of tables, they could see Monterey Bay filled with waves that cut the cobalt blue waters like spears of white ice. They ate a hot meal in case their home remained without power. Carmelita enjoyed her lunch. The restaurant was her favorite one because of the small ice cream cone given to children for dessert.

"Let's drive around Point Piños," Mike announced, and after they passed the old lighthouse, they stopped at one of the parking pullouts to watch the ocean swells.

"I like the big horn," Carmelita said after it blared, and Mike drove beyond to Asilomar Beach."

"Shall we take the Seventeen Mile Drive and stop by your mother's house? She asked about Carmelita the other night. Maybe she'd like to see her," Mike suggested.

"Let well enough alone," Rita replied quickly. "I need to get back to the house and prepare for tomorrow. I might be in the shop by myself tomorrow, and I think it's going to be a big day. Not everyone's going to be out on those soggy golf courses in this chilly weather, and they're bound to come browsing around the Pebble Beach Shops. I have a lot of things to do."

"OK by me," Mike answered good-naturedly. "There's a great basketball game I want to watch."

"Don't get your hopes up. We might still be without power," Rita remembered.

"Then I'll take another nap,' Mike laughed.

When they returned home, the telephone was working. Rita called Dolores Espinosa and asked her to help at The Old Booktique for a few days. Dolores was well acquainted with books on California lore and history, as she had a premium book collection of her own. Dolores and Rita were distant cousins. Since she was a widow and her children were away at college, she often had time to help Rita at the store. She had been the first to call Rita when she heard about the burglary and the missing *Carmelo Diaries*. Rita had often discussed the project of the proposed television series with her. They talked about it like mutual grandmothers discuss a family wedding.

"When you make your presentation be sure to include the part about how Clarita and her *Yanqui* circumvented the conventions of marriages in Alta California," Dolores advised her.

"It was one of Clara's favorite parts, but I don't know how much truth there was to it," Rita sighed.

"Just write it down as you remember it from her and we'll discuss it some time in the next week."

"When Tessa comes back she can help me out. She was one of my friends at Santa Lucia that were invited by Clara to her story teas."

"Oh, I remember her famous high teas that she served in the library. Since they usually included fudge brownies, fruit tarts, and little finger sandwiches, I bet the girls came without to much coaxing."

"I think that's why they came. They stuffed themselves with food while Clara elaborated about Spanish strict social customs. Once Tessa told Clara that they were very snobbish."

"What did Clara answer?"

"Clara was never at a loss for words. She would say, 'Yes, they were very class conscious and continued to be so for many generations. Even their playmates were selected for them. You need to remember at what time they lived in California. Their manners came from the early nineteenth century. Tessa, you seem to think that history took place just a few minutes before you came down to breakfast.'"

Dolores laughed. "Rita, you must tell the story and just the way Clara told it. How we look at history usually depends on who our ancestors were."

"Exactly."

"I'll be glad to help you out this week. And feel free to tell me about the story of your ancestors. You know, we have mutual cousins somewhere. See you tomorrow." Dolores promised.

As soon as Rita said goodbye, she began to write, and she started out as if Clara were in front of a small group of listeners.

"Now Mariano was said to have told the story differently," Clara would begin. "You know whom I mean. It was Don Mariano Guadelupe Vallejo."

Rita remembered that Clara talked slowly and carefully while pronouncing his name in a soft Spanish way. This made it sound musical and the word Vallejo sounded very liquid.

"But, of course they say that Don Mariano made every story a little grander that it really was. When he talked he possessed *duende.* That is Spanish for something that is even better than charisma. He was a master of nineteenth-century oratory. When Don Mariano talked about Clarita de Segovia, he was always complimentary, and he would tell everyone that she was of pure Castilian heritage. He bragged that not even one generation of her family had come from Mexico. This was true. Clarita was the only daughter of María Isabel de la Luz y la Vega and Bernardo Cárlos de Segovia. They lived on a large ranch situated in a valley near the mouth of the river Carmelo near the Spanish mission San Cárlos. Don Bernardo considered himself the owner of the ranch although it was really a cattle and land concession from the King of Spain. Mission San Cárlos, founded by Father Junipero Serra, dedicated to the glory of God and the King of Spain."

Rita began the next part of the Carmelo story just as her grandmother Clara had related it. She started with a reference to Mariano Guadelupe Vallejo. It was known that his life paralleled the pivotal events of the history of nineteenth century California. He, as well as Clarita, lived from the time it was a Spanish colony to the coming of statehood in the United States of America and into the time of the California Gold Rush.

"The power is on," she heard Mike call, and she telephoned Anita to find out if all was in order at Stonecrest.

"Oh yes, an hour ago," Anita said hurriedly, "I'm watching my favorite television show. I'm watching a biography of Gloria Swanson right now, so I'll talk to you later."

"No need to do that, Mother. I'll be busy fixing dinner since we have electricity now."

"Oh yes, and Charles called to say he would be down here during the middle of next week. I asked him to stay here. Bye for now," Anita said in one breath.

During dinner Rita told Mike about her call to Anita.

"Did Charles say why he was coming?"

"She didn't say. She wanted to get back to her TV show. Charlie is a scratch golfer. He probably wants to come down to watch the tournament."

"It's more than that. I think it's strange that he's coming back so soon."

After Carmelita went to bed, Rita said to Mike, "You've heard my grand-mother tell her story about Clarita. I wrote down how I remembered she started when she wanted to tell her story. Do you have time to read what I have written?"

"OK, I'll do it now, but I won't have much time to do this kind of thing next week. I'll be busy during the tournament. Remember, we have parties to attend almost every day."

"I have everything under control. Marquita is going to take care of Carmelita, and Dolores is helping at the shop.

"And let's keep our distance from Brother Charles," Mike added.

"That I can promise," Rita said smiling as she handed him what she had written. "Be sure to make some comment."

CHAPTER 19

▼

Clara Torelli's story about Clarita was usually told it to an audience. After a preamble, such as the one about Don Mariano Guadelupe Vallejo, she would start.

"I think that Will and Clarita always knew they would be together no matter how difficult it was for them to marry. Will said he was an American, but he had no papers from any government, because he had left the ship on which he arrived to the coast of California in 1824. He said he was part of a small rowboat scouting party that was sent to find a landing place in the waters around Point Lobos. Ships frequently off loaded some of their cargo at places on nearby shores. Later the ship's agent would barter for hides, and transactions were made without the boat needing to pay the high Mexican tariffs at the customhouse in Monterey. Will was sixteen, and it was his first voyage out. His parents, both from Ireland, had died a few years before. After his aunt in Boston died, he was truly alone. Not accustomed to the harsh treatment under Captain Trever Smith, he probably decided to jump ship when his rowboat capsized, and the other man was drowned. The ocean was and is treacherous in the coastal waters of what is now known as Carmel Bay.

"Clarita was the only daughter of María Isabel de la Luz y la Vega and Bernardo Carlos de Segovia. They lived on a large ranch situated in a valley near the mouth of the river Carmel near the Spanish Mission San Cárlos. It was located on the north side of the Carmel River, which was often impossible to cross. Don Bernardo considered himself to be the owner of the ranch.

"Clarita had been brought up in a traditional Spanish fashion, strict in social manners and deeply religious. She had never seen her father use his hands for anything manual, except to hold the reins of his horse. She lived surrounded by many Indian. Mission converts, who lived on their ranch. She observed an amazing amount of hard work in the corrals and fields and in the many rooms of the *hacienda* where she lived. The neophyte women did all the household tasks of grinding corn, washing clothes, cooking, and carrying loads of wood to the outside ovens while her mother, María Isabel, embroidered, made lace, and directed the household servants. Her mother was diligent about teaching her two children, Estéban and Clarita Isabel, to read and write, and she accompanied them to the Mission for religious instruction and mass. Clarita's mother was not robust, and she did not enjoy horseback riding. She was accustomed to a large family with brothers, sisters, cousins and grandparents in Spain, and she found life on the ranch to be lonely. Her greatest pleasure was going to visit her cousin, Loretta, who was married to the captain at the *Presidio* at Monterey. Clarita's mother had deep auburn hair and dark blue eyes, and Estéban, Clarita's older brother, was said to resemble her. Clarita's mother died during the year that Clarita turned twelve. Soon after her death, Clarita found Will O'Farrell in the surf and saved his life.

"Clarita had wavy brown hair and it was said that her eyes gleamed with a lively sparkle. Later, after they were married, Will insisted that she have her portrait painted. It was a formal painting showing a lady with her dark hair gathered and held on top with a large tortoise shell comb. If one looks at it closely, one can see her refined features and the animation in her eyes."

Grandmother Clara Torelli always told this background to the love story. It was sometimes long and sometimes quite short. She always used the name, Will, when she referred to Will O'Farrell. Because his name was difficult for the Californios to pronounce, they called him O'Farol or Guillermo. After Clara described Clarita and the setting of her ranch home, Clara told the following story that Rita remembered. She used Clara's words as much as possible in writing the presentation she planned to present to Dave Goldman.

"In Alta California there was a strict code of behavior to follow in courtship for the *gente de razon*. Even after Mexico was free from Spain, this code was followed. It was necessary for all military men to procure permission to marry from the government of Mexico. Even when the gentleman was not military, he needed to obtain permission to marry from his family and the government officials. Young girls were accompanied everywhere by the *dueña*, who walked behind when a young couple strolled down a path. The *dueña* was supposed to sit and make lace in the patio or the *sala* when the suitor came to call. However, with glances, motions, and the tapping of fans at a *fandango* or *baile* there was sufficient communication between a young lady and her suitor. It is said that in Alta California, there was greater freedom than in Spain or Mexico.

"None of this decorum was followed by Clarita and Will. Their life together was different from the beginning. After Clarita's mother died, Don Bernardo took a greater interest in the ranch and had simple little shelters built so that his *vaqueros* could have a place to live in the rolling hills to the east. Sometimes he accompanied them as they followed the river through what is known today as Carmel Valley. When Estéban de Segovia started his lessons at the Mission with Father Antonio, Clarita thought they had forgotten about her. Though she was small in size, she was agile, and she insisted on always riding a particular horse all over the ranch. Often she could find Will, and she would talk to him without shyness. They talked about losing a mother, and they formed a mutual concern for the other's welfare. She thought of him as someone to care for. She appointed herself to be the person who would teach him to speak Spanish. When he arrived at the ranch, he had been put to work immediately, because he told Don Bernardo he could do the work of a carpenter. The ranch manager soon found him willing to do everything. Will lived among the Indians at the ranch, although he went to mass with the family. When he learned to speak some Spanish, he was invited to accompany Estéban when he rode to the farthest pastures. Sometimes when Don Bernardo was away, Will ate a meal with Clarita and Estéban. He enjoyed being a part of the ranch family.

"Will and Clarita formed a bond that endured all during their lives. While Will was learning to speak Spanish, he taught Clarita words and sentences of English. He started with his name. He told her how to pronounce his first name. At first all she could say was *O'Farol.*'

"At the end of that year, Clarita's father had become a solitary person. He seldom went to Monterey, and although he went to the Mission for a dinner with the Fathers, he did not seek other friends. Gradually, Don Bernardo became aware of the quiet charm and devotion of Esperanza. She was a fair skinned girl, with straight brown hair, which she braided, and she had an open, broad friendly face. Although she talked very little, she sang with a melodious voice. It was after Estéban sailed away to Spain to become a priest, that Esperanza, now a girl of sixteen, and Don Bernardo were married in a simple ceremony at the Mission San Cárlos.

"Esperanza became a good wife and devoted herself to Don Bernardo, who now saw less of Clarita. In that way, she depended on Will's friendship even more. Will was put in charge of training Ramon to be a groom for Don Bernardo's horse, and on good weather days, Will and Clarita went together by horseback up the valley of the River Carmelo. With a leather bag full of food, they often had a picnic lunch after they explored the lands around the river."

At this point Grandmother Clara would pause to see if she still had an audience. She wanted to explain that the lives of young Clarita and Will were different from the other colonists of Monterey. She would continue with authority and earnestness.

"There were no *dueñas*, fluttering fans, and flirtatious eyes to complicate the friendship of Will and Clarita, who always felt those sunny days in Carmel Valley were the happiest of their lives. However, there was one day that was unusual and gave them both in a special bond. It was a bright day in spring when the weather was warm, and they rode up the valley to a place where the river narrows. It was very shallow, and they decided to wade. Clarita took off her leather skirt and held up her petticoat. Will took off his chaps and rolled up his pants. As they walked upstream, they turned a bend and met a series of little falls. They were quickly up to their knees in rushing water, and before they could reach the banks, a strong wind arose and blew through the narrows with great force. Clarita began to falter and soon was swept into the current. Although Will was ahead of her, he was always looking back, and he quickly put his arm around her shoulders and towed her to a little beach ahead. Clarita regained her breath as she sat there and when she recovered, they began to laugh together. Clarita was wet from head to toe and looked very much the way she did on the day when she rescued will from the surf. They exchanged their first kiss.

"When my grandmother Isabel was about to be married in 1885, Clarita told her about that first kiss with Will. Clarita told her that both she and Will knew they wanted to love each other as a man and a woman. Although they both felt strong emotions, they did not embrace again. They planned to ask her father to give them his permission to marry when she was sixteen. Being aware of a strong mutual attraction, they did not ride far up the river again, but they talked of their future and of living together on Rancho Carmelo."

Clara always stopped the story here and made an explanation to her audience.

"I was told by my Grandmother Isabel, that Clarita always loved Will in the most special way. She always spoke of him with a different tone of voice. She said they talked in both English and in Spanish. Will told her that *enamorada* and *amoroso* were the most beautiful words he ever heard. He wanted to know all the words of tenderness in the Spanish language. Clarita said their first kiss was a new experience for both of them.

"Not long after the first romantic encounter of Will and Clarita, her friend and cousin, Consuelo, became betrothed to Lieutenant Miguel García, and a celebration was held for them at Rancho Carmelo. Besides the feasting, there was dancing with violins and guitars playing music at intervals for more than a day and a night. Clarita, dressed in her finest red silk skirt, danced exclusively with Will, who looked like a gentleman in his black velvet pants and short silk jacket. When Don Bernardo saw them dancing, he pulled them aside, and within an instant, he banished the man he called 'Guillermo' from the ranch. Clarita had just turned fifteen, and Don Bernardo soon told her that she was already betrothed to Felipe Vargas with plans for a marriage as soon as formalities were observed. That is when *The Carmelo Diaries* were begun."

Rita stopped. "That's as far as I have written. What do you think, Mike?"

"Let's talk about it tomorrow."

"I know this is your busy time. We'll talk about it later."

"Better read to me as you go along, but remember, I'm not a literary critic." He gave her a little pat.

"You always say the right thing," Rita laughed, and they went upstairs.

CHAPTER 20

▼

January 31, 2000

Monday began with a golden winter glow. Then the early morning sun cast a blazing shaft of light across the lawn. Rita left early while Mike was still wandering around the house looking for his favorite sunglasses. Carmelita had already eaten her breakfast. Rita drove by the Carmel Mission and arrived at a perfect time when a shaft of intense ochre light bathed the top of the church. She parked near the entrance, and walked toward the large wooden gates. They were closed and secured with a large conspicuous lock. Peering through the portals she looked toward the entrance to the basilica. Enclosed within the mission walls were stone statues, native shrubs and plants, and a shed made of adobe walls. She walked around the outside walls and crossed the street for a better view of the illumined bell-tower. With no tourists around, Rita could imagine it as it once was at the top of a hill. Clarita de Segovia and her family had worshiped here. New thoughts emboldened Rita, and soon she drove off, invigorated with a new enthusiasm.

When she arrived at The Old Booktique, there were crowds of people milling around the golf pro shop. The golf tournament was already in play. Although it was the first day of the qualifying rounds, there were many spectators who chose to attend at this time.

Rita could hear the telephone ringing as she entered The Old Booktique. "Dave Goldman here," Rita heard when she picked up the receiver.

"Here, like in Pebble Beach here?" Rita said.

"No, I'm still in Beverly Hills. I'm calling to tell you I'm coming up your way on Wednesday."

"Oh that's great," she said in a somewhat coaxing voice, momentarily forgetting to be on her guard. She was about to ask him to lunch at the Shore Club, but instead she waited.

"Have you heard anything more about the stolen *Carmelo Diaries?*" Dave asked.

She swallowed. "No, but it really doesn't matter. I have a great copy of *The Carmelo Diaries*. It's a translation that was made by my grandmother."

"OK. But I like the idea of the authentic diaries. It gives the story a real charm, and if the series is a success *The Diaries* can be auctioned or sold for a big price."

Rita was now becoming hopeful about the production of the story and at the same time she had less regard for Dave's intentions. "I reread the story this last weekend. Also I wrote up what I recall from my grandmother's stories. Do you plan to see any of the old adobes and historic places around here when you come up?"

"I'll be pretty busy. I'm really coming up to see the tournament, and I have a golf date with Roger from the Disney Studios."

"In other words, you are not in a hurry to talk about *The Carmelo Diaries*," Rita said trying to sound casual.

"Or something like that." He paused. "Oh, I'm interested, and I think the publicity about the missing *Carmelo Diaries* will be good. Yes, did you know the Monterey sheriff's office called me?"

"They've been tracking down every lead."

"Totally unnecessary, I think"

"They have been very active."

"That's what I mean. I think they're stretching."

"I'm glad they are active. I think *The Carmelo Diaries* are important. Whoever did it also took other books too."

"Rita," Dave said emphatically, "The burglary bit is really great for a promo for the story I am going to tell."

"I don't see it that way."

"Trust me, Rita. This is what I do. This is a business and there's something in it for everybody. That is, if you still want to be a part of it."

"Well, now I know more where I stand," she said, hardly keeping her indignation controlled.

"I'll give you a call," he said quickly with a fast cadence in his words.

Before she could think up an answer, he had hung up, and the telephone immediately began to ring again.

"This is Captain Lewis, Mrs. Minetti. Did you make an appointment with Dave Goodman?"

"No. I've just talked to him. He thinks the burglary is as important as the contents of the *Diaries*. It's all about deals with him. Personally, I don't want to rush into anything right now."

"That's a good idea. By the way, our department was notified that a few things from your inventory were found. There was an autographed copy of a book by Ambrose Bierce, three first editions John Steinbeck books, and autographed copies of Wallace Stegner's *Angle of Repose*. They were found in Las Vegas of all places. I think we're getting close to some real evidence. I hope you find some clues as you move around your shop."

"Why are you telling me this?"

"No reason. Let me know of any developments I'll call tomorrow." He finished.

Annoyed with the conversations with Dave Goldman and Captain Lewis, Rita put down the phone and told herself not to let anger interfere with her thinking. She was disappointed with Goldman's attitude. She had a growing feeling that the stolen *Diaries* were somehow connected to his production of the early California mini-series.

Dolores Espinosa had arrived a little before 9:30 when the shop opened. The atmosphere at The Old Booktique assumed a new calmness. Dolores stood with erect excellent posture and moved with the grace of a dancer. The facial characteristics of her distant Spanish ancestors were predominant. She moved with a quiet ease from the bookshelves to the tables. When a few customers arrived, she gave each some attention without intruding in their pursuits. Rita observed with satisfaction. Looking out toward the putting green near the entrance of The Retreat, she was amused with the activities of the hotel guest golfers. The phone rang again. It was Mike.

"Yes, Dave called," she answered him, "and he's being cagey. He skirted around the subject of making a definite appointment. I tried not to be too eager. I didn't volunteer to take him to lunch or show him around."

"Do you think he's still interested?"

"Yes, but he wants to let me know that he can do the deal without me. He's intrigued with the idea of stolen *Diaries*."

"I thought you said this was going to be a project without the usual Hollywood hype," Mike replied

"I thought so. I guess I was gullible. However, I don't think Dave realizes that *The Carmelo Diaries* are only part of the story."

"What are you planning to do?"

"Keep working on a presentation," she said. "Mike, I have letters and more diaries in my possession. I'm going to put my attention on the whole story. *The Carmelo Diaries* doesn't tell it all."

"Play it cool with Goldman, Babe. How's it going at the shop?"

"Couldn't be better. Dolores has such class. She knows antique books, and she certainly exudes her love for our collection of books. I'm going to ask her at The Booktique on a regular basis. Maybe we'll do a monthly book tea."

"Don't jump too far ahead. This is a busy social week for us."

"Do we have to go to all the parties? Carmelita will feel like an orphan."

"I think we need to go to most of the parties, at least the ones involving clients. It's important for me. This week is usually the busiest week in our year. Particularly if the weather is good. I'll see you at 4:30, hon."

The telephone rang again and she heard a voice she did not recognize. "This is Mel Stern from Beverly Hills. I'm coming up to the Pro Am tournament, and I read about your shop in *Antiques of America*. I'd like to know more about your books"

"Do you have any particular period or type of book in mind? We do specialize in the Western United States and particularly California," Rita offered.

"I might as well be upfront with you. I know Shana Tyrone, and she told me about the prospect of doing a story about your family in early California. I'm often interested in the projects of Shana Tyrone. She told me that a few years back a national magazine did a ten-page feature article called 'California's Land Grant Aristocracy.' Your grandmother even had the feature picture on one of the pages. They called her 'A Grande Dame of high society' and a mighty good-looking lady she was."

"So this isn't really about antique books then?" Rita laughed.

"It could be. I own several books that were published in the nineteenth century. I particularly like geography books. Since I'm a native Californian, I like to collect books about early California."

"That's our specialty, and if you know the location of The Retreat, you can find us easily. It's a glass gazebo near the putting green." Rita became enthused. "Where were you born, Mr. Stern?"

"Cedars of Lebanon Hospital, and I've lived in Beverly Hills all my life."

"I lived in Los Angeles a little while, but I consider myself a northern Californian."

"I have another reason to be interested in Shana's project. It involves Dave Goldman."

Rita was amazed and silent until she said. "Really."

"I must tell you we are friendly rivals. We've always been rivals since our days at Beverly Hills High School. Afterwards he went to USC and I went to UCLA. And so forth."

Rita said, "Really" again.

"Oh, don't be turned off. Dave and I are friends. We go to the same parties and belong to the same country club. We just do things differently. I've had more experience than he's had in the actual production of documentaries. He's more into public relations and advertising. I've spent some time being a professional photographer. When I realized there were a lot of people who were really good at photography, including my wife, I decided to go into the production part of the business. I've been lucky, and now I can pick and choose the kind of projects I want to do."

"Mr. Stern, I find this all so interesting that I'm speechless. My husband would say it's pretty hard to make me speechless."

"I think I know what he means. My wife would say that too. We plan to come up to the tournament this week. Maybe the four of us could get together."

"Mike and I would enjoy meeting you. We could take you around the historical spots that are in the story of *The Diaries*."

"We'd like that. We don't know much about Monterey. Ellen and I have mostly lived around Beverly Hills all our life. We knew the town when Rodeo Drive was just another street in a small town. I had a paper route when I was a boy and knew where all the movie stars lived. Do you know Beverly Hills, Rita?"

"A little. We occasionally visit friends there."

"I'll give you a call soon," he ended with a cheerful voice.

When the telephone rang again, she thought of asking Dolores to answer it, but looking across the room, she saw her with a customer.

"I talked to Mr. Goldman again," Captain Lewis said immediately and without a salutation. "You didn't tell me all that he said to you." There was a silence.

"I'm tired of questions, and I don't know what you are referring to," Rita said.

"Now, Mrs. Minetti, you want the police to find your *Carmelo Diaries*, don't you?"

"Of course, but it always seems you are always quizzing me."

"Mr. Goldman told me he was a busy man with many projects. He said you overestimate your importance to him. He said he told you not to think you were his top choice to work on the historical series."

Rita could feel herself becoming angry again. She had not been angry like this for years. She took a deep breath. "That's not really true. I don't remember his words to be like that. However, he has changed his attitude toward me since we first started talking several months ago. He thought the idea of stolen diaries would be good publicity. If I were you, I would do some investigating of him."

"Good girl, now you are thinking. In other words, something has made you suspect Mr. Goldman?"

"No, I didn't mean that either. I'm as much in the dark about him as you seem to be, but I am telling you that he is still interested in using *The Carmelo Diaries* and not interested in anything I have to do with it."

"I think I'll continue to investigate and find out who else he's been talking to," Captain Lewis said.

"I don't think he's a criminal. However, he probably loves to cut a close deal. Maybe he's not too fond of working with a woman who is an authority on a subject." Rita tried to change the subject. "Thank you, Captain, for persisting."

"By the way. Can I talk to Tessa?"

"You may not, because she's not here."

"During the AT&T tournament?"

"She had a few days of vacation coming. It's usually a social time here during the tournament. There's not much serious book buying."

"But you're shorthanded. With the burglary and research and all that."

"There you go again, Captain, questioning me about my daily life."

"I just want you to think of the larger picture instead of tripping merrily down the yellow brick road to Oz. It's strange to me that Tessa is taking some time off now. Have her call me when she comes back. No. I'll call again. I need to talk to her about her part in all this."

"I think you're being overly suspicious."

He laughed. "Now you're telling me about my business." They both laughed. "That's enough for now." He ended without a goodbye.

It was noon. Only one customer remained in the shop, an elderly man who was sitting at the Chinese library table pouring over a vintage Bret Hart.

Dolores said, "No wonder you need more help. You're always on the phone. And it's almost lunchtime. Here's your guy to take you somewhere," and Rita looked toward the door and saw Mike.

"Boy, I'm sure glad to see you, hon.," Rita said. "It's been nothing but phone calls. As one door closes there's another one opening."

"Let's pick up a sandwich from the little deli over there and go watch the waves. You can tell me all about it."

There was so much traffic congestion around The Retreat, that extra private security officers had been hired to direct traffic. Mike and Rita had parked their cars in a special enclosure, so they walked to a quiet spot near the outer most hotel cottages. They sat on a flat rock, watched the cormorants on a far rock and ate.

"Mike, Dolores is wonderful. She can handle whatever happens at The Booktique this afternoon. I'm going home. I'll escape the phone, and I'll write down what I am remembering about the rest of Clarita's story while it is still foremost on my mind. I've got some good ideas."

"That's a good move. You'll have time to change clothes so you can look really stunning at the party. I'll come home, and we'll go to the party together. I have some clients from San Francisco I want you to meet."

A giant wave leapt against the rock just below them and sprayed a shower of sea foam that exploded like a Roman candle on the Fourth of July.

"That's still a stormy sea out there. I think there's more rough weather to come," Rita said, and she gave Mike an affectionate kiss. He put his arm around her.

"I'll use every minute of my time writing this afternoon. Call me when you leave the office. It'll give me just enough time to look stunning for you."

When Rita arrived home, Marquita told her that Carmelita had just gone to sleep.

"I'm going to be working in the upstairs office," Rita said to her. "If you want to do errands for yourself, go ahead and then come back about four o'clock as we planned."

After Marquita left, Rita decided on her clothes for the evening. She liked sport clothes the best, but she knew this was an important event for Mike, so she chose tonight's outfit to please him. The subject of clothes was always a controversial topic of conversation between Rita and her mother. Anita preferred what she called 'outfits' from certain specialty boutiques in San Francisco. She thought Rita was often dressed too casually. Anita had given her a lapis blue silk skirt that was tastefully beaded in a pattern of black jet at the hemline. Rita decided to wear it with a simple black cashmere sweater. Then she would wear her sexy high heel shoes that Mike liked so much. With this decision made, she sat down at the computer and began to write some of the anecdotes she found in Isabel's notebooks. She quickly jumped into the present when the telephone rang.

"Rita, I'll be in for work tomorrow," Tessa said. Her voice sounded depressed and without emotion.

Rita was surprised. "Tessa, I'm covered at the shop. Dolores is coming in every day this week. Go on and enjoy yourself."

"No, I want to come back to work." She sounded as if she about to say more, and then she said cryptically, "I want to be busy. I'll tell you about it later. I'll sort it out, and then tell you."

"You sound mysterious."

"I'll tell you about it, believe me," she said quietly before she hung up.

CHAPTER 21

▼

Rita went back to her research about Clarita's life. She consulted a journal written by Isabel, after her grandmother, Clarita, had come to live with her. She thought it an important addition to the Carmelo story. Now Clarita does not say O'Farol but refers to him as Will. Isabel quotes Clarita in her story.

"'What I have to tell you happened in the year of 1834 after Ardo and I left the home of Consuelo and Miguel García. Governor Figueroa had given me permission to take Ardo to live at Rancho Carmelo with the family of my father, Bernardo de Segovia. Although Ardo and I lived in a bedroom at the edge of the big *hacienda*, we participated in the life of the ranch, and we felt part of all that happened there. We ate with Papa and Esperanza and their daughters and we all went to mass together. At that time I had only two dresses, my shawl and my jewelry. Later, some of Captain Garcia's soldiers brought trunks that contained my books, clothes for Ardo, and many of the black dresses that Cousin Consuelo had given me to wear during the mourning of my husband. However, when I settled into living at the ranch, I no longer wore dresses of mourning. Instead I wore a leather skirt or a skirt of bright material, and. I wore a simple cotton blouse because I wanted to be active around the ranch. I began riding a horse and took an interest in what was planted in the vegetable garden near the house. I spent many hours with Ardo.

"We had almost no visitors. Will came to the ranch to make drawings. This was done to show the boundaries of Rancho Carmelo. He spent many days riding all over the ranch with *vaqueros*, and he made a map showing all the features of nature. This was for our petition to the governor. After he presented the drawings to Papa, he was invited to visit the ranch as a guest. He did this with regularity. When he arrived, he brought us news from Monterey, and he stayed for our noon meal. Papa enjoyed his stories.

"By the end of summer, Will rode to the ranch to tell us the governor was going to grant us the land that Papa had requested. However, our ranch no longer included the lands to the south of the River Carmelo. These tracts had been given away. Will told us that more *Yanquis* were arriving in Monterey. He worked for one *Yanqui* in particular named, Tomás Larkin, who was a half brother of Captain Cooper. Will believed that Don Tomás was a man of the future. He told me this when we rode our horses to the valley of the River Carmelo. It reminded me of former days when we rode together, but now there were deeper feelings between us. It was a serious love, and I already knew we both wanted to express it, although neither of us said anything to each other in spoken words.

"Then there was soon a day when this changed. Somehow we knew it would happen. Even when I was married to Don Felipe, I continued to love Will, although I still called him 'Guillermo' at that time. We stopped by the river where the valley narrows. After tethering our horses, we crossed to the other side of the river. We looked for the shallow places to cross the river and stepped from rock to rock. Then he took my hand to help me. We found a dry spot where we sat together beneath the large spreading oak trees and sat on a soft pile of leaves. Will told me that he loved me. He said that I was always the woman in his life.

"Everything was different than when we were young and lived on the ranch. Life had been simple then. Now we knew that our lives could be in danger if we let our love be known that we had become lovers. We pledged to each other that we would find a way to marry. He told me he would talk to Don Tomás, who would know the best way to make it legal. We knew that we could ask one of the fathers at the Mission to perform the marriage rites, but the legality of the marriage was a different matter. Will had no citizenship papers. When he left the next day, I was happier than I had ever been in my life. I did not tell Papa about us. I had learned to be careful. I let him enjoy the good news about the governor granting us title to the ranch. I told him that we would need to go to Monterey to make it official with the signature of the governor.

"I did not know what was to happen next. On that very morning, *vaqueros* who worked for Don Diego were setting out for Rancho Carmelo. They must have camped overnight in the grassy headlands near the sea at the mouth of Carmel Bay. The river was easy to cross at that time of year.

"In the afternoon, when *siesta* was over, I took Ardo and some of the children of the ranch to a shady spot near the beach. Two young Indian maids accompanied me. Then I heard our horses whinny, and I saw several strange *vaqueros*. They surrounded us and after dismounting, the men rushed toward Ardo. I caught him, and I pulled him close to me, but there were too many of them, and they took him away from me. They carried him to one of their horses and rode off. When another *vaquero* came towards me, I reached down to the sand, and I found pebbles beneath the trees. I threw rocks at him and shouted to my Indian girls. I told them to pick up rocks and do as I had done. I could hear Ardo calling to me as his captors galloped away with him. It was an impossible situation.

"Although I could not reach Ardo, I had kept myself from being abducted. I knew that Don Diego was the hidden leader of the kidnapping. I knew I was to be the next victim. Since only one horseman had remained to carry me away, I was able to escape, and we quickly fetched the little girls and other children and galloped back to the ranch. Papa was brokenhearted. Ardo was the most important person in his life at this time.

"Ramon and his family now lived on the ranch. I wrote a letter to Consuelo and asked Ramon to ride to Monterey and deliver it. I did not know where Will was working, but I gave Ramon a letter and told him to deliver to Señor Guillermo. Captain García was not in Monterey, and Ramon could not find Will. Ramon understood that he was to give the letter only to Señor Guillermo. As the days passed Papa became more and more sorrowful. He would not leave his bedroom, and I could not discuss going to talk to the governor in Monterey

"There was always the threat of my abduction. I was afraid to venture out or even to go to the mission to pray, because I was afraid of meeting some of the *vaqueros* from the ranch of Don Diego. Finally I knew that Will must be found. I told Ramon to go to the house of Señor Larkin and give him a letter from me. Again I instructed him to take several *vaqueros* with him as protection. I was afraid that the *vaqueros* of Don Diego might harm Ramon if he went alone."

Here Rita stopped and added an explanation. "To have a perspective of the outside influences in Clarita's life, we need to fix the dates of 1834 and 1835 in our minds. The breaking up of mission lands was of foremost interest to everyone in Monterey and Alta California. In 1834, the local California Assembly called for the confiscation of all the properties of the Mission San Cárlos, and this required a detailed inventory. Many historians think this inventory was not very accurate. There is very little recorded, except the notation that one-half of the moveable property was to go to the natives, and the other to the secular administrator to distribute for other purposes. Since this event happened over fifty years after the mission was founded, there were many discrepancies in the rights of possession. The mission had received monies from the Pius Fund at the beginning of the colonization period in 1770. In the later years, Mission San Cárlos had been the sole source of finance for the local militia and colonial government at the capital, Monterey. Governor Figueroa wanted each mission to have an adjoining rancho for the support of the mission, but there was a difference of opinion as to whether this was a decision that should come from the governor.

In 1835 everything was in a state of change, and the governor had already made land grants of land south of the mission, namely, the Rancho el Sur to Juan Bautista Alvarado, the Rancho San Francisco to Catalina de Munras, and the Rancho San José y Sur Chiquita to Teodoro Gonzales. It ran from San José Creek to the Little Sur River. This left the remaining mission lands and the lands of Rancho San Cárlos yet to be settled. Land was to be distributed to the neophytes, but many of the Indians were in no way prepared to farm their own lands. Some were eager to leave and live a free life in the hills and the river country to the east. The padres had quarrels with the civil administrators, and there were disagreements even among padres, because the new Zacatecan order of missionaries, who arrived with Figueroa, did not understand the older priests. Later that year, there was an added confusion because of another change in the government in Mexico. The ambitious dictator, General Santa Anna, repealed certain laws to give himself more power, and land distribution became subject to whims of many officials and much misunderstanding. These were confusing times, and yet this fact made it possible for Clarita and Will to marry without following the customary pattern of Spanish courtship.

Rita stopped writing and tried to put herself in the place of Clarita who was now a twenty-two year old widow. She had become a mother twice and had now lost both her children. Clarita never wrote this in her diary, but when she finally told her story to Isabel, these words explained her feelings.

"I could have accepted the loss of Ardo as God's will if he had died and received the last sacrament. But I felt ashamed of the terrible reality of having him torn from my arms. It was something I could never forgive of those who caused it. I continued to attend Church, and yet I did not ask to be absolved of my sins of unforgiveness. I constantly prayed to the Blessed Virgin because she knew my feelings. Ardo was my sole reason for living. Now I wanted to remain at Rancho Carmelo the rest of my life."

Rita read this journal with tears. After glancing at her watch, she put the story away. It was almost time for Mike to be home. She gave Carmelita a bath and assembled her own clothes. Carmelita played with Rita's fancy shoes in the closet until she saw her mother putting on a skirt. "Mommy, mommy, don't go out" she said

"Just for a little while. Then we'll be back to have supper with you. Did I ever tell you about my big black poodle that always went to the corner and howled when he saw me take out a party dress?"

They heard Mike coming up the stairs. He tossed a package on the bed and proceeded to open it. I'm going to be in style," he said as he unwrapped a deep blue dress shirt. "You're always ogling at some good-looking anchorman who wears these kinds of shirts."

"I thought you'd never notice," Rita replied with a laugh as she threw her arms around him. "Not to worry. You're much handsomer. Those silver streaks in your hair make you look so distinguished. I'll stick with you."

The Minettis left as soon as Marquita arrived to stay with Carmelita. They drove to the home of Johnnie Brasconi, the executive president of The Retreat. His house was perched on a hill with a panoramic view of the Pacific on one side and a sweeping vista of a championship green on the Spy Glass Golf Course in the other direction.

Rita told Mike about her day. "Just before you came home, Tessa called. She said she would be back to work tomorrow. She is still being mysterious, so I don't think it went as well as she had hoped in San Francisco. When I told her to stay and enjoy herself, she said something about needing time to think. Anyway, with both Dolores and Tessa at the store, I decided to stay home tomorrow. I'll make a few phone calls and play with Carmelita in the morning. Mr. Goldman will be in town Wednesday, and then I'll find out if he is avoiding me or if he intends to offer me a contract. I'll have plenty of time to join you at the tournament in the afternoon."

"What a temptation. Let's go to Maui or Tahiti."

"Did I ever step into that one," she laughed. "And I should know better. You're the man with the ready comeback."

"I was really hoping you could take it easy this week. Have some fun. I think you're juggling too many things."

"That's why I'm going to have both Tessa and Dolores in the shop."

"There's still the unsolved burglary and Captain Lewis. Maybe we can skip the Annual Crosby Clam Bake," Mike suggested.

"No, Mike. We should do it all. We're a team. The Clam Bake is one of the only traditional events left from the early days. This tournament used to be a just a hometown event. Even when I was growing up, I can remember Grandmother Clara giving a party and hoping that Bing and Cathy would come. Stonecrest was host to celebrities like Phil Harris, Clint Eastwood, and Arnold Palmer. I was too young for those kinds of parties, but I distinctly remember when Sean Connery showed up. I insisted on coming downstairs to see him, because I thought of him as James Bond, Agent 007."

"I went to a few of Aunt Clara's famous Crosby parties myself," Mike remembered out loud. "It was the only time Clara allowed golf talk. I'm glad you reminded me about Aunt Clara's little whistle stops, as she called her parties. I hate to be a name-dropper, and yet I think my clients love it when I tell them about the old days around here."

"Do you have a script for me tonight?" Rita questioned.

"Of course not. Just be you. However, I especially want you to meet Ed and Shirley Roja. I know you'll like them, and they're really serious about finding a house to buy in Pebble Beach. Shirley grew up in Southern California. They have lived in Venezuela for the last ten years, and now he is retiring from Miromar Oil. He's already been invited to join the Cypress Golf Club."

"That says it all," Rita murmured. "You know I like to meet new people."

They drove by a house under construction. "I remember when this was a rambling country house," Rita sighed as they turned the corner. "The original house was built like a California Bungalow, and it was tucked into a grove of eucalyptus trees. It had two guesthouses for the seasonal overflow. Grandmother's eccentric friend, Carrie Jamison, lived there."

"It went for five million when she died. The new owners gutted the property. They showed us their plans for a new mansion they planned to build." Mike gave a brief whistle. "Phew. Sixteen rooms. We thought the project would stretch into the eight to ten million category."

"Were you in on the deal?"

"Yep. We shared it with another agency but it turned out that the new owners went bankrupt. Then the property became vacant for a while until the Raff Ambrusters came here on a visit. They attended a party in Pebble Beach, and when they saw this property they bought it. They started building and haven't stopped yet. It will have eighteen rooms and is built in a semi-circle. At least they've saved the remaining trees, which gives it great privacy."

"I like it when you talk to me about your business," Rita said. "And especially right now. I don't want my problems to monopolize our lives. Do you know the history of all the old mansions in the Del Monte Forest?"

"You exaggerate, Babe, but it sounds good anyway," Mike laughed. They were nearing the gated entrance to a steep driveway that led to an enormous contemporary home. The mansion had a magnificent view of both land and sea. Valet parking made it possible for all the guests to approach the house without having to walk up the hill. So many guests had already arrived, and Rita and Mike could not find the host. "I think everybody in the real estate business is here," said Mike quietly to Rita as they walked out to the front verandah. Soon a roving waiter served each of them a glass of champagne.

They chatted with a couple from Palm Springs and someone else who had just flown in from Dallas. Mike thought he had heard the voice of Ed Roja, so he strolled in that direction. He returned with Ed and Shirley and introduced them to Rita. For a few minutes they all stared at the deep flamingo colors and the afterglow of the ocean sunset.

"It's really spectacular tonight," Rita exclaimed, and she began to talk to Shirley, while Mike and Ed Roja started discussing how to fit in a golf game tomorrow.

"I'm always interested in why people come to settle somewhere. I guess it's because we've lived in so many places," Shirley commented to Rita. "Were you born here?"

"I spent most of my childhood at my Grandmother's house at Stillwater Cove. It's just around the corner."

"Then you don't get lost on these winding roads. We've been taken on so many rides since we arrived, that I'm completely turned around. Ed gave me the car to use while he played the Cypress course yesterday. Then I couldn't find my way for a lunch at The Shore Club. I made all the wrong turns. It was a good thing for me I had my cell phone. I called and followed a new set of directions." She paused. "And how did your grandmother happen to live here?"

"My great grandfather was Gustavus Schaeffer," Rita began with animation. "He was famous for his Nevada silver mines. It made him extremely wealthy. Gustavus Schaeffer was aware of what Samuel F.B. Morse was doing with the Pacific Improvement Company on the Monterey Peninsula. He wanted his children and grandchildren to have a place for vacations, so he bought several lots here just about the time the United States entered the First World War. My grandmother Clara was his daughter and she inherited several choice pieces of land overlooking the ocean. After Clara Schaeffer and Leo Torelli were married in 1926, they built Stonecrest. It remained a vacation house until Clara moved to Pebble Beach after she was widowed."

"This is so much better than talking golf," Shirley told Rita. "Let's move to one of those seats over there and get more acquainted. Do you have children? A career?"

"How about you?" replied Rita who did not want to monopolize the conversation.

"Our four children are practically independent. Two are in college, one in prep school, and one is married," Shirley said simply. "We haven't put down roots, since we've moved around so much. Caracas was our longest residence. When we lived there, I was very busy entertaining Ed's business associates and their families. I'm looking forward to living in one place and having a life of my own."

"You'll find plenty to do here. It is certainly not like The City. I mean San Francisco," Rita corrected herself. "Amazingly, you can find yourself quite busy here, particularly if you like nature and animals or art."

"That's good, because I like all three. Was your grandmother partial to anything in particular?"

"I suppose one could say, history, particularly California history." Rita became more animated again. "In her later life the Big Sur Trust was very dear to her heart. She was able to coax several donations of land from her lifelong friends."

"And you?"

"Mike and I have a wonderful little girl, who is almost three years old, and I actively manage and own a little business."

"Oh that sounds wonderful. We can't stay long this time, but we'll be down again soon. Can you get away for lunch? I'd like to hear more about what goes on here," Shirley said spontaneously.

"That's easy to arrange," Rita replied. "Do you know how to reach me?" she paused and then reached inside her purse. "I just happen to have one of my cards here, and she handed her one from The Old Booktique. "I go by Rita Atherton just to keep my own identity," she explained.

Shirley looked at the card. "It's good that you have your own business. That's great. And yet, I imagine it's harder for you to take off at lunch than if you weren't the boss."

"I'll make time. Just let me know when you'll be in town, and I'll arrange it."

The Rojas left the party soon. Mike and Rita mingled a little and then departed to keep their promise to Carmelita.

CHAPTER 22

▼

February 1, 2000

Mike left early for golf. The prophecy was for fair weather.

Rita stayed home as she had planned. Soon, she received her mother's call. "I'm so glad to find you home dear. Was the party fun last night? What did all the ladies wear?" Rita's mother said as soon as she answered the phone.

"It was fun but rather like a three rings circus. Mike really went to connect with some clients named Ed and Shirley Roja. I enjoyed meeting them. Shirley Roja is just the sort of person I like to know. I'll tell you about it later. I am staying home today to be with Carmelita."

"Oh, that is even better," exclaimed Anita. "Charles just called and told me that he and Missy are reconciling, and they are on their way to Pebble Beach today. They will stay with me tonight. I agreed with their desire to stay at The Retreat for the rest of the time. I called to invite you over for lunch today. And bring Carmelita. You know, they haven't been down since she was a baby, and she's a regular little person now. Put on that cute little outfit I bought her for Christmas. Missy always dresses their girls so carefully. And they are well behaved, although they say that Darcy is in those sullen teenage years now."

"Are you sure it won't complicate things. Carmelita's attention span is that of a normal child who's almost three years old and I don't..."

"She'll be just fine. Besides it's a good icebreaker. She will entertain all of us. I'll expect you at 1:30."

When this conversation was over, Rita received a telephone call from Missy. There was a preemptory tone and sound in Missy's voice. "Rita, I know we can be friends. I suppose you've heard that Charles and I are getting back together."

At first, Rita did not know what to say. It had been three years since they had talked. "I think it's wonderful, and of course we can be friends, Missy. There may have been differences between you and Charlie, but you and I can be friends."

"And I do want to thank you for always remembering the birthdays of our girls. Charles wouldn't let me send anything to you when you had your child. It is a little girl, isn't it?"

"Carmelita is her name."

"Rita, I'll come right to the point. I need you to help me keep Charles away from that woman who is constantly inserting herself into our lives."

"Missy, I'm entirely unaware of what has been going on in your lives."

"That may be true, but I know you've been a mistress to a married man, so you could really help me."

"Missy, what is this call about? Not my life, I hope."

"Oh no my dear, but I hope you can be understanding. Now that you are married, I think you can understand my position as a wife."

"Missy, I just found out about your separation last Thursday when Charlie called Mother."

"I didn't know that. You see, I thought you didn't care about our marriage," Missy said peevishly.

"Please listen to yourself. You are calling me early in the morning. You are talking in riddles and saying things about my life that are not true."

"Rita, I could give dates and places where you had secret meetings with your married lover, so don't give me any talk about your innocence. But I don't want to talk about your life. I'll forgive you everything and will let you see the girls if you'll just encourage Charles to go through with this reconciliation."

"That's pretty hard since Charlie has never been influenced by anything I ask of him. However, he is my only brother, and I really do want the best for both of you. If he asks me, I'll tell him he should do his part to preserve the marriage," Rita answered.

"He's invited me to come down to the AT&T with him. We're still living apart, you know. He told me he thought there was a chance for us to have a romantic interlude, and he hinted that together we could work things out beween us. Your mother invited us to stay at Stonecrest, but we decided to be by ourselves. I found someone to stay with the girls. Charles and I want to have a romantic tryst. I want a chance to show him I am sexy as," she stopped. "Well, you know what I mean."

"Sounds great to me."

"Oh, Rita, I'm so glad we're friends and that you haven't said anything against me to Charles."

"Until Mother invited us all to dinner last week, I haven't seen or talked to Charlie since Grandmother Torelli died."

"That may be true, but I didn't know how far you would go with revenge. Charles has been bitter about how you treated him."

At this point Rita wanted the conversation to end, so she didn't ask any more questions. She knew her brother. He could very well have a mistress. He was often charming when he wanted to be. Girls always wanted to date him in college and women thought him handsome with his sculptured straight nose and prominent cheekbones. He had matured into a distinguished looking man. A little gray hair enhanced the image.

"I can assure you that I have no need for revenge. I can also assure you, that I know nothing about his love life either with you or anyone else. You have two great daughters. They are my nieces. And that's where things stand with me."

"I'm glad to hear you say that, because you know I really want another child. I just turned forty, and Charles has always wanted a son. It could be Charles Atherton, the third."

"I think Charlie would like that," Rita said hoping that Missy had played out the scenario. And she had. They ended the conversation with a familial goodbye.

This conversation changed her morning. Anita had insisted that she and Carmelita go to Stonecrest for a lunch with Missy and Charlie. Although Carmelita was hardly the age for an adult gathering, Anita sincerely wanted to have her come. Rita called her mother when Carmelita woke up from an early nap. "We'll be there soon," she promised. "Go ahead with cocktails."

"Be sure to look elegant. Missy is wearing a new Chanel suit," her mother said in a half whisper.

Rita did not change from what she was already wearing, tailored gray slacks and a turquoise blue cashmere sweater set. She brushed Carmelita's wet hair, and it curled by the time Rita started to put a dress on her.

"Are we going to a party?" Carmelita queried.

"Sort of. We're going to Stonecrest. You'll meet your uncle and auntie, and then we'll all have lunch together. I'm sure that Nonie will give you an ice cream cone if you eat a little bit of whatever is served to you."

Because of the sunny weather, there were already many extra cars at the entry gates of Pebble Beach. Rita had a resident guest pass, which allowed her to drive to Stonecrest with ease.

When they arrived, Charles greeted them warmly. He lifted Carmelita high in the air, and putting her on his shoulders, he carried her into the dining room where Missy was standing at the window and looking out. Anita was talking to Alma about the service, and then she quickly moved to where Charles had deposited Carmelita on a special chair that Anita used for her.

"This is a party," Carmelita said happily looking at the table with flowers and candles and gleaming crystal.

"Yes, it is a party, dear, and I have a new doll you can play with while we are talking. If you are good, you may take the doll home with you."

"I like parties," Carmelita said.

"My but you are chatty for such a little girl," Missy said coming forward. "I'm your Aunt Missy." Rita noticed that she looked impeccable in a mauve gray suit with entwined C's on all the buttons. Her blond hair was worn in a soft pageboy, and only her steel blue eyes had not changed since Rita last saw her. Both Missy and Charles appeared to have been going to gyms and spas. Missy gave Rita a European greeting of kisses in the air on both sides.

"You look lovelier every time I see you, Sis," Charles said. "I think we'll all agree that marriage certainly agrees with you. We're glad Mike's your one and only."

"Where is he, Rita?" Missy asked. "We would really like to know him better."

"The AT&T tournament is a busy time for him, and with weather like this he's probably out showing property on the Seventeen Mile Drive," she answered.

"Your Mother is thinking of meeting us in the Fiji Islands. Maybe you and Mike could get away and join us," Missy went on.

"When you own two businesses, there is always one of them that is having a busy time. There are several antique book shows coming up, and winter is the time that my clients like to look for books. It's just not vacation time for us now."

"By the way, have the police uncovered anything new? Have any of your books been found?" Charles asked Rita.

"A few editions turned up in Las Vegas," she replied and was going to say more. Then she decided to let him pull it out.

"And *The Diaries*?" he asked.

"Nothing. It's like they disappeared from the face of the earth."

"Do we have to talk about disagreeable things, children?" Anita said in a coaxing and yet petulant way. "I want Alma to serve her soufflé while it is perfect," she said as she smilingly rang a little bell. Charles was pouring a vintage Sancerre wine into their glasses while Carmelita was busy eating a breadstick.

"You'll have to replace your books soon, dear. Better go to some of those book fairs very soon," Anita said as she patted Rita's hand.

"I think I'll attend some estate sales around here," Rita commented.

"What do we have on our agenda tomorrow morning, darling?" Missy said to Charles, who was sitting across from her.

"You have the morning free, dear. I have an unexpected early morning golf game. It could be the business deal I've been coaxing along. I'm the host of the game."

"Oh we know what a workaholic you are," Missy said supportively.

"I thought it best to get my business out of the way. Then Missy and I can have some time to ourselves," he said jovially and winked at Rita.

Carmelita was quiet as she sat between her grandmother and mother.

Alma served them a tropical fruit salad of mango, fresh pineapple, and papaya, and she thoughtfully gave Carmelita a small toasted cheese sandwich and her own dish of sliced banana and oranges.

"Did Mother tell you that we have asked her to fly with the girls and meet us? I know a wonderful resort in the Fiji Islands. It will be on our way back from Australia. We'll make a real family holiday."

When Charles was in charge, he was positively radiating with charm. Then Missy brought her hand up from beneath the top of the table and showed them a sparkling new diamond and ruby wedding band. "We're making a new start all the way," Charles announced.

"Rita, since I have the morning free tomorrow, I think I'll drop by your little shop about eleven, and then we can lunch together at some nice place," Missy turned to say.

Carmelita hugged her grandmother and asked, "Can I call you Nita?"

"Oh you can't do that, dear. You see, my girls call her, Nonie, and it would be too confusing if you called her Nita," Missy said.

Anita wanted to please everyone. She was happy that Carmelita liked the doll and wanted to sit by her, and yet she wanted the lunch to be a personal welcoming gesture toward Charles and Missy. Rita wanted to help her mother, so she leaned over to her daughter and said, "After lunch we'll go upstairs to the room where I used to play with my grandmother's dollhouse."

"I want to take my cream cone there?" Carmelita exclaimed.

"Carmelita, it is not nice to interrupt our party. I was talking to your mother, and we were making plans for tomorrow," Missy continued.

Carmelita pouted and looked down at her dress.

"Anita, could you ask Alma to take Carmelita upstairs?" Missy continued. Then she turned to Rita. "When you've been a mother a little longer, you'll learn when and where to bring your child."

"Carmelita is here because Mother thought you'd like to see her.

Charles had gone to the sideboard, and before Missy could answer, he held up a slim square bottle of amber liquid, "I've brought one of the earliest bottles of my next venture. We will market a true California Eau de Vie. It will be understandably expensive because of the immense amount of fruit needed, but after a little education of the public, I think there will be a market for it." He poured the heavy amber liquid into four small crystal glasses on a tray and ceremoniously brought it to the table.

"I hope we will all see each other after the AT&T is over. Maybe next Monday evening. That will give us a chance to talk to Mike," Charles continued and turned to Anita. "Mother, after the dessert course, Missy and I will need to run off. Missy and I have some catching up to do." He looked at Missy as she nodded.

Dessert was a simple flan served with cookies that Alma called *dulces*. She gave Carmelita a little cone filled with strawberry ice cream, which was her favorite flavor at the moment. Then Charles served the liquor.

"I haven't decided on a name yet. Maybe it should be Eau de Marielle in honor of Missy. That's her baptismal name you know."

Rita toasted with the others and was quiet. She wanted to remember everything that occurred so that she could relate the conversations to Mike.

Anita talked quietly to Alma and then she turned to Carmelita, "When you finish your ice cream, dear, Alma will wash your hands and take you upstairs to look at the dollhouse."

"We'll come up soon. Then we can play together," Rita assured Carmelita.

After their compliments, Charles and Missy soon departed. As soon as the door was closed Anita began, "I am so happy for those two. Missy was right to ask for all that alimony. Although she has money of her own, she thinks she has learned how to keep Charles interested. Dangle money. Do you know that she found out that Charles had a mistress?"

Rita shook her head as Anita continued. "She hired a detective as well as a special lawyer, and they really made Charles understand that if he continued with his affair, he could lose a great deal of money. I'm sorry to say he takes after his father in that department. He wanted a wife and a mistress. They even traced two purchases of expensive jewelry that he had charged to a special account. He doesn't know that Missy told me all this, of course. Has she said anything to you about it?"

Rita nodded as her mother continued. "Anyway, I think when he found out that there would be no money to pursue his new wine project, he decided to win Missy back, and it looks like he's done a good job. Charles needs a lot of money to bring out his private label. All of his reputation is wrapped up in that enterprise. He wants to take an active part on the board of the Wine Institute, you know." She stopped and looked thoughtful. "He is my son. And I know how he is. He wants to top what the Torelli Brothers have done."

"Charlie is competitive. I know that." Rita agreed.

As Rita listened to her mother, she observed that Carmelita was careful with the miniature furniture in the dollhouse.

"Of course, Missy doesn't know that she will eventually lose Charles. The wealthier he becomes, the easier it will be for him to play around," Anita said with a firm jaw and a tone of voice stronger than usual. She put her hand on Carmelita's shoulder. "And I really like to be called 'Nita' better than Nonie, dear, but right now we should be nice to your auntie."

"Easy there," Rita intercepted Carmelita's hand as she was reaching far back into the dollhouse and into a fancy bedroom. "These are not toys, and we can't go to the store and buy another one if we break something."

"I like the pretty bed," Carmelita said.

"Nevertheless, it is good that we are all a family again." Anita said to Rita. "I think it would be nice if you invited us to your house for dinner the after the Crosby is over. Oh dear, I mean the AT&T," Anita said.

"Not this year, Mum. Right now, I have too much going on. Mike suggested that I slow down. When I entertain, I want to do it right, and I can't do it just yet. You're a tough act to follow, you know. And particularly after that beautiful lunch, Mum."

On the way home Rita and Carmelita stopped by The Old Booktique. Rita learned that Mr. Goldman had not called. However. Mel Stern had called and left a local number for a return call. Captain Lewis had interviewed Tessa.

"He stayed quite a while," Tessa said.

"I told you he often asks about you. Maybe you've made a conquest there," Rita remarked. "We've just been to lunch at Stonecrest. Charlie and Missy are together again, and they came down for the tournament." She thought Tessa would be amused with all the posturing of her family and the wooing of Charlie and Missy. She refrained from saying much more because of Carmelita's presence.

"I'll call you later and tell you a little more," Rita promised her when they were leaving.

When Mike came home, he looked exhausted. He was quiet. Rita told him about their lunch and what she could remember of their conversation. She thought he'd laugh at Carmelita's decision to call her grandmother 'Nita', but he remained quiet.

Finally he said, "Your day wasn't as upsetting as mine. I received a letter with no return address. Hell, I'll show it to you and see what you think of it." He went to his brief case and pulled out a plain envelope with a San Francisco postmark. He handed it to Rita.

When Rita opened the envelope, she took out a standard piece of computer paper without any salutation and just the words, "How much have you and your wife discussed about her relationship with 'The Senator?' Does she still see him or hear from him?"

"This is ridiculous," Rita exclaimed, and she could feel her hand shaking. "We've both told each other enough about our pasts. I've seen enough marriages where people wed and have stayed married when they were miserable. I never wanted a marriage to be like that. I married you because I love you thoroughly, and I'd rather be with you than anyone else in the world." The more she said, the more emotional she became until she put the letter down and threw her arms around Mike and started sobbing.

Mike stroked her hair and almost nervously patted her until he gently pulled her closer to him and kissed her tear stained face. "What ass would send such a thing? It sickens me that there are people in our life who would send a letter like this," Mike remarked.

Rita slowly stopped crying and ran her fingers through his hair. "Honey, maybe we don't want to go to the Clam Bake tonight. Let's just stay home. Carmelita's had a big day, and she'll go to bed early. And," she stopped, "we'll go to bed early.

"Fine by me," he said. He picked her up and pulled her close to him. "You're my lady, and that's all I want.

Carmelita came running from the other side of the room and was clapping. "Now my turn," she said as Mike carefully lowered Rita and then put Carmelita on his shoulders and trotted around the room with her.

"Whee," she cried.

It was now Rita's turn to clap. "We don't need to go anywhere to have fun. It's so good to be home. How about waffles and scrambled eggs for dinner?"

"Waffles, waffles," Carmelita repeated.

Right after dinner, the phone rang. "I was all set to put a message on your machine. I thought you were going to the Clam Bake," Tessa said.

"We're both too tired," Rita said while remembering that she had said she would call her.

"Well, I'm tired too. We had a bunch of people come in the shop just before closing time. Besides I think I'm coming down with a cold, and it's better that I don't come to work tomorrow. I told Dolores before I left the shop. She said it was OK. I think she likes being at The Booktique."

"Originally I told her I wanted her for this whole week anyway. And remember that when you went to San Francisco, you didn't know how long you'd be gone."

"Well it all turned out different, didn't it," she said sounding rather forlorn. "Do you really think Captain Lewis is interested in me? It would be fun to date someone new."

"He can't ask you out or anything like that while the case is still open. So he'll just keep finding reasons for coming around to see you."

"I hope he wraps it up soon. I really need to talk to you about my life. Right now I better take care of my throat."

"We'll find a time soon. If you feel better tomorrow, we could do lunch, and then I'd have an excuse not to have lunch with my sister-in-law."

"How did Missy look?" Tessa asked.

"Oh, all buffed and polished. She's still a cold fish, especially in her gray Chanel suit."

"Glad to hear it," Tessa agreed and quickly said goodbye.

When she hung up Rita went back to where Mike was sitting. "Tessa has been acting very strange this week," Rita said to him.

"Let's forget everybody and have the rest of the night to ourselves." Mike said.

CHAPTER 23

▼

Early the next morning, Rita went to the office near their bedroom. Before she continued to write the story of Clarita's life, she reread her grandmother Clara's description of Clarita.

"It was known that Clarita was a lively and active person with abundant chestnut brown hair and soft brown eyes. Her skin was fair, as she always wore a wide-brimmed hat to protect her complexion when she was outdoors. Since the family kept the dress she had worn to the wedding of her granddaughter, Isabel, it was evident that she was of slight build and quite short. At present the dress is periodically on display at the Monterey Historical Museum. The only portraits of Clarita were painted after she was a mature woman, and these hung in a small old-fashioned sitting room at Stonecrest. This is where Clara had always kept certain pieces of the family furniture that had come from her childhood home."

Picturing Clarita helped Rita visualize the following story, which Isabel recorded in one of her blue satin journals.

"I wish you could have seen your grandfather at that time. He was never anything but handsome and had clear blue eyes and reddish gold hair. My brother, Estéban, had blond hair and eyes of blue like those of my mother, but the eyes of Will were intense like the ocean. His American friends called him 'Will', and that was hard for me to say at first. The *vaqueros* and *Californios* called him Guillermo. He could read and write both Spanish and English, and he was good with numbers, but he didn't read many books. He was tall and stood straight. He could make anything with his hands. He was of a man of good deeds and ready to help others, and he usually did so. He was not a person who sat on a bench and let others do things for him. Above all, I could always trust him.

"The second time I sent Ramon to Monterey, he found Will and delivered my letter in which I explained my plight. After reading my letter, he immediately went to Don Tomás Larkin and told him what had happened at Rancho Carmelo. He explained to him about the character of Don Diego Vargas and my great fear. Don Tomás must have advised him that this was a time for action."

Thomas Larkin never became a Mexican citizen. Instead, he obtained a carta, which was similar to a passport, and this was renewed from year to year. He was allowed to stay in Alta California without being subject to Mexican law. This made it possible for him to marry an American lady, Rachel Holmes, a widow, in a protestant ceremony aboard a ship anchored near Santa Bárbara.

"Señor Larkin told Will that he would ask a friend, the U.S. consul in Honolulu, to make up the correct documents for William O 'Farrell, a Yankee, who had lost everything when his landing boat capsized. Señor Larkin advised him to follow his own example and register for a *carta* as a citizen of the United States. After asking him if he wished to wed the 'fair lady of Rancho Carmelo', Don Tomás told Will that it was fortunate that we were both of the Roman Catholic faith. He advised Will to tell his intentions to the *padres* at the Mission San Cárlos. Don Tomás also loaned him money so he could give the *padres* gold for their cattle hides. He told Will that it was especially important at this time because the missions were losing revenues. Will found a fresh horse and returned with Ramon to Rancho Carmelo.

"When Will arrived at the ranch, after his talk with Señor Larkin, he took charge of everything. He gathered a band of men who would fight for us and guard me. Then he went to the Mission San Cárlos to talk to Padre Real who took care of the inventory of the mission. He never told me what they agreed upon, but when he returned he told me that we would marry the next day after we had been to confession and attended mass. He cautioned me to tell no one. Not even Esperanza. My father was in a deep sleep and unable to speak, so there was no need to observe tradition. I had not been courted in the Spanish manner. In fact, we said very few words that day. We went into the inner courtyard and knelt by a statue of Our Lady of Tears beneath a giant oak tree. It was a quiet place where my mother had put in a small rose garden. Will was the first to speak, and he said, 'I love you, Clarita Isabel. I have always wanted you to be my wife. If you are not ready to marry, I will understand, and if you wish, I shall stay here and protect you with my life. I will defend you and Rancho Carmelo as long as you wish. It is for you to decide.'

"I remember looking into his eyes and saying, 'I want to be your wife.'

"We sat holding hands for a very long time, and then he pulled me up and kissed me. I had never been kissed like that. I already felt that I was a part of him, and yet he was so gentle. Then he showed me a simple gold ring and said, 'I wish this could have been the ring of my mother, but nothing will be of tradition in our wedding. Tomorrow morning you must dress in a plain black dress that is the style that you wear when you visit the mission. We will ride on two separate horses. Some of my men will follow. No one is to know what is to take place, and for that reason not even Ramon will be aware that it is more than a visit to the mission to pray for your father and make arrangements for a *padre* when it is time to give your father the last rites.'

"Early the next morning, I put on a simple black skirt and wore a white blouse without embroidery. I took a plain black shawl, and the only piece of jewelry I wore was the gold cross that belonged to my mother. Then I knelt at the little altar in my room and prayed. The time passed quickly. I went to the other end of the *hacienda* to the rooms where Papa and Esperanza lived. Esperanza was completely devoted to Papa and seldom left his room, except to direct the maids in their cooking and to tell them about their chores. I told her that I must go to the mission to arrange for a *padre* to come to Papa. She told me that she would stay close to Papa. We embraced each other. Through the open doorway I saw a *vaquero* with my horse, and he told me that he would ride by my side to the mission. I saw Will in the distance and in the company of several other *vaqueros*, most of whom had grown up on our ranch. Our horses followed the trail by the River Carmelo. The morning fog had just lifted, and I could hear the ocean as we neared the mission. I was allowed to go to confession first. Then I waited in the shadows while Guillermo was with the *padre*. After mass was recited, Will and I slipped into a small room near the altar. Padre José María Real met us and quietly conducted a brief wedding ceremony. Then he asked Padre Juan to come into the room for a blessing. We were invited into the library that Padre Lasuen had once used. There we talked about the health condition of Don Bernardo. We all agreed that Padre Real would visit Rancho Carmelo on the next day. He wrote our names in a register with other names and he gave us a piece of parchment on which he had written his name, the date, and the words of the *contracto matrimonial* that he had performed at the Mission San Cárlos. Both Will and I signed our names, and Padre Juan came forward to add his name as witness to our signatures. It was all very solemn until he went to the corner of the room and brought forth four small glasses and proceeded to pour brandy from a tall bottle. He then asked us to kneel, and he pronounced another benediction. Only then did I realize that I should give him something. As I started to open the clasp on the chain of the cross that was given to me on first communion, I realized that I was wearing two chains. It was a sign that my mother wanted Padre Juan to have her cross, and I gave it to him with gratefulness in my heart. *Gracías Santa María.*

"Our *vaqueros* were waiting for us, and Will and I rode back on his horse while they rode at our side. When we arrived at Rancho Carmelo, Ramon was waiting for us. He told us to come quickly to Esperanza. She was crying and told us Papa had become awake after three weeks of sleep.

"'You must see him now. I think he will die soon. I want to send Ramon for a *padre*.'

"We went from the extreme joy of our marriage to the depths of sadness. Together we entered the room, and Papa was propped up on a mound of lace pillows and talking in a clear voice, although no one was in the room.

"'María Isabel,' I heard him say the name of my mother. 'We are not like all the other people in Monterey. They do not know the Spain from which we came. That is why I have always liked to talk to the Spanish fathers at the mission. The new Zacatecans do not know our Spain. And now even they will be leaving us. Let me come to you.'

"I wondered if he would recognize me. He seemed quite well, and I hoped he had made a miraculous recovery; however, as he talked I could tell he was in the past and not much in the present.

"'There is someone with you, Clarita Isabel,' he said. 'Is it someone I know?'

"Will came forward, and since Papa did not recognize him he introduced himself.

"'I am Guillermo O'Farrell, and I lived here at your ranch as a young man. I am your friend,' he said. 'I have come to tell you that the governor has granted you the rights to your ranch. Your daughter, Clarita Isabel has become my wife, and I will protect and cherish her. We will stay here to help you manage the ranch.'

"Will was truthful and full of courage. I was fearful of what would happen with Papa and I was determined to be strong. I wanted to be worthy of his bravery.

"Papa blinked and looked at us as if we were on the shore and he had sailed out to sea.

"'Yes, you must stay here and take care of the cattle and all the people who live on the ranch,' he said. 'I am on my way to Spain. María Isabel is already there. We are going to see Estéban.' He laid back his head and closed his eyes. He was breathing and appeared asleep.

"Guillermo and I held hands and were very quiet, so that he did not stir. When he appeared to be awake, he smiled at us and said nothing. He lifted his hands and covered his mouth. As I drew nearer, I could see that he was shaking his head slowly, and when he opened his mouth he tried to talk and could not do so. I bent over and touched his face. Then I kissed him. He made a low humming noise and continued to smile.

"What shall we do now?' I whispered to Will.

"'Ramon has already been sent to the mission. We must take turns with Esperanza and stay by the side of your father. If there is any change, we should all gather around him,' he answered.

"I called Esperanza. I showed her my wedding ring and told her that we had been married this morning at the Mission. I said that we told Papa about our marriage. I told her that Papa wanted us to stay at Rancho Carmelo. I told her that Papa talked of leaving soon. Esperanza nodded.

"Padre Juan arrived late that afternoon, and he said he would pray by the bedside of Papa. I went to my bedroom and found two beautiful necklaces that Don Felipe had given me. I gave them to Padre Juan with instructions that he give them to the statue of *Nuestra Señora de Belen* (Our Lady of Bethlehem) to wear as she graced the altar of the mission church Then I told him that food would be brought soon, and that we would return to the bedside after we had rested a little. Esperanza said she would sit outside the room. As soon as Will saw me go toward the little house where food was cooked, he caught up with me.

"'Clarita, we must be together. It may be long before we can do so again.'

"I quickly thought of the room I had occupied as a little girl. It was now a storeroom for linen. I told him to follow me and we went up the stairs at the far end of the house. Although we were very tired, we cleared a small space and found happiness with each other before we both fell asleep. Nothing in my life had prepared me for such happiness. We did not sleep long, and we returned to Papa before the sun went down.

"Papa was still breathing but not easily. I found Dulcera and Felicia, so that if Papa awakened, he could see all of us. I asked Ramon to be present at the side of Esperanza. The bedroom could hold no more. It had been a warm afternoon, but the thick adobe walls kept the room cool. I was the one who sat closest to Papa. Then I saw him try to raise himself up and say something. He opened his eyes, laid back and looked contented. I am sure he was thinking of Spain. Then he stopped breathing and I motioned to the *padre,* and we all knelt in prayer. Esperanza put a beautiful lace coverlet over him. After some time, Padre Juan asked me if Papa had made a *testamento.* I knew that he had done so when he was last in Monterey, but did not know where it was located, so I excused myself to find it.

"Near the *sala,* there was a small library of books. In this alcove, there was a table from China across the seas. On this table was a leather chest. The room was a little dusty, as no one dared enter it except Esperanza, who had been with Papa constantly during the last few weeks. I became bold. I opened the chest where I found a collection of letters from Estéban. Then I caught sight of a small prayer book that had belonged to my mother. Inside it was a piece of parchment folded into quarters. As I opened it I could see that it was his last will and testament. I dared not read it, but my curiosity overcame me when I saw that the year was one thousand eight hundred and thirty-four. I also saw my name and the name of my son, Felipe Bernardo Vargas. I would read no farther as I wanted to bring it to the *padre.*

"My son Ardo, I thought, with a pang of sadness. I must get the word to him concerning of the death of his grandfather, and he should be allowed to come to the funeral. Then I thought of what the word funeral meant. There must be a ceremony. My father was the owner of a great ranch and he was a fine Christian gentleman. I must send riders to Monterey and the neighboring ranches to inform them of the event, and Esperanza must begin to prepare immediately for a large group of people who will be arriving at the ranch. Guillermo must see that cattle are slaughtered so there would be meat for cooking a generous meal for our guests.

"I brought the *testamento* to Padre Juan, and when I told him where I had found it, he suggested that we go in the *sala* for the reading. Only Will and I were present. Padre Juan told me that I was to inherit Rancho Carmelo, including all the land, houses, cattle, and horses. Upon my death, Felipe Bernardo Vargas was to succeed me in this inheritance. I was to provide a home for Esperanza, Dulcera, and Felicia, and see that the girls would have a correct religious education and a proper dowry of fine linens, dishes, and silver, and I was to find them good husbands who attend mass. Papa asked to be buried at the Mission San Cárlos beside María Isabel. He asked that four hundred *varas* of *rancho* land be given to Ramon. There were provisions for the church, and I was to make small gifts to the *vaqueros* and others at the ranch. I was to be appointed as the one who would see that all this was carried out. The *testamento* was very legal. It was signed and witnessed on the fifteenth day of June of the year one thousand and eight hundred and thirty four. Miguel García and Juan Bautista Sepulveda were witnesses. Padre Juan pronounced that all was in order and again we knelt in prayer together. He told me to keep and prize the document with our marriage certificate that he had given us this morning. He said that no one knew what was going to happen to the mission records now that José Antonio Romero had been appointed the majordomo of the mission. This man had already taken many of the mission sheep and cattle to his own *rancho*. The neophytes of the mission were running away and Padre Juan said he might be leaving for Mexico in order to serve another community.

"I told him that I wished him to officiate for the funeral and burial. He did not know our family well, so I informed him that my father was the youngest son of a large family living in Spain. All of his sisters and brothers had passed on. My father had lived in Alta California much of lifetime and the *gente de razon* of Monterey were to be informed of his death. I told him that I thought even the governor would come to the funeral. Father Juan told me that there would be hard times ahead for Alta California. He gave his blessing and we both knelt in prayer.

"After I returned to Esperanza, who was keeping vigil near Papa, I took command of the household. I gave orders for candles to be brought from the storerooms for the all-night vigil and told her to inform everyone on the ranch. We held visitation in the large *sala*.

"Padre Juan and I set the date for a funeral and arranged to have Papa taken to the mission. At last, Will and I were alone with Papa, and after we prayed, we silently held hands. Others would soon be coming to pay their respects to Papa. Then we went to my bedroom. Will and I had not even established a place at the *hacienda* where we would live. I wondered if anyone would believe that we were truly married?"

CHAPTER 24

▼

February 2, 2000

Rita was startled when her business phone rang. Looking at her watch she found that it was already six-thirty. Mike heard it and looked into Rita's office while the phone continued to ring. In a sleepy voice, he said, "Oh I thought you were downstairs exercising and couldn't hear the phone."

"I hope it isn't Missy," Rita sighed.

The answering machine picked up the message. Tessa's voice was heard. "You know I won't be at work today. Call me if you have a minute before you leave for the shop. Bye."

"That's not like her. Even her voice sounds different. I wonder if something is wrong," Rita said. She closed down the computer and gave Mike a kiss before going into Carmelita's room. Since Carmelita was still sleeping, Rita quickly returned to Mike who was shaving.

"Another early golf game?"

"No, thank goodness, but after a quick breakfast, I want to get over to the office, check my messages and see what they've scheduled for me. Remember we have a late afternoon party at the tent of Central Coast Savings and Loan. How about you?"

"I'll be very busy, and Missy seemed insistent that she visit the shop and then go to lunch with me."

"Do you have to do that?"

"I think so. She's oversensitive about family relationships right now. I told you she and Charles are back together, didn't I?"

"You told me plenty."

"Yesterday there was a call from Mel Stern, the other person who might be interested in some kind of a production of *The Carmelo Diaries*. What's on our schedule tomorrow? Just in case the Stern's want to meet us?"

"Try to call me when you have some definite information, Babe," Mike replied.

Rita made Mike what she called his "jump start breakfast" of a banana, cranberry juice, and vitamin-enzyme powder whirled in the blender. Then she went to take care of Carmelita.

As Mike left the house he called out, "Take it easy, Pal. Give me a call if there are any big changes today."

The phone rang again. "Did you get my message?" she heard Tessa's voice.

"I was going to call after Carmelita's breakfast," she said.

"I figured. I'm in a better mood, but I just can't come in and work. I want to meet you for lunch and explain. Let's not get tangled up with all that traffic around the golf courses. How about meeting at that cute little pasta place in Pacific Grove?"

"Tessa, I can't meet you. Remember I told you that Missy almost commanded me to go with her for lunch after she came into the shop this morning."

"Rita, this is important. I have to tell you some things, and this may be my only time," her voice was becoming firmer.

"O.K. then. Twelve-thirty at Peppi's Pasta. I'll tell Missy that I already have a lunch appointment with a client."

After Marquita arrived to take care of Carmelita, Rita dressed in a soft gray-green woolen skirt and a narrow ribbed pistachio sweater. She arrived at The Old Booktique before the customers arrived. There was a message from a well-known historical bookstore in Ferndale, and it said that some of the stolen inventory had been found. There was no word from Dave Goldman. She called the number that Mel Stern had left and found it to be a spa hotel resort in Carmel Valley. The Sterns were out to breakfast. Mel soon called back and asked Rita and Mike to have lunch with them tomorrow. He suggested that they meet at the spa hotel. Rita accepted immediately since she had heard nothing from Dave Goldman.

Dolores arrived well before the store opened. She was looking elegant even in a casual straight skirt and white blouse. Perhaps it was her upright posture. Her presence was calming to Rita, and they looked over the changes in the morning agenda.

"I don't want you to think I always run my business this way," she explained, "But nothing has been as usual since we had the burglary last week. Thank goodness, you're here. I don't know what I would have done without you," she finished.

"It's actually been good for me. It makes me realize that I like to work with collectors and find something special for them."

"Oh yes." Rita said, "My sister-in-law will be coming in. She's never seen The Old Booktique, and she wants to buy a special book for my brother. I was supposed to go to lunch with her, but something else important has come up."

Dolores needed no extra explanations. Rita called Captain Lewis.

"I have finished interviewing," he told her. "I'm going to leave your case now, and we'll inform you if any more of the inventory is found. Feel free to call me or use the number on my card if you get any ideas or leads. We've gone as far as our information takes us. There are too many closed doors."

"I'm glad to be off his daily calling list," Rita told Dolores.

Missy arrived. She was wearing a navy-blue tailored wool suit. She wore kid gloves and looked less casual than all the golf spectators in slacks and windbreakers. Some of the spectators were circulating around the area of the Retreat and putting greens as well as the shops. They hoped to see celebrities.

"I want to buy something meaningful for Charles," Missy said to Rita. "He has really become interested in nineteenth century California this last year. The California wine business started in Napa at that time, you know," she added in a tone of confidentially.

Dolores was nearby, and Rita took Missy's hand. "This is Dolores, my expert. She'll help you find the right book."

Missy turned and began telling Dolores about the new tasting room at their winery. "When people from Moët et Chandon come to visit from France, we want to have something that reflects our history to show them. They were so gracious to us when we were in Éperney a few years ago."

"Here is a rare book, written by General Mariano Vallejo. He tells about his first attempts to grow grapes for his own wine." Dolores suggested. Missy flicked through the pages impatiently.

"Where should we eat, Rita? I can call the concierge at The Retreat. He will get us a good table at the Sanderling, if you want to go there."

"Not today, Missy. When I arrived this morning, I found I had a previous lunch appointment with a client."

"But, Rita, you promised," she said while looking around the shop. "Don't you have other employees who could do things like taking a client to lunch?"

"I'm not on vacation this week. It's unusual that I took the day off yesterday."

"Then I should tell you now. Charles and I decided to host a dinner on Monday night. It will be after the tournament. I want to personally invite you and Mike to attend. You will pick up Anita won't you?"

Rita quietly said "Of course, Missy."

The phone rang, and Dolores summoned Rita to take the call.

It was Mike. "The Rojas will be in town next week. They want to see us for lunch."

"Anytime is fine except Monday. We are invited to a dinner party by Missy and Charles on Monday night."

"OK, if we have to. Love you, Babe." Mike hung up quickly.

When Rita returned to Dolores and Missy, they were both engrossed in the comparison of autographs of early California governors. The Mexican governors signed their names with elaborate rubrics that were almost illegible with their flourishes of penmanship.

"I'm leaving you in good hands," Rita said as she gathered her briefcase and leather jacket. She made a quick exit.

Peppi's Pasta was located on a narrow street in old-fashioned Pacific Grove. Rita walked up the wooden steps to enter a restored house of the late Victorian era. The menu attested to pizzas of an uncommon variety, such as artichokes and sprouts or Mexican chorizo sausage and fresh red peppers. Tessa arrived. She had a new hair cut. She looked best in short hair.

"You look great," Rita said as they walked in together. She was hoping to hear great news.

"You look great too. But then you always do," Tessa replied. "And thanks for meeting me."

They glanced at the menu of traditional pizzas and pasta dishes. The choice was easy when they found that the specialty of the day was a thin crust pizza with a topping of artichokes, sun dried tomatoes, and Fontina cheese.

"This lunch is on me," Tessa said brightly "and I'm ordering a bottle of Cabernet."

"No wine for me," Rita quickly said. "This has to be a short lunch. I have so much to do. I have to be sharp this afternoon."

"Then I'll drink most of it. I came by taxi, and I can go home by taxi. Let's have a salad while we're waiting for the pizza."

"They ordered. The waitress brought a bottle of vintage Cabernet Sauvignon and poured some wine in Tessa's glass.

"Just have a sip with me," Tessa urged Rita, and the waitress poured a glass for Rita.

"It sounds like you have great news. Is it your mysterious Mr. X?" Rita said touching her glass with Tessa's.

"Well yes and no," she replied. "I want to toast to a new life."

Rita took a sip. "I'll toast to that, but I want to hear more."

Tessa took a long thoughtful taste, and then she said, "I'm leaving tomorrow for Scottsdale, Arizona."

"Just like that. Did he ask you to meet him there?"

"No, I'm going by myself. I think I'm going to live there. A month ago I applied for the position of manager of the boutique and apparel shop at the Sirocco Hotel. I wanted to go at that time, but now I have a different reason." She took another taste of the wine. "Yesterday afternoon, they offered me a job to work as an assistant in the hotel boutique. They said I had to come right away. So I took it."

"This is sudden. I didn't have the slightest…" Rita stopped. She was going to say that she needed Tessa, but she realized that sounded selfish. "I didn't know you wanted to do something else," Rita said.

"You know I'm not very bookish," Tessa said quietly.

"I think you've been great at The Old Booktique, and I like working with you. I don't want to stand in the way of what is best for you," Rita said while knowing she could not disguise her disappointment.

"I was going to wait until I got the job and give you two weeks notice and all that." She paused and took another sip of wine. "This is an emergency. When I was offered a job I decided to go."

"You said this had something to do with Mr. X?"

"Well, it does. You see, I've decided to give myself a trial period of being away from him. If I like it in Arizona, I'll stay. And if we still love each other, it will be easier for us to see each other there. It's a decision we both have made."

The food arrived. "I'm really going to miss you," Rita managed to say as they started eating. Tessa began another glass of the Cabernet.

"There's more to it, and I didn't want to leave here until I told you how sorry I was that it has to be on such short notice. I didn't think I would really do it until I went up to San Francisco last weekend. Getting this job, any job, was a sign for me to leave."

"The main thing is that we're good friends. Best friends," Rita said.

"Maybe you won't say that when I tell you the rest."

"There's more?"

"Don't you want to know more?"

"That's up to you. Especially since you said you may not be seeing him for awhile."

"I just can't keep it a secret from you any longer. I've been in love with your brother since the first time I saw him when I visited you at Stonecrest while we were in high school."

Rita was stunned. "Charlie?"

"I know he's not always your favorite person. Because of your grandmother's will and all that, but I know him in a different way."

"I'm sure you do."

"We've been lovers for a long time"

"Real lovers?" Rita said without thinking how absurd that sounded.

"Of course. He was the first boy to make love to me. We did it that summer before he went to college. I was staying with you at Stonecrest."

"We were in high school then," Rita gasped. She took a look at the beautifully prepared pizza. She wanted to eat it. Incongruously, she wished that Tessa had told her after she had eaten lunch.

"That was the first time. And I fell in love with him right after the first time. We made out whenever we could, but there were lots of years that I didn't even see him. Although there were a few times he looked me up when I was at UCLA. He would take me to a late dinner and we would go back to his hotel. I knew it was a fling, but it was so exciting."

"You were married for six years."

"Nothing much happened then. Although he did surprise me once. It was in Washington D.C. after Dad's funeral. I was alone, and he found out I was there. He said he wanted to cheer me up. He can be sweet, you know"

Rita looked at her in amazement.

"I don't imagine he said anything to you about me, because you two were never really close. And I am wise enough to know that Charles is the kind of a guy to play around, but about a year ago he called me and told me he was going to get a divorce. He asked me to meet him in San Francisco He said he had been going through therapy, and that made him feel worse. He knew I'd gotten a divorce, so he thought we could talk about it together. I met him at the Redwood Room. He had a bottle of Dom Perignon waiting for us. He said his grandmother said a bottle of good champagne could cheer up anybody. He asked the waitress to bring appetizers. Then we had martinis. He put his hand up my skirt.

He knew that always gets me going. I moved his hand a little farther up. Then he said, "Let's have the next bottle of Dom Perignon sent up to our room."

Rita tried to stop Tessa. The waitress kept filling up her glass with water after she poured a little more wine for Tessa.

"I'm going to the bathroom," Rita said.

"I'll go with you," Tessa continued, and she continued talking all the way. "Charles has always been my ideal lover. And you know, Rita, some jerk would have seduced me in my first year at college anyway. Let me tell more."

"Not here in the rest room," Rita said. "Let's go to my car."

After Tessa paid the bill, Rita carefully walked her to the parking lot and helped her into the passenger seat. They just sat while Tessa continued talking. "We went up to one of those wonderful hotel rooms that look down on all of San Francisco. It was a room where you can see all the lights, the Bay Bridge and the Transamerica building. I don't know if I really saw them, though. I do remember the maid had turned down the bedspread and I ate the chocolate on the pillow. I found the chocolate on the other side of the bed and put it down my blouse. Charles watched me and told me he liked his chocolate that way."

"Tessa, I don't have to know the details," Rita said as put her hand on Tessa's arm.

"But I want to tell you. I don't want you to think this love is some little fling. He was separated, and I was divorced. We stayed in The City for a week. That proved to me that it wasn't a one-night stand. Missy had taken their daughters to Aspen for the Christmas holidays. Charles was supposed to meet with his therapist the next day but he canceled the appointment. We went shopping. He bought me a bracelet at Neiman-Marcus. We took a ride on a cable car and he bought me flowers from a street corner vender. He bought tickets for a play the next night, but instead we decided to have dinner in the room and get more acquainted. I hadn't brought a suitcase, so I had to buy some clothes, and he insisted on paying for it. He said he had always wanted to have a mistress. I felt so special, but it was really more than the sex. I was always in love with him, and now he was starting to fall in love with me. I liked the idea of being his mistress. I didn't care about anything as long as I was with him. He said he loves having a person all to himself. If you think Missy is a pill, you should have heard the things he told me about her. She must have ice water in her veins."

Although Tessa had drunk almost a bottle of wine, she was coherent. What she was telling Rita came tumbling out with the elated emotion of remembered feelings. She had never told anyone about this before, and she became enraptured with her own story.

"We continued to be lovers whenever we could. We flew to Cabo San Lucas on weekends. We went over to Hawaii to see Bebe and your Dad. Then Missy found out that he was having a 'sordid little affair' as she called it, and she filed for divorce. Charles said it was just as well, but to protect me he wanted us to be more careful. He didn't know if she really had a detective as he had suspected. They were starting to haggle over a financial settlement. He is very serious about his creating his very own wine label. After Missy hired the detective, we had to plan our escapes better. In a way, this just made it more exciting and special. It was then Charles told me he loved me for the first time. That was about six months ago. He bought me a beautiful emerald solitaire ring."

Rita gave Tessa some bottled water that she kept in her car. "Do you feel all right for me to take you home?"

"Rita, I still love Charles." she said and started crying. "Last weekend in The City, in our favorite room and in our favorite hotel, he told me that he and Missy were getting back together. They are probably not getting a divorce. He said it was the only way he could make it financially. He has some other ideas, but he said they might not work out. I told him I might move to Scottsdale, and he thought it was a good idea. He said it would give us time to think. He even told me he loved me, and said that if I had been his wife, he would have been faithful to me."

At this point Rita started thinking of her own life and of her father leaving them every few months when she was small. She remembered moving into Stonecrest with Grandmother Clara. She felt lonely and alone in that big house. She wished Tessa hadn't confided in her.

"Rita, when I got the call for the job in Scottsdale, I thought I should leave now. I'm going to try to make a new life. I even want to forget about Charles for a while. I'm wise enough to know it will take a lot of money and years for Charles to be free. I don't know if I'm strong enough to resist him when he wants me to meet him. Maybe I'm kidding myself to think I'll ever have him. He needs to succeed with his specialty wines, and he can't do it without Missy and her money."

"You poor baby," was all that Rita could say. Tessa's confession made her feel sad. "I'll take you home now. You'd better get yourself ready for Scottsdale and a new life."

Tessa was asleep while Rita drove her to the Carmel cottage she had rented. She sat up when the car stopped, and after Rita walked with her to the house and made sure she was well, she hurried back to The Old Booktique.

Dolores had much to tell her. Missy had decided to buy Charles the seven-volume original edition of Bancroft's *History of California*. Mike left a message about meeting him at the Hospitality Tent, and Captain Lewis had already paid a visit to the shop. "He said he really wanted to see Tessa." Dolores said.

Rita had to catch up on what she had planned to do today. She had four hours of work to accomplish in two hours. "It is the end of the month, and I need to get some figures ready for the accountant," Rita told Dolores. She spent the rest of the afternoon at her computer. She tried not to think about Tessa. She didn't want to tell Mike about Tessa and Charles, although she knew that sometime she would.

At five Rita closed the cut glass door that was the main entrance to The Old Booktique and walked to the party at a corporate tent where she agreed to meet Mike. When she walked through the entrance, Pete, Mike's associate, greeted her. "Hi, Pretty Lady. Mike is over there. Rita looked at the gathering of guests. There was already a high-pitched hum of voices. After the near pathos of Tessa's confession, this all seemed like a cartoon video. "How's it going, Rita?" someone called loudly over the noise made by the party-goers.

"Just great. And the weather looks better," she answered as she glanced around the tent and realized how many of her friends in Pebble Beach were involved in some part of real estate.

"Good to see you. Where have you been? Let's get together," she heard almost simultaneously, and one of the directors of the Forest Shore Mortgage Company gave her a hug while another poured her a glass of Chardonnay.

"Say, I read about your break-in. Did they take much?" Said Debbie, a friend from tennis days.

"Not too much. And I think we'll recover most of it," Rita answered.

Mike was soon at her side. "How was your lunch? Any juicy tidbits about the Atherton reconciliation?" He whispered.

"Plenty," she laughed. "Plenty."

Rita ate some stuffed mushrooms and baby cheese pitas. Mike was a little surprised.

"Are you hungry, Babe? I bet you had one of those no-calorie designer salads for lunch."

"We had artichoke and sprout pizzas," she said.

"Then let's pick up some Chinese food to take home for dinner," Mike suggested. "We can leave here in a just a little while."

"Let's talk to Vic Armbruster a few minutes. I know he was the one who invited us," There are so many people milling around, I don't think we can talk to everyone we know." Rita told Mike. Together they made their way through the crowd. After a short conversation with Vic, they left.

When Rita and Mike arrived home, Carmelita was impatient to show them her new finger paintings. Then, she eyed the cartons of food that her father placed on the kitchen table. "Can I open the little boxes?" she asked as she stood on a step stool and looked at the array.

"It's Chinese food," Mike stated. "Marquita said you've already had your dinner. Do you want to try some of this food with us?"

"Right now," she said, as he helped her unfasten a white carton with a wire handle.

"Let's eat now, then" said Mike and together they opened all the boxes while Rita put plates on the table. Carmelita ate some rice while watching her parents use chopsticks to eat snow peas, Shrimp Foo Young, and Mandarin Pork.

Mike could wait no longer. "Rita, I wanted to hurry us home because I wanted to hear about your lunch."

"It's quite a story so I'll tell you latter this evening," she smiled. Soon she took Carmelita up to bed.

When Rita came downstairs, she called out, "Espresso, tonight?"

"No, don't go to all that trouble. I'm eager to hear about your lunch?"

"To start out. I didn't go to lunch with Missy. She wanted to take me to The Sanderling, and I told her I had a previous business engagement."

"Good."

"Just after you left, Tessa called and reminded me that she couldn't come to work and begged me to have lunch with her. She said she wanted to explain something," Rita began.

"And did she?"

"Yes. Lunch with Tessa was quite an awakening. She's going to Scottsdale, Arizona, tomorrow. She's going to start a new job, and she'll probably live there."

"Is she out of her mind? She has a nice cozy cottage in Carmel, and she doesn't have many professional skills to offer."

"Apparently she's been thinking about moving for quite awhile."

"Does this have anything to do with her romance?"

"I think it is everything."

"Did he drop her?"

"Not exactly, but she found that he wanted to stay married."

"So, if he is married, she should have thought about that possibility."

"She wants to get away now. She's pretty broken up."

"Did he give her the 'I'm going to get a divorce bit, so he could get her into bed?'"

"I think he was officially separated, but now there's going to be a reconciliation." And Rita stopped not knowing how to say the rest.

Mike had been munching on biscotti, and he put it down. "Are you talking about some people we both know? Some people in your family we are supposed to see next week?"

"Yes," she said quietly and put her hands together almost like a prayer.

"Oh, for God's sake. Tessa's such a pushover and especially right now. I hate to say it, but any guy could get into her pants since her divorce. What a louse he is. I think even less of him right now. What did you say to her?"

"It isn't that simple, Mike."

"I think so."

"She told me she encouraged the affair."

"That's what I mean. She's eager for anything, but he didn't need to take advantage of the situation."

"No of course not, but,'

"She's the kind of a girl that guys love to play along."

"Oh you males. Are we all pieces of meat to you guys?"

"No, Babe, and please don't get involved with her problems or your brother's."

"Mike, she told me she has loved him ever since her first year in high school. That's when she first had sex with him. I'm still in a state of shock. I didn't mean to tell you all that, but it does explain some things I've wondered about."

"I'm glad you told me. I don't want you to keep all this worry to yourself. Didn't you have the slightest indication of it? You've been buddies a long time," he changed the tone of his voice.

"There were years we weren't at the same schools or even in the same country. She was often with her dad during the summers. He was in the diplomatic service, you know."

"Yes, but do you think they really had sex when you were in high school?"

"She was a boarding student when we went to Santa Lucia. I wouldn't put it past Tessa to have climbed out of the window after hours. I sure didn't suspect anything was going on with my brother. After all he was in college then."

"Didn't you have an inkling?"

"I told you, Charlie and I were never close. I was pretty tame in those teen years. I really didn't even consider such a possibility of Tessa and Charlie 'doing it.' Grandmother Clara always inspected my white party shoes for grass stains and, come to think of it even my underwear. She and Mother probably watched me with far more suspicion than the nuns at the convent. I was intimidated by what Grandmother expected of me."

Mike threw his head back and laughed. "So you were really a 'little goody two shoes' in spite of yourself."

"Yep, they had me in every horse show, dance recital, and fencing tournament so I was lucky to have enough time to go to school dances."

"And that's what we're going to do with Carmelita?"

Now it was Rita's turn to laugh. "I hope it's not your past that is haunting you."

"Seriously, Rita, this puts a whole new spin on your brother's actions. Do you think this has anything to do with his recent appearance in Pebble Beach?"

"Do you think he came here to see Tessa?" she questioned

"I was thinking about the burglary."

"Do you think he's involved?"

"Some detectives say there's no such thing as a coincidence. Listen to this. Charlie comes to town for a wine conference. The Old Booktique gets burglarized. Charlie buddies up to Anita," Mike enumerated.

Rita continued. "Charlie gets interested in nineteenth century California history. Charlie mentions the name Dave Goldman to me,"

"And then you had some weird feelings about something missing in your home office."

"That's why I wanted to go to Mothers for dinner. I wanted to watch him. I don't see him as a thief, but he could be involved in burglary in some way. If it turns out that he does business with Mr. Goldman," she paused. "Then I'll really know. You realize, this isn't anything I want to share with Captain Lewis. I'm going to be very careful about what I say to him."

"You said the good captain keeps asking for Tessa. Do you think he suspects something about her?"

"Not really."

"You told me that he says he is shelving the case."

"Yes, but when I returned to the shop today, there was a message that he wanted to talk to Tessa."

"Could she be a suspect?"

"I really don't think so. But I won't be surprised by anything now. Maybe we can get some clues from what Mel Stern has to say, or maybe Charlie will drop some remark at dinner next Monday night."

"I thought you said we were have lunch with them."

"Now it's dinner."

"I am not forgetting how he behaved when Aunt Clara died, and I think he's scum for playing around with Tessa all these years. If I really think he had anything to do with the burglary, I wouldn't trust myself to be in the same room with him."

"Let's wait to see what happens when we go to that dinner. In the meantime, we'll have an interesting lunch with the Sterns tomorrow. I'm going upstairs now and I'll write some more about Clarita's life during the Larkin era when she was first married to Will O'Farrell. I want to have some good material to show Mr. Stern. Of course, you'll be with me, and we won't commit ourselves to anything until we talk it over."

"Well then go write it up," he laughed. "I'm going to be your slave driver. Get into that time machine of yours and flip back to your illustrious ancestors."

The phone rang and Mike answered it. "OK, Tessa, I'll tell her, and lots of luck and all that in Scottsdale."

When Mike entered her office. Rita looked up from the computer. "Was it for me?"

"It was Tessa saying she was on her way to a new life, and I told her I'd tell you about it.

"I won't be too long. I have Isabel's blue satin notebooks to help me. I'm writing about the year, 1835."

"Is this your only real source of information for those years?"

"Yes. Clarita lived with Isabel and her husband in her later life. Isabel quotes her grandmother in her books."

"Then use Clarita's words"

CHAPTER 25

▼

Rita went to her office and continued writing Clarita's life story. She used Isabel's blue satin journals and Clarita's own words.

"Papa died in 1835. I had never arranged an important funeral; however, I was determined the event would be worthy of Papa. I needed Consuelo to come to Rancho Carmelo as soon as possible. I told Captain García to inform the important people living in Monterey. I used my precious supply of paper to write a special note to Consuelo in which I told her that Padre Real officiated when Guillermo and I married at the Mission San Cárlos. Then I sent Ramon to the Garcías.

"As soon as she arrived, Consuelo told me I had married too soon and without a proper ceremony. She said some of our friends would not consider it correct to marry within the first year of my widowhood. She reminded me of how long even Mariano Vallejo had waited to obtain permission to marry Francisca Benicia Carrillo. She also told me that Guillermo was a man who worked with his hands and not a Spanish gentleman. All this would have made me angry, but I knew that Consuelo was truly concerned for my welfare and wished only the best for me. She put her arms around me, and I cried as she told me I must make sure we obtain permission from the governor to marry again, perhaps at the San Cárlos Chapel at the Presidio.

"Consuelo was of great assistance in helping me make arrangements for the guests who would stay at the ranch. Esperanza worked everywhere as she directed the maids who were making *tortillas*, cooking *frijoles* and harvesting summer vegetables. The men of the ranch hastily constructed tables. We found linen table-clothes to cover them. The entire courtyard was used for festivities. Will ordered a slaughter of cattle and told the men to dig pits for the fires that would cook the beef. We found wines in the storehouse that would satisfy the thirst of honored guests. When I had an opportunity, I told Will that Consuelo thought we should ask Padre Real to make a proclamation concerning our marriage. She said Padre Real should inform everyone at the funeral that we were married with Papa's blessings before he died. Will rode to the mission to arrange this with Padre Real at once.

"When he returned, he told me that Padre Real would make the announcement of our marriage. In former times, we would have been asked to donate a new bell for the Mission as Joséfa and Enrique Fitch had done when they came back to California after their elopement. But now that the Mission was being closed, other arrangements were made. Will told Padre Real he would buy the remainder of the cattle herds that belonged to the mission. This purchase took the entire sum of gold that was loaned to him by Señor Larkin. This arrangement satisfied Padre Real, who assumed that Will was a Mexican citizen or would be one in the future. I knew that Will had already promised Señor Larkin that he would remain an American. I knew there would be many sins we would confess later, but we needed to make decisions for that moment in time.

"I wanted Ardo to come to see Papa in the coffin, and I wanted to tell him of his inheritance. I did not know the location of the Vargas family. When I told Consuelo of my worries, she said it was of no importance now. She had recently learned that Ardo, Doña Eulalia, and Don Diego left on the ship, *Estrella*, for Mexico. Eulalia was to stay in Sonora with Ardo, and he was to attend school there.

"We were saddened to hear of the ill health of Governor Figueroa. He could not attend the funeral. José Castro took his place as the official government representative. He had been appointed the acting *jefe politico* for the governor during his illness and whatever time he was resting from his official duties.

"Consuelo brought me one of her best black dresses. She could not wear it, as she was with child again. Although Consuelo said it was not necessary, I wanted to have Esperanza and my little sisters, Dulcera and Felicia, sitting near me during the services for Papa. I found some suitable clothing for them, and one of the maids altered the garments to fit them. They looked proper, and I was proud of their manners. I wanted all of the de Segovia family to be as elegant as people in Monterey. I knew that despite the teaching of the Padres, many of the Indians had run away and become savages. This was true for those who did not marry in the church, but it was not true for all of the Indians. Esperanza and Ramon were faithful Christians, and much of their life was been spent with our family on Rancho Carmelo. Our good Governor Figueroa proved that men with Indian blood were capable and performed well in even in the highest of offices. Although I am proud that I am Castilian Spanish, I know that much of what I am is due to my early training and the ideals of my parents. This is what I wanted to pass on to my children.

"When the day came for the funeral, there was a constant procession of horses and *carretas* coming from all directions. Encarnacion and Captain Cooper, as well as Juan Bautista Alvarado, were first to arrive. I was introduced to the wife of Señor Larkin. She wore a bonnet on her head. This is the first *Yanqui* lady I had ever seen. She seemed pleasant and had even changed her name to Raquel from Rachel. She spoke a little Spanish with us. There were members from the families of the Vallejos, Estradas, Castros, and the Munras. Many of them told me they had not visited our ranch since I was married to Don Felipe Vargas. Later, after Padre José María made the announcement of my new marriage, those who did not know us well expressed some amazement. After I told them that we would be living at Rancho Carmelo, they were cordial and said the proper words of welcome, asking us to come visit them in Monterey.

"Señor Larkin surprised all of us with an invitation. He announced that when the period of mourning for Papa had passed, he would give a *fandango* at the Custom House in Monterey, and it would be in honor of our wedding. He used the name, Guillermo, and his praise of him gave us a new standing in the community. Although I wished Ardo could have been with us, I knew how jealous Don Diego could be. It was best not to make him angry, as he was a fearsome man. Those who came for the funeral were satisfied that all the local customs were observed. As they left, they again invited Will and me to come to Monterey. We were accepted as man and wife.

"For a few days after the funeral, Will and I took long rides up through the narrow valley of the Rio Carmelo. Sometimes we started in the morning before the fog had lifted from the folds of the hills. We spread quilts under the shelter of broad oak trees and sat there while we talked. We were always happy when the two of us were together and alone. Then we would gallop back to the *hacienda* and drink our morning chocolate. During the remainder of the day, we went about our separate duties. Often we would express our love by a gentle look across the dining table.

"Will was needed to finish building a storehouse for Señor Larkin, who conducted his growing business in the family house. It was built in a different style than the other adobe homes in Monterey. The Larkin house had an inside stairway, red wood floors, and more fireplaces than any other house in Monterey. Will often worked for Señor Larkin, because he wanted to pay back the gold that had been loaned to him. I wanted to keep the ranch prosperous, so it was decided that I would stay at Rancho Carmelo to make sure that the *vaqueros* followed the orders of 'Don Guillermo', as he was now called He returned to Rancho Carmelo from Monterey on Saturday afternoons. With the help of Ramon and the loyal *vaqueros*, we finished the autumn roundup and the Mission cattle were mixed in with our own. I paid many visits to the Mission San Cárlos, and I always asked the fathers how we could give them further aid. I can tell you that every time Will went to Monterey to help Señor Larkin, I was not happy until he returned to Rancho Carmelo.

"Time passed quickly, and we were very happy. Near the end of September when Guillermo and Señor Larkin were inspecting a finished building, there came word from the governor's quarters that he had suffered another attack of his illness and the governor suddenly died. What a blow to all of us. It was already decided that José Castro and Nicolas Gutierrez would take over the temporary rule of Alta California. Guillermo rode back to Carmelo with the news, and after we packed a trunk of clothes, which we sent by *carreta*, we galloped back to Monterey to attend the funeral. We stayed with the Garcías, although we saw little of Miguel who was in charge of the military formalities. Times were sad. I had lost my father, and a now the governor whom I trusted to give us our land grant. However, I had the love of Will to keep me strong. We knew we had much to accomplish. I was almost certain that Will and I would become parents.

"The news of the death of Governor Figueroa reached Mexico, and instead of a governor with a moderate temperament, we learned that we would be sent a man whose fits of anger were well-known, namely Don Mariano Chico. He was to arrive by ship in the spring. When he heard the news about the arrival of the new governor, Don Diego did not stay in Sonora. He returned to Monterey with a bride, and he briefly introduced her to the important families living there. She was a girl of fifteen and from a good family. They lived at Rancho Rincón, and went to mass at the Mission San Juan Bautista.

"In another month I returned to Monterey to attend the baptism of the new son of the Garcías. While in their courtyard I was alarmed to see Don Diego. He had come to pay a visit to the Garcías. He brought a gift for the child and also sought me out at the far end of the garden. He bowed deeply to me and invited me to come to visit my son when he returned to Rancho Rincón after a term of school in Mexico. It was more difficult to answer his politeness than if he had said cruel words to me. I was caught without a reply, and as I lowered my head, I saw the scimitar knife he often wore at his side. I did not trust him.

"I told him that I did not wish to trouble him, and I asked him to bring Ardo to Rancho Carmelo for a visit. I told him that Ardo would like to see the place he spent many happy days and where he could visit the grave of his grandfather.

"Then he told me lies. He said Ardo knew that I had abandoned him. Don Diego said Rancho Rincón was my rightful home and told me I could be with Ardo at any time if I returned to my home there. He said he told Ardo that I chose to live in sin with the *Yanqui, O'Farol*.

"I was in despair when Don Diego said this, and without any more conversation, I turned and left his presence. I went to Consuelo and asked for paper and ink so that I could write the words of our conversation. I wanted to remember what I had said. To this day I know they are the true words that were said. I wanted Ardo to know why I had not come to see him.

"With the good Governor Figueroa dead and the prospects of a governor, who is unfriendly to *Californios*, I avoided seeing Don Diego. I feared that he would seize an opportunity to accuse me of disobedience to the laws of Mexico, and he would take this accusation to the new governor. I did not go into Monterey, and I did not ride into the hills of Rancho Carmelo or up the river. In the meanwhile, the political and military powers of government were divided between Señors Gutierrez and Castro. They performed their duties well and offended no one.

"When the new governor, Mariano Chico, arrived and was installed May 3, 1836, there were many important colonial affairs to address in Monterey. The ruling families of California were, for the most part, very much against the authority of the government of Mexico."

Rita made a notation here that this was the same period in time (1835–36) when the Americans in Texas were in revolt against the Mexican government.

"Governor Chico repeatedly lost his temper in extreme ways. He shot and killed a young and innocent Indian boy, and he failed in all attempts to placate the differences of the northern and southern *Californios*. He made little progress with the appointment of qualified men to distribute the land of the missions and he was unable to quell the Indian uprisings. We did not want to attract attention, and we lived quietly at Rancho Carmelo. This was easy as there were far more scandalous things happening in Alta California. There were marital judgments for the governor to decide. His solutions were not wise.

He was not a good governor. A series of charges were brought against him by the local city council, and he angered all the townspeople when he placed the *alcalde*, Señor Estrada, under arrest. Monterey citizens rose in defiance, and Governor Chico began to fear for his life. He chartered a ship, and after being denied landing in Santa Bárbara he sailed for Mexico. He never returned.

"Will and I spoke the English language to each other most of the time. Will insisted on my calling him by his American name, Will, and I loved him more every day. In Monterey and at the ranch, where only Spanish was spoken, everyone continued to call him Don Guillermo. I was contented with our life, and both Will and I looked forward to the birth of our first child."

Rita put down the blue satin book and yawned. She didn't realize until now how tired she was. She had finished an important part of the presentation for the Sterns.

CHAPTER 26

▼

February 3, 2000.

Thursday is always Round One of the simultaneous play on the three golf courses chosen for the AT&T Pebble Beach National Tournament. For several years, the AT&T had been plagued with rain. This year was no exception. A new storm developed during the night. The local television station covered the weather as an international catastrophe. It was violent enough to postpone the day's tournament play. Rita and Mike listened to the wind as they were dressing in the morning. It lashed at trees in the yard and howled as if begging to enter the house. Rita cooked Irish oatmeal, and just before serving, she added raisins. As Rita, Mike, and Carmelita sat eating the warm nourishment contentedly, Mike said, "I wish we could all stay home and be comfortable, but I need get to the office early. There will be no play anywhere, and I may have some eager customers."

"I hope it doesn't rain every day," Rita said with a sigh.

"This storm is just blowing through. It probably will clear up this afternoon," Mike said, and tried to sound reassuring. .

"We're always busy at the shop during stormy weather. I'll go in as soon as Marquita gets here. Shall I meet you at the office? Then we can drive out to the valley together."

"Fine by me. Did you get your writing finished last night?"

"It's not complete by any means, but I have enough to show Mr. Stern. I don't want to bore them with details, but I want enough material to entice them. I'm writing about a confusing time in California history."

"What years are you writing about now?"

"Last night it was 1835 and 1836. California had seven governors, if you count Castro and Gutierrez twice because of their two short terms."

"They had political problems too," Mike commented.

"It's rather complicated, and an abbreviated telling of the story makes it sound like the plot of a comic opera. I was trying to weave the ongoing politics with the events that were happening in Clarita's personal life. You know, the deaths and funerals, births and baptisms, weddings and domestic intrigue."

Mike looked at her. "Would you have been delving into all these diaries and history if there hadn't been the burglary?"

"Probably not this soon. However, last month you remember, I was already contacting people who might want to produce a television show."

"Do you think the Sterns are really serious?" Mike asked.

"Yes, I think so. Mr. Stern sought me out because of Dave Goldman as well as Shana Tyrone. Stern has produced several documentaries for PBS. He is interested in telling history from the viewpoint of someone who lived during the time. Clarita certainly qualifies for that. She was a contemporary of the Vallejos, J.B. Alvarado, and Thomas Larkin."

"Does your mother know you're doing this?"

"I haven't told her much about it. I think she'll be interested in our meeting with the Sterns, although I'll bet her first question will be about the clothes."

"And what are we wearing? By the way?"

"The Valley is always casual. Slacks and a sweater. Right now, I'm dressing for rain. I'm wearing my good old yellow slicker. I want to buy one for Carmelita"

The weather was clear by eleven when Rita and Mike took the Carmel Valley Road from Carmel. They could see big puffy cumulus clouds in the distance near the far hills that border the Salinas Valley. They stopped at a security gate and made their way up to the Valley Spa Hotel. The buildings were contemporary with a traditional California feeling and the atmosphere was pastoral. When they stepped inside the flower filled courtyard lobby, Mel Stern came forward to introduce himself and his wife, Ellen.

"Too bad the weather spoiled your golf," Mike said after the introductions.

"Oh the AT&T was just an excuse to get away. We've spent the whole morning relaxing here at the spa," Mel said with a smile.

"We love it here in the country. It's a great place for city people to get away. Our room has a panoramic view of the whole valley and a nearby ranch," said Ellen, who was a petite, well-proportioned woman just a little older than Rita. She wore a short denim jacket over a red tee shirt. Rita made a mental note to tell her mother that Ellen's tailored denim jeans had a rhinestone trim on the cuffs. Anita was always interested in detail.

"We really don't like crowds. The main reason for the trip was to meet you," Mel continued.

"That's terrific," said Rita candidly.

"We thought we could talk about how you envision the project, get acquainted, and then we'll go have lunch. Would you like a drink or something?" Mel asked as he gestured to both of them.

"Oh, no thank you, not right now," Mike responded.

"How about if I interview you?" Mel said getting right to the point. "It's the best way to get answers to what I want to know."

"I have some questions, too," Rita replied.

"What made you want to find someone to produce a television story about your ancestors?"

"We've just celebrated the year of the Gold Rush sesquicentennial. There's been a lot of publicity about it. I think there's more to California history than missionaries and miners."

"So this is personal?"

"I grew up at my grandmother's house on Stillwater Cove. She was always telling me stories about the person we were named after, Clarita Isabel de Segovia. In our family she is important. Her life parallels all the things that happened around Monterey from the beginning of the Mexican era in 1822."

"So, it will be her story?"

"Hers and all the daughters who followed her."

"A woman's story?" asked Ellen, suddenly more interested.

"Yes, I suppose so. Nineteenth-century California was a man's country, and yet there were strong women here who made their own imprint. These women had many children; then many were widowed, and after a *Californio* husband, they often married a European or an American."

"Did all this information come from your ancestors' diary? I understand these diaries were stolen."

"Yes, and they are still missing. I do have a translated version. Also I own other journals written by Clarita's granddaughter, Isabel. My Grandmother Clara inherited it all, and she also took great delight in telling stories about Clarita's life. With her encouragement, I read a great many history books and majored in history at Stanford. Grandmother Clara wanted me to put my degrees in history to good use, so with her help I own a bookstore that sells rare and antique books."

"How did you come to own the original diaries?" Ellen asked Rita.

"Clara willed them to me." Rita stopped talking and looked at Mike before she continued. "You're finding out things about me. I thought you wanted to know something about the story?"

"I think you and the story go together. Besides, you said you wanted to be a consultant or have something to do with the production."

"That's right. Without me, it might be just a story like Zorro, without the sword fights."

"Mr. Stern why do you want to make a television production of the story?" Mike said, because he thought Rita might digress from her intention to find out his plans for the project.

"That's a good question. I'll take my turn at answering everything you want to know. And please call me Mel. Do you know these stories too, Mike?"

"Rita's Grandmother Clara was my great-aunt by marriage. Clara married into the Torelli family, who are part of the Minetti clan in Napa County. We all go to the same weddings and funerals. Everyone who knew Aunt Clara was given a recital of what was written in *The Carmelo Diaries*. She was masterful at storytelling. I'm familiar with the stories. Rita is passionate about the whole thing, and I support her all the way."

"That's great. What do you think about the *Diaries* being stolen? I understand the store was trashed and other books taken?" Mel turned to Rita.

"We are puzzled. And it's annoying and creepy." Rita said impulsively. "Many of the books have already been found in various cities, and they will be returned to us. As yet, *The Carmelo Diaries* haven't been found."

"Do you think they will be found?"

"I hope so. The local sheriff's office is investigating, and I'll let them do their job."

"And if they don't solve it?"

"The *Carmelo Diaries* are insured. I have a copy of them, and I feel that owning the diaries doesn't make any difference to my telling the story. The burglary gave me an incentive to write up the entire story," Rita said with enthusiasm.

"Is she always this positive?" Mel asked Mike.

"Yep, except when she isn't," Mike said, and they all laughed.

"When is it my turn to find out why you are interested in the story?" Rita said looking at Mel.

"Actually I first heard about it through Dave."

"Frankly, I wonder if you're interested in this because of Dave or whether you really think it has merits," Rita said.

"Probably both. I wanted to meet you to see if we could collaborate. What did Dave tell you?"

"We've only had a few conversations about making a documentary. Nothing definite. In fact I expected to be seeing him this week."

"He's a busy man. He spreads himself out pretty thin." Mel added

"And you?" Rita asked.

"You can see I'm more relaxed. I only do one project at a time. Ellen has worked as a nature photographer. Sometimes we work on projects together. I think we could film this story and have something special. The setting for a docudrama in this area is outstanding. Also I like the idea of telling an authentic story of how people's lives were affected by the sweep of history. After Dave told me that you no longer had *The Carmelo Diaries,* I wondered if you could continue it without them?"

"Now you can see that I'm capable of supplying you a full story."

"Do you look anything like your Clarita?" Mel asked with interest.

"We only have one portrait of her when she was around my age. Her husband, Will, found someone to paint her portrait, and I understand it always hung in the *sala* of the *hacienda* of Rancho Carmelo. It was partially burned and recopied later. It is quite a formal portrait, and she doesn't look like the lady who loved to ride horses and at times directed much of what went on at the ranch. It shows a lady with glossy brown hair parted in the middle and wound around her head. A black lace mantilla partially covers her hair. She is pictured with long earrings and a cross on a chain at her throat.

The artist painted her eyes a dark gray and made her complexion a pearly ivory."

"She was Spanish?"

"Both of her parents came to California from Spain. They were Castilians, whose ancestors were probably Iberians and Visigoths. I think my auburn hair comes from her Irish-American husband. The rest of my ancestors were English, German, and Italian. I'm a hybrid."

"Do you have any more questions?" Mel asked Rita.

"Oh lots. Do you think the burglary made any difference in Dave's plans?"

"He thinks the burglary might put you out of the picture. He envisions something entirely different than what I have in mind."

"Is yours longer or shorter?"

"I think it is something that could also be made into a video. When it is televised it could be shown in six episodes. I'd like to go beyond the time of the California Gold Rush. You said Clarita left Monterey for San Francisco in the 1850s. If this all goes well and you have the material to give me, we could include her life in San Francisco. We could even include the 1906 earthquake. If that's too much, we'll do it in two parts."

"Now you're dangling a carrot for me to follow."

"Sure. Think of how great this could be for your store and the California history business."

"Can we discuss the next step over food?" Ellen said impulsively."

"Maybe Rita wants to know more about Dave?" Mel put in.

"I think I know quite a bit about him now. I know that he's not the person for my project," Rita concluded.

"I understand there's a couple of restaurants in the Village. One called La Palma and another is Zen Pasta," Ellen said.

"Maybe Zen Pasta would be more in keeping with your spa regime," Mike suggested. "I haven't been to the place yet, but I hear it's good. Everything's fresh and organic."

"Let's try it then," Ellen agreed. "Tell us how to get there."

"It's just past Los Laureles Grade," Mike told them. "Do you know where that is?"

"I saw it last afternoon when we were driving around," Mel said and they left separately.

Rita knew the drive was an opportunity to hear what Mike thought about the whole situation. As soon as they drove down the hill to the Valley road, Mike spoke. "Babe, you're coming to a point where you need to make some definite decisions. Remember you have a business to run, and you no longer have Tessa to help you. Do you really want to see your diaries made into a T.V. series?"

"The answer to that question is, yes. I have ideas about who can manage the shop, and I'm all for doing something new," Rita said with conviction. "I'm ready to tell a story about all the generations of my family in California."

"Do you want to have the Sterns take it over?"

"Yes, I think they are qualified. I like them. Was I too impulsive? I need your feedback. Do I need more time to think about all this?" Before he could answer, she said, "I do know I'm not going to work with Dave Goldman. I have a feeling he plans to meet with Charlie sometime this week."

"Why do you say that?"

"It all adds up. It suits both of them," Rita said.

"You know both of them better than I do," Mike concluded.

"Do you really think I'm taking on too much?"

"If you get Dolores to work at The Booktique full-time and you keep us from having any more togetherness meals with Charlie and Missy, I'll be happy."

"You drive a hard bargain."

"Are you going to say anything about this to Captain Lewis?" Mike asked.

"No. Let's not say anything to anybody. Let's wait and see how it plays out. I think we're going to hear more from Tessa."

"Here we are. Would you mind if we needed to go to South while we work with the Sterns?"

"Hell no. I'm going to sell the Rojas a five million dollar house. I can take off a few months and just enjoy being with you and Carmelita."

"I think we'll know what we want to do after we're with the Sterns a little longer," Rita concluded. Mike nodded as they pulled into the parking lot of The Zen Pasta.

CHAPTER 27

▼

The Sterns and the Minettis arrived at the restaurant within minutes of each other and they walked together to the entrance of a rustic stone house. Wandering red bougainvillea flowers surrounded the open doorway, and near by the name Zen Pasta was painted on a discreet sign hanging from a large bamboo pole. After they were seated, and had time to leisurely study the menu, Mel asked the waiter about the ingredients in the pizza sampler.

"We can make a sampler combination with almost everything we serve, or you can choose three different kinds of small pizzas in the vegetable category." came the answer.

They decided on a Venetian fish soup, a vegetable pizza combination of portabella mushroom, dried tomato and basil, and a Japanese noodle dish. Mel had noticed that Rita had brought a zippered black notebook into the restaurant." Did you bring something for me to look over?" he asked Rita.

"Just a draft that I wrote up last night," she said.

"By the way do you have a working copy of *The Carmelo Diaries*?" Ellen said from across the table.

"At our house."

"We would like to see it. Also, we hoped that you could show us the location of the ranch you described to me last week when we first talked on the phone."

"You mean the place where Rancho Carmelo used to be. There is nothing left of it now. We know from our sources that at one time Rancho Carmelo extended for several miles in each direction of the flood plane of the Carmel River. It included the gentle hills that surround the Carmel River. Are you familiar with Monterey and Carmel, Mel?"

"We've stayed at The Retreat at Pebble Beach several times, but I really wouldn't say we are familiar with The Valley."

"Then you are in for a treat," Rita exclaimed happily.

"I bet you wonder what kind of jokers we are. We really don't know the area, and yet we are interested in producing a television series about this area." Mel laughed.

"Then we'd like to show you around a little," offered Mike.

"Good. We already agree on important things. And I'm glad to see you are involved in this too, Mike," Mel said.

"I'll even be your chauffeur," Mike continued.

"I think this project will start to take form, soon. Mel said with conviction "Before we go back to L.A., we might be able to make some decisions."

"Do you want to look at the countryside or visit old historic adobes?"

"First the scenic, the photogenic, the unique. We can visit a house or two, but you know, we have old adobes in Southern California."

They eagerly ate the freshly prepared food and talked about how the weather might affect the next day of tournament play.

"It's going to clear," Rita said jauntily.

"Oh, and how do you know?" asked Ellen.

"We have our own informal way of predicting a storm. We do it by looking at the direction of the wind from the sea," Rita offered.

"We'll have some sun soon. Let's drive around together this afternoon. Then you can take in the tournament or whatever you want to do tomorrow," Mike suggested.

"Then we should go back to the hotel and leave our car. It'll be easier if you take us to see some of these places," Ellen suggested.

After the Sterns parked their car, they all drove back to Carmel in Mike's roomy Mercedes sedan. "To your left is the Carmel River," Mike said. "It's a respectable running river only in the winter. When they mapped Rancho Carmelo, they used the river as a point of reference. It flows towards the ocean. Rita tells me that the Rancho Carmelo included land on both sides of the river."

Rita continued. "The ranch *hacienda* and ranch buildings were built on the north side of the river, within walking distance of the Mission San Cárlos Everyone on the ranch went to the Mission for mass. The neophyte Indians walked and the family rode horses. Don Bernardo enjoyed his association with the Spanish fathers who were in charge of the mission.

"The Mission is still in use today, isn't it?" Ellen asked.

"Very much," Mike agreed. "We attend mass there. The Basilica is also used for concerts and non-catholic choral groups"

"But not at the time Clarita inherited Rancho Carmelo, "Rita hastened to add. The Mexican government closed the Mission and it was literally abandoned. Everyone left. People even took the roof tiles for their own houses. Others took anything they could find since building materials were scarce. There are old walls in Monterey made from the stones, and tiles of the Mission."

"That's hard to believe. It looks quite beautiful today," Ellen said.

"It was slowly reconstructed sometime after the American Civil War, when the mission properties were given back to the church." Mike told them. "It assumed the look it has today sometime in the nineteen forties."

"So you know the history of this Mission also? Ellen said to Mike.

"It is our parish church. It's really quite authentic. A man named Harry Downie made the restoration his life's work."

"Will you allow us to look over all that you have written?" Mel asked.

"After we take a look at the Mission, we can swing by our house and pick up what I have finished. Of course, you realize I consider my writing to be just a rough draft," Rita said apologetically.

They left the green rolling hills of the river valley and entered a suburban environment on a road through a shopping center of disparate one-story buildings and stores.

"Anywhere U.S.A." Rita announced.

"Do you want to stop at the Mission?" Mike asked.

"That depends on how much time we have," Mel said thoughtfully. "Now that we know where the sights are, we can always come back on our own."

They approached the Mission San Carlos, its sturdy basilica and prominent bell tower. It was built in a primitive Romanesque style and the basilica is set apart from the surrounding walls and garden.

"Some of the walls are original," explained Rita. "There has been a great deal of excavation done around here. From the Spanish records, we know a great deal about how it was built."

The parking lot in front was filled with cars and tour busses, and Mike and Mel agreed it was not the time to go inside. Mike drove around to the next street at the rear of the church where other mission buildings stood.

"There is a huge interior courtyard at one side of the church. It is still used for large gatherings and church *fiestas*. In the missionary days there were blacksmith and carpenter shops, dormitories, and other community rooms inside the court-yard," Rita said.

"And did your Clarita come here often?" Ellen asked.

"Almost every day when she was growing up. Later when she lived in Monterey, she went to the San Cárlos Chapel for mass with the other colonists."

Mike turned onto Dolores Street. "We're officially in the town of Carmel now. Let's drop by our house. We can pick up the material Rita wants you to look over."

"Maybe you'd like to come in," Rita invited.

Rita and Mike lived in a two-story house built in what is known as the Monterey style, which is a combination of New England and California. It was built of stucco with dark wood trimming with an overhanging roof on the sec-ond-story. Mission style red clay tiles covered the roof. A sprawling aged Cypress dominated the front area that was mostly brick paving and raised flowerbeds.

"You can freshen up and relax while I go up to my office. I'll bring you what I have. However, I need to warn you, we have a young daughter, and she plays all over the house on a rainy day."

"I'll get us some water. You must be thirsty," Mike offered.

"Mel and Ellen sat in a room that had an eclectic mixture of heirloom tables with bouquets of flowers, a large, comfortable leather chair and ottoman, and Carmelita's toys.

"These are likable people, and Rita is truly enthusiastic. I think whatever they tell us is authentic even if they don't have the original diaries," said Ellen.

"We've been wanting to do a project together," Mel agreed. "There could be a lot of good photography shots around here, and with her story as a basis, we might even want to make it a fiction one."

"Let's see what the real Clarita turns out to be like," Ellen commented.

Rita returned with her diary translations, notebooks, and her own latest addi-tions to the story. "I'll explain what I can before Marquita brings Carmelita back from a walk. Then you can take some of the material and read it at your leisure."

Mel glanced at the photocopied pages gathered into a binder. "You say these are the translations of *The Carmelo Diaries* that were stolen?"

"Yes, my grandmother had this done quite a long time ago by one of the teachers at Monterey Institute of Foreign Studies. It isn't exactly literature. At times it's pretty literal. The translator included some of the Spanish words because my grandmother thought it gave more flavor. Since you're from Califor-nia, you are probably familiar with Spanish words."

"Does anyone else have this translation?"

"I don't know for sure. I don't think anyone else has really cared about it. If the original *Carmelo Diaries* are returned, I plan to have them translated again."

"I think I'll look at what you have written. You say your material is from stories that your grandmother told you and also a diary of Clarita's granddaughter?"

"That's right. Isabel's journals are written in English. Here is also a wedding photograph of Isabel. You can see she was very pretty. It is said she had dark brown eyes, blonde hair that was tinged with gold and a pearly complexion. She had a tiny waist that was so important then. She captured the heart of Edward Butler Shaw. He was a wealthy gentleman who made a fortune in shipping and finance. After they were married in 1885, they led an active social life in San Francisco They often spent time in Europe during the summer. When Clarita was widowed, Isabel insisted that she live with them. Isabel wrote the reminiscences of Clarita and Isabel gathered her notebook material from their many conversations."

"Do you have copies of this?" Mel wanted to know.

Rita nodded.

"I've already decided that we want to develop the project. How comfortable are you if we make any changes?" Mel wanted to know.

"What sort of changes?" Mike said when he heard the word, 'changes.' He was just returning to the room with bottles of Evian and Perrier water.

"Nothing that violates the historical integrity, but we might want to add a fictional character or two, if we decide to go that way," Mel explained.

"Wait until you have read both the early Spanish diaries and what I have written," Rita said empathically.

"There will need to be that option in our contract," Mel said.

"If it seems consistent with the story, I will consider it," Rita consented.

"Now there are a few other places where I would like to go. Could you drive us to Monterey, Mike?" Mel proposed.

"I don't know how long you plan to stay on the peninsula, so I'll give you my abbreviated tour," Mike offered. Rita phoned Marquita to give her a choice of activities for Carmelita's afternoon and they all climbed into the Mercedes.

"Please first take us to where the sailing ships arrived and to the Monterey Custom House. I understand you have a *Presidio*. Is it near the shore?" Ellen asked.

"The building called the *Presidio* today belongs to the U.S. Army," Mike explained. "It isn't in the same location as the original and historic one. That one was located near where the San Cárlos Church is found today. The first *presidio* was a stockade of wood and adobe and housed soldiers, their families, and it housed the governor. Nothing remains of it today. We only know what it was like because of some excavations made in the 1970s."

"Since I'm good at reading in the car, I'll look over your story as we go. It's a way to save some time," Mel told them.

"What about the Custom House?" Ellen asked.

"We're headed there now. It's near the shore of Monterey Bay and is part of a State Historic Park that includes several restored buildings."

"Sounds good. Something we can see and use to visualize the past." Ellen agreed.

Mel grew quiet as he read pages from the translated diary, and at one point, he exclaimed, "It sounds like a hard place for the women to live."

They arrived at Monterey by way of Pacific Street. Mike drove around the block where the Larkin house was situated and pointed out various adobes that belonged to people whose names Mel would soon recognize.

With her Leica camera, Ellen snapped pictures out the window. Rita and Mike said very little. Soon Mike entered the big municipal parking lot near Fishermen's Wharf. He parked the car as they eagerly began looking at the wharf. There were visitors in town for the golf tournament enjoying the pleasant turn of weather and many became sightseers crowded near the Custom House Plaza.

"This area was quite a hub of activity in the Mexican era," Rita offered. "Monterey was the capitol of the Spanish colony, and there was always a custom house here. It was important for Spain to impose import duties."

"Is this the original building?" Ellen asked as they proceeded to walk toward it.

"Each new structure was built on the original site."

"Was this one built during the Mexican era?" Ellen continued.

"Yes. The Mexican government encouraged trade because of the revenues it brought to the government. The present building was originally constructed in 1841 when the harbor shoreline came to the edge of the building. Thomas O. Larkin contracted to build it and Will O'Farrell might have supervised the construction.

The Sterns and the Minettis paid admission at the door, looked into the furnished rooms, then walked through a large storeroom that contained a varied assortment of items from stiff cowhides to bottles of French wine, wooden bird cages and even a ten-foot saw hung from the ceiling.

"The middle section of the building was the social center where Monterey's important people held their dances. The music was provided by military bands from the visiting ships," Rita said.

"That would make a good scene for social action," Mel said to Ellen. "And what about your ancestors? Did Clarita and Will dance here?"

"Undoubtedly, because dancing was a very important pastime in early California. It gave the people an opportunity to dress up. The ladies wore colorful skirts and shawls and on their feet they wore silk shoes from Paris. The men were equally resplendent in short velvet jackets, embroidered shirts, and red sashes."

Ellen was taking notes, and both Mel and Ellen nodded in agreement.

"When can we see you again?" Mel asked Rita.

"Tomorrow would be fine. We are invited to an informal lunch at a home situated on the eighteenth fairway of the Pebble Beach golf links. It's an informal party. The hosts are very good friends of ours. You'll be welcome to come as our guests. I'll telephone your names to the security headquarters at the Pebble Beach gate."

"Sounds interesting. I'll bring a preliminary proposal. Don't talk to Dave if he calls. He'll want to worm information out of you," Mel said.

When they parted, the Sterns promised to call to finalize plans the next morning.

"I think it went well," Rita said to Mike as they drove home. "I like them both. They're not afraid of enthusiasm."

CHAPTER 28

▼

February 4, 2000

Rita was accustomed to waking up in the dark at this time of the year. This morning she awoke to daylight, and the first things she saw as Mike, who was dressed and putting on a tie. The clock said seven-thirty.

"Wow, I overslept," she exclaimed. "Is Carmelita up and everything?"

"And everything. She's not dressed yet, though. That's your department."

"I must have stayed up too late reading Isabel's journals. I'm still a little groggy. And I need to be at The Old Booktique early."

"I'm going over to the office. I want to get the Roja paper work started before my first client comes in. Meet you at the party at noon, Babe. I'll call Stern and give him more detailed directions concerning getting to the party today," Mike continued.

"Why not meet me at the shop? It's easy to find, and I already told Ellen where it's located," Rita suggested.

"Good idea. If there are any changes I'll give you a mid-morning call. Now I'm on my way." He came over and gave her a kiss.

Rita abbreviated all her morning routines and dressed Carmelita for her Friday playgroup. It was a neighborhood gathering of two-years-olds who played together in supervised games with a teacher. Mothers rotated duties such as bringing mid-morning snacks and helping with activities. Rita dropped Carmelita off, and Marquita picked her up, unless it was Rita's turn to help.

The sun was almost blinding as it climbed higher, and the prospect of fair weather put Rita in a good mood. Cars were already lining up at the Pebble Beach tollgate, and because of yesterday's delay in play, it promised to be a record attendance day. Rita found everything in order at The Old Booktique, and she silently blessed the presence of Dolores, who promised to help at the store for at least two weeks. Then she listened to her office voice mail.

First, there was a brief message from Tessa. "I really like Scottsdale. The job is a little boring."

Then there was a message from Captain Lewis. "Please call me about a short appointment." A second message from him said, "I'll be at The Booktique on Friday at ten o'clock for a few questions."

"The preview of the San Francisco Book Auction will be February 18th at the Mosconi center," came an unknown voice.

There was only time for a short conference with Dolores as many customers were now arriving, and the store was filled with people. Dolores helped some of them find the books they specified, while the others seemed content to peruse the selections placed on the big table by the side window.

Rita was startled to see Captain Lewis standing nearby at the table devoted to books about the California Gold Rush.

"Your autographed copy of *Life on the Mississippi* was found yesterday in Sacramento," he said. "Tessa still not back?"

"No. And I don't know anymore than that." Rita shrugged her shoulders. "Tessa told me she wanted to give it a try."

"Is there any place you and I can talk privately?"

"Not here. The store is full."

"How about stepping outside with me and walking over to look at the names on the AT&T tournament Hall of Fame?"

"Sure. I'll tell Dolores that I'm going out for a few minutes. I can't believe all these customers."

They went out the side door in the direction of the golf pro shop and stopped near a large bronze roster with the names of those who had won the tournament in all of the past years.

"How well do you know Tessa?" Captain Lewis asked her.

"Heavens, since high school. We both went to Santa Lucia School in Monterey. She was a boarding student and often came home with me on weekends."

"I thought you said something like that. Don't you think it's a little strange she suddenly moved away and took another job?"

"A little unusual, yes, but Tessa doesn't have any ties or career plans here in Pebble Beach."

"I told her not to leave while the investigation was going on," Captain Lewis informed Rita.

"Is she critical to your case?"

"No. Probably not. However, just think about the part she could have played. You left The Old Booktique at three in the afternoon on the day before the burglary. She was the one who closed up. She was the last one in the shop."

"That is what she's supposed to do. She closes up. I went home to be with Carmelita about three o'clock," Rita explained. "You told me that our fingerprints were all over the place and that is normal for people who work in the shop."

"Yes, of course that makes sense. And certainly her fingerprints were everywhere as well as yours." The captain paused. "I am following up on everything."

"I'll be glad to cooperate. Just not today," Rita said earnestly.

"Is your store going to be open tomorrow?"

"At first, I thought I might close, but if it's like today I intend to be open all day. I am really delighted with all the customers. Any sales will make up for the days we lost after the burglary."

"Good, then I'll drop by around eleven. You might be thinking about any conversations you've had with Tessa in the last few weeks. Does she have any new boyfriends? Did something upset her? She doesn't know anybody in Scottsdale, does she?"

"I don't think so. But I told you she doesn't have anything to tie her down here. Maybe she's tired of the rainy weather."

"Well, you've narrowed it down a bit. I've been doing some checking, and I may have some new answers tomorrow. I am planning to ask your mother a few more questions."

"Good God, you don't think she had anything to do with it, do you?"

He shook his head and said, "It's not quite like that."

"She certainly wouldn't mind talking to you. She said you were nice to her. But with Mother, be sure to use your best manners. Make an appointment. Don't just barge in," Rita paused. "Why am I giving you advice? I guess for my mother's sake. She sort of lives in another world."

"My visit wouldn't be for interrogation. I just want to sound her out about a few things. She's lived around here for a long time. Is she as connected to the *Carmelo Diaries* as you are?"

"No, she tells me that I'm obsessed with *The Carmelo Diaries*. But we've always had different interests."

"Then I'll see you at eleven. Tomorrow," he said.

Rita nodded, and they both walked off in different directions.

"I can hardly wait," Rita grumbled to herself as she entered her shop.

There was no time to ponder about what Captain Lewis had said. As soon as she entered the door, she was busy with customers. She answered questions about the authenticity of her autographed copies and found some rare books listed in several auction inventories.

"We're early," she heard Ellen's voice. "Are you always this busy?"

"Not usually during tournament time. But then with all these concession tents and the carnival atmosphere, everyone seems to be in a buying mood," she answered.

"Do you have your books displayed by topics?" Mel asked.

"They start out that way at the beginning of the day. Often some one lays down a book as soon as another one meets the eye. The books migrate."

"Do you have anything on the early motion picture industry in California?" Mel continued.

"You would ask for something I don't have. Over the years there has been any number of films made around here, particularly in Pacific Grove and Point Lobos, and we might find a book showing old photographs of those times. I'll research it for you, if you like."

"It was just an idea. You go on with your customers. Ellen and I will browse here, maybe walk outside a little, and when Mike comes, we'll carry you off."

At noon, nearly all the customers were gone. Rita talked to Dolores about how they would manage the shop during the afternoon. "Mike and I are going to a party over at the Milton house. It's near The Retreat. Not far at all. You can reach me on the cell phone if something special comes up. No matter what happens, I'll be back in an hour and a half. You can have the rest of the afternoon off."

"It's such a beautiful day. Maybe I'll just walk around and watch people," Dolores commented.

"If you do that, remember to wear one of those special badges in plain sight. Otherwise, a volunteer will stop you and ask you to buy an entry ticket. Tomorrow, I'll make other arrangements for us."

Rita went into the small private powder room and changed from her sweater to a simple white silk blouse. She slid into a forest green leather jacket that would keep her warm and put on walking shoes. After peering at herself in the mirror, she applied a little gloss to her lips and ran a brush through her hair.

Mel, Ellen, and Mike were waiting just outside the shop, and together they took a shortcut through The Retreat guest parking lot to their destination. The crowds were in a holiday mood. Yesterday's weather and the cancellation of play only served to heighten the level of anticipation and excitement of today's spectators.

This was the first day of official scores and all the players, and their spectator followers had high hopes. Mike knew Bill and Betsy Milton well and had attended their porch parties since the years when the tournament was affectionately known as' The Crosby.' The Miltons greeted the Minettis heartily and made the Sterns welcome also. Betsy also told Rita she was sorry to hear about the burglary at The Old Booktique. As others were arriving, they quickly made their way toward a wide verandah that stretched the length of the house. It had a sweeping view of the famous eighteenth fairway that sloped toward the turbulent waters of the cove. Beyond this, lay Point Lobos and a panoramic view of ocean waves with white caps.

"I've always wondered what it was like to be a spectator from a place like this," Ellen said as she let her eyes follow the players. "Here we are at a private home on this famous golf course. This is quite a privilege. And what a sunny day. Sorry to take you away from selling houses, Mike."

"There isn't anywhere else I'd rather be. Life is to enjoy when you can," Mike said. He glanced at Rita, and when she smiled at him, she could see satisfaction in his eyes.

"We're glad you can be with us," Rita added. She could be relaxed at this informal party, and she watched the Milton granddaughters playing a game with a soft plastic ball on the lawn in front of the porch. Guests of all ages were enjoying themselves.

"Betsy always expects her friends to help themselves to the food. You'll see tables set up soon, and there will be everything you'd want to eat from grazing food to fried chicken and potato salad. A little later they'll roll out a cart, and someone will serve Italian gelato and frozen yogurt in cones. The foods are the same every year and nothing could taste better," said Rita.

"And where is this Stonecrest that you refer to in your story. Can I see it from here?" Mel wanted to know.

"Take your binoculars and look right over there," Rita said while guiding his hand. "At the edge of the cove you'll see a high stone wall and the upper story of a large house. That's it."

"And you grew up there? That's pretty-high class," Mel laughed.

"For everybody but me. I was rather like the family pet that was kept for amusement, but under strict orders to be clever, entertaining, and obedient. I always enjoyed going to some other house where I could be sweaty and loud and have adventures."

"Just goes to show that we're never satisfied. You came out all right, though," Mike said as he gave Rita a playful nudge.

"We'll just walk out on the lawn and look up and down the fairway," said Mel and he took Ellen with him. "I can see a golf team coming with a whole gang of followers." Mel was excited

"Is there anyone in particular you want to see at the party?" Rita asked Mike.

"Oh, I might just mingle a little. I'll say some hellos around, you know," he answered. "But tell me what our dear police captain said. Is he still circling around us like a vulture?"

"He seemed annoyed that Tessa went to Arizona. He said he wants to talk to her. He also said he's going to talk to Mother again, and he insisted on making an appointment with me tomorrow. What do you think he has in mind?"

"Maybe he thinks the burglary is faked. What proof is there that *The Carmelo Diaries* were really in the safe?"

"I never thought of that," Rita said with surprise. "Well, it's absurd."

"Maybe he thinks you wanted publicity for your business."

"You just ruined a perfectly splendid afternoon. Don't say any more, Mike," Rita said scowling but with a half-smile on her face.

"You asked and I just gave you the worse case scenario," Mike said honestly. "You're right. Let's enjoy ourselves. This is such a comfortable party, and look at the Sterns. They're having a good time."

Mike was quickly part of a group where they all knew one another. Rita talked to Betsy's daughter, who lived in San Francisco and always came for the event. In little while, Ellen found Rita and talked about taking pictures of the golf course next week when the tournament was finished.

"I told Dolores I'd be back in an hour and a half. I think I'll go back now. Then I can be back for the lunch," Rita told Ellen.

"Shall I find us a table?"

"That would be great. Some of the most famous players are scheduled to pass by here soon. The fun is just starting. I'll tell Mike to look for you," Rita concluded.

Mike was easy to find. He always had a congenial group around him. "Everything's going so well with the Sterns," she whispered. "Ellen's over there at that table with the red-striped umbrella, so please don't let her stay alone too long. She's already enthused about taking pictures of the scenery and the golf course next week. Mel is out there standing against the ropes on the lawn."

Rita walked over to Betsy. "It's always a treat to be here. I'm going back to the shop to close up. I'll be back soon," she said.

"Come hungry," Betsy called.

When she returned to the shop, Rita collected several cryptic messages from Captain Lewis and Dave Goldman. There was a short "Hello, and I'll call again," from Tessa. Dolores was delighted that she could spend the sunny afternoon in the fresh air. She agreed to come to work tomorrow, even though it was Saturday morning.

"I really enjoy being with people who have a passionate interest in rare books," she commented. "And they always tell me a story of why they want a particular book. I wish I could work for you permanently, but I do have commitments right now. Have you been looking for a permanent assistant?"

"Not yet," said Rita truthfully. "There's been too much going on. Tessa left at the worst possible time. I don't know what I would have done without you. I know it sounds cliché, but you know I really mean it," and Rita put her arm around her shoulder.

"You'll be able to manage once the AT&T is over," Dolores consoled.

"And after the investigation is over," Rita added. They both left the shop at the same time.

Rita found Mel and Ellen at the designated table, and Mike soon arrived with two more plates of food.

"It must be the sea air that makes me so hungry," said Ellen in between bites of chicken breast and deviled egg.

"Are you free the rest of the day?" Mel asked Rita.

"I'm playing hooky from myself."

"Did you bring me any more material to look over?"

"If you're really interested, you can stop by our house, and we can go over some material together," Rita said quickly.

"I might as well come out with what we've decided. After I talked to Dave this morning, I decided to move fast. I'm ready to make you an offer."

"Can you tell me more about it?" Rita exclaimed.

"We want to do this thing for the Biography Channel. I'll interview you several times and make you a part of the show. It helps that you're good-looking. We think you have a good speaking voice, too. We'll do lots of photographing around here, and make it all very real and authentic. How does that sound to you?"

"Really wonderful. What does Dave have to do with it?"

"I told you. We're friendly rivals. He thinks we don't have a story yet, and I know we do. So I want to move while we're on top of it. I want you to come down to Beverly Hills next week and bring everything you have to contribute to the project. We'll take it up to the era of the Gold Rush. If you have more information that is significant to history and your family, we'll take it farther."

Rita's head was full of questions, and she was just about to pour them out when she looked at Mike. "I'm all for it," he said. "Of course, it's Rita's call, and she can think it over if she wants."

"Dave must have really pushed your buttons," Rita said smiling.

"Not really. I just know when he's bluffing. He's someone who'll take the offensive position unless you're ready to call him on it. That's why I want to go ahead now."

"Come on, Mel. Let's go get some gelato and see if that big crowd is following Tiger Woods. You promised you wouldn't talk business all the time," Ellen coaxed.

"You still haven't said you are with us, Rita," Mel said looking directly at her.

"Then the answer is 'yes,'" she said throwing up her hands. "And all the details will work out," she added.

"Ellen's right. Let's go get some gelato," Mike agreed.

"I'm still worried about the burglary thing," Rita softly confided to Mike as they walked across the Milton lawn toward the roped-off area near the golf cart path.

"That's what you have me for, Babe. If somebody's trying to intimidate you, it's not going to work," Mike said and he squeezed her hand.

For the next half-hour they ate gelato and watched golf with the rest of the Milton guests. As predicted, an excited parade followed the most popular Pro Am team on this first day of play. The excitement was contagious, and when they posted the score for the round and the score for eighteenth hole, a loud cheer could be heard from the crowd that had gathered on the ocean side of the hotel.

"Shall we go over to the Divot Dive and have a drink to celebrate our pact?" Mel suggested.

"It's too busy and noisy there now. I just happen to have a bottle of Dom Ruinart '88 champagne on ice at The Old Booktique. It's even better than Dom Perignon," Rita invited.

"We accept," said Mel and Ellen.

Early evening shadows were beginning to slant across the golf course as they walked toward the shop. When they sat down in anticipation of enjoying the rare vintage, Rita drew the blinds a little. She kept four Waterford fluted glasses chilled in the little refrigerator of the kitchenette.

"Well, it seems I don't have that bottle," she said with a shrug. "We'll have to do with Dom Perignon, after all." She wrapped the bottle in a linen towel and handed it to Mike for opening. She opened a box of savory cocktail biscuits, and the group was ready for a taste of the clear and precise sting of heavenly bubbles.

"To us," said Mike as he carefully eased the stubborn cork and poured the pale amber liquid into the glasses.

They had each taken a sip when the telephone rang. "I'm taking the afternoon off," Rita announced. She knew the message would be recorded on her voice mail. After they finished the bottle, they again verified the time of their next appointment. It was to be early afternoon tomorrow at the home of the Minettis. The Sterns left and walked toward The Retreat.

"Before we go home, Mike, I want to hear what's on my voice mail," Rita said.

"The crowd will have thinned out more by then, anyway" he said as he went over to a table and examined some of the books.

Rita listened to her messages.

"Rita, I want to remind you again that we are all having dinner together next Monday before we leave for Napa. Oh yes, this is Missy of course. Don't call back. Charles and I are incognito tonight," she finished in a well-modulated, high-pitched voice.

Next came a plaintive voice that she recognized as belonging to Tessa in one of her moods. "Rita, where are you when I need you?"

"This is Captain Lewis. You and I don't need to meet tomorrow. I decided to subpoena Tessa, and she will be back in California this weekend."

"Mike, I want you to listen to these messages with me," Rita called. She replayed the tape and when the words were repeated, they sounded less ominous. "It's the next chapter, isn't it?" she said to Mike. "I'm glad that I have Dolores to help me next week."

CHAPTER 29

▼

February 5, 2000

Since it was Saturday, Mike planned to stay home with Carmelita. Rita asked Amy, who lived next door, to play with Carmelita in the backyard while the Sterns were at the house in the afternoon. Hoping to avoid traffic into Pebble Beach, Rita left early for The Old Booktique. Spectators were beginning to trudge along the cart paths, while others were staking out a viewing position for themselves. It was already promising to be a busy day at Pebble Beach Golf Links. Almost as soon as Rita arrived at the shop, she saw Captain Lewis approaching.

"Glad you're here alone," Captain Lewis began. "I enjoyed talking to your mother again. She was most helpful. She said she had known Tessa for a long time. She told me that Tessa's father was a career diplomat with the U.S. State Department. She said he had been in charge of consulates and embassies. all over the world. Tessa lived in many exotic places while she was growing up. Does Tessa know everyone in your family?"

"I doubt if she knows my father."

"Your brother?"

"Of course."

"Why do you say that? You told me that he was older than you."

"Tessa often stayed at Stonecrest with us during school vacations. We were best friends when we were students at Santa Lucia."

"Was Tessa a friend of your brother's?"

"I guess so."

"Oh, I remember now. You don't see much of your brother anymore."

"Our paths don't cross."

"Your brother stayed at the Retreat for The Vintner's Conference last week. Did you see him then?"

"Yes, I did. Mother had us all to dinner while he was here."

"I know your store is now open, but I'd like to go over some ideas with you." Rita led the way to a table on which there was a magnifying glass and some vintage maps. Lewis drew up a chair for himself.

"Did your brother see Tessa when he came to the conference?"

"It's a small world around here, and since The Booktique is across the putting green from the hotel, it's possible he stopped by the store."

"I mean, did they meet for a drink or something else?"

"They could have done so, but I can't give you a definite answer."

"I thought she might have mentioned it to you."

"Since Grandmother Clara's funeral, Charles has not been at the top of my list for a conversation."

"Tessa told me she saw your brother."

"Then you already know."

"And it was the day before the burglary."

"So?"

"You're a hard person to talk to. I think you are holding something back."

"Where did you get your information about this?"

"I asked around at the Divot Dive, and one of the waiters said Tessa and Mr. Atherton were together having drinks the night before the burglary. He said they stayed quite late. He said he saw them every night of the Vintner's Conference. I thought she might have confided in you."

"She knows how I feel about Charlie."

"I think Tessa's activities are something we should investigate, don't you?"

"This sounds like an investigation into Tessa's personal life. Do you usually do this for every case?"

"Sometimes I do. Your brother's wife hired a detective to find out what he was doing during the last few months. What do you know about that?"

"Missy and Charles have been separated for awhile. However, they are staying together at Pebble Beach this week. There is hope for a reconciliation."

"Yes, your mother told me that, too. She's happy about it. Are you?"

"Do you know what I'm going to say now?" Rita stopped, as Captain Lewis bent forward "I won't answer any more questions unless they are directly related to the burglary," she said emphatically.

"I think this is related. When we gathered fingerprints right after the crime, we were puzzled that there were so many of Mr. Atherton's fingerprints at The Booktique."

"You never mentioned it before."

"I wanted things to play out a little more. When Tessa suddenly went to Arizona, I figured that she and your brother were playing around, and you wanted her out of your life, hm?"

"That is preposterous," Rita said with disgust. "Don't you have somewhere else to go? I have a business to run. I purposely came here early to get ready for customers. You left a message that you didn't need to see me, and yet here you are. Your message said you had subpoenaed Tessa."

"Yes. I figured that was the best way to talk to her."

"OK, then I don't need to be questioned anymore."

Captain Lewis gave her a sheepish little grin and shrugged his shoulders. "You can't blame a guy for trying. I was really planning to put the case aside for a while. Then I got a lead from the bartender that led me to believe Tessa and your brother knew each other pretty well. I thought you might give me some tips on how best to talk to her about this."

"I'm the wrong person for that."

"Rita, you really are a difficult person. Life has been good to you. What are you guarding? Why should you be so careful about your answers? You could take a lesson from your friend, Tessa. She is more spontaneous," he finished.

Rita was not sure if she wanted to defend herself. Although she wanted to ask him if he had contacted Dave Goldman, she thought better of it. "Let's both of us stick to our own business," she said in an acerbic tone.

"You're on the defensive now," he laughed, and she waved to Dolores who was coming up the path to the store.

"Just in time for a rescue," she greeted her. Rita realized that Captain Lewis was more complicated than he had first appeared. She thought it wise to end the converstation. "You'd better go now. Here come some customers."

"Then I'll give you an assignment. Find out what Tessa and your brother were doing at the shop the night before the break-in. If you can't do that for me, I'll begin to wonder whether this whole thing is rigged up so you could make an insurance claim or just to get publicity."

"We're going to be busy this morning. I can feel it," Rita said turning to Dolores and away from Captain Lewis. She walked towards her desk in the back of the shop and then came back to Dolores after the captain left.

"I'm going to help you out here until you find a permanent assistant," Dolores said. "You are under a great deal of pressure right now. I was a little stressed out yesterday myself. I'm not used to crowds, but after a good night's sleep, I decided to see you through until things return to normal."

Rita immediately went over to where Dolores stood and put her arms around her friend. "That's the best thing I have heard for several days. Frankly, I don't know what's going on with Tessa. Captain Lewis just paid me a call. He told me he subpoenaed Tessa. She had to come to Monterey this weekend, because he wants to ask her more questions. A few days ago he told me that he was going to shelve the case for lack of information. I think he's using this interrogation for his own purposes."

"It's an imperfect world," Dolores laughed. "Frankly I like being here. I enjoy the variety of customers However, I have my own commitments too."

"I really appreciate what you have done here. The tournament has made the place a zoo. We'll close at two. We'll both avoid the traffic if we go home at that time. I need to get back to Mike and Carmelita. The Sterns are coming over to the house at three."

After Dolores finished with a customer, she consulted Rita. "What do think about putting the early edition of Mark Twain's *Roughing It* in the locked vitrine near the window? It's sure to attract attention. I'll print up a small card about it. Also I saw a Bernard De Voto book on one of your tables That should be in evidence. I overheard a lively discussion about the book on public television."

"Which brings me to something you do best," Rita agreed enthusiastically. She unlocked the vitrine and placed Twain's book, on a shelf that displayed antique bifocals with round metal frames. "I'd like to have a monthly teatime discussion of different topics gleaned from California writers. We could use an historical viewpoint. We could host a discussion about California from a modern and sociologic point of view."

"And," said Dolores who stopped straightening a small bookshelf and cocked her head toward Rita.

"I want you to be the moderator. You can even choose the topics, and we'll have a book special on any book we sell. How about it?"

"I think I could try it. We'll talk about it when "She looked towards the door, "Here comes a customer," and she greeted a slender woman who wore a tweed coat at least one size too large. She had a red, beige, and white Burberry plaid cashmere scarf wrapped around her head. It appeared that her hair was wet underneath the scarf.

"I made my escape this morning and went swimming," she said. "While the others are walking the course behind the leaders, I've decided to have the day to myself." She sat down at the table and glanced through some special editions of Harriet Beecher Stowe's *Uncle Tom's Cabin* and Charles Dana's *Two year's Before the Mast*.

"Did you have any particular book or place in mind?" Dolores asked.

"Something that is putting forth a partisan point of view," the customer said. "Frankly I don't care who it favors. It could be about the Franciscan missionaries or John C. Frémont. Personally I care about these things, but I like to own books and diaries with a biased point of view. I use those kinds of books to gather different points of view. The truth in one era can be dead wrong at some other time."

"Then you'll enjoy our small collection of nineteenth-century geography and history books," Rita said as she brought out a worn leather-bound book that was no larger than an eyeglass case. "This one was written during the presidency of Andrew Jackson and lists at least twenty-three kings as sovereigns of their countries in Europe."

"Is this for sale?" said the customer holding up a small, embroidered red Chinese shawl that Rita had arranged near a book about Spanish place-names in California.

"Almost anything we have is for sale but that," Rita answered. "That's something personal that was handed down in my family."

When Rita saw the customer's look of disappointment, she continued, "We'll do a search for out-of-print publications to your specifications, if you wish."

"I think I'll stay here until lunch," the customer announced, and she took off her coat. She wore a simple black woolen jumpsuit. "We're staying at The Retreat, and I grabbed my mother's coat when I decided to walk over to the pool at the Shore Club. I'm not interested in golf like the rest of my family."

"You're welcome to browse and ask Dolores any questions. Otherwise we won't bother you."

The customer arose, and leaving her coat thrown over a chair, she silently scanned the shelves. Rita was called to the phone.

"Rita?" came a familiar voice. "I'm in town just for today. I've got to see you today. Alone! I want to talk to you." It was Tessa.

"How about very late this afternoon? If the weather's still nice, we can take a walk together. If not, we can talk in my upstairs office."

"Do you know that Deputy Dog wants to talk to me again?"

"Who?"

"Oh that's my name for Captain Lewis."

"He stopped by the shop this morning to ask questions about you," Rita sighed.

"I think I'll sue him for invasion of privacy." Tessa said with a saucy voice.

"What sort of questions has he been asking you, Tessa?"

"Intimate things about Charles and me."

"Did he come right out and say that?"

"He said he had been talking to people around The Retreat. They said I was with Charles a lot last week. The Captain said I was lying when I told him that I didn't know Charles very well."

"That wasn't very smart on your part. You could have said you and I are good friends and you've known him for a long time."

"It's Missy. I know it is Missy. She's trying to stir up things. She kept a detective on her payroll as soon as she and Charles were officially separated. I know she wants to make trouble for me, and especially now that she thinks she's got Charles again. She probably called Deputy Dog and gave him some tips and told him to go talk to the bartender at the club. Everybody there knows that bartender is a snoop and a blackmailer."

"For everybody's sake, you'd better play it cool, Tessa."

"Did I tell you that Deputy Dog said he really wanted this case to end because he wanted to ask me out to dinner?"

"And what did you say?"

"I just giggled and said he was funny."

"So when is he going to officially question you?"

"In a about an hour. He told me to come to his office He says it's private there."

"If he really wants to take you to dinner, you have an advantage. But be careful. Just tell him anything vague. Something to confuse him, but don't make flat denials."

"What if he comes out and says, 'Have you and Charles been lovers?'"

"Say, 'Shame on you. You're being nosy for your own curiosity.'"

"Have you ever had to answer a question like that?"

"Yes, I have. I actually said that on certain occasions in my past."

"You said, 'Shame on you?'"

"Yes, because I have never told anyone about my intimate life."

"But I know you were the senator's secret girlfriend."

"Tessa, that was someone's romantic story you wanted to believe."

"When I heard that a well known senator who was a Bourbon drinker ordered Pol Roger Brut Champagne for his girl-friend at the Paris Ritz bar, I knew it was you. Long ago Charles told me that particular champagne is a winegrower's favorite."

"Pol Roger makes a great Champagne, particularly the Cuvée Sir Winston Churchill. The rest of what you say is a romantic story you want to believe."

"Rita, you are exasperating. You're not helping me at all."

"I think I am. You need to think up a few ready answers right now, before you see the captain. Think up some answers that will work in almost any situation."

"Do you really think he is interested in me?"

"I don't think getting involved with him is a good idea."

"OK, I'll just play dumb."

After a pause, Rita said, "Gotta go, pal. We're having a busy morning at the shop. Come by my house after five this afternoon. You can tell me about the interview then. I'll have a little time to talk, and then I need to get ready for the dance at the Shore Club tonight."

"Thanks. I didn't want to bother you, but I'm kind of scared about saying the wrongs things to Captain Lewis," Tessa finished.

CHAPTER 30

▼

Rita looked up and saw a familiar customer. She was dressed in a casual, black jumpsuit, and in a hysterical tone of voice, she hailed Rita. "Can I charge these books to our bill at the hotel?"

"We take all major credit cards."

"What shall I do? I don't have any credit cards?

"The Old Booktique doesn't have any affiliation with the Retreat. I'll hold a few books for you until Monday afternoon, and you can decide if you want them."

"I definitely want Bernard de Voto's signed copy of *The Year of Decision 1846*. My father has a birthday coming up. I'll think about Hittel's Volume Three of his *History of California*. It was published in the year my great-grandparents were married in San Francisco. My family goes way back, you know. Ciao," she shouted and snatching her coat she hurried out of the store.

Satisfied with a full morning of sales, both Rita and Dolores left the shop early and avoided traffic as they headed in the opposite direction of most of the spectators and traffic.

Carmelita and Mike were both napping when Rita returned home. After a quick lunch of fruit and cheese, she went to her office to finish putting together her presentation for the Sterns.

When Mike awoke, Rita said, "I wonder if Dave Goldman really intends to do something about the first proposal he sent to me?"

"Let's hear what Mel and Ellen have to say," said Mike as he saw the Sterns coming up the stone path towards their covered patio.

Mike opened the door and after calling, "Welcome to the Minettis" he gave Ellen a hug and grasped Mel's hand with fervor.

"We're a little late. It's hard to tear ourselves away from watching golf." Mel said after Mike's affectionate reception at the door.

When they were seated, Mike offered them drinks, and Rita went upstairs for her material. She returned with her arms full of notebooks and boxes. Mel laughed. "I can see the only other person we're going to need for this project is an editor. We'll have more than enough material."

Mike returned with a tray and glasses of ice tea that they requested.

"It's your fault, Mel, that the volume has grown. You suggested that Clarita might have a San Francisco story, and now I have included that story. It's from one of Isabel's journals."

They poured over the pages of a translated *Carmelo Diary*, and then examined letters of Consuelo and Clarita.

"Somehow we need to include the part that 'Grande Dame Clara' played in all this. Maybe we could start the saga with a scene that shows her telling the story to all of us. I think Clara is the link with the distant past and today's world,' Mike commented.

"'Grande Dame Clara.' I like that name. What did she look like? Did she look like you?" Mel turned to Rita.

"I don't think so, but then I knew her with silver hair. I have some old photographs showing her with very dark hair, worn in the nineteen twenties bobbed style."

Mike spoke again. "My first memories started about 1959. Aunt Clara and Uncle Leo came to stay at Silverado in Napa. Mama first took me to San Francisco to get a new suit to wear to the dinner they had arranged for all the Torellis and Minettis. We are related a couple of generations back. Aunt Clara had dark chestnut hair and vivid blue eyes. Her clothes looked different than those of Mama and her friends around Napa. In fact, I had never seen a lady like her."

"Was she more fashionable?" Ellen asked.

"Her clothes weren't exactly fancy. The Minettis pride themselves on being good dressers. The clothes of Aunt Clara were different. They had a sophisticated sort of elegance, and although she was the same age as Mama, she had a figure like my older sister."

"Wow," said Mel. "Now you tell me, Rita. What kind of clothes did she wear?"

"Mostly Chanel suits. I'm told she often went on buying trips to Paris and had her clothes made there. If the year was 1959, it was just before my mother was to married Rexford C. Atherton in1960."

"What was Clara like when you lived at Stonecrest, Rita? Was she fun?" Mel asked.

Mike was eager to talk. "I always thought she was fun. A real Auntie Mame type. Of course, I only saw her at parties and weddings. We always knew when she was in the room,"

"Rita, was she fun?" Mel turned to her.

"I knew her most of my life. We went to live with her at Stonecrest in 1970," Rita began. "I don't know what she was like before Grandpa Leo died. I do know that Grandmother ruled at Stonecrest. I had lots of boy cousins from Uncle Pauli and Aunt Gina. My only girl cousin was almost grown up when I came along, so I think I became Grandmother's favorite grandchild. I thought my grandmother was wonderful. She showered me with toys and stuffed animals, and I was usually with her almost every day at teatime."

"Would you say she was domineering?" Mel asked.

Rita shook her head. "Not exactly. She was generous and outgoing. She was often like a chameleon. She could pretend to be many things. When she discovered a person's particular usefulness, she would draw them into her sphere. It was then she became the dominant one."

Rita looked at Mike, and he looked at her with surprise.

"No, no," Rita said. "That makes her sound cruel. She wasn't that, but she liked to have her own way. She was concerned for others and listened to people tell her things. She invested her fortune well, and made a great deal more money, which she distributed everywhere. She put up all the money that went into the Torelli wineries. And best of all for me, Clara was my earliest friend and advocate. Mother doted on my brother. My grandmother championed me."

"She sounds like a superlative woman," Mel agreed.

"There you have it. She always said that she was Spanish, Irish, English, and German and took the best of all three."

"What did she look like when she was older? Did she change then?" Ellen asked.

"She never seemed really old to me, although. She became more demanding as she reached ninety. And I think this was hard for my mother to understand."

"You knew her in her last year?"

"Oh, yes. Right after Carmelita was born, she began to admit to me that she lacked her usual energy. We often sat and talked about what she wanted me to do. She talked about *The Carmelo Diaries* and told me she wanted me to take the story to the world."

"You've started me on a new track, Rita," Ellen said looking at Rita and Mel. "This may be absurd. How about putting some of the present in the video?"

"How about producing this as a drama. What about you playing the part of your grandmother, Rita?" Mel continued.

"Mike drew quite a picture of Clara. Begin with 'Grande Dame Clara.' If you don't mind being made up as an older lady, you could play the part, Rita." Ellen continued.

"It might even start with one of her soirees where she amused an audience with her stories and served Dom Perignon," Mel said.

"It could be staged in the library where she told her stories. Rita would be familiar with the surroundings," Ellen suggested.

Rita was truly taken aback. "Oh, no, "I'm not the type to play Clara. We need a professional actor for that," she managed to say.

"But Rita, you're a pivotal person," Ellen persuaded. "You are the one who knows the whole story."

"It might be more than I could handle right now."

"You won't have to write the story, Rita. You can dictate it to someone else. I'll find someone to make it whole," Mel said.

"I might have said yes before the burglary. It hasn't been solved you know. I've been thrown off balance ever since."

"That will play itself out," said Mel with assurance. "Our production won't be started right away. You'll have time to hire a competent assistant for your shop in the interim. After the tournament I'll read everything you give me about Clarita's whole life story."

"You make it sound so easy," Rita sighed.

"That's our business. Ellen and I have resources, and by the end of next week we'll have a new proposal for you to look over. That gives you a whole week to get back to normal. How about it?" Mel said.

"That's a whole new agenda," Mike said thoughtfully.

"Not new, but an expanded and a better one," Mel agreed heartily.

"I hate to bring it up," began Rita, "but what about Mr. Goldman? What if he calls me and wants to do a deal and wants to use just *The Carmelo Diaries*."

"Let me handle that. Trust us. I know Dave better than you do," Mel said.

"If Mr. Goldman calls, we'll tell him we are undecided. But should we say anything about what we've talked over with you?" Mike ventured.

"Just trust us, Mike. That part will all work out. I understand Rita's reluctance to take a more active part in the production, but we may think it is necessary. At the very least, we need Rita as an adviser. She knows Clara's style and mannerisms and probably even has some of her clothes she can loan us."

Mike looked dubious, and Rita crossed the room to where he was sitting on the sofa and put her arms around his shoulders.

"It's up to you, Rita," coaxed Mel.

"I'll even close the shop for awhile. Carmelita is at a good age to take with us, and we'll all go South for that part of the production," Rita offered. "What do you think, Mike?"

"Give us a few days, Mel. We'll think it over. If we decide to do it as you now envision it, we'll come down to L.A. to talk with you. Give us at least a week to decide," said Mike.

"If you happen to make up your mind earlier, you can reach us at the Valley Spa Hotel. Otherwise I'll expect a call in L.A. on Friday, Rita."

"I think you'll like the part I wrote last night," said Rita. "It's very photogenic." She handed him a bundle of the pages. At that moment Rita saw Amy and Carmelita coming up to the front patio. Carmelita was chattering, while Amy carefully placed the tricycle under its cover in the garage.

"We saw a new puppy down the street," Carmelita said as she opened the front door and began to walk in. When she saw the Sterns in the living room, she stopped in the doorway and waved her hand bashfully.

"Come in and meet our new friends," Rita said as she took Carmelita's hand and led her toward the guests. She hung back a little, and Rita carefully glided her toward Ellen. "This is Mrs. Stern, and this is her husband Mr. Stern. We will probably see them when we drive down to Los Angeles in a few weeks."

Carmelita lowered her head shyly, and then came in and made a little curtsy that Rita had taught her. "I'm Carmelita Antonia," she said softly, almost in a whisper.

"That's a big name for a little girl," said Ellen as Carmelita quickly ran to Mike and after jumping into his arms, she nestled her head into his chest. Rita excused herself to walk outside to Amy.

"I think it's your playtime with Daddy," Ellen continued and Carmelita looked up and nodded.

"It's been great seeing you people again. When you come down to L.A. we'll get together at our place. I'll arrange something special for Carmelita," Mel continued.

Carmelita looked at Mel. "What is it?" she said with interest.

"It's a surprise, and it wouldn't be a surprise if we told you," Ellen said.

"Oh, I like that," Carmelita commented and settled back against Mike.

"Then it's all set. We'll hear from you soon. The more you think about it, the more you'll like it," Mel finished. "We'll be going now."

"Yes, and thanks for every thing. We'll talk soon," Ellen said as they were leaving.

After they picked up the glasses and walked into the kitchen, Rita looked expectantly toward Mike.

"I know you're excited by the thought of putting Clara into the story, but I spoke up because I thought it was better if we didn't move too fast," Mike explained.

Just then the doorbell rang. Rita had forgotten about Tessa.

"Oh, my God, Mike. I completely forgot that I told Tessa to come over after she had talked to Captain Lewis. I thought we would take a walk, but it's too cold for that now. We'll go up to my office I want to hear what she has to say. She wanted it to be private."

"Don't take too long. We are expected at the Shore Club party at seven-thirty."

"I'll be ready for the party. Tessa doesn't have much time She's planning to fly back to Scottsdale this evening."

Rita opened the door and gave her friend a hug. "You look terrific, pal. Everything must have gone well."

"OK, I guess. But as usual, my life is now more complicated. Rita, I think you're right. Maybe Deputy Dog really wants to have his way with me. He started to ask me questions about what I do at your shop, and I sort of led him on. I said I thought he was a great detective, and I told him I would cooperate in any way I could. I purposely wore my skirt with the split that shows my legs. If Captain Lewis is really interested in me, it might be fun to see what develops. Let's go upstairs, and I'll tell you all about it."

When they were in Rita's office, Rita closed the door and Tessa sank into a large comfortable wicker chair. She wore an enthusiastic expression of childish exuberance. "Someday, I'm going to be your sister-in-law. Charles told me so last night."

Rita looked at her friend in amazement. Tessa's eyes sparkled. Her soft seamless skin was without wrinkles. Although she was usually a little over-weight, she was now trim. Tessa still had the vulnerability of an adolescent. Rita understood that Tessa's devotion to Charlie was equal to his ego: however, what he needed now was a wife with more material assets.

"You're better off as his mistress."

"Rita, how can you say something so vulgar? We're the best of friends. I thought you'd want us to be sisters."

"I'm giving you good advice."

"Don't you want me to be happy?"

"Charlie has always been the classic example of a person who wants what he can't have. You've known him a long time, and you'll always have him in your bed if you don't marry him."

"We don't even need a bed. We've been good at doing it anywhere," she exclaimed "But I don't want to wait too long. My biological clock might run out."

"If you two get married, it won't be for your biological clock. Charlie is in the midst of an ambitious expansion right now. He needs Missy's money and he's going to stay married to her."

"I shouldn't talk to you. You don't know Charles the way I do." And I have it all figured out. My mother is still living. I can kiss up to her and get all the money Charles wants. As for the playing hard to get," Tessa paused and looked forlorn for a second. "Well, it's too late for that. He knows I live for him. Everything I know about sex, I learned from him. I know the way he likes it and I do it for him."

"All the more reason not to live with him. He likes the adventure of meeting you on the sly."

"No, it isn't that. I know he likes flattery and all that, but you see he knows that I don't flatter him. It's real devotion. I can give him every kind of love he needs."

"If you really love him, just stay cool right now. He deliberately set up this second honeymoon stuff with Missy for a reason. If he told you he loved you last night, then it's best for you to be scarce for a while. Going to Scottsdale is a good thing."

"Do you really think so? You're not just telling me that because you and Charles are always competing. You know he thinks you've got it pretty good now. A business and Mike and all that."

"He isn't thinking that much about me. He has other things on his mind. He's envious of the Torelli brothers. He wants to make it big time in the boutique wine business. Missy filed for divorce because of his affair, but now he figures that he needs Missy to achieve his goal. He wants it all, the business success, social position, and you on the side. You're one of the pieces."

"That's disgusting, Rita. Charles is right. You are against him. You don't think he has any good motives."

"Is this what you wanted to see me about?" Rita said realizing that the conversation had become personal and emotional.

"Not really. I don't mind staying in Scottsdale. It's best for me to be out of the way, right now. That's what I really wanted to talk to you about. Captain Lewis is asking me some personal questions."

"I need someone to be with while I'm waiting. It might be fun to have a fling with Captain Lewis."

"Tessa, that's not wise."

"I think it could help Charles, if Captain Lewis was dating me."

"What do you mean?"

"He talked to me about the burglary. He asked me if I had ever slept with Charles?"

"In a formal questioning?"

"Not really. Well, I don't think so. But he asked me to tell him about what I did with my whole evening on the night before the burglary."

"And did you?"

"Not yet, but I'm afraid of what he might ask me tonight. I'm supposed to meet him at the Coast House for dinner before my plane leaves at ten. What do you think he'll ask me about?"

"He'll ask you when you left the shop on the day before the burglary. He'll ask you if anyone else was in the shop with you after you closed up the shop. They found fingerprints belonging to Charles. Captain Lewis will ask you if you stopped anywhere before you went home, and if there was someone who could verify it."

"What do you mean, 'If there was someone who could verify it?'"

"You know, like a waiter at the club or checker at the market. Someone who saw you on your way home. Captain Lewis will ask you to describe what you ate and maybe what you saw on TV that night."

"Tessa's facial expression changed. "He could ask all those things?"

"He can, but you're not under oath yet. If he suspects something, and it goes to trial, than he can ask all kinds of things and what you answer at a trial has to agree with what you tell him tonight."

"Then I'd better not meet him. He might wheedle something out of me."

"Didn't you say he asked about your whereabouts the night before we were burglarized?"

"Yes, and I told him I went to my place and watched television. I told him I stopped at a tiny market on the way home. I go there a lot, and they know me." Rita watched Tessa crossing her legs nervously.

"That was a good answer."

"But I know he's going to ask for more. Do you really think I should just leave?"

"It might be fun to have a fling with Captain Lewis."

"Tessa, that's not wise."

"I think it could help Charles."

"What do you mean? Rita commented. Before Tessa could answer, Rita continued, "Excuse me. I have to use the bathroom."

"Go ahead."

When Rita returned, Rita said, "I told you this morning that Mike and I have to go to a party. I need to get showered and dressed. You'd better go back to Scottsdale on an earlier plane. Go through LAX, if you need to. You have a lot of things to think over, and I don't want you to tell me any more about it now. I don't want to know any more than I do."

"Sometimes you scare me, Rita."

"You scare me too, girl," she shot back. "You've got a lot to lose."

"What if Deputy Dog asks you about our conversation?"

"What you told me just now is personal. It doesn't concern him. I won't let you tell me anything else. So that's that." Rita put her arms around her friend. "Just get the hell out of here and go to Scottsdale, even if you have to drive all the way back tonight."

"That's a good idea," Tessa said giving Rita a hug. "And don't tell Mike about the things that Charles and I do."

"As little as possible," Rita assured her as she was leaving.

Rita had time to dress and she and Mike went to the Shore Club to the Gala Tournament Ball. They made an early evening of it.

CHAPTER 31

▼

The next morning Rita arose early and read the translated Carmelo Diary of 1837.

"Will rode from Monterey back to Carmelo today. He brought me a special present. It was a leather bound book filled with paper. I am going to write about our life at Rancho Carmelo. I thought I would try to write in English since I have been speaking English to Will and Raquel Larkin. I call her Rachel now." *It was written in a different color of ink and written in Spanish.*

"I have tried to write in English and have decided to continue my writing in Spanish. I cannot express myself in English the same way as I do in Spanish. It seems that I lose my soul when I write in English. I cannot write about the things closest to my heart in English. The language of the *Yanquis* is not as beautiful as Spanish. I remember that my brother, Estéban, liked to write in Latin. I am certain that now he writes in Latin all the time. The last letter I received from him said that he is a secretary to a bishop in Madrid, and he hopes some day to go to Rome as a secretary to a cardinal. Papa would be very proud of him. I wish Papa had been blessed with more sons. It is now my responsibility to keep alive the names de Segovia and de la Luz and give these family names to our children.

"Near the last day of 1836, our daughter, Patricia Isabel, was born. We used the names of both our families. Patricia has a happy disposition. As the months go by, she keeps her reddish-blonde hair, and it curls well. My mother would have loved the name of her granddaughter, and she would have said the name with her soft Castilian lisp. After the birth of Patricia, the weather became warm and pleasant. I was able to be out in the fresh air, and I enjoyed the courtyard where we have vegetables and some flowers. I sat outside in the shade of the patio and held Patricia in my arms while I sang to her. Will likes to hear me sing the Spanish songs of my childhood. He sometimes plays a little on the guitar while I sing. Don Felipe would never allow me to sing to our son, Ardo. He said it would not help him to grow up to be manly. He did not want me to spend so much time playing with him, and he insisted that Ardo stay with the Indian maids in a small room next to the *sala*. I often think about the time when Ardo was a small child, and I never stop wondering what he is doing now. I can only guess what he is thinking. Even if Will and I have many sons, I will continue to dream of Ardo. Does he really hate me? Does he really believe that I abandoned him? No. The Blessed Virgin will whisper to him when he hears the wind in the sycamores. She will tell him that his mother, Clarita, is singing to him. She will tell him to be brave and kind. I would like to see him, but it would not be safe. These are troubled times between Alta California and Mexico.

"Now that I am married to Will, I never want to be far from his side. This is especially true when we are away from our ranch. Will is not a Mexican citizen, and the government could do fearful things to him. We are fortunate that Don Tomás Larkin is our friend. Will says that Don Tomás receives newspapers from all the ships that come into our port. That is how he knows what is going on everywhere. He also has *Yanqui* friends in the Sandwich Islands, and they tell him how things are in the other parts of the world. When the son of Don Tomás and Raquel is ready for school, they will send him to the Sandwich Islands. This year, we were asked by the Larkins to come to Monterey for a visit. We stayed in a house that Will built for the guests of the Larkins. They entertain often and give their most festive party on the Fourth day of July. This is the greatest day of celebration for all the *Yanquis*. It is the anniversary of the day these people of America declared their freedom from the land of the English. The Larkins asked all the best people of Monterey to come to a special dinner, and afterwards there was a general *fandango* for the townspeople. Consuelo and Miguel García have kept their adobe in Monterey, and although it is too small for all their family, they like to come to town for special events. Sometimes they bring their older children. It was at the time of the *fiesta* of the Americans that I heard about Ardo from Consuelo. First, she told me again that the Vargas family is very powerful in Sonora, Mexico. She said that Ardo is staying there to be educated. Then she confided that Antonio Vargas has asked for the hand of their daughter, Prudencia. She is my godchild and is very beautiful. She has deep blue eyes and soft brown hair. This Vargas man is many years older than Prudencia. I had hoped that she would not marry someone who lived so far away.

"We wanted Esperanza to come to Monterey for the *fiesta* of the Larkins. She stays very much to herself, and she says very little. One of the men in the regiment of Miguel is interested in marriage with Esperanza. Next time we go to Monterey, I am going to insist she come with us. I do not know what it would be like to be without Esperanza at our *rancho*, but she will make this man a capable wife and she will have a man to protect her. This would be good for my oldest little sister who is already eleven. It would help her find a good husband when she is fifteen. This would fulfill my obligations to my father in regards to one of my little sisters.

"Don Tomás tells my husband that he is disappointed in the Mexican rule of California. They always want to send us governors from Mexico City. Most of these men do not know our land and our ways. Don Tomás is hoping that my lifelong friend, Juan Baustista Alvarado, will stay on as governor. He tells Will there are many families in the South of Alta California who want to have the power of Monterey. Some of the Carrillos want to take over the territorial government. I do not understand why they think they know what is best for all of Alta California. The seat of the government has been here since 1771, and many of the Carrillos have family in the north. I am thinking of the wife of Don Mariano Vallejo, for example.

"Consuelo says the most important thing is to own land. All of us who were born in California must obtain the titles to this land. So we must support Juan Bautista Alvarado and do what we can to keep an army in Monterey to defend him. She does not like *Yanquis* as she has seen many of them who are rough and angry men. They drink much strong liquor and yell at us in loud voices. This frightens her. When Mariano Vallejo came to Monterey last time, he paid us a call, and although he and Juan Bautista Alvarado are related, he encouraged me to listen to the words of Don Tomás. He says that California is alone in the world, and many foreign governments want to take us over. Even the Russians have not given up their claims to the northern coast. Don Mariano knows about this because the headquarters of the Russians is near his great ranch north of San Francisco Bay. Don Mariano has been occupied with Indians who are more savage than the ones we have around us in Monterey. Don Mariano thinks we need a strong government to help us keep a good way of life for our families. He asked Will and I to come pay a visit to their ranch. However, it is very far away from here.

"July 1837. When I told Will that we would have another child in January or February, he gave me the most important gift that a wife can have. It is a large carved oak bed that will take up much of the space in the *alcoba* that he is building for us. He has found us a real cradle of the same wood as the bed, and it will stay beside us He has taught some of the men how to be carpenters, and they will make a large cupboard for our special clothes. The Mission San Cárlos is beginning to fall apart, and we sent some of our men to bring back stones and bricks for our new buildings. The first thing we added to the *hacienda* was a small chapel, near our bedroom. I can say my prayers and observe daily devotions in this chapel, when the time grows near for the birth.

"A happy golden month has passed. We had no visitors, and there was much work to be done in the pastures. Will directs all the branding of cattle. We had our own *rodeo*. Afterwards, we sang and watched the young children of the ranch do a Spanish dance. This has been the happiest time of my life.

"Summer is over, and I have been feeling safe and contented as I do when I am with child. I decided not to ride out to the pastures with Will or go to *meriendas* with my young sisters, so I did not accompany Esperanza to instruct the younger Indian maids in the activity of washing clothes by the river. I must say this to explain a sad day in our life.

"It seems that Dulcera, my sister who is eleven years, had gone upstream a little way. She had taken two other little girls with her. At this time of year the current of the river is not swift, and children love to play in the gentle water. It is not unusual for some of the horses to be wandering nearby, so the children thought nothing when they heard a whinny. It is said that the little girls saw two men jump from their horses, and one took a *serape*, waded in the water, and picked up Dulcera and rolled her in the *serape*. They carried her to a waiting horse and rider and galloped off. The little girls ran to tell Esperanza and their mothers, but it was too late to get help.

"When Esperanza came back, she told me what happened. I asked her if the children knew the men. She shook her head. I asked if the men were Indians And she said shook her head The *vaqueros* were strangers. We all were in tears.

"I sent Ramon to find Will, and when he returned from Monterey, he was very angry, which is unusual for him. He organized our men to go on a search, but he did not leave my side. It was at least a week before Xavier, the soldier who has expressed a wish to court Esperanza, came to tell us that the *vaqueros* were from Rancho Rincón de Gavilán, where I had lived when Don Felipe was alive. Esperanza said nothing, but she often shook like a sapling tree in a storm. We must see that Padre Mateo knows about this and that he allows Esperanza and Xavier to marry sooner than was planned.

"There is no way that we can accuse anyone of the abduction. Later we learned through some of the Indians on our ranch that when Don Diego went back to Sonora, Mexico, he took Dulcera with him. I believe the vulgar gossip about Don Diego and know that he has always bedded with the serving girls at his ranches. Dulcera is too young for that, and yet I know Don Diego and his evil ways. Will went to Señor Larkin and told him of the abduction. Will told him of the possibility that Dulcera will be taken to Sonora, Mexico. Will asked him what could be done, and he asked him if we could get our governor to help with the return of Dulcera.

"Don Tomás told Will that an accuusation would be useless. Juan Bautista himself has a mistress, who has borne him children. He cannot accuse powerful men of these offenses. Juan Bautista needs friends who have much gold and who influences the men in Mexico City.

"It was not comforting when Consuelo told me that Dulcera would be safe if she learned to please Don Diego. Her very words saddened me. 'Dulcera is so young. He will teach her his ways, and she may grow to be his favorite woman. Then she will lead a pampered life.'

"He is a cruel man," I said. 'This will not be a good life,' I told her, but Consuelo said it was the only way she could survive. I prayed even more to my patron saint, and yet I was not comforted.

"I have failed to keep the promise I made to my father. I told him I would watch over my little sisters. Now Dulcera will never have a good husband. She is lost to me, and as with Ardo, she is under the rule of Don Diego. We were able to persuade Esperanza to wed Sergeant Xavier Vega, and yet I think she only consented in order to protect herself and my other little sister, Felicia. They all went to live at the army post of General Vallejo in the land north of San Francisco Bay.

"My life has shifted even more away from my past. My heart was wounded because Consuelo could not understand my grief. She does not express concern or care about my dear Esperanza. She has never thought of Dulcera as my true little sister, because Esperanza is her mother. I began to be suspicious that she thinks less of me because I am the wife of Will O'Farrell, a man who works with his hands and speaks Spanish like a *Yanqui*. She thinks Will is not a gentleman because she does not understand what makes a man truly noble. I must find a way to tell her. I need spiritual advice. I should find a way to attend confession and mass, but I am afraid to go anywhere without my husband and the band of six loyal *vaqueros* who he has trained for our safety.

"Although, we are living at our ranch all of the time, we have an invitation to stay at the house of the Larkin's, and we are going to Monterey soon. Without Esperanza, I would have many more duties of directing the work of the house. She is a great help to me. On the visit to the Larkin's, my good friend of Rachel told me she was also with child again. She told me about her earlier life and how she was once married to a sea captain. She was on her way to join him in the Sandwich Islands, but he died before she reached her destination. She met Don Tomás on the voyage to those islands. She told me she gave birth to a child who died, and I realized that it was selfish of me to cry only for myself. I asked Raquel to come to mass with me and we went to the church that had been the Royal Chapel San Cárlos. We both prayed for our children and for a safe place for them to live.

"Raquel is a dear lady, and she shows me her clothes that are different from what I wear. She has six bonnets and only one lace *mantilla*, which is what we wear to church. The colors of her skirts are dark, and she has almost no jewelry. She writes letters, which go by boat to the American part of the world, and I know she misses her family. She also reads books when she has some time. Although she does not direct servants to make *tortillas* and work at the chores of a ranch, she has much to do with entertaining and directing the making of food to serve to the officers of ships visiting the port of Monterey. She says that Don Tomás wants to build a new customs house on the shore by Monterey Bay.

"September 1837. We were called to Monterey to sign the papers for the grant deed to Rancho del Rio Carmelo. The ranch is what I inherited from my father. Governor Alvarado gave Will a league of land located on the far side of the Rio Carmelo and farther up the valley. He also made a land grant to the Munras family. They have lived in Monterey for many years now. Don Tomás says Don Juan Bautista wants the good will of the *Californios*, because the governor now worries about the ideas of the rough Americans who helped him take control of the government last year. One of the men is named Graham, and he makes the cheap whiskey that gets the Americans drunk. They yell cruel words at Governor Alvarado and he thinks the Americans are plotting a revolution against him. When we are in Monterey, Raquel, although she is not of our faith, sometimes attends mass with me. I also visit with Encarnation Cooper and my other friends, who admire the beauty of our Patricia.

"Monterey is filled with intrigue. I need to be quiet during the last months before the birth of our next child. At this time, Will and I returned to Rancho Carmelo for the rest of the year. Will invited a friend of Don Tomás to paint my picture. He insisted that I wear a black *mantilla* and the new earrings he bought for me. They told me to think of something beautiful while I was being painted, so I thought about Ardo. I hope I do not look sad in the painting, because I am truly happy with my life with Will, and we are safe at Rancho Carmelo.

"It will soon be the season of the *Navidad*. Will has asked Don Tomás and Raquel with their children to visit us at Rancho Carmelo. As the weather is still fair, I can sit out on a bench in the *patio,* and I have directed some of my maids to tell us the story of *Las Posadas.* One of our maids has a young baby, and he will be held in her arms. Some of the young boys will be dressed as shepherds. They will act out the story of the *Natividad* I think it will be a good *fiesta* for all of us.

"After our guests returned to Monterey, we asked Padre Mateo to hear our confessions, and he conducted mass for all the true believers at our ranch. It was held in what is left of the mission chapel. We will not to go to Monterey until after our child is born, because we know there are strange *vaqueros* taking cattle from our upper pastures. Our *vaqueros* must be on guard. Will trains them to protect us.

"Our son was born soon after the day of the *Natividad.* I had a very easy time at birth, because he was so small. He came before the expected time. Will wanted to name him Liam Cárlos, but since he is not well, we waited for the naming until after Padre Mateo arrived. Then we decided on the name of Cárlos Antonio de Segovia O'Farrell. We wanted to honor the names of my family as we had promised Papa. If it was a girl, the name we chose was María Isabel after my mother.

"Young Cárlos would not take any nourishment. Merced, the wife of Ramon, has abundant milk for her six months old daughter, and she tried to suckle him. It was to no avail. He became weaker and quietly died soon after midnight of the old year and only an hour into the beginning of 1838.

"The beautiful Mission San Cárlos has been completely abandoned and strangers came to take what little was left. We had a simple service at the ranch and buried Cárlos Antonio in an area that has been fenced for this use. It is a beautiful place under a large oak tree. Padre Mateo already blessed the land for us. Those of us who live on the ranch can use the consecrated land for our families. Will promised to stay at the ranch with me and he will protect me from outside sorrows. We have much to be thankful for. We will pray for more children."

CHAPTER 32

▼

"It is the summer of 1838. We are thankful we live at Rancho Carmelo and want another child. I have prayed to the Blessed Virgin for this to happen. It comforts me that I can go to the little chapel that Will had built for us. I place flowers on the altar every day. I do not wish to see any of my friends in Monterey. My health is improving, and by next year we will surely have another child. Will and I have always shared our sorrows when there is a death of a loved one. After Will learned to speak Spanish, he told me of his early life in Boston before his parents died. He became an orphan. We both have had tears to shed. Now we pray together for strength to bear the loss of our son.

"We trust Ramon, and we send him with the loyal *vaqueros* when we have hides to sell Don Tomás. The happenings of the government really do not interest us. It is better for us to spend our days and nights in this peaceful place where the land tumbles down to the sea. On sunny days, Will has the men making adobe bricks for the buildings that will be erected near our house. I teach the women to work at making candles and soap. Some of the maidens work in our garden of vegetables. The herds roam all over the nearby hills. As soon as it rains, there will be tender, green grass for them.

"When Will went to Monterey last week, he learned that Governor Juan Bautista Alvarado has had many more political troubles with the Carrillos of the south. They want the capital to be located in the *Pueblo de Los Angeles*. Miguel was called back into the militia of the governor. He will take our soldiers to the South. Cousin Consuelo sent a letter by messenger to tell me that my goddaughter, Prudencia, is to be married to Don Antonio Vargas, and they will live in

Sonora, Mexico. Consuelo would like to see us, but she has much to do at their ranch, since her husband is away with the troops.

"When the boat, *California,* arrived, the governor announced that Mexico had become a republic, and it is now divided into twenty-four departments. Alta and Baja California are now separate departments. Monterey has been declared the official capital of Alta California. We are now eligible to elect a *diputado* to the congress in Mexico City. The ship brought documents from Mexico, and there were pardons for past political actions. Juan Bautista Alvarado will remain governor of Alta California. Mariano Vallejo was appointed *comandante general* in consideration for his services. Don Juan Bautista and Don Mariano proclaimed this to the *gente de razon* by public pronouncements and private letters. Now all the people of Monterey can enjoy a good life again. The ship, *California,* even brought new uniforms to the officers and men of our militia.

"1838 came and went. Patricia grew quickly, and as soon as she learned to walk, she was riding her own horse. Many of our friends came to see us at the ranch, and I began to entertain with *fiestas* and *bailes.* Don Tomás Larkin and his wife, Raquel, as well as Encarnacion Cooper brought their children when they visited Rancho Carmelo. Patricia was never without a playmate from Monterey.

"Governor Alvarado gave Consuelo another grant of land to the south of the Pájaro River. She is delighted. She wants each of their twelve children to have a ranch. 'We *Californios* must have legal rights to our property before the vile *Yanquis* come to take over everything,' she told me.

"Martina María Castro is now married to our friend, Juan Bautista Alvarado. It was a strange ceremony. Juan Bautista has become a disillusioned man with so many political problems, and he is drinking more than he should. In fact, he said he was too ill to attend his own wedding, but everyone knew that it was because he was drinking the night before. His half brother, José Antonio Estrada, acted as a proxy at the wedding ceremony, which was held at the Mission Santa Clara. Eight days later, the bride came to Monterey, and there were many days of customary wedding celebrations.

"We attended the marriage of Prudencia María García and Don Antonio Tiburcio Vargas. I wondered if Don Diego and Ardo might come, and I learned that they are living permanently at the Vargas Ranch in Sonora, Mexico. The newlyweds will remain at the ranch of the Garcías the first month after the wedding. While they are there, they will prepare for the long journey to Sonora. They will travel part of the way by ship, so that Prudencia can take her maid and her trunks.

"After two months the newlyweds were ready to leave, and Consuelo announced that she would be a grandmother next year. There was much rejoicing, and Don Antonio promised to bring Prudencia and their child for a visit next year. We continued to hear nothing of Don Diego Vargas and Ardo. Perhaps when Prudencia visits next year there will be a time for me to talk to her and learn of the fate of Dulcera.

"Sometimes I am fearful of the world beyond Rancho Carmelo. Will would like to stay here all the time, but when Don Tomás summons him by messenger, he quickly leaves for Monterey. Don Tomás says that although Will is not good with *negocios,* there is no man in California whom he trusts more. He wants him to help with cargo inventories when an important ship comes to port. Will always brings presents to us when he returns. Now we have a beautiful set of glazed dishes from China and a teak-carved table for our *sala.* He brought me another pair of red dancing slippers.

"We have removed ourselves from Monterey even more. Will and I now have time to take our horses and ride beside the Rio Carmelo. We ride beyond the place it winds up the little canyon. We enjoy family times in the evening when we sit under the oaks by the courtyard. We watch Patricia play with the children of Ramon and sometimes we sing. When we look at the curve of the bay near the mouth of the river, we say that only the curve of the body of Patricia is more beautiful. We also compare the blue skies of autumn to her shining blue eyes, and we tell her that the rays of the sun rising over the hills are like the gleam of her golden-red hair. We talk to her in English and in Spanish so that she will speak both languages.

"It is 1839. Will was full of joy when I told him that we are going to be parents again. Since Xavier is no longer needed at his post in the north, he will bring Esperanza and their little sons to the ranch to live. I will be able to see my younger sister, Felicia, again. I pray that this will happen before I give birth to our child. We will ask the governor to give Xavier a small plot of land near us. Surely he has given enough service in the militia to receive this reward.

"I have always felt different from the other ladies who live around Monterey. Consuelo tells me that the entire community calls me, '*La Señora de España*', although I was born on Rancho Carmelo. This is because both my parents were born in Castile. I have had friendships since childhood with the Vallejos and Estradas and have been invited to the homes of the oldest important families of California. Because of this, it was thought that I would be married to one of the *Californios* after Don Felipe died. No one can understand my marriage to Will. Even Consuelo calls him a *Yanqui.* Sometimes she looks at me with disapproval when I talk in English to Raquel Larkin, whom I often call Rachel. There is another matter that makes me different. Consuelo does not understand my love for Esperanza and my little sisters. They are daughters of Esperanza and Papa. Consuelo does not understand my emotions.

"Will and I have a special bond, because we shared an early life at Rancho Carmelo. It was different with my first husband. We never really knew each other. Will and I have always been friends who can talk together, and I have never been afraid of him. I know that *Yanquis* come in different shapes and dispositions, just as our people. Consuelo is right to fear Isaac Graham and his men. They are not gentlemen. Don Tomás does not go to church with us, and she does not think he is good. I know that he has helped the community of Monterey by bringing trade and supplies to us, and he is generous with his entertainment of our people. I pray for our friends who do not go to mass, and yet I trust their word and accept their sincere friendship. As more people come to California, we will need to learn to look for the best qualities in everyone.

"When Will learned about our coming child, he started construction for another room, and he drew plans for a verandah like the one that he added for the house of Don Tomás in Monterey. Patricia is almost four years old and a great companion for me. When Felicia comes to take a reading lesson, Patricia wants to sit by her side, and she pretends she is reading. I really think that soon our Patricia will be reading also. After the lessons, Patricia takes a nap and then plays with the daughter of Ramon in the late afternoon.

"We are a complete community here at the ranch. I find much pleasure in the out of doors. I have one man and two maids who plant and tend my vegetable garden. I have books from one of the late mission fathers that tell about growing fruits and vegetables. Padre Mateo often comes to hear confession and to say mass for all of us. After the service we serve a meal to everyone. It seems that we are in constant preparation of food. When Padre Mateo stays for the meal, I like to serve him a flan that he likes. He says it reminds him of his childhood.

"The workers at the ranch always address Will as Don Guillermo, and on the occasions of celebration he wears one of his velvet jackets decorated with silver buttons. I will not wear my new dance slippers until after our child is born. I have found a maid who is very good at brushing my hair. I now wear my hair in a womanly way and need someone to carefully arrange it for me. Will says this style goes well with me.

"Xavier is a trained soldier, and he teaches the *vaqueros* how to defend the remote parts of our ranch. Because of this, it will be safer for us to stay here when Will goes to Monterey to help Don Tomás. The last time he went to Monterey, he stayed at the home of the Larkins. He told me that the dinner conversation was about the arrival of a certain Captain Juan Sutter. This Sutter immediately met a *yanqui* David Spence, who offered him lodging. Don David is influential, and Captain Sutter was able to have an audience with the governor. The Captain showed him the same letters of introduction that he showed Don David. He told them that he wanted to settle in the valley of the Rio Sacramento, which joins the Rio de Los Americanos. This interested Governor Alvarado, because he wants to have a settlement in the wilderness that is built by a capable person. He wants to have a place of defense against the savage Indians and the American trappers who come over the mountains. Don Juan Bautista warned Captain Sutter about the dangers of the wild empty country by the big rivers, and also he advised him to stay away from the lands north of San Francisco Bay, as this land is in the realm of his uncle, Mariano Vallejo. Captain Sutter was certain that he could build a good settlement, and when he told Governor Alvarado that he had carpenters and artisans, the governor promised him all the land he wanted. Don Juan Bautista also gave him a letter of introduction to Don Mariano. Will thought that Señor Sutter would probably be given title to the lands if he could show a good beginning.

"In the spring of the year 1840, we were blessed with a healthy child. She was born a large baby Her name is Anita María. Before the new babe was born, I had fears of another early birth and of having a child who is too tiny to live. We did not need to fear this. Anita is a very healthy child and is hungry all the time. Esperanza asked to be of help, and this was fortunate because it was a difficult birth. I lost much blood because my body was torn with such a large baby. I do not remember much about the birth as I was ill afterwards. Padre Mateo came from Monterey, and he sat by my bed to pray for me. Will sat on the other side and held my hand much of the nighttime. I heard the sounds of the *padre* praying and of Will crying. I wanted to comfort him, but I was without energy, and knew I must summon my strength for the recovery. We decided to have her baptized in the San Cárlos Chapel in Monterey. Señor Larkin has offered his home for a celebration of the event, when I am well and can participate in the festivities. Although we are simple people, Don Tomás has always been generous to us with his hospitality.

"For many days I could not leave the bedroom. Esperanza found someone who could nurse Anita and satisfy her appetite. Will did not leave my side unless there was a maid in the room to summon him if I needed him. Esperanza cooked soups made of beef and vegetables with little strips of *tortilla* floating in the bowl. She made cups of hot chocolate as my mother had taught her, and she served it to

Will and me every morning. It became a ritual with us even after I regained my strength. The more we prospered at Rancho Carmelo, the more we wanted to live only at the ranch. Every parcel of news was disturbing, be it from Monterey or from Padre Mateo, who told us about the problems in the former mission districts of San Gabriel and San Diego.

"It is the summer of 1840—Anita grew so fast that my first task was to help in the making of new clothes for her. Patricia plays with the small children of Esperanza and Xavier, and there is a tranquility that blesses the entire ranch. We move at our own pace. This is a time of serenity. We have over two thousand horses and fourteen hundred head of cattle, and we are prosperous because we spend all our days at Rancho Carmelo.

"Now that I am in good health, Will goes to Monterey to work for Don Tomás, and he always brings us back something to amuse or delight us. I had asked him many times about the land of the *Yanquis* and he brought me a small book written in English about geography. It once belonged to a captain of an American ship. It is not new. It does not tell that Mexico is separated from Spain. It does not even mention the Californias. It tells much about North America and not much about other countries. I asked Will to find me the part that tells about Spain, and he found two pages. There is a picture that shows a bullfight. I have never seen a bullfight. The book says that Spaniards are temperate, grave, polite and faithful to their word but proud, superstitious, and full of revenge. I think that could be true. Most of all, it tells about Boston. It says it is a large city, noted for commerce. There is a picture of people called the Pilgrims who were landing on shore by boat. They are all dressed in clothes that look strange for a landing party. The men all wear long jackets down to their boots and the ladies wear bonnets like those of Raquel. Boston must be a wonderful place to see. I do not know all the English words in the book, and I need the help of Will to read it. When Patricia gets older, it will be a good book for her to read The pictures are drawings and show animals that are said to be a tiger and an elephant. Will says he knows of no one who has really seen such animals.

"Don Tomás was true to his word and gave us a *fiesta* to celebrate the birth of Anita María. Raquel is with child and is not feeling well. I had a conversation with her when all the others had left the *fiesta*. She says that life is changing in Monterey. More and more Americans are arriving, but they are not the polite men who have married the women of our finest families. They are loud ignorant men who never dress in fine clothes and who do not observe the customs of California. Don Tomás does not like to have so many of these men in Alta California.

They are trappers and hunters and have no manners. That is why they are sending young Tomás to school in the Sandwich Islands.

"When I was at the evening *fandango*, it was the first time I had seen Consuelo in many months. She is full of happiness because a boat just arrived in port, and she received a letter from Prudencia with news about her life. At one point in the evening, we were able to sit in the garden at the side of the Larkin house. I asked her if she ever heard anything about Ardo, and she told me much. She said that Prudencia saw him once and he is a handsome young man. He has been sent to Mexico City for schooling. It is far from Sonora and he stays there all the time.'

"I asked Consuelo if she ever heard what became of Dulcera.

"She sighed. 'Gatita is what Don Diego called her. Don Diego wanted to give her to his wife, who could train her to be her chambermaid. He thought she could make a good servant of her, but she was like a stray animal, and they found her with child before the year was out. They took the child away from her, as she did not know how to take care of it. Soon she was with child again and had the child early. Someone was able to find a priest to baptize the baby before it died and they were both given last rights,' Consuelo finally stopped talking.

"I crossed myself. This was a sad story for me to hear. It was dark in the shadows of the trees in the Larkin garden and I could hide the sadness of my face.

"'She was already a lost soul,' Consuelo added.

"'*Pobrecita*,' was all that I could murmur.

"The name of the man Isaac Graham was everywhere in Monterey. Don Juan Bautista heard of a warning about this *Yanqui*. It is said that he is gathering his rough trappers, and he intends to take over the town and countryside. Don Juan Bautista does not like this Graham, although once several years ago, Graham helped him when Juan Bautista needed a private army to menace Señor Gutierrez, the temporary governor. Now things are different, and Governor Alvarado sent his men to seize this man, Graham and his rough men. They will be sent to San Blas as prisoners. As yet, nothing has been settled, because this Graham says he is innocent, it cannot be proven either way. Since this is a current topic of conversation, I asked Consuelo about what she had heard about Graham, and she said that she was not interested in what *yanquis* do

"I was glad to return to Carmelo with Will and to give my attention to our young family. We have been given good fortune in our life, and I will dedicate more time to teaching the children to read. We also sing together and Esperanza teaches Felicia and the daughters of Ramon the stitches necessary for sewing. The Blessed Virgin will give me guidance as to how I can bring improvement to all the children of our ranch. I have vowed to form a small school for us here, and I will find ways to keep all the children safe on our ranch. Strange *vaqueros* have been riding in groups of six or seven to scout the various ranches in the valley of the Rio Carmelo. No one recognizes them as men from our community. Since we do not know their motives, we must constantly protect our land and the people."

CHAPTER 33

▼

February 6, 2000.

Dave Goldman called Mel at the Valley Spa Hotel on Sunday morning. "Dave, here. I didn't know whether you two were planning to go out to Pebble Beach?"

"No, we don't want to be in all those crowds. We're going to do some spa things here. Ellen's arranged a couple of appointments. What's up, Dave."

"Let's meet for a late breakfast. I know a great place in the Carmel Valley Village. They serve *huevos rancheros* in the old style. Originally, I wanted you to meet Charles Atherton. I'd like your opinion about him, but he's not available. He's on a second honeymoon. He and his wife have some family matters to attend to tomorrow. Charles said he had some-fence mending to do with his mother. Those were his words. He's kind of a strange guy. First he's like all those ex-prep school schmucks, and then he tries to talk like a regular guy. I found out about his wife, Missy. She's blue blood all the way. He says she knows the social crowd in San Francisco. Anyway, I guess you're tied up."

"I suppose I could meet you tomorrow morning."

"I'll pick you up at your hotel. Bye the way, you've met Rita. What's she like? What does Ellen think of her?"

"Ellen likes her and I think she's great. She's very enthusiastic. As for looks? She has wavy auburn hair and a great curvy figure. She's younger than I expected, and Ellen thinks she's genuine"

"Do you think she's got more than The *Carmelo Diaries* to give you?"

"We've come up with a whole new idea of how to present it."

"Tell me about it."

"I won't discuss it with you until you tell me what you plan to get from Charles Atherton."

"I may just let go of the whole thing. Do you really have something that sounds good to you?"

"Yeah. And it's something Ellen and I want to do together. Our girls went away to college this year, you know."

"Frankly, I think Atherton has lost interest now. He cooled off after he went to that big shot wine convention at The Retreat. He tells me he made quite a hit. Now, all he talks about is developing a designer wine with his own label. He says in two years, he'll be ready to market it. He's made a bid for more acreage in the Carneros region between Sonoma and Napa. He'll take over an established vine-yard. He and his wife were separated, but now, they're back together. They're going on a trip to Australia in a few weeks. I think he's been a bad boy. He had a hot little number on the side, and he's willing to give her up, because he wants to expand his vineyard. I think he needs his wife's financial backing."

"Does his wife know that he has been talking to you about a T.V. series that takes place in early California?"

"Yeah, but I don't think she takes it seriously. She thinks we're pretty sleazy in the 'Southland' as she calls L.A. I told you she is San Francisco upper crust with an holier than thou attitude."

"What does she see in Atherton?"

"She wants to hang onto her husband. He's a good-looking guy. Wavy hair and intense blue eyes. Quite a gentleman when he wants to be. And besides his grandmother was an important grande dame of the old guard of San Francisco society as well as Pebble Beach. The grandmother knew Samuel F. B. Morse, who developed Pebble Beach and all that. His grandparents built a mansion in Pebble Beach quite a few years ago, and Charles lived there when he was a boy. I think his grandmama sent him to all those fancy prep schools. His mother's inherited the mansion. He told me Rita wanted it and she made a big fuss at the funeral. Rita turned his mother against him, but his mother really dotes on him, so he made up with her when he came to that wine conference, last week."

"Did Atherton say anything about the *Carmelo Diaries*?"

"Sort of brushed it off as incidental. You still didn't tell me much about Rita."

"I think you'd like her. She told us she talked to you about producing a T.V. series. She has been expecting to hear about a proposal from you."

"I'm going to let the project go."

"I think you ought to tell her that."

"Why? I don't owe her anything."

"Dave, do I always have to tell you to be nice to people. Call Rita. She thinks something is strange, because you didn't call her back. After she had that burglary at her shop, she's been kind of edgy about a lot of things."

"She's taking the missing *Diaries* all wrong. Since *The Carmelo Diaries* have disappeared, the story is all the more interesting."

"We'll talk about that tomorrow, Dave. What time and where?" Mel asked.

"I'm not quite sure. I'll call you back. I'll leave a message on your voice mail if you're not in. Ciao, man," Dave finished with a flourish.

The Stern's day was filled with a reflexology massage, aromatherapy, and a seaweed foot wrap treatment for Mel. At the same time Ellen had a collagen mask facial, a gommage body treatment, and a pedicure. They passed up the hot stone body therapy and Swedish massage and returned to their room exhausted.

Mel wanted to see the finish of the tournament on T.V., and had just closed the French doors to the balcony when the phone rang. It was Dave.

"Mel, you'll have to take a rain check on that breakfast tomorrow. I'm going to fly back to L.A. right away. I found out I have a late date tonight."

"Don't tell me you got lucky."

"It's even better than that. She says she's in love with me."

"Who is the lady?"

"Maggie Storm. You may not have heard of her yet, but you're going to. You know that new movie that's coming up for production about the life of Lena Horne? She's going to play Lena when she was young and just starting with singing jobs. I know the movie's going to be a winner. Anyway, I met her about a month ago at a party in Vegas. It was love at first sight for me. I think she might be farsighted or nearsighted or something, because she really took to me that first night. It wasn't long before we got physical, and she's clung to me like a kitten ever since."

"Well, good for you. So you're too busy to care about *The Carmelo Diary* story. Is our bet off?"

"What do you mean?"

"You know, our bet about who's going to produce a show about *The Carmelo Diaries?*"

"You don't have them. You can't produce the show."

"I don't need them. I have Rita."

"You may be sorry. She could be difficult to work with."

"Why do you say that?"

"Her brother says she's temperamental."

"That's just what her brother says. Anyway, I think you're giving up because of your girlfriend, Maggie?"

"Yep, it's about Maggie. We're a real item. I figure if Atherton and I worked on a production, we'd have to have dinner together sometime. Missy would take one look at Maggie, and after she got over being jealous as hell, she'd make some cutting remark. Maggie isn't famous yet, so Missy wouldn't see Maggie as a celebrity. She'd just see her as one helluva foxy looking, leggy, black girl. Atherton keeps saying she's really into prestige."

"So, you want to protect your little sweetheart. That's a real switch for you."

"Is that Dave?" Ellen called. She had heard the first part of the conversation.

"He has to fly back to L.A. right away for a heavy date, and we won't see him until next week."

"Let me talk to him," Ellen said and Mel handed her the phone.

"You old rascal. Why didn't you bring her up here? Then you wouldn't have to go back so fast."

"She's a busy lady. She takes singing lessons almost every day, and she's getting fit for her wardrobe in the new movie about the life of Lena Horne. She's got the part of the young Lena. I'll have to adjust my life for her."

"Dave, you're kidding. Love 'em and leave 'em Dave. This doesn't sound like you."

"Ellen, this is the real thing. I'm trying to take it slow because I want to marry her."

"You married? That would really be something."

"Don't make me sorry I told you. I've got to be smooth," he said as he drawled out the word, smooth.

"Have you asked her to marry you?"

"Not yet, but I've made up my mind. I want to have kids with her. We both knew it was special last week when we flew to that island resort in the Caribbean. You know, the one that's near to the private island that's so big with European royalty. It was our first weekend together, and I told her I loved her. I know there's an age difference, but she told me she always wanted to love a guy just like me. She said she even dreamt about it before she met me."

"Well, if that isn't love it'll have to do," Ellen hummed a little.

"And I've changed my mind about doing a show around *The Carmelo Diaries.* That way, I don't have to do a get together dinner with the Athertons. I don't want to tip toe around that Missy Atherton when she meets Maggie."

"You think Missy would hurt Maggie's feelings?"

"Hell, no. But it wouldn't be good for my business. There'd be the biggest cat-fight you ever saw. It would even be in the *National Inquirer*. Missy would say some catty thing, and then my little girl would tell her where to go in the kind of language you hear from those old mamas who sit at the slots in Vegas. They'd just go on from there."

"Dave, you are so funny," Ellen laughed.

"You think it's funny? I know women. Mixing two kinds of women is danger-ous. I lost a good lay once, by having her come to dinner with my sister."

"So the bet's off?" Mel called from across the room.

"That's what we need to negotiate," Dave told Ellen as she gave the phone back to Mel.

"Do what you want to do with your new idea, Mel," Dave continued talking. "But I better warn you about Rita, Mel,"

"You told me that before. Just exactly what did her brother say about her?"

"He said she's one spoiled babe. She's got a husband who watches her pretty close, because he knows what's she's like. Atherton told me she was the mistress of some famous senator when she lived in Europe. The family was really upset about it. The rich grandmother almost disowned her. She was proud of her ancestors. They claim to be descended from Spanish grandees and all that. Any-way, Atherton told me all about Rita and the senator."

"Is that all?"

"Well, her brother said she was extra cozy with the rich grandmother a few years before she died. Because of that she walked off with most of the family assets. In particular, a fabulous library of books and some jewelry. She let her grandmother set her up in that little book business of hers." He paused. "At least Atherton's mother inherited the mansion, which is worth at least twelve million in today's market."

"I guess the grandmother would be Clara Torelli, the grande dame of Pebble Beach."

"The one and the same. Anyway, you've got to watch that Rita. She's a con-niver."

"She seems pretty normal to me," Mel put in. "She's awfully busy juggling a business, a little girl, and her husband."

"Yeah, and that, too. The husband? Atherton doesn't know what she sees in him. Maybe he's like a manager to her. Atherton says the husband has always been crazy about her. He fell for her while he was married. That was long before his first wife died. It seems the wife turned out to be a pretty sad case, though. She was diagnosed schizoid, and she was an alcoholic too. After the husband put his crazy wife in a sanitarium, he found Rita, and they had a torrid affair. Charles said the old grandmother interfered and had Rita cool it. Then as soon as the wife died, the grandmother insisted they get married and have a kid. Charles says she set up a big trust fund for their little kid, right away."

"Atherton told you all this?"

"All that and more. So that's why I am warning you."

"You must know Atherton pretty well?" Mel asked.

"In a way I do, and in a way I don't. He's hard to know. He's unpredictable. He's certainly not one of us. However, he really knows about premium wines and even studied at some college in the south of France. He likes to drink fine wines, too. That's how we met. It was at the Cellar Master's Wine Festival in Europe. It was then that he told me about his plan to enter the private label wine business. His cousins carry the Torelli name. You've heard of Torelli wines, of course. It's not the greatest wine, but they're the biggest wine outfit in California. Their biggest seller used to be what we called 'Dago Red', and they make 'Wine in a Box', the picnic stuff. Now, they've branched out a little and have a small line of vintage wines. Atherton used to manage that division, but they never went to the estate-bottled level. Atherton told me that he was always in the shadow of the Torellis, so he convinced his other grandmother to give him a start with his own vineyards.

"A generous lady."

"He and Missy have two girls, and the grandmother liked the idea of them all living in a big house on an estate in Alexander Valley. It's up in Sonoma or Napa County. Missy liked the idea of the big house because of the prestige. It was something she could talk about with her ritzy San Francisco friends. That's how Charles started a business on his own. He says he's always in need of more money for the venture. It took time for the new vines to mature, and he had to find just the right winemaker. Charles has a master's degree from some big name business school, and he's familiar with the venture capital scene. Last year he contacted me in regards to doing a mini-series on T.V. He said it would be about early California in Monterey, and we could use material about his well-known family. He said his grandmother had some old diaries that go way back to the time of the Spanish. He told me he could show me those diaries."

"I get the picture. He wanted to sell you his ideas and information from the historic diaries. He needed to get money for his premium wine venture. Now you're not interested because you've got a new girl friend."

"Correction. This is the love of my life. This one's a keeper. I'm going to win this lady, and she's going to be my wife."

"I heard your voice clear across the room when you were telling Ellen that you're crazy about some show girl," Mel agreed.

"She's not a show girl. She's a serious actress and a singer. And this is different than anything else in my life. She's really got class as well as being good looking. She's really serious about her voice. She doesn't just yell into a microphone. She's got a great future, and I want to spend it with her."

"So what about *The Carmelo Diaries?*" Mel asked him.

"I told you. That bet is off. Produce a show on your own. I'm not competing. Tell Ellen all the things I told you about Rita. She might be hard to work with. Even from the angle of her busy life. She might not have time for you."

"What about the real *Carmelo Diaries?*" Mel continued.

"I guess they aren't important to me now," Dave said cryptically.

"OK, we'll have to find something else to bet on," Mel continued good-naturedly.

"I'll call you no later than next Thursday," Dave finished. "I've got to call a taxi and go right now. Wish me well."

"Mazel tov," Mel concluded, "Congratulations."

CHAPTER 34

▼

February 6, 2000.

Teams of golf professionals and amateurs with the lowest scores played only the Pebble Beach Links on this last day. The crowd was large, although many people preferred to see the closing rounds at home on television. This included Mike. While Carmelita took a nap, Rita continued reading Clarita's story.

This is what the diary said.

"1840. There are only a few days left in the year. I am writing a summary of my life during this year. The children are doing well, and I am directing the maids and discharging the duties of the household. Anita María is a robust healthy baby, and I have regained much of my health. However, I was either too tired or too involved with my duties of supervision to write about what has happened from day to day.

"This has been a prosperous year for Rancho Carmelo. We have had little rain in November and December, and Will says that we may have a drought if we do not have rain in January. However, he knows where to move the cattle so there will always be something for them to eat. He takes his most trusted *vaqueros* with him, and they are constantly riding over the *rancho* looking for small valleys where the grasses stay green for a longer time. Will tells me of the wondrous view from the top of the ridges on the mountains to the south of us. He promises to take me there after the spring rains have passed. He says that from the top, I will see the shining waters of the vast Pacific Ocean. Also, our *vaqueros* continue to ride all over the ranch, and they look everywhere for strangers. Will has supervised the building of bunkhouses for the *vaqueros* to sleep on his little rancho located in the river valley, and he has given them permission to hunt for game birds for our table. We allow them to keep some of the game for themselves.

"This autumn, after the annual roundup, we decided to have a celebration. For this *fiesta*, we added two rooms, and we have furnished the rooms with mahogany bedsteads for our guests. Consuelo arrived at our *Fiesta del Otoño* with the Hartnells. Miguel is still on active duty somewhere with his soldiers. Sometimes the governor needs him to lead men to the Southland and settle a quarrel. Since it is dangerous to ride on the trail to Monterey without an armed escort, Consuelo traveled with the Hartnells to our *fiesta*. Governor Alvarado appointed Señor Hartnell to be the *visitador general* of the missions, and he has been faithful in his duties. He is intelligent, well educated and a good husband to Teresa, as already evidenced by their nine children. Over the years they have suffered the loss of four of their children. Teresa looks well and told us that she was expecting another child by summer.

"Soon after Consuelo arrived, we talked together, and she encouraged me to have another child soon. Consuelo brings children into the world with much ease. I did not explain to her that I was injured internally by the birth of Anita María. She would not understand my fears. Will talked of my weakness to a friend, who is a ship's doctor. He told him that I must give my body a few years to heal.

"The Larkins spent two nights with us at the ranch. It was after the *fiesta*. They did not bring their children, except for the youngest. The Coopers, the Estradas, and the Castros all came to the fiesta for three days. We had sleeping spaces for everyone. All the children slept together in the nursery room. Anita María, of course, still sleeps in the cradle close by our bed. There is now a grand *sala* for dancing. It takes up the space of two rooms, and is part of the original house of my childhood. This *sala* is now the middle of our residence. The other *sala* is for our private family use.

"Every time Will goes to Monterey and a ship comes in, he continues to bring something home for us. Much of our furniture comes from China, which is the direct route for the ships that come into the port of Monterey. Will has always wanted me to have a pianoforte. Not long after he returned from his last trip to Monterey, he came to the vegetable garden where I was directing my maids to tear out weeds. He looked happy, and after he tied a handkerchief over my eyes, he led me to the grand *sala*. There stood a handsome piece of carved mahogany furniture, which encased a musical instrument. I admired the beautiful keyboard with white and black keys that made sounds when I pressed them with my fingers. Will said he had waited a long time for a pianoforte to arrive. This one came all the way from Boston around the tip of South America to Alta California. Will wants me to learn to make music on our Pianoforte. When our girls are older, we will find a teacher for them. Before the *fiesta*, I learned to play a few simple tunes that sounded like the songs my mother taught me. On one of the days of the *fiesta*, I dressed in my finest black taffeta skirt and wore a lace blouse with long sleeves. After dinner, when the men went out to the courtyard to talk and tell stories to each other, I entertained the ladies with simple music on the pianoforte.

"'Little Cousin, you look like a grand Castilian lady of the olden days. Our mothers would be proud of you,' Consuelo said to me in a rare moment of congratulations.

"When I told her that the pianoforte was a gift from Will, she said, 'Guillermo is becoming a good husband, after all.' Those who speak only Spanish cannot say 'Will', so they continue to use his Spanish name, Guillermo."

Rita stopped reading and pondered about the changes that were to come to California. Many of her ancestors had a story to tell about what had happened. Rita had customers who were interested in buying or obtaining books that would clarify some of the issues of land ownership over the years. She made it her business to collect books that told the story from various viewpoints. The books published in the beginning of the twentieth century were usually an American version. Californios were described as idle, pleasure seekers who danced on Sundays and were uninterested in educating themselves or their children. In the last part of the twentieth century, more books written about the clash of cultures. Rita stocked books of all persuasions, including the ones that claim that California was invaded and occupied by a foreign people who were indifferent to the society and the races living on the land before their arrival. There were buyers for all interpretations.

After supper, when Carmelita was asleep, Rita and Mike talked about the project. "How shall I present the story to the Sterns?" Rita asked. "Sometimes I think California is a place in our minds and not a piece of geography at all. Everyone's experiences are so different here. This is a story of the last two hundred years in California history."

"Where are you in the story, Babe?"

"1840–1846 and not many people here wrote about themselves."

"Is that important to the Sterns?" Mike asked.

"They want to know what it was really like then."

"Do you want me to listen to more of Clarita's diary?"

"I want you to be part of this," she said in a pleading voice.

"OK Babe. But I may give you some uneducated answers."

"You weren't born yesterday, Mike. You're a native Californian. The Minettis came to San Francisco in the 1880s."

"They were poor, and they started cultivating grape vines. Soon they bought some land. It has always helped to be a family who owned land. Those Anglos who first came here, married into the landed Spanish families," Mike answered.

"Wealth was measured in land until the Gold Rush" Rita quickly added. "The *Californios* had big families and there was always much celebrating."

"Sounds good to me," Mike laughed.

"There were lots of small battles going on in the 1840s. Every governor had to fight some self-made leader with his little group of followers. Tempers ran high, and there were even duels and a new governor from Mexico," Rita added.

"Can you tell about Zorro?" Mike commented with a wry smile. "Look, Babe, you need to enthrall your audience."

"My grandmother did it with Dom Perignon. I want to do it by telling about the real people who lived here."

"Then get to the exciting parts in a hurry," Mike advised. "Feuds and duels."

"Mike, you're making fun of me."

"Not really."

"It's not as simple as the Mexicans and the Americans want to tell it."

"Things seldom are."

"There were some people in California, like Clarita and Will, who were trying to manage their land by creating a self-sufficient community of people who worked together."

"And it was feudal. Everyone owed service or protection to someone, and Rancho Carmelo had its landlords, the *hacendados*. Don't forget the ranch hands called your ancestors, Don Guillermo and Doña Clarita."

"Yes, but they didn't take the land from anybody," Rita said earnestly.

"How did they get it?"

"Clarita inherited it from her father," Rita looked at Mike, who cocked his head and said "Well."

"Her father received Rancho Carmelo, with rights to run cattle, from the king of Spain, who gave most of the land to the missionaries." Rita explained.

"And?"

"When the Spanish came, there were Indians living up the valley. They hunted all over the area, but they didn't exactly own the land. And don't you dare ask me about anyone else."

Mike got up and put his arm around her. "Babe, I'm sorry if I interrupted your story. Just tell me what happened to your family."

"OK. Here is a copy of the diary that Clarita wrote. She's telling about their life, and she doesn't realize that with every passing year, they are coming closer to a time when California history takes a dramatic change." Rita pronounced every word with more emotion.

"What would that be? The American conquest or The California Gold Rush?"

Rita continued talking. "I suppose the person who most understood what was going on was Thomas Larkin. He was playing it pretty cool. He never became a Mexican citizen. Most of all, he wanted to make money, and he made money under the rather ineffective Mexican system of governing California. He was a great reader of newspapers that arrived by ship, and more than anyone else, he knew about what was going on all over the world. He liked the gracious living of the *Californios*, but he was also an American, and he never wanted to give up his own culture. He was known to be a shrewd trader at the same time as he was generous with his hospitality and life long friends with the *Californios*."

"Are we talking about the very same Larkin whose house is on the Adobe Tour of Monterey?"

"The very same. I love that house because it is such a mixture of cultures. The house was built with adobe bricks for the ground floor. Larkin added a sturdy redwood frame to support the second floor and added an upper porch, like a New England house He used genuine panes of glass, shipped from the East Coast of America.'

"It was also his store," Mike added

"I think he was a practical man. I tend to see a lot of good in him. Maybe because he liked Will and gave him a job after he was exiled from Rancho Carmelo."

"Will was your great-great-great-grandfather wasn't he?"

"That's where my red hair comes from," Rita answered.

"Say, not to change the subject, but what's going on with Tessa? Is she in some kind of trouble?"

"Tessa's always in some kind of trouble. She does things before she thinks about the consequences."

"I thought she was living in Scottsdale?"

"She is, but Captain Lewis subpoenaed her. He said he wanted some more information, but I really think he wanted to get to know her."

"That would figure. I knew there was reason he was spending so much personal time on this case. And did she take him up on it?"

"He asked her to meet him for dinner before she flew back. I warned her that he might ask her questions she didn't want to answer. When she left here, I think she was going to see if she could fly to Scottsdale on an earlier plane."

"I think a little romance would do her good. She really hasn't had a relationship since the divorce," Mike commented.

"A new love would be great for her. I'm sure we'll hear from her tomorrow."

CHAPTER 35

▼

The following morning, Rita arose early and went into her office to finish reading the third Carmelo Diary written by Clarita.

"I have not traveled to Monterey much this year, and our *fiesta* was very important. It was my only opportunity to find out what is happening among the people of Monterey. Encarnacion Cooper had news from the Vallejos. Everyone said that Don Juan Bautista has been a generous governor. He has given at least thirty grants for *ranchos*. Some *ranchos* consist of open grassland, but many *ranchos* are already occupied with homes of *Californios* and their families. The Espinosas, the Borondas, the Castros, and the Soberones are some of these families. The closest land grant to our Rancho Carmelo is San José y Sur Chiquito, and those lands have already changed ownership again. There are no buildings on the land.

"For all his charm and ability to win friends, our governor has his dark side and behaves badly when he is under the influence of strong drink. Encarnacion Cooper is his aunt, and she only speaks kindly of him, so she tells us he has mostly good days and nights, now that he is married to the lovely Martina of the Castro family.

"A group of ladies gathered to admire our new pianoforte. Consuelo advised them. 'Do not forget Juan Bautista Alvarado is one of us. He needs our support. A vile man, who is called Graham, constantly menaces him. Although Miguel has retired from active duty, he has offered his services to Juan Bautista. Miguel can easily gather a group of soldiers to put down a riot,' Consuelo assured us.

"I made certain that I talked to Rachel Larkin. Although she knows all the ladies present, it is hard for her to be part of a conversation in the Spanish language. Also I know she recently lost a child before it was born.

"'I am always amazed at the elegant appearance of all the Spanish ladies,' Raquel said to me while we were sitting together at a corner table. 'We live in such a wilderness, and yet I attend more balls and parties than any of our relatives in the East.'

"'What do they do with their evenings?' I asked her in amazement.

"'Dancing is frowned upon in some circles, and no one would dance on a Sunday,' she told me.

"'I am glad that we are not that kind of people.' I told her. 'Your July *fiesta* in honor of your country is always a wonderful gift to Monterey, and at *Navidad*, you serve imported Champagne at your *bailes*. We appreciate your hospitality.'

"When all talked together, the conversation turned to the bad *Yanqui* named Graham. Teresa said he plots to overthrow our government. The warning came from Padre Suarez del Real, who heard it in confession. The governor acted immediately and arrested the perpetrators. Then he rounded up the foreigners who were not married to California ladies, and he shipped them off to San Blas, Mexico. This included the *Yanqui* Graham. None of us thought it too severe, but it was said that some Americans were worried about who would be banished next.

"I am writing about our special *fiesta* for our friends in Monterey, because this was the only real party we hosted during the year. As much as Will and I enjoyed the company of friends and the compliments for our beautiful little daughters, we were glad to be quiet after all the guests had gone to their homes. I tire easily, and I take a long rest every afternoon.

"Now I have time to pray again and make decisions for the ranch. The Blessed Virgin saved my life, and I plan to do more and more for the education of the children on the ranch. Not everyone will read and write, but I shall help all those who show an interest. Felicia reads very well, and she even reads a little English. She spends more and more time in prayer. I wonder if she is happy. She never talks about Dulcera. I know she misses her sister. I will ask her to teach with me. She can teach the smaller children, especially those of the household of Ramon. She will not be so timid when she is in the company of the young ones.

"After the *fiesta del otoño*, Will and I had time to enjoy life together. We watched our children play, and we practiced songs on the guitar and piano. I cannot ride far distances yet. Life here at Carmelo is so different than the loneliness I endured when I was living in the household of the Vargas family. At that place there was much hostility between Felipe and his sister. Here there is happiness.

"Will does not go on long voyages to Chile or Mexico City the way the other men do. Captain Cooper still sails the seas and leaves Encarnacion to manage a large household consisting of many generations. Don Tomás often goes by ship to Acapulco or Mazatlán to see other Americans or talk to the Mexican officials. Señor Hartnell must journey all around Alta California to visit the missions where the *padres* hold mass. Will spends most of his time at our ranch, although I am lonely when Will goes to Monterey for a few days. I have been blessed with good fortune to have the love of this man who is often by my side. Although I may never see Ardo again, I must not think of what I have lost. I will pray to be strong about this."

In some ways Clarita was like many women in any other era. When she was young and without responsibilities, she had time to write. As the years followed, she led a busy life with children and the supervision of a large household. She and Will shared the management of Rancho Carmelo. The journal was often put aside. After lapses of several months, she would resume her narration. Paper was a valuable commodity. Clarita's diary in the 1840's became a collection of family anecdotes and political updates.

"Spring 1841. Anita is the easiest child of all. There is always someone to play with her. She has auburn hair and large blue eyes, and Felicia is her favorite person. I am so glad, since Felicia no longer has periods of silence and sadness. Now she is always singing.

"It is only when I hear of something unusual happening in Monterey that I understand how much my own life is completely centered around Will and the household of our ranch. All of us at Rancho Carmelo are praying for late rains this spring. This will make the meadows greener. We will need to slaughter even more cattle to be able to feed a smaller herd. Will is always watchful for an opportunity to make us more independent of the uncertainties of selling cattle hides. His friendship with Señor Larkin gives him the most opportunities for this. Governor Alvarado is friendly and courteous to us and never causes us trouble, but he cares little for what happens in the countryside surrounding Monterey. Every time I see him I am amazed that he looks so much older. Consuelo tells me that he continues to drink strong spirits a great deal, and sometimes he falls and hurts himself. Poor Martina. She has been his wife only a short time. I'm glad we do not live in Monterey to see it all.

"Don Guillermo Hartnell has been the guest of our ranch on several occasions. He takes his post of *visitador* seriously. I think he likes to come here because he enjoys our mealtimes. At noon dinner, we often include Esperanza and all the children, and he says we remind him of his own big household with their many relatives and all their many children. Will talks to him both in Spanish and in English, and later he told me that Señor Hartnell has been responsible for the dismissal of those administrators who have stolen goods and livestock from the missions. There has been a small increase in the number of *padres* in other missions of Alta California. Some are more important than others. Our own Mission San Cárlos is in complete ruins.

"Privately, all of us born in Alta California are disappointed that Governor Alvarado does not take a more active part in his duties as governor. Señor Hartnell knows that Mariano Vallejo has written a personal letter on this subject to President Bustamente of Mexico. Juan Bautista and Mariano hardly speak to one another now, and although everyone knows that Mariano can be haughty, they also know that Juan Bautista has long neglected his duties. He has held public *fiestas* by using profits he gained from selling mission property. I am certain we will hear more about all of this.

"Consuelo has gone to visit Prudencia and her baby who live in Mexico far to the south of California. No doubt she will have much to tell when she comes back, near the end of summer. She knows I always want to hear about Ardo, who is now thirteen years old. He goes to school in Mexico City. I think Consuelo would like to arrange another good marriage for her next daughter.

"Every time Will comes home from Monterey, he tells me of more foreigners in town. No wonder Encarnacion is never seen except at mass. She does not speak any English and is uncomfortable with these strangers. She likes Will to visit because she says he is polite and speaks to her in Spanish. Life in Monterey is different than what we knew in our early years.

"August 1841. I wish that Will did not need to go to Monterey at this time. Our life on the ranch is so satisfying. When we have good fortune, we have a *fiesta* with much food and games for all who live on the rancho. When there is a drought, we still manage to eat well, and we have a simple *fiesta* for the workers and their families. We always invite the *padre* from Monterey to bless our animals, and he takes part in other blessings of the ranch children. My greatest pleasure comes when Will and I have a day to be by our selves. Our favorite pastime is always a small journey with our horses up the river valley to a bend where we sit and eat a little food. We laugh and talk as we did when we were younger, and we pretend we are young lovers. I also enjoy holding classes in reading for the children of Esperanza and Xavier and Ramon and Merced.

"Felicia reads very well, and she continues to help me. Soon it will be time to have Patricia read with us. She says she wants to be a nun and teach children. However, I hope to find her a good husband so that she can have children of her own. For this I will need to take part in more activities in Monterey. Then I will know something about the disposition of the men in Monterey who come from the families of Spanish blood. Felicia is a de Segovia and a devoted Catholic. I think she is very beautiful with her black hair and blue eyes and quiet ways.

"Perhaps, we will find a small house to occupy in Monterey during the week of *Los Pastores*, and I can take Felicia with me to some of the festivities. Raquel Larkin decorates her stairway and doors with pine boughs, and she serves tea and hot chocolate with special sweetmeats. Her friends and their daughters are all invited, and Felicia and I will enjoy this.

"Late fall, 1841. Every time Will returns from Monterey he brings stories of more that is happening. Most of it is disturbing. He follows the advice of Señor Larkin, and he listens and observes. He stays away from those who would make trouble, and also he is very careful to avoid taking sides. He only goes to Monterey to be of help to Señor Larkin, who although not a Mexican citizen is highly respected by the *Californios*, and we know that he considers California his home.

"It is clear that Governor Alvarado has given up all his leadership because of poor health. He had offered to resign, and we think that the new president of Mexico will send us another governor soon. The Russians have departed from the lands north of San Francisco Bay, and other men from foreign countries are arriving to make their fortunes. Will says Señor Larkin says California may need the protection of the *Yanquis*. He does not mean the *Yanqui* men who come here to trap animals, but the men of their government who write to him. Will tells me to call these men 'Americans.' The true name of their country is the 'United States of America.'"

There were no other entries in the journal until 1844. Rita knew California history and had a general idea of what was happening in the Mexican territory of Alta California from 1841–44. Mariano Vallejo resigned his position as military comandante. There was lack of money in the treasury to pay those officials who had been working with diligence. The Mexican government appointed Manuel Micheltorena, an adjutant general, to be governor and commanding general. He arrived in the south of Alta California with a fleet of four vessels. After being welcomed there, he officially took office in Monterey on December 31, 1842.

Also in 1842, Commodore Thomas ap Catesby Jones, commander of the U.S. Pacific fleet, heard rumors of a war between Mexico and the United States. These rumors grew after the annexing of the Texas Republic to the United States. Jones thought that other countries might try to seize California, so he set his course for Monterey and upon arrival took command of the port. This incident included raising the U.S. flag and marching some of his men through the streets of Monterey. Thomas Larkin was the principal figure in achieving a peaceful solution to this misunderstanding. The whole incident ended peaceably, and after the American flag was lowered, the people of the town celebrated with a round of parties and all the officers of foreign ships danced with the ladies of Monterey, even at their private balls. This incident changed the life of Thomas Larkin.

From as early as 1833, there were attempts to have an American Consul in Monterey, but something always intervened. There was already an official consul in Oahu in the Sandwich Islands and Mazatán, Mexico, but the population of Americans in California was growing. In 1843, the U.S. government recognized Thomas Larkin as the most influential citizen of Monterey. He spoke Spanish and knew all the important leaders of Monterey and the lands to the north. He became the official consul to Mexico in 1844. He had many duties and looked after all legal matters and the general welfare of American citizens in Monterey, whether they were residents of California or seamen with problems. Since he had no predecessors, he often had to follow his own evaluations of matters between Americans and the government of Mexico. The diary continues.

Spring 1844. We need to make a permanent home in Monterey where we will live for several weeks each month. Since Señor Larkin has become an official of the United States government, he has asked Will to work full time at his office and store. Señor Larkin promises to find a permanent assistant. He is petitioning the U.S. government to issue papers of citizenship to Will. I am being pulled in opposite ways. I have seen many Americans whom I do not like or understand. They do not care to learn our ways or customs, and most of them do not attend church or try to speak any of our language. When I am in Monterey, I sometimes listen to them talking, and they do not know that any of us can understand what they are saying. They say many bad things about us. I love Will more than anyone, except my children, so I want him to be an American citizen, because it is dangerous to live in California without papers from any country. Señor Larkin has been kind and generous to our family and I think he understands the California people. I wish more Americans were as *simpático*.

"My other worry is that I am away from my duties of managing Rancho Carmelo. My little daughters are happier at the ranch; however, I always bring them with us to Monterey. I have resolved to have them near me at all times. While in Monterey, I must find a good husband for Felicia, and we participate in social gatherings with the families of eligible men. I have not prayed as much to the Blessed Virgin as when I was younger. When we are living in Monterey and near to the *Presidio* Chapel, I can do my daily devotions. Although we are crowded in a small adobe with two bedrooms and a small *sala*, there are many advantages to living in Monterey.

"The first *fiesta* after the New Year was attended by Governor Micheltorena. I have seen him at church. He is a handsome, mannerly man, and he looks very Spanish. Already Señor Larkin has sailed to Mazatlán on business with other influential *Californios*. Although we have already heard that some of the *Californios* want to rebel against the new governor, we want to see what he will do for us. He has said that he will establish schools in Alta California. He promises he will find teachers who will be sent to these schools, and he will aid the bishop in Santa Clara who wishes to establish a seminary. I sent a letter by one of our *vaqueros* to Consuelo and Miguel. I encouraged them to attend the New Year *Fiesta* and become acquainted with the governor.

"During the last few years, there have been a few newcomers who have arrived from Mexico and who are educated and want to make California their home. Some are distant relatives of Miguel García. They are part of the large Alonso family in Mexico. Consuelo tells me that there are many young men in this family who will want to marry only girls who are of Spanish heritage. She has finally counted Felicia as one of these young ladies. After I help Felicia to be more comfortable on the dance floor, we will have a *fiesta* at our ranch and celebrate some anniversary. I will make sure that there is dancing for the young people. Meanwhile I must find a lady who will accompany Felicia when she is asked to go walking after church. It would be best for Felicia to have a husband she knows. She would be frightened of a marriage with a total stranger.

"All of the *Californios* here have not forgotten the humiliation of the raising of the American flag in Monterey when Commodore Jones of America came to Monterey. The commodore sent a letter of apology to Governor Micheltorena, but that did not really settle their fears of a sudden American takeover. We do no think the small army at the *Presidio* can protect us. There are always foreign ships in port, and the business of Señor Larkin does well. We do not rely solely on the cattle hides. A new wharf is being built, and the Custom House has been reconstructed to be suitable for all the gatherings of the many people in Monterey.

Will is at his best when he is supervising construction. Since this new governor is agreeable and the business of Señor Larkin has been good for us, we do not want to be any part of the people who want to force the return of Governor Micheltorena to Mexico.

"I am not thinking much about the future, as my most important duties are with my family and this includes Esperanza, who has been by my side so much of my lifetime. She cared for Papa in his hours of need and I will always value her devotion. She was surely sent to us by God. Although I am fearful about our future, there is one thing that I have learned, and that is to be thankful for all our daily blessings. I want to always have Rancho Carmelo as our own. I have made a promise to the Blessed Virgin. It will be my duty to find ways to teach the children who live at our ranch. I believe it is more important than any gift of gold I can give the *padres*."

CHAPTER 36

▼

February 7, 2000

Rita was downstairs starting breakfast when the phone rang. "Hello dear. I wanted to reach you early, so you could tell all this to Mike," came her mother's confidential tone of voice. "Tonight is very important. First of all, Missy and Charles are officially together again. This dinner is very special for them. Charlie has invited Andres Duncan and his wife. You know, they are one of the earliest winegrowers in the Carmel Valley, and now they have built a quaint little place for wine tasting that resembles a farmhouse in Provence. What do they call those things?"

"That would be a *mas,*" Rita supplied.

"Oh, yes," Anita continued quickly, "Anyway, their tasting room is something really special. Upscale wine tasting and yet informal. You've probably seen the Duncans at the Shore Club. You may not know them, but you've heard of them. They have lived on the Monterey peninsula a long time."

"Is anyone else going to be at the dinner?"

"Missy was able to contact her brother, Stanton, and he is flying his plane down, just to be at the dinner. That is why I wanted to reach you before you planned a strenuous day for yourself. Did you?"

"I think it will be quite a normal day," Rita said trying to assure her.

"Normal for you is busy. Maybe you could lighten up your schedule. Have you given any thought to what you are going to wear?"

"Frankly, no. I want to see what the weather is like."

"Missy is always understated and chic. So don't wear anything too colorful. How about that deep sapphire blue blouse I gave you for Christmas?"

"Did Missy give you any indication of what she would be wearing?"

"Oh no, dear. She never does. Anyway, she is the hostess and can wear whatever she likes. She said she has something to show us. Do you think Charles bought her a new wedding ring?"

"I'm sure she would like that," Rita commented.

"And they are postponing their trip until the girls have winter break in February. Then the girls will meet them on their way home from Australia. That will be in the Fiji Islands, at that new resort. They are still trying to coax me to accompany the girls."

"I think you should go, Mother."

Anita ignored Rita's reply. "Missy put Charles on the phone to talk to me. He never sounded happier." Then her mother lowered her voice and talked in a deep whisper. "Do you really think that Charlie had a mistress? I mean the kind that gets jewelry and lingerie? When we went to lunch the other day, Missy told me that her detective found out about the mistress. But he was never able to identify the woman. It's good that Charles has turned over a new leaf. He says he's given her up. Do you think so?"

"Who knows? Anyway it's their life."

"Now, dear, don't be flip. This is a time for family conciliation. And you know there is nothing that would make me happier than you and Charlie being good friends. Like in the old days. Even Rex and I are talking to each other again."

"You know how different we are Mother," Rita said softly while she was thinking of the old days and of how her brother teased her and took her favorite toys.

"Of course I know. But blood is thicker than water. What is good for him is good for all of us. This wonderful new wine venture is so prestigious. Do you know Petra Duncan?"

"No, Mother. The friends I see now are the mothers in the neighborhood toddler play group," Rita replied.

"You must be in a silly mood. I know you meet important people on the peninsula and Mike does, too."

"What are you wearing, Mother?" Rita replied and changed the subject.

"Oh, I really don't know yet. I love my Escada suit although it's quite dressy. However, this is an important occasion. I may buy a new blouse when I go into Carmel to get my hair done. When will you pick me up tonight?"

"Missy said seven o'clock for cocktails. The Residence in the Pines is rather far away, so I think we should pick you up at six o'clock."

"Oh, that would be lovely. I hope Mike will enter into the conversation. Does he know Stanton?"

"He may know him. Mike knows a lot of people in the Bay Area. And Mike is a talker. He's always in the center of a conversation at a party."

"The other night when I had you over for dinner, he wasn't very talkative. However, he certainly looks happy, now that he is married to you." She paused. "After that awful ordeal he lived through with Gloria." There was a silence.

"Yes, I know, Mother." Rita said solemnly.

"And how's Carmelita? When can she come and spend the morning with me?" Anita went on.

"Just let me know your free days and I'll bring her over."

"I'll have Alma make some cookies, and we'll have a real tea party. Do you know, I still have the doll dishes that I played with when I was a little girl? My mother kept everything. Little by little we are finding various items. Do you have tea parties with Carmelita?"

"Not yet. We usually do something active. She has a lot of energy."

"Then it will be good for her to have a tea party with me. I'll be ready for you at six tonight. Ta ta."

Carmelita was now awake, and Mike was downstairs before Rita made coffee or prepared breakfast. "That was Mother on the phone. She's really excited about tonight. She said there might be eight of us. Missy invited Andres and Petra Duncan and also her brother, Stanton. Mother says that Charlie and Missy want everyone to know they are reconciled. Missy will be part of their new company. Missy can help with the publicity for their limited edition of connoisseur wines."

"Good. Then she'll be occupied. Do we really have to go tonight?"

"Definitely. We're to pick up Mother at six."

"You mean I'll have to be charming for an extra hour before and after the dinner."

"And to three more people who have been invited to the party."

"I think I'll go up to Carmelita's world while you fix me a power breakfast. I have a big day."

After Mike left, Tessa called. "You won't be able to guess where I am, so I'll tell you. I only drove almost all night and I'm in Palm Springs. I'll take off tomorrow for Sedona. I'm going to see Mother and then drive down to Scottsdale from there."

"What about your job?"

"I called them, and told them I would be in next week. I'm only temporary help anyway."

"Captain Lewis will be looking for you."

"I know. I called my apartment in Scottsdale for my messages. He had telephoned me, and he didn't sound official. I think he has a nice voice. He said he would be coming to Scottsdale soon. He said he really wants to see me."

"And I think he does. He has a new theory about the burglary, and he thinks you might be involved."

"Gee, and I thought he wanted to make out with me."

"Maybe that, too. You can juggle both."

"It might be fun. I'm ready for a fling. I haven't given up Charlie, but it might be a while before he gets out of Missy's clutches. In the meantime I need somebody else."

"Whatever you do," said Rita. "Be smart. And if you were involved in the burglary, I don't want to know about it. Captain Lewis is sure to ask me."

"Do you want to know all that happens with me and Deputy Dog?"

"Only if you seduce him." Rita laughed.

"I think I can do that."

"I bet you can," Rita laughed again although she was puzzled.

Two hours later, Rita was at The Old Booktique and checking her appointment book. She looked up and saw Captain Lewis.

"Have you heard from Tessa?" he asked.

"Hello?" Rita answered. "Don't you say, Good Morning, Ma'am?"

"Lady, I'm busy. I was being nice to your friend, Tessa, and asked her to have a light snack with me before her flight to Phoenix, and she didn't show up."

"Maybe she took an earlier flight."

"There wasn't any. Not even a flight to LAX. I checked with the airport."

"She has a job and an apartment in Scottsdale, so that's where she'll go."

"I need to talk to her, but I don't want to be tough. I may just go there and bring her back here for questioning. I can do it legally, you know. I now have reason to suspect she had something to do with your burglary."

Rita took a quick breath. "I don't know why."

"Your lack of information is phenomenal, lady."

"You can keep me informed," Rita said lightly as she waved to Dolores who was entering the door

"I might have to involve you as a suspect too, you know."

"Then I had better not talk to you anymore."

"Oh, lady. You never make it easy. I'll see you soon."

"OK, give me a call, Captain Lewis," she said with a tone of finality.

As soon as he left, Dolores put her arm on Rita's shoulder. "What does he want now?"

"Any number of things," Rita laughed. "Publicity, closure of the case, or maybe Tessa."

"Really?" said Dolores rolling her eyes.

"That gives us a pretty wide choice."

The conversation ended with the dramatic entrance of the eccentric client who had wanted to charge books to her hotel room. "We have to leave today, so I'm ready to do business. I brought my credit card," she said waving it in the air and throwing down her cape, walking stick, and scarf. "I need to get some special books as presents for my mother and three backgammon addicts."

Dolores led her gently to the Chinese table and settled her accessories beside her. Rita continued making the store ready for customers. The morning went quickly. When Rita was ready to leave for lunch, Dave Goldman called.

"Rita, I really planned to see you when I was up there, but something came up that's pretty great for me, and I left in a hurry."

"I always like to hear good news," she answered a little puzzled.

"You'll probably hear about it from my friend Mel in a few days."

"That would be great."

"Yeh, I thought you would say that. I have another big deal that I'm going to promote. I flew back to L.A. last night. I really intended to see you, but this other thing came up. Give my regards to your brother."

Rita hardly knew what to say. "Well, thanks for calling to let me know," she managed.

"Mel said that you and your husband would be coming down to L.A. sometime soon. Maybe we could all have lunch together?" Dave said as he sensed coolness in Rita's voice.

"Maybe," Rita said.

"O.K. then. I'll tell Mel that I called you. Dave finished with "I gotta go."

CHAPTER 37

▼

Monday evening, February 7, 2000

"Anita, you look lovely." Mike said as he escorted her out the door of Stonecrest toward the car.

"I wanted to wear a suit, but it is so cold tonight. I had to wear something that went well with this coat," she explained to Mike. "What is Rita wearing?"

"I know she looked perfect, but I really can't describe it," answered Mike. "When she gets here, you two can sit in the back seat and talk about clothes on the way out."

"We don't often have a chance to do that," Anita agreed as she carefully entered the car. When Rita arrived, Anita complimented the shimmering turquoise pantsuit that her daughter was wearing. However, she worried whether it was appropriate. "I hope that Missy doesn't think you've upstaged her. You know this is their big night."

"She won't notice anyone else. She'll be occupied by all the details of the party," Rita said. Hoping to end the topic, she steered the conversation toward speculation about what the evening might bring.

They took the Carmel Valley Road toward The Residence in the Pines, which was where Missy and Charles decided to have their dinner. They drove by the Valley Village, and crossing the Carmel River, drove up a steep hill. Soon they found The Residence Club and Resort. It catered to equestrian tastes, and all the guests stayed in cottages. The dining room was famous for its old world charm and available to members of The International Residence Club. An attendant at the gatehouse took their names and made a ceremony of their admittance.

Mike drove up a winding road lined with tall pine trees, lit with amber spotlights. "Ah, it lives up to Missy's description," Anita commented. "It is such a shame her parents were killed in that accident. They liked Charles so much, and they would have been so glad that they are back together. The Residence in The Pines is a perfect place to celebrate."

Charles greeted them at the entrance, and Missy, in a red silk Chanel suit, took them to a room they called 'The Map Room.' She seated Anita in a comfortable English wing back chair near a contented fire. "Rita looks lovely tonight, Mother, and those pearls are becoming to you." Missy gushed with enthusiasm as she patted Anita's hand.

"They belonged to my mother," Anita said quietly. "Pearls pick up light from the fire, you know," she said as she settled into the chair and accepted a cut crystal snifter of cognac from an attentive waiter.

Missy wanted Anita to be discreetly settled and comfortable in case Rita and Charles were not overly cordial. "I need to join Charles at the entrance gallery," Missy said.

Andres Duncans entered The Library. As soon as Andres saw Mike, he said, "Mike Minetti, I haven't seen you since that tournament at the Sierra Lake Country Club a few years ago. Are you still winning tournaments like you did at that Invitational?"

"It was just my lucky day," Mike shrugged.

"Seriously Mike, you've got a natural swing, but I bet you don't play as much as you should. My club has an Invitational coming up in a few months. Why don't you get serious about your game and plan on being my guest."

"Sounds like a great idea."

"Good. I'll call you."

Missy entered with Petra Duncan, and she smiled when she saw Mike and Andres in a conversation. After Petra and Anita greeted each other, Missy introduced Rita. "I don't think you two know each other. Petra Duncan, may I present Rita Atherton, Oh I mean Minetti," she laughed. "She was Rita Atherton so long. Stanton called. He said that the weather had changed, and he had to land in Salinas instead of Monterey. He'll be just a little later than he expected. He's bringing our cousins from Piedmont with him. I think we should all go to the Vineyard Room and have another drink." She turned to Anita. "Do you want to come with us, Mother?"

"I want to be with all of you, of course," Anita said.

They walked toward a large room with many conversational furniture groupings and a baby grand piano at the far end. A musician was playing familiar show tunes and a few guests at the Residence were sitting around the edges of the room as if it were all a stage set for Missy's party.

Charles entered the room and walked to where Mike and Andres were talking about golf. He stood beside them a moment and then said, "Pebble Beach golf links are dear to our family. My grandfather Atherton had my dad on course even before he was in high school. When Dad was courting Mother, he played Pebble Beach every weekend."

"Clara Torelli was quite a player herself. There's a picture of her in the Grillroom of The Retreat. It's one of those old time ones where the ladies wore long skirts and straw hats," added Mike.

"Do you get down here often, Charles? We should have a game at The Cypress together," Andres suggested.

"I don't come down as much as I should. I've been focusing on my own vineyards in the last few years. I've been venturing out from under the protection of the Torelli Brothers. I love the challenge, but its hard work."

"Nobody knows what a taskmaster the vineyard can be," Andres agreed.

"How do you find time to represent Northern California vintners all over the world?"

"I have a son who is active in the business, and we hired the best of winemakers."

"And your reward is a prestigious product," Charles complimented. "I know you come up to Napa, so I'll expect you to call me when you do. I want you to come to Holly Ridge, where we expect to make the best Cabernet Sauvignon in California."

"How does your wife feel about the wine business?" Andres continued.

"She's encouraging me now that I've branched out on my own," Charles said with enthusiasm. "She thinks the Torelli Brothers were too overpowering and agrees that I need to be on my own."

Andres turned to Mike, "Do you know the Torelli Brothers?

"The Minettis are related to the Torellis. Actually I grew up around Napa."

"Then you and Rita are some kind of cousins," Andres laughed.

"All by marriage," Mike replied.

"I guess the one Mike is referring to is Celia Minetti who married Pauli Torelli, our uncle. Get's complicated, doesn't it?" said Charles as he affectionately put his hand on Mike's shoulder.

"What appellation are you using, Charles?" Andres continued.

"Holly Ridge Reserve. Missy thought it up when we decided to call our little estate 'Holly Ridge,'" Charles explained.

"And you live in the vineyards?" Andres asked.

"On one of the hills nearby."

Andres realized that Mike had not said much, so he leaned his way. "Mike have you ever thought of being in the wine business?"

"Not really. My family had to take bankruptcy during prohibition, and it changed his opinion about vineyards. Dad did all right in real estate in Napa, and when I came down here, I just gravitated toward that profession."

"You have someone in your office who handles wine properties, don't you, Mike?" Charles asked.

"I found a good man for that. He has so much business he has several agents working with him. We have a Salinas office, too."

Stanton arrived, and after introductions all around, Missy quickly ushered everyone down a wide hallway to a private dining room and told them to find their place cards. The table was filled with a multiplicity of glasses that shone like Christmas ornaments in the candlelight. Candles were also a part of the small flower arrangements that accompanied each place setting. The room was long and narrow. The whole atmosphere was intimate and festive, although formal. Charles sat at the head of the table with Anita and Rita on either side. Missy sat at the foot of the table with Stanton and the cousins. Andres sat at the right of Rita.

"I've always wanted to meet you," Andres said with a wink. "Tell me about yourself."

"That's hard to do except to say that I seem to be always on the go."

"Where do you spend most of your time?"

Rita saw Charles was standing and about to say something, so she leaned her forward and said, "Charlie wants to make a toast."

Just then, two violinists strolled into the room, and five waiters entered bearing bottles of champagne and silver buckets of ice. The sommelier of the Residence ceremoniously walked up to Charles with a magnum of champagne, and Missy rose from her seat to be with Charles.

If Mike had been sitting at her side, Rita would have whispered, "and now the Olympic Torch will be lit." However, she sat with dutiful expectation while the cork was carefully removed from the bottle. A waiter gently poured the effervescent liquid while Charles nodded his approval.

The violins played the "Anniversary Waltz" as Charles and Missy looked at each other in rapture. The waiters then stood behind the guests and stepped forward to fill the glasses with Champagne.

Charles began to speak. "Here's to my wife, Melissa, whom we all know as Missy. Next week will be our fifteenth wedding anniversary, and we are celebrating tonight with our family and good friends. To commemorate this event, I am giving Missy a ring." He took a blue Tiffany box out of his pocket and opened it carefully. He then removed the ring and placed it on Missy's left hand ring finger. It was a circle of marquise diamonds. Everyone clapped, and Charles and Missy touched glasses.

Stanton jumped to his feet and said, "Let us toast to their happiness."

Everyone took a sip, and Charles continued. "We also want to announce our new joint venture. Holly Ridge has acquired a new piece of property a little to the south and west of us in the Carneros region. Its superior location is well known. We will use traditional farming methods to produce a Cabernet Sauvignon that is polished and has a depth of mystery in its rich flavors. Our aim is to make a complex wine that requires both our expertise and the cooperation of nature." Charles stopped, and he turned to Missy so she could speak.

"We chose this project because we know it is a worthy commitment. It will take some time to attain, but the product will be a wine that connoisseurs will savor and want. Maybe, it will be chosen for vertical tasting in years to come. Charles and I will be in this together. So let us make a toast to our supreme Cabernet." Missy and Charles touched glasses before they sipped.

"Now enjoy the dinner that Missy has dreamed up for you," Charles added and sat down in his seat at the head of the table.

Missy took her seat at the other end while each guest was served a small nest of toasted grated potato with a dollop of creamy foie gras. This was presented on gold-bordered porcelain plates. The five waiters appeared again and served Beluga caviar from an iced bowl that was elegantly displayed on a mahogany trolley. Each course was an art form in presentation, and all the portions were served on large plates. Curley endive held tendrils of lobster placed on thinly slice beets. A pear eau de vie sorbet preceded the pan-seared monkfish topped with a tomato glaze, and it was served with a vintage Shiraz wine. After the cheese course, the diners were offered a choice of various petits fours and paper-thin chocolate mints with various coffees.

"I am glad to know Charles is serious about his place in the wine business," Andres said to Rita. "He told me how much he admired his Grandmother Torelli. She was a legend around here, you know. Was she part of your life, also?"

Rita nodded.

"I had the pleasure of being with her on a few occasions. I even attended one of her famous Dom Perignon circle of friends when she told about some of the people who were her ancestors," he continued.

"That was her greatest pleasure when she grew older."

Stanton was talking to Missy at that end of the table, and Andres turned to talk to the lady on his other side, who had been introduced as Missy's cousin, Fanchon. Anita was talking to Mike who was seated at her side. Charles took the opportunity to ask Rita about Carmelita.

"She's a very active little girl," Rita started. "She…"

"Sis," Charles interrupted, "you know Missy and I are serious when we say that we're going to live a different life. We will probably stay home more. I bet Carmelita would love to come visit us in the country."

Missy had just invited everyone to gather for some cognac in the Music Room, and while Andres stopped to say something to Petra, Charles turned to Rita. "Missy has come around and wants to put all her assets into producing a premium Cabernet. Sis, let's put our differences aside, too. I think you and I can do that."

"Charlie, we've always been pretty independent of each other. You're not asking me to put my assets with yours, are you?"

"Oh no, Rita. I don't want us to have any bad feelings about each other, although I used to have some bitter feelings about your getting *The Carmelo Diaries* from Grandmother. I knew if I had them I could make some big money. I have good contacts through some of my Hollywood type neighbors in the wine country. *The Diaries* tell a great story, you know."

"We can agree on that," was all that Rita could manage to say.

"Lately I've changed my mind. Do whatever you want," said Charles, and he stopped. When Rita didn't comment he continued. "Anyway, when I looked at the bigger picture, I decided to win Missy back, and just about that time the Carneros property came on the market."

Charles stopped again, and now Rita knew she had to say something. "Sounds good," she said trying to be noncommittal She knew she was playing a game with Charles. There were still missing pieces in the puzzle. At the beginning, she saw only a small section of the solution. Now it just a matter of a little more information.

"Anyway, what I'm really saying," Charles said slowly as if he were searching for words, "I want to show you that I'm sincere about being friends. I'm not interested in *The Carmelo Diaries*. I've taken my life to a new level in a different direction with this new project in the Carneros." He stopped again, and when

Rita nodded, he said, "Go ahead and promote your stories about Rancho Carmelo. I've made some contacts in Hollywood, and I can throw some your way."

"I have my own plans," she said.

"Oh, I know all about some of your attempts, but frankly the guy that used to be interested in your ideas isn't interested anymore."

"Then I'll find somebody who is," she said, realizing he didn't know about Mel and Ellen.

"You know I'm talking about Dave Goldman." Charles said. "Sis, I can hardly picture you all settled down. You always said you wanted to be independent. Otherwise, I thought you would have married that senator who was in love with you. At least when his term was over."

"Charlie you fantasize, and you don't really know that much about me. I like my life as it is today. I like being part of my own little family. Mike's a wonderful husband, and Carmelita means everything to both of us."

"So it's all going to turn out OK. I'll have my famous vintage wine, and you can find somebody to help you tell a story about the diaries. By the way what did you want to do with them?"

"Charlie, things are just starting to get OK between us. Don't say any more. Let's be friends for Mother's sake and let the rest alone."

"But we don't often have a chance to talk," he insisted. "I guess now's not the time, though."

"After what I've been through with the burglary, I don't want to talk about *The Diaries* any more, Charlie. This has been a beautifully orchestrated dinner. I'm glad you have Missy. You need her."

"What do you mean by that? She's not perfect, but things are good for now."

"You're like Dad"

"Don't start that now, girl."

"What do you mean?"

"I mean, I think we should try to understand Dad. Mother never went through with the divorce, you know. If Mother's willing to take him back now, I think I know a way to do it."

"Money?"

"Of course. Mother has more of it than she knows about."

"Then for her sake, I hope she keeps it."

Missy came back to the edge of the dining room where Charles and Rita were talking. When the conversation sounded as if there might be some antagonism, she was soon standing by his side.

"Your Mother is beginning to look tired, Rita. Maybe she would like to go home. We're going to stay here tonight, otherwise, we would be glad to take her back."

"It was a beautiful party, Missy, and this is a perfect time for us to leave. Are you going back to Napa tomorrow?"

"I don't think so. Charles says he has a surprise for me. The girls aren't really expecting us yet."

Missy walked to where Anita was sitting, "Mother," she addressed Anita. "Rita said you would be leaving soon. We want to drop by to see you before we leave tomorrow, but we haven't finalized our plans yet. Anyway, we will call you tomorrow at a decent hour," and she gave Anita an air kiss on her cheek.

"Oh, I would love that," Anita murmured.

On the way home, Anita was very talkative. "I have never seen Missy looking so radiant. The red Chanel silk suit was perfect for her. So vibrant. It just goes to prove that blondes can wear red. It was a lovely party. Just the kind that those glossy magazines photograph when they do a story about the 'Beautiful People.'"

"Then we must be the 'Beautiful People,'" Rita agreed because she knew her Mother's interests.

"I'm proud of my little family," Anita went on. "Do you really think I should go to Fiji with the girls?"

"It's totally up to you. It would give you a good chance to get reacquainted with them."

"But what would I do with myself there. Everyone will be swimming and snorkeling, and they will be busy with all those water sports. I'd rather take the girls to Europe next summer."

"Wouldn't that be quite an undertaking?"

"Oh no. My friend, Betsy, did it with her granddaughters, and they were just fine, because they took one of those well-managed tours that plan everything for you. They even include the tipping."

"You have time to think about it," Rita reminded her.

"I saw you and Charlie talking together after dinner. I hope you two will let bygones be bygones." She sighed. "He says you have not stopped blaming him because he used to tease you when he hid your toys."

Rita made a face, but her mother did not see it. "It was worse than that," Rita replied. "He buried my toys behind the house. I can still remember the horror when I found my Barbie doll after a year or two. I was doing a garden project for school, and I was digging holes to plant pansies, when I uncovered her. The face was ruined with dirt and mildew, and it was really very scary."

"Rita, you are a grown woman now. What a silly thing to hold against him."

"Obviously he remembers it, too."

"That is not a reason to avoid seeing each other. Now that they have included us in their new life, we should continue to be a part of it."

"I don't think they'll want much of Mike and me anyway. Rita finished."

Anita was in such an exhilarated mood that she went on talking and disregarded Rita's remarks. When Anita was young, she loved to be present at her Mother's parties. She enjoyed the decorations, the unusual foods and interesting people. Missy's dinner party fed into her fantasies.

"I wish we could have given you and Mike a lavish wedding reception. But Mother was not well, and I hesitated to ask if I could use Stonecrest. My little cottage in Carmel was too small for entertaining."

"Mike and I didn't want anything elaborate. Just planning it would have taken a year, and Grandmother had become too fragile for that. We wanted her to attend our festivities. She attended our wedding and that was what we wanted."

"I'll give you a big anniversary party in a few years. Maybe sooner," Anita continued. "Do you know what Charles is giving Missy as a surprise?"

Rita shook her head. "No, he didn't mention it."

"He's treating her to a week at the Emerald Garden Spa. I know it is the most exclusive spa in California. He has some business appointments this week. He has a meeting with the editor and publisher of the most prestigious wine magazine. I don't know if the main office is in New York or Los Angeles. Then he has to go to Scottsdale. Anyway, he will be busy all the rest of this week while Missy is at the Spa."

"He's going to Scottsdale?" asked Rita in astonishment.

"Yes, I am sure that is what he said. He said that he owns a little corporation in Scottsdale and it takes up too much of his time. He's thinking of becoming a silent partner. Anyway, he is going there for a meeting." Anita finished.

"That's very interesting," Rita said. "In more than one way," she whispered to herself, and she wondered if she should tell Mike about it.

When they reached Stonecrest, Mike escorted Anita into the house. On the way home Rita said very little to Mike. Finally he said, "We can relax now that the dinner party is over. You're quiet. Are you OK?"

"I guess so. At the end of the party Charlie came over and wanted to talk to me. I hate to admit it, but Charlie can still bug me."

"He brought several issues. He even mentioned *The Carmelo Diaries*."

"Is that all?"

No, there are lots of things. I'm apprehensive about what Charlie and my Dad may be planning," Rita said. "And wait before you answer. There's more. Mother said that Charlie is going to go to Scottsdale this week before he and Missy leave for Australia."

"Scottsdale, Hm. Maybe he is just going to end his affair with Tessa," Mike said.

"He'll never quite end it. He won't give up the attention of someone who is obsessed with love for him," Rita sighed.

"Do you think that Captain Lewis is interested in her?"

"Sounds that way to me. I hope she uses some judgment with the way she handles it. Yet she really needs a new love interest. Even though I don't think he's her type."

They reached their home. It was long after Carmelita's bedtime and after looking into her bedroom, they went to their bedroom.

"It's too late for me to think about Charles or your Dad who I don't know. I'm really sleepy right now." Mike said as he yanked off his tie.

"Me too." I decided to take it easy tomorrow, after I open up the shop with Dolores. I think we should go to Los Angeles right after Carmelite's birthday."

"Good idea. Tomorrow I'll come home early, and there'll be just the three of us here."

"That's the best news yet."

"Love you, Babe," he said as he brushed his hand across her hair and she kissed him.

CHAPTER 38

▼

Rita persuaded Dolores to be the manager of the Old Booktique for the next few months. Anticipating lassitude that follows a spectacle dinner of unusual foods and wines, she had planned an easy day for herself. She took Carmelita to the Children's Library in Carmel, where they chose five new picture books to bring home. After lunch and while Carmelita was napping, Rita began to read the last *Carmelo Diary.*

"November 1844. We are now living much of our time in Monterey, where I hear more about the changes taking place in Alta California. I do not like these changes. Will prepared me for this, by telling me about the many foreign boats coming into our port. There is also the problem of the *Yanquis* who arrive by way of the overland trails from other places in America. These men walk around in our town and yell at us with loud voices.

"Many missions in the Southland have retained their buildings, and the resident *padre* still conducts mass for the people. Our dear Mission San Cárlos Borromeo del Carmelo is no more. It has been torn down by storms and men have carried off the stones. Padre José María Real, who lives in Monterey, visits the ruined Mission occasionally. His brother, Padre Antonio Real sometimes conducts a service for the few neophytes who live near the Mission. I used to take the ranch children with me to see the *padre,* but they became frightened when they heard the wind blowing through the skeleton walls. It was the sound of flapping of loose boards when the wind blew from the ocean. For this reason, I asked the good father to conduct services for us at our chapel at Rancho Carmelo.

"Felicia, Patricia and Anita live with us in Monterey, and we attend mass at the Chapel near the house of the governor. Anita stays at home with my maids. After the service, the girls enjoy walking with our neighbors who attend church. There is often a happy parade of young boys and girls who run forward and around us. When the children reach their homes, they call out *adios y hasta luego* to one another. Although Felicia is very shy, Patricia joins in the merriment.

"Sometimes Señor Larkin asks Will to travel very far away to the Fort of Captain Sutter in the Valley of the Sacramento. It is over a day's ride to the east. Will takes several men with him and we always have one or two of our trusted ranch *vaqueros* to guard us in Monterey. Because Will leads an active life, he dresses in his leather clothes much of time; however, he follows the customs of the *Californios* and wears elegant dress clothes at the *fandangos*. He is very tan from working outdoors. Although Will now has his papers to prove that he is an American, most of the new *Yanquis* here believe that we are a Mexican family. Sometimes they shout rude words at us. They try to scare us, because it amuses them.

"Above all, Señor Larkin wants Monterey to remain a peaceful place for those who live here and for those who do business in Monterey. He tells us to keep our trusted *vaqueros* close by. We found a barn near the Larkin house where they can sleep. Will built a small addition to our adobe for my maids to sleep. It is a satisfactory arrangement because our life is simple. I do not entertain very much.

"On Wednesdays, I often go to the house of Rachel Larkin for a custom she calls 'taking tea.' Sometimes she entertains a group of people, but often I am the only one and so I bring Felicia, who enjoys playing with the babies, Carolina, who is two years old and the new one called, Sophie. Rachel tells me that in the homes of Boston, they serve tea everyday. She has a collection of China teapots and beautiful painted teacups. She also has a sugar bowl and a large cream pitcher. All of this is set on a silver tray. She usually serves little cakes and a variety of dried fruit and nuts. This is a time of day to talk about events and happenings. When Rachel and I are alone, we talk about our homes and children. We usually talk in English with a few Spanish words added here and there. She helps me if I do not know what word to use. The word 'home' is one of those words. When the Spanish use the word *casa*, it is really not the right word to describe what the *Yanquis* mean when they say they want to go home. It can mean a place that is bigger than one building. It can mean the town of Boston.

"Rachel says that the *pueblo de Los Angeles* in the south will become more important than Monterey, if Don Pío Pico takes command of the government. I told her he was born into a large family of soldiers in the south of Alta California. He owns ranches there, and now he is president of the *junta*. Once Rachel asked me what I meant by the word *junta,* and it was hard to find just one English word to tell her. It means a group that meets together. I often complain about the wild *Yanquis* that dress in mountain clothes all the time and talk and yell in loud voices. Rachel says there are different kinds of Americans just as there are different kinds of Mexicans. Although her husband encourages Americans to come to our land, he says the wild mountain men are not good for his business. He wants the type of people who will make their home in Monterey. He wants families who buy from his store. Much of the furniture in the Larkin house is from all parts of the world. Rachel favors the kind of furniture she would use if she lived in Boston or a place called New York.

"In early December, Will returned to Monterey from the fort of Captain Sutter. I told him I wished to return to Rancho Carmelo for a month. There are many days of fair weather at this time, and I want the children to ride horses and play in the fresh air before the season of rain arrives. I always feel safe at Rancho Carmelo and enjoy the privacy of our house within the large courtyard. Many years ago Papa found a good location for his house, which is near the top of a hill. On one side we look out toward the sea, and on the other side we can see the mountains of Santa Lucia. I enjoy watching the cattle standing on the hills, and seeing the young calves running in a graceless gallop. I feel lonesome for the ranch when I am in Monterey.

"We plan to have a small *fiesta* for all who live at the ranch. I asked Padre Real to come to bless the animals, and we will choose several of the ranch children to take part in our own presentation of *Los Pastores.* December is a quiet month. Will is here with us at the *fiesta* and celebrations. He sometimes takes his carpenters to his little ranch in the Valley of the Carmelo River. They will repair the buildings. When *Natividad* passes, I want to return to teaching the children of Ramon how to read. I will teach them some simple English words. Since I have been writing some of this journal with English words I know how difficult it is to write in another language. I want to teach the children while they are young.

"December 15, 1844. Soon after we arrived at Rancho Carmelo, Señor Larkin summoned Will because he thought there might be a revolution against Governor Micheltorena. The governor makes promises to everyone and does not keep a promise to anyone. Don Juan Bautista Alvarado wants to get control of the government again, and he knows that everyone in Monterey wants the unruly soldiers of the governor to be sent back to Mexico.

"Señor Alvarado is forcing Governor Micheltorena to take actions, but it might become a riot, and this would give the foreigners a chance to fight. Some of the foreigners favor Alvarado because they think he will give them land grants.

After a week, the people quieted down because the governor signed a statement that he would send the bad soldiers away in three months. I want to stay at Rancho Carmelo, where we are safe.

"January 1845. We celebrated a quiet *fiesta* for the New Year, and are content to be together as a family. Esperanza, Xavier, and their young boys live near to us in a small adobe. *Padre* Antonio from Monterey arrived before the Holy Night, and he said prayers with us. In January, Will continued to stay with us at the ranch. It is a time to ride out to the different pastures with his men. There is not so much to do here in the winter. Secretly, I am only completely happy when he is at Rancho Carmelo with us.

"I wish we had a son for Will to teach to ride. He would use the little corral near the outside wall. He is proud of how well the sons of Ramon use the *lasso* and he is planning a contest for the *vaqueros* who use the *reata larga*. This is the longest *lasso* of all. I suggested that we have a contest for the younger men so they can gain experience. On rainy days, it will give them something to do. I continue to teach the children reading and their numbers. I want to teach writing, and so I sent our rider who goes into Monterey, to the house of the Larkins. I asked for some paper. And Raquel is always kind and sends these supplies to me.

"Sometimes I hear from Consuelo. She sends her letters to me by a rider who travels back and forth to the house of Encarnation Cooper and the Larkins. Consuelo is planning for the marriage of her second daughter. She does not want her to live so far away, and she is glad that Rosita has been chosen as a bride for the son of a prosperous family. The Alonso family has many ranches near Monterey, and Enrique already owns his own ranch near the trail to Mission Santa Cruz. Consuelo always writes about Prudencia. She continues to live in Sonora, Mexico, and is with child again. She wrote to Consuelo about Ardo. He is planning to be a priest and will stay in Mexico City. He does not attend the Vargas family gatherings, so she has not seen him this year. I read this with both happiness and sadness. Ardo will always be in a special place in my heart. I may never see him again.

"In Monterey, I know that our people do not think we have a strong man for governor. He seems to be friendly and well educated, but he cannot make decisions. If Governor Micheltorena had been governor in earlier times, he would not have had these rough *Yanquis* around. In the old days there were only the Indians for the soldiers to fight. Now there is a large group of foreigners. We do not understand them and they do not understand us. Now that our *Californios* have tasted power, they do not want to accept the governors Mexico sends us. They are going to insist we have a *Californio* for governor. This is a confusing time to live.

"There is a special reason why we are safe at Carmelo. Our ranch lies just beyond the road to Monterey. Stray riders rarely travel this way. There is no one living south of us, because the River Carmelo often floods, and it is difficult to cross. After the first light rain, in autumn, we have our men gather the cattle and drive them to the north side of the ranch. In the winter, the water of the river runs very swift and the dirt from the banks often falls into the water. Our Carmelo *vaqueros* can watch for strangers from our buildings on the hill. Since we live on what we grow for food, and Will brings us tools and other things we need from Monterey, we are free to live a good life.

"February 1845. Will rode to town and returned back to Carmelo with much news. Señor Larkin thinks that Don Pío Pico will be governor of Alta California soon.

Don Pío has been active in local government in the south. He is well known in Mexico, and their government will give him the position.

"When Governor Micheltorena left Monterey with his soldiers. He first marched his men north toward Mission Santa Cruz. Will told me the governor did this to find more soldiers to join with him. However, he told everyone in Monterey he was on his way south to the *Pueblo de Los Angeles* to see the *politicos*. Does he know that the Picos and Carrillos and many other families who own ranches will make him leave Alta California? In Monterey José Castro and Colonel Alvarado are gathering loyal men to follow the governor and make sure that he does not come back to Monterey. José Castro will take some soldiers on a march to the South and show everyone that he has much power. Señor Larkin has a good friend in the south named Abel Stearns. He is married to a daughter of the Bandini family. This is where he gathers this information that he tells to Will.

"Señor Larkin has decided to give a large *fandango* at the new Custom House. It will bring cheer to the people of Monterey. He asked Will and I to attend. And so we are going to Monterey. He told Will to bring our children with us. Because of the unrest, we decided to travel in the company of our most trusted *vaqueros*. Señor Larkin also told us to bring our valuable possessions and documents with us. We will make quite a procession as we take our *carretas* and extra horses over the hill from the ranch down into Monterey. Yes, the Larkins invited Felicia to attend the *fandango*. We know that Consuelo and Miguel will be in town with their family, so it will be another opportunity for Felicia to meet the young people of her own age.

"When we arrived at Monterey, I visited all my friends in town and also there are other families who have come for a visit and to attend the *fandango*. They all talked about a new American who came to talk to Señor Larkin. When we attended the *fandango*, we learned more about this man. His name is Juan Frémont. He is said to be handsome. Although he dresses like all the mountain men, it is said he has better manners. Recently he spent much time with Señor Larkin. It is natural that he would seek a fellow *Yanqui* as he needed supplies for his small band of soldiers. He came from over the tall mountains east of here. He first stopped at the Fort of Captain Sutter. This Frémont says he is on his way north to a place called Oregon. He even met with General Castro and Colonel Alvarado. Perhaps I can take tea with Rachel and find out what she thinks of him. When I was alone with Consuelo the day after the *fandango*, I asked her about this new stranger named Frémont. She said, 'It doesn't matter to me. I do not care to know him. I dislike all *Yanquis*.'

"'Even Señor Larkin?' I asked in amazement, because she goes to his store every day when she is in Monterey.

"'Yes, Señor Larkin,' she insisted. 'And you must be careful. He will lure your Guillermo from you. Isn't he always sending him somewhere?'

"I could not say much to her, because she had already decided what her feelings would be. I was without an answer because it is important that she invite my little half-sister to the wedding of Rosita. I do not dare tell Consuelo that I hope Felicia can marry into a good family like the Alonsos. Felicia has such a delicate face with some good Castilian features. Most of all she is willing to please everyone, and she will make a good wife. She loves children and is more educated than some of the other California young ladies. I have a lovely yellow dress of silk that she can wear at the *fandango*. My dressmaker can make it smaller for her. I will give her one of my tortoise combs for her hair, and I will personally arrange her glistening black curls. I think that Don Fernando Xavier Alonso is less than thirty years old. He may be twenty-five. He will surely be part of the wedding of his brother. He might dance with Felicia.

"During our stay in Monterey, we heard the name of Juan Frémont many times. When I talked to Rachel, she told me that he had come to measure land and find the best way for Americans to pass through Alta California. She said this Frémont had talked to General Castro about his passing through the lands. Later, when I asked Will, he said that Frémont is also collecting men to add to a group of followers. Will met him at the Fort of Captain Sutter. He liked him at first and found his stories about crossing the high mountains very interesting. Then Will began to think he was a man who told false stories. Will met some of his followers and thought they were not men of the best conduct. Will would tell me no more. I learned from Isabel Brown y Sepulveda, who lives near Encarnacion, that some of the soldiers of Frémont did not honor the hospitality of Angel Castro. He is an elderly uncle of General Castro. After they appeared at his ranch, the men drank too much *aguardiente* and forced their attentions on one of the ladies in the family of Don Angel, who ordered the men to leave. It was necessary for Don Angel to draw his pistol to make them go away. This insult does not please the *Californios*. The husband of Isabel Brown is a man who came from England. He became a Mexican citizen in order to marry Isabel, and he is now a landowner. He met with Señor Larkin and several ranch owners to discuss what to do if they decide not to trust Mr. Frémont."

"When we returned to Rancho Carmelo, it was nearing the end of the rainy season. Will and the *vaqueros* had much work to do with the cattle. Some were brought down from the upper meadows. They will be led to the pastures on the other side of the river later in the spring. There are buildings and corrals to be mended. The younger men always like the active work. It is well that Will spent some of his early life on this ranch, because he knows how to tell the men to do these tasks. He is patient when he teaches others. Will says that being a *vaquero* is an honorable occupation. He respects our *vaqueros* and always remembers the cruelty of the captain of the ship he sailed on before he reached our coast. He does not punish a man unless he has warned him or unless the man disobeys the rules of the ranch. Most of our men had parents who were neophytes of the Mission San Cárlos.

"March 1845. We stayed at the ranch for all the spring season. Consuelo sent many short letters by rider to tell me of the preparations for the wedding. The couple will marry at the Mission San Juan Bautista. Three days of festivities will be held at their ranch. The Garcías have built two simple adobe houses for their guests. Consuelo says that these houses will be a place for Rosita and Enrique to stay after they are married and come to visit them. When I told her that we were bringing Patricia, Alicia, and Felicia, she invited us to stay at one of these houses. Prudencia cannot attend the wedding, as the birth of her child is near. Sonora is far away. After the wedding, Consuelo wants us to spend several weeks at their ranch, because she will be lonely without her married daughters.

"We made many preparations for the happy event. Not every lady has such good fortune to marry someone who has courted her properly, and Rosita loves him. Consuelo has made sure that every Spanish custom will be observed, and Rosita will receive the required gifts of six pair of slippers, six mantillas, six dresses, six *rebozos* and six jackets. I am bringing her embroidered linens for their bedding.

"Summer 1845. It is a pleasure to write about such a beautiful traditional wedding. The closest friends and the family all assembled at the García ranch on the day before the ceremony. On the wedding morning, the bride left the house with her father and together they rode on one horse. It was quite far to the little pueblo of San Juan Bautista. Soon after the bride and her father departed, Consuelo and her six sons rode their horses to the Mission. After confession Rosita changed from her black gown into her lovely white silk wedding dress.

"Soon after the family arrived at San Juan, a long procession of guests filled the little plaza by the Mission. All were on horseback or riding in *carretas*. Felicia, Patricia and Anita all sat on large pillows in a specially constructed *carreta*, and flowers were placed on the horns of the oxen. I insisted on riding a horse beside my children when I made the journey. Will rode just ahead of us, and Ramon rode several *varas* behind us. Will wore his long red hair pulled back underneath his soft gray sombrero. He wore velvet pantaloons, a white linen shirt, and a pale gray leather bolero. It was decorated with silver ornaments. He likes to wear the clothes of a gentleman. Every time he makes a present of jewelry to me, I give him a new ornament for his clothes. I, myself, like to sew silver buttons on his pantaloons. I was proud to see him sitting so tall in the saddle. He was easily the most handsome man at the wedding.

"The family of all the Garcías and the members of the Alonso family were seated in the front rows of the church. Everyone felt near to God as they glanced up from their prayers to the old altar in front of the painted *reredo* with the carved holy figures. Much of the furniture has been taken from the mission and the walls are cracked; however, I always feel calm at Mission San Juan Bautista. I worshiped here in the days when I lived at Rancho Rincón de Gavilan. Very little of the Indian population is left, and yet the church survives and serves a little group of people who come from nearby ranches.

"After the service, we ate some simple food, and all returned to the García rancho, where we took a *siesta* and rested for the later festivities. I had hoped that Don Fernando Alonso would see Felicia and be captured by her quiet beauty. But this was not to be. Consuelo told me he had already asked for the hand of a young lady of the Estrada family. The musicians gathered, and as soon as the music began, the bride and groom began to dance. When everyone was dancing, I noticed that Felicia danced gracefully and was never without a partner. Timoteo García glided with Felicia to every corner of the dance floor. I was pleased by her manners and satisfied that she was enjoying herself, so I accepted the invitation to dance with my husband. We Spanish take great pride in our dancing, and yet I must say that Will is the best of all dancers. There is something in the way he dances that reminds me of a light feather making a circle. He told me once that some of the Irish are kissed by fairies, and it makes them light on their feet. His father taught him to dance the jig of Ireland. In that dance he jumps high in the air. Perhaps Patricia will dance like that. She is always twirling around as she runs through the paths in our garden. She wanted to dance at the wedding, and since he was waiting for the arrival of his bride-to-be, Don Fernando Alonso was kind enough to ask Patricia to dance with him. She is tall for her age and dances well for a girl of nine years. They even danced the *sardana*, a Catalonian dance. I suppose he did not want to dance with the grown ladies, since his intended bride was not yet present.

"During the remainder of the wedding day, various families from Monterey arrived, and by late afternoon everyone was eating the beautiful food prepared for the wedding supper. When the Estrada family arrived, Don Fernando escorted his intended bride to an arbor in the garden. I used my fan to cover most of my face so I could watch them. I do not know if they are well acquainted.

"After all the wedding festivities, I talked to Felicia. Her eyes glowed as she told me about dancing with Timoteo. I think she likes him, but she did not say. I am sure she will not be considered as a *novia* for Timoteo, because Consuelo has already decided that Timoteo will marry someone from the Vallejo family. During the next few days, I watched Felicia and Timoteo, because I am concerned that Felicia will think of him with too much love. Timoteo has soft gray eyes and dark brown curly hair, and he plays the guitar well. Consuelo noticed his attention to Felicia, and told me to send Felicia to a convent for schooling in Mexico. I am always surprised when Consuelo thinks she knows best about everything for everybody. Her words made me sad.

"I want to go back to Rancho Carmelo as soon as it is polite to leave. I shall talk to Will about leaving the next day after Sunday mass. Tomorrow, I will tell Consuelo that we are needed at Rancho Carmelo. Meanwhile we will enjoy one more day of festivities."

There was nothing more written in this diary. There are only empty pages.

Rita knew there was more to Clarita's story. What about enigmatic Captain Frémont? What became of the entrepreneur, Thomas Larkin and his wife, Rachel? Were the powerful Vallejos, the Alvarados, the Estradas, the Coopers, and the descendents of the other pioneer families able to keep their lands? How did the American Occupation of 1846 affect Clarita and Will? Rita needed to find other sources for her answers if she was to continue the story of Clarita's life. There were more letters and the note-books of Isabel.

CHAPTER 39

▼

Charles and Missy resumed living together in their Mediterranean style house situated in Carneros vineyards. After the elaborate dinner party, it was necessary for Charles to make a trip to New York to speak at a three-day exhibition called the California Wine Experience. It was the first time this event had traveled from California, and wine makers and winery owners from all over the world were expected to attend. Charles hoped to bring his own wines to this event within two years.

Captain Lewis went to Scottsdale to interrogate Tessa, and when he returned, he briefly informed Rita that he was satisfied with Tessa's answers.

Tessa called Rita to tell her about the situation. "Guess what? Rita," she said. "It seemed more like a date than anything else. He didn't ask any questions. We went to dinner at the Scottsdale Princess Hotel, and we made plans for the next weekend. I bought a new dress. I think he's interested in me."

Rita worked on store inventory at the Old Booktique, and business was slow, which gave her time to recover from the last two weeks.

Rita and Mike had their evenings free for talking. Rita kept him current with Tessa's life.

"So Captain Lewis is dating Tessa. "Maybe that's the reason he wants to wrap up the burglary case." Mike remarked.

"I'll be glad to get all this past us, so we can live our own life. Are you ready to hear more of Clarita's story?"

"How much is there?"

"Plenty. There's enough for more than one television series. But *The Carmelo Diaries* don't tell it all."

Mike looked quizzical. "What is missing?"

"Claritia stops abruptly in 1845 and doesn't tell about the rest of her life."

"But you said you had a lot to tell."

"It's all in Isabel's notebooks."

"How did she know it all?"

"She is Clarita's only granddaughter. She married Edward Shaw and lived in a mansion in San Francisco. She had time to paint porcelain, play the piano, and write in satin covered notebooks. Clarita lived with her in the later part of her life.

"Do you have these notebooks?"

"Yes, and I started reading them this afternoon. They tell what happened to Rancho Carmelo."

"Aunt Clara always told me that the de Segovias lost their extensive land holdings around 1850. She said there was nothing left of Rancho Carmelo. Just some maps showing the approximate location. The family blamed it on the Americans. Was it really that way?" Mike asked.

"Not quite," Rita continued. "The first disaster happened before the Americans and the Mexicans went to war with each other. It is easy to blame the marauding Americans who roamed the countryside, but the first disaster at Rancho Carmelo was a fire that could have been caused by *vaqueros* from Don Diego's ranch near the Salinas River. Clarita always said that it was an act of revenge."

"That makes a better story," Mike agreed.

"Thomas Larkin had warned the O'Farrell family to protect themselves with their own trained *vaqueros*. He told them to keep their valuable possessions in a safe place. Clarita always took her jewelry with her when they traveled to Monterey. She also kept her few books and diaries in her possession when she moved back and forth from the ranch to Monterey. Grandmother Clara said she kept these treasures in a large leather box with handles. She called it a *cofre*, which is a Spanish word for trunk."

"Do you have this box?"

"No, but I remember seeing it when I was growing up. I thought it was old and ugly. "I think Grandmother Clara gave it to the museum at the Carmel Mission."

"What happened to the contents?"

"Scattered, I think."

"Aunt Clara told me the de Segovia legacy only existed in the form of descendents. All their land holdings, their cattle and horses and the early furniture are gone. No town was named after them. Not even a street anywhere," Mike said. "At what time does Isabel take up Clarita's story?"

"From the time the O'Farrells left the García *rancho* in July 1845."

"How did Isabel learn about the story?"

"Isabel became Clarita's closet confidant."

"Was Isabel acquainted with all the people in the story?" Mike sounded interested.

"All the old, Spanish families knew one another. The daughters of Clarita and Consuelo married the Alonso brothers. Enrique and Fernando. Isabel was an Alonso.

"When did she write her notebooks?"

"In about 1886 after she was married and when Clarita came to their mansion near Pine and Taylor in San Francisco."

"Is that one of the books?" Mike asked as he saw a light blue satin book in Rita's hand.

Rita gave him the book. "Take a look at this one."

Mike carefully turned over some pages and gave it back to Rita. "Why don't you read me some of the pages to me?"

Rita opened a small satin book and read, "Almost every day, *Mamacita* and I sit near a large bay window in the upper drawing room. We watch the people below, or we talk about the events of the day. When we take tea by ourselves, she talks about the past. This is what she said.

"'We lived on a cattle ranch near the River Carmelo, and your grandfather managed the ranch while I supervised a big household. We lived by the rules of my Spanish parents with a certain formality of manners and much attention to our family, which included many servants. Thomas Larkin often asked your grandfather to oversee the construction of his many buildings in and around Monterey. It was Thomas Larkin who advised us to prepare for the coming of more Americans.'"

Mike saw Rita squinting. "Is Isabel's fancy writing hard to read?"

"A little, but I want to read it to you, because it tells what happened when Clarita stopped writing in her diary."

"Go on as best you can."

Rita began reading aloud again.

"Your grandfather and I took our daughters and Felicia to the García Ranch to attend the wedding of Rosita, the second daughter of Consuelo and Miguel.

Rosita was to marry Enrique Alonso. And our family became acquainted with the Alonso family at that time. Your mama met your papa there. We remained at the García ranch for several days after the wedding and were planning to return to Rancho Carmelo the next week, when suddenly Ramon came riding into the García courtyard. I can still hear Ramon shouting, Don Guillermo to your grandfather, and his words tumbled out as he told us that strange *vaqueros* had ridden into our courtyard and set fire to our beautiful *hacienda*. The house quickly burned down. A beam of wood fell on Esperanza and she died in the fire. Your grandfather and I immediately departed for Rancho Carmelo by horseback, and Ramon followed after he was given some food and a fresh horse. Our children and my maid remained at the García ranch.'" *Here, Isabel made a notation that Clarita cried a little and said she would tell her more the next day, and she continues with the story.*

"'After riding several hours, we arrived at the charred and smoking ruins of all the buildings that were enclosed by the courtyard. Esperanza had been pulled out from the debris and taken to her own house. My beautiful pianoforte and exquisitely carved bed were badly burned and all our furniture was reduced to ashes. The only things we owned were in the trunks we had taken to the Garcías, that is, my jewelry, books, diaries and some gold coins. We had only the clothes we brought for the wedding visit. Horses had trampled through my gardens and swords had torn whatever was left to destroy. This was an act of revenge or hatred. Someone had set the fire, and they meant to destroy us. We could think of nothing to do but made sure that no embers remained to catch on fire again. We went to the little *casa* where Esperanza lived with Xavier and the boys, and found there was nothing we could do there except to contact Padre Real in Monterey. Since it was near nightfall, we found shelter in the bunkhouse on your grandfather's little ranch in the hills. When we returned to the García ranch, we rested, and then we took the children to our house in Monterey. Your grandfather went back to search for anything of value, but he found very little. We were saddened and full of grief. I did not have the heart to write anything more about the Rancho del Rio Carmelo in my diary.'"

Rita looked up from the satin book and said to Mike. "The O'Farrell family lost all their possessions except what they had taken to the wedding *fiesta*. It is well that Clarita always traveled with her jewelry, legal papers and books."

"That's some story. Did they ever find out who did such a thing?" Mike asked quietly.

"I think there was so much anti-American feeling at that time among the *Californios*. Almost everyone blamed the *Yanquis*. Clarita was certain that Rancho

Carmelo was destroyed by orders of Don Diego, although he was living in Sonora, Mexico at the time."

"What happened next?"

"Isabel writes that the O'Farrells continued to live in Monterey. She doesn't tell more details. I suppose Will was very busy riding back and forth to his little ranch and building more bunkhouses for the *vaqueros* who stayed there to help with the fall roundup. Since the fire occurred in the summer, all the cattle were out on the range and on the higher hills up the valley."

"How far do Isabel's journals take the story?" Mike asked.

Rita turned the delicate old pages to the end of the first journal. "I think it goes through the 1860's. Isabel doesn't tell much about the actual conquest of California by the Americans. She observed that Clarita and Will avoided involvement with the war between Mexico and the United States. Will had papers to prove he was an American citizen, and Clarita was a Mexican citizen. Thomas Larkin probably advised them to avoid crowds and to lead a quiet life. He loaned Will the money to buy lumber for an addition to their house in Monterey, and Will paid him back with his sale of cowhides in the autumn."

"I always thought that the *Californios* did not suffer much in the Mexican— American War," said Mike.

"You learned your California history a long time ago. I've done some reading lately and have found several tragic events that happened to the *Californios*. They had true reasons to distrust the Americans."

"Can you prove it? Mike questioned

"Some incidents are verified fact. One event in particular is outstanding. It happened in 1846, just before the outbreak of war between Mexico and the United States. When Frémont and his men were scouting around the area north of San Francisco Bay, they were expecting some opposition from General Castro. When they saw a small boat crossing from San Pablo, John Frémont sent Kit Carson and a few others to meet it. Carson was heard to ask Frémont if he should take prisoners. With a wave of his hand Frémont said something like, 'we can't take prisoners.'

"There were three men on the boat, and while on their way to the mission church nearby, they were deliberately shot and killed by Kit Carson and his men. The *Californios* who were killed were important citizens of Alta California, the de Haro twins, about twenty years old and their great uncle, José de los Reyes Berreyesa. It was considered a brutal murder. This saddened and angered all *Californios*."

That's awful. What did Mr. Larkin do in the war?"

"Isabel did not write about Mr. Larkin. From my research, I know that Thomas Larkin found it hard to be the peacemaker he wished to be. He was both a representative of the American government, a consul, and he was a personal friend of many illustrious *Californios*. From the beginning, he found Frémont insensitive to the *Californios* and found his words and promises were not to be trusted by anyone. What Larkin really wanted was the annexation of California to the United States. He thought this could be done without a war. At one time, Larkin was a captive of General Castro and taken to Los Angeles as a prisoner of Mexico. Larkin was treated as a guest and an enemy at the same time. Clarita told Isabel that it was a trying experience for the Larkin family at home. One of his daughters was very ill, and his wife Rachel was pregnant. His own health deteriorated from worry. The daughter died and everyone was concerned for the health of Rachel Larkin.

"Isabel wrote in another journal about the visits of Clarita to Rachel during the invasion of the Americans. Rachel feared that her husband would be killed either by the soldiers of Castro or by some drunken American. Rachel had to endure the death of Adelaide without her husband to comfort her. Clarita often took Rachel to San Cárlos Chapel, where they prayed, and were comforted by Father Real. Most of the *Californios* were glad when the war ended, although we knew that American soldiers would take over the town of Monterey."

"Do you think you'll include this in your presentation?" Mike asked.

"I really don't know, but I think it's best to include whatever I can find. There are many versions of the American Conquest."

"Let's finish talking about the story this weekend," said Mike wearily.

"It will still be here on the desk." she said and patted the journal."

"To amuse us and perplex us," Mike added.

CHAPTER 40

▼

February 9, 2000

Rita arrived at The Old Booktique early the next morning. February was inventory time and she wanted to begin early. There was a pleasant calm to the area around the Retreat. When she looked across the putting green, she could see the two doormen chatting with each other. Rita liked the leisured atmosphere that had returned to this five star resort.

After attending to a few orders that had arrived over night on her e-mail, she went to the table that featured California history and became engrossed in searching for information about the American Conquest.

"Is that you, Rita?" came a distinctive voice.

She turned around and looked up in shock to see a familiar face. It was a face she had not seen for several years.

"Monty," she exclaimed. "Belmont Peerless Bates," she said slowly trying to gain composure.

"Clarita Isabel Atherton," he said in the same tone and as slowly.

"What are you doing in Pebble Beach? It's a long way from Illinois, or is it still D.C.?"

"I came for the last day of the big tournament, and the weather is so great that I decided to play some golf. Peoria is cold at this time of year." He paused. When Rita didn't speak, he went on. "Also I wanted to look you up."

Rita took stock of how he looked. He did not seem any older, and he was not so painfully thin. His face was the same, slightly tanned with well-defined features, and soft brown eyes that could focus on whomever he was addressing. His hair was just a little grayer, and it suited him. As usual, he looked well groomed and wore a maroon cashmere sweater, dark-gray tailored slacks, and a navy blue blazer.

"Welcome to my quaint little store. Are you interested in any special kind of books?"

"Not really," he grinned, and stopped as if he had more to say.

Rita took in a quiet breath while she was thinking of her next words. She had once been very much in love with this man. She knew his face from every angle. She had memorized his features. Their times together were always short and not long enough for either of them. He was usually tired when he arrived in Europe from Washington D.C., and after he went to sleep, she often stayed awake and enjoyed the contentment of being near him. She always tried to make the most of the time they had together. She remembered watching CNN during an international oil crisis. She hoped she would catch a glimpse of him being interviewed with other government officials in Geneva. Now, she stopped herself from thinking of the past and willed herself into the present.

"I specialize in California, but I have some rare English classics in prime condition."

"Please show me a rare book." He said, and quickly went on. "However, I was hoping you would be here and that I could take you to lunch."

"I can't take off for lunch today. I'm the only one here today"

"It's your store. You could close up for the afternoon." He looked at her as if he expected to persuade her. "For old times sake," he coaxed."

"Monty, I, really," Rita started to say but didn't continue.

"When my second term of office was over, I didn't seek reelection. I went home and took a lovely cruise around the world with Karen. She died a few months ago. Since then, I've been out of touch with everyone."

"I'm sorry to hear about Karen," Rita quickly said. "Are you a man of leisure now?"

"No, I'm quite busy. I'm writing up my years in the senate and particularly my work with energy committees, particularly the passage of the National Energy Act. It's pretty dry reading, but I was advised to write it up"

Someone entered the store and asked Rita a question.

"You go and help your customer. I'll just browse here until you're free," Monty said.

Rita nodded and tried to listen to the customer. She was amazed at herself. She had really forgotten what a strong attraction there had been between them.

In the past, she had wanted to be with him under any circumstance. She had, in fact, changed the direction of her life for him. She first met him at a time when she was doing graduate work at the Sorbonne in Paris. When he told her he loved her, he had been honest, and he also told her he was married. She loved him, and she changed her own career plans in order to be with him whenever it was possible. They wanted to keep their meetings private, so she lived in Europe when she had finished her courses in Paris Although she did not like all the things she had to do to keep away from the press, she met him wherever he asked her to meet him. She remembered going up service elevators in various hotels so that she would not be recognized. Once when she was staying in his suite, she had to occupy one of the bathrooms for over an hour while he had an emergency meeting with a government official from Kuwait. Monty told her he would marry her in a minute if only Karen were well, but Karen had a rare blood disease that baffled medical authorities. Monty was a well-known political figure, and public opinion would be against him if he divorced his invalid wife. He was running for reelection.

"I have a better copy of that Mark Twain," Rita told the customer, an earnestly timid lady, who asked her about the copy of *Life on the Mississippi,* displayed on the history table. "Excuse me, and I'll find it for you."

As she hurried toward the back of the store, she continued to think of Monty. She knew it was silly to be emotional, and she didn't want to analyze the reasons. At that moment, she was overcome with a sweep of nostalgic longing for the past. It sometimes happened when she heard a half forgotten love song. So many memories were crowding to the surface. Again willed her mind back to the present.

The customer continued looking at books, and when Rita returned with what she thought was a better copy of the Twain book, the lady's shyness was overcome with an exclamation of approval. "I'll take it. I'm in a little hurry. Just put it in this sack, and I'll give you cash." She then drew out a wad of hundred dollar bills.

As soon as the customer left, Monty motioned to the chairs by the window. "Let's sit down," he invited. "Let me look at you" he said warmly. "You are a person I have visualized all this last year. You know, I don't think you've changed at all. Maybe you are just a little more beautiful".

"Monty, you always know what to say. And always you're the diplomat. Of course, I've changed." Rita chided.

She was about to tell him about Mike and Carmelita when he rose and pulled her up from the chair. "It's twelve o'clock. There are no customers now. I first thought I would call for my car and take you down the coast, but if you are really short on time, we can just cross the lawn and have a lunch outside on the hotel patio."

Rita knew that no matter what he said, she was not going to accept his invitation. For once, she was glad to see Captain Lewis approaching the shop. "There's always something to keep me busy," she exclaimed. "Here comes Captain Lewis. Did you know that I might be accused of faking the burglary we had a few weeks ago? I really think it's just because the captain can't solve the case."

"Do you have a good lawyer, Rita? That's an area in which I can help you. I know a great lawyer who specializes in just that sort of thing. Let me handle it for you."

"Oh no, Monty," Rita said quickly, realizing she was getting herself in even deeper. "The whole accusation is preposterous."

"All the more reason to get a lawyer. Just when you think you don't need a lawyer." He paused. "That is the time you really do need one."

"Right now I need to talk to the inspector, but thanks anyway."

"Go ahead. I'll wait. I have all afternoon. You are the reason I came to California. Just point me to the direction of your biographies. Do you have one about Robinson Jeffers?"

Rita was ready to panic. She was thinking that she should have told him about Mike and Carmelita immediately. She wondered if she should call Mike right now. She could tell him to drop by, and yet that would be unfair to Mike.

"Can I do something for you Captain?" she called as he entered.

"Not today," he said a little mysteriously. "Well, yes you can," he corrected himself. "It's a little private. Can you step outside to talk?"

"Yes I can," Rita answered quickly.

"Your case is closed. At least for now. It doesn't look like *The* Carmelo *Diaries* are going to turn up, and Tessa assured me she was the one who locked up when she left The Old Booktique the night before the burglary. Have you talked to Tessa lately?"

"I think she called me yesterday."

"Did she say anything about me?"

"Yes, she said you didn't make her feel like a suspect."

"Anything else?"

"She said you were coming to Scottsdale to see her."

"This coming weekend. You may think that being a professional law officer makes me sophisticated, but in truth I lived a routine life as a city policeman in a small town in Idaho. My wife died five years ago, and I went back to college so I could upgrade my career. I've been to busy with my job to date much. Now, I'm ready. I think Tessa is interesting, and I want to know her better. You're good friends. I thought you could tell me what she likes. "And you could put in a good word for me?"

Rita was taken aback at this turn of events. "Of course," she said. "Tessa is interesting if you to get to know her. Especially since you told her that you're not suspicious of her involvement in the burglary. She's a generous and spontaneous kind of person. Show her a good time. Bring her flowers." Rita knew she was stalling, and as they walked back to the shop, she could see Monty, idly thumbing through the books.

"Do you know if she's seeing anyone special right now?" Captain Lewis continued.

"Not that I know of. I think she would like a new boy friend. Don't tell her I said so," Rita spoke softly to him.

"Do you think I'm moving too fast for her?" he asked.

"Not at all. Sweep her off her feet. She'd like that. I have a customer over there, so I really need to see what he wants," Rita went on. "Let me know how it goes."

When she went back to Monty, he quickly put the book down.

"Have you thought about where we should have lunch?" By now, I know you're thinking about what you want to say to me." He laughed. "Maybe even some things I don't want to hear. I will always remember your last words when we said Goodbye. It was at Heathrow, and we were taking planes in different directions. We made a pact, you know."

She remembered saying "I will love you always and forever darling" and now she forced herself to say something else. "That was in another life. I'm married now, Monty. And we have a wonderful little girl."

"Then your name is not Atherton? Monty looked visibly shaken. She knew she had told him none too soon. "What is your married name?"

"I am Rita Minetti. When I opened The Old Booktique my name was Atherton. That is a well-known name around here. I thought it best to keep it for business reasons."

"The same Minetti who grows the famous wines? Is it your home town, and Mike has been in business here for a long time?"

"The same name. All his family live in Napa, except…"

"Rita this shocks me. You said you were never going to get married unless it was to me."

"I said that in another life. You see, I really have changed, Monty. It has to do with being part of my family. I am even thinking of taking part in a television special about my family ancestors."

"That's wonderful. All the more reason we should have lunch. We'll talk about your plans."

Rita shook her head.

"I will be true to my word, Rita," he said. "We'll just talk. I won't try to seduce you just because I take you to lunch."

"I seem to remember about the first time we had lunch," she laughed, and now she was feeling better.

"How could I help myself? You were the most beautiful and sexy woman I have ever taken to lunch. Let's see, we were both passengers on the last flight from Nice to Paris. Remember? Then the flight was canceled. The weather was dreadful, and we were stranded. It turned out to be the luckiest day of my life."

"Monty you are full of Blarney."

"You told me you had some Irish blood, too, way back. By the way, what is your little girl's name?"

"Carmelita."

"That's a very California kind of name. I like it."

"How did you know that I had a shop here?"

"Your brother told me. I met him at a food and wine festival. He's quite an enthusiastic speaker. I recognized the name, and told him I knew a Rita Atherton once. We had a good talk. In fact, he encouraged me to look you up and told me you had an upscale place located by The Retreat at Pebble Beach. He is a very ambitious young vintner, you know."

"Yes, he's certainly ambitious."

"That's what he said about you."

"Charlie and I often have different opinions about the same thing," she answered immediately.

"I wondered about that. I also realized that you had never mentioned your brother to me. It sounds like you two are in touch now. He said he was going to have dinner with you this week. I thought he might have told you that I was here in Pebble Beach."

"I think the dinner he referred to was a dinner to announce the reconciliation of his marriage with Missy. He was quite occupied with all his guests."

"He said that his wife had become interested in a purchase of some prime land in the Carneros region between Sonoma and Napa. They are going to create a grand cru vineyard. I'm sure you know all about it," Monty continued.

"The new vineyard will be good project for both of them," Rita commented, and she wondered why Charlie had encouraged Monty to look her up. What was her brother scheming about now?

At that moment Anita came walking into The Old Booktique. She was wearing a red, pink and beige tweed suit and only her low-heeled simple shoes gave her a casual look. She had remarkably supple skin of a light olive cast. As she grew older, her dark hair had grayed to a salt and pepper. Now, she often changed the color to find the one that made her strong Mediterranean features a little less predominant. Her looks favored the Torelli side of her family.

Anita approached Rita and Monty, and when there was a pause in their conversation, she said, "I just thought I would drop by to invite you to lunch, dear. That is when you have a lull."

"Oh Mother, this is a busy day for me. I really can't do it. I even had to turn down lunch with an old friend here," she said gesturing toward Monty. Rita looked back and forth at both of them. "Mrs. Atherton, Mother, may I present Belmont Bates," she said in a manner that would have pleased her grandmother, who had coached her on introductions and manners.

Anita looked at him with interest. "It is a pleasure to meet you, Mr. Bates. Somehow you look familiar."

Monty nodded his head slightly and said, "Mrs. Atherton, I am very pleased to meet you. I used to be a senator. You might have seen me on television a few times."

"That must have been it, Mr. Bates. Don't you think we can persuade Rita to pop into the Grill at the Shore Club for a light meal? I don't see anyone else here, right now."

"I think you can persuade her, Mrs. Atherton."

"Go get your coat, dear. Mr. Bates and I will talk while you freshen up."

Rita hurried off toward the powder room and tried to plan what she would do. At first she was dismayed with her mother's invitation to lunch, and then she decided that this was the best way out of Monty's invitation. They could all go to lunch. She would leave early, and she would have even more to tell Mike tonight.

They walked from The Old Booktique to The Shore Club, a short distance down a path toward the boat pier. Anita and Monty walked ahead and talked about the clouds and the rain of yesterday.

"We will oblige Rita and go to the Grill today," Anita chattered as they walked through the door of the club. "I know Rita loves the Croque-Monsieur they make here. That is the first thing she wants to eat when she gets to Paris. It takes her back to her student days. Do you know Paris, Mr. Bates?"

"Yes I do Mrs. Atherton. If I may make a suggestion, maybe she would rather have a Croque-Madame."

Rita gave Monty a circumspect look. "Yes, I prefer chicken to ham," she said.

Anita ordered the salmon quiche with a salad of mixed greens. Nathan, who usually waited on Anita, assured her that they would make a Croque-Madame, which both Monty and Rita ordered. Anita and Monty decided on a glass of local Sauvignon Blanc, and Rita asked for a pot of green tea.

The lunch was filled with small talk. Anita was delighted that Monty made a hobby of collecting wines and had already met Charles. "He has just hired the best winemaker in the business for his new venture." Anita told him. "Mind you, Charles has put in years of hard work learning the business from the Torellis. That is my side of the family, you know. However, my brothers have their own sons in all the management positions, so I am delighted that Charles is now branching out with his own label. He is very capable."

"There's a great deal to learn about in the wine business," Monty managed to say.

"Are you familiar with Pebble Beach, Mr. Bates?"

"It has been several years since I have been here. So far I've enjoyed the golf very much. If it doesn't rain, I'm to play Cypress Point tomorrow."

"Did you know that my father was one of the earliest members there? He met Mr. Rex Atherton Senior at the Forest Country Club. That is where I met Rex, my husband." Anita paused as she looked at Monty with new interest. He had trained himself to be a good listener. "Well, Rex and I really met when we took riding lessons together at the Equestrian Center as teenagers. Isn't that quaint?"

Monty took all of Anita's chatter as amusing entertainment, and occasionally looked at Rita for her reaction to what he perceived as her mother's mix of mindless enthusiasm and conformity. By observing Rita's glance, he decided that Rita had long been accustomed to these characteristics. Rita had previously told him that living in Europe was a welcome change from her family. At that time, he did not know quite what she meant. He remembered their long talks when they told each other about their earlier lives. At this moment, he fervently wished that he had been able to have a long lunch with Rita alone. They could have shared what had happened in their lives since they were last with each other. He mused on how they were not so far apart in age now. In some ways, they had changed roles. She had chosen a way of life she wanted to protect. She obviously valued her family more now than she did when he first knew her. He understood her and realized that she did not want to change her life now.

When Nathan came to announce the desserts, Rita ordered an espresso coffee. Anita insisted on ordering the mango parfait. "It's the only place around here that makes it the way I like. Real mango fruit with grapefruit ice. I think you'll like it Mr. Bates."

Rita drank the espresso from the small cup rather quickly, and as soon as the desserts arrived, she said, "Excuse me, but I really need to get back to the shop. You two can stay and be decadent."

"I'll see that you are escorted home then, Mrs. Atherton," Monty volunteered, and Anita looked flattered and pleased. "We will let Rita have her way. She's rather determined about it," she said looking at him flirtatiously.

As Rita walked quickly back to the shop, she smiled to herself in amusement at the unusual turn of events that occurred in the last two weeks. The day had become warmer, and she was in no mood to sit at the shop and work. She decided to go home and make her business calls.

Rita called Mel and told him that she had been reading all of Isabel's blue satin notebooks. "I think the material will be a real addition to the story. The books tell Clarita's story after she leaves Monterey. That is when she goes to San Francisco in the last half of the nineteenth century."

Mel and Rita decided to meet at the Stern's home in Beverly Hills in early March. "Right after Carmelita's birthday," Rita told him.

"Did you know that Dave actually decided to get married?" Mel said after they decided on a meeting date. "He announced it at the Friar's Club. No one ever thought something like this would happen. Dave says the wedding will be very private and on some tropical island. He wished us well on the Carmelo project and said that Ellen and I were the right people to work with you. He's not going to take on any new projects so he can spend all his time promoting Maggie's career."

"And Ellen?"

"She's so excited about working with you that she can't talk of anything else. She's down in La Jolla right now. She wanted to visit with our twin daughters who started college there last fall. Then she'll have lots of free time."

"We'll see you soon," Rita finished. Then she dressed Carmelita for outside play on the swing set. As Rita pushed Carmelita into the air she heard her daughter's happy shouts of joy. This was the best part of her day. Later, she would be telling Mike about what happened this morning and at lunch. She thought it would be easy as they had always talked about their past lives. Rita had met Mike's former wife when she was still a very beautiful woman. Gloria was outgoing and vivacious and enjoyed giving parties. Gloria and Mike led an active social life and were often photographed in the social section of the *Monterey Sentinel.* It was good for Mike's business. However, Gloria was in and out of sanitariums during the last ten years of her life.

When Rita and Mike became serious, Rita told Mike that she had a serious love affair when she lived in France. She had not gone further into explanations. Now, she knew she would need to give him a few more details. Although Rita and the senator had been able to keep their lives private, Grandmother Clara had learned of the gossip about Senator Bates with her granddaughter. Grandmother did not like it.

"Don't think your sordid little love affaire isn't talked about," Grandmother Clara told Rita as soon as she heard about it. "The party chiefs are going to make him give you up no matter what he says. I want you to do it first. I insist you come home. At my age I really need you. I will see that you have your financial independence," Clara told her.

At first, Rita would not agree to leave Europe. All she wanted was the living arrangements that she and Monty had agreed upon. However, she soon realized that the longer they met and lived a secret life, the more the odds were that a reporter would see them and print it in some article. She knew her Grandmother was right, and that she, Rita, had to make other plans and leave for California. At first, she did not know what to say to Monty. She had decided not to drag it out. When she told Monty of her decision, he told her that he would divorce Karen and marry her. She knew that making her his wife was too high a price for him to pay. His career would be over. Eventually, he would be unhappy to leave the senate.

Because she continued to love him, Rita told him she did not want to see him until after the next election. As a compromise, she promised to meet him for a weekend in a secluded place outside of London. Once there, he tried to persuade her to change her mind, but she stood by her decision. She asked him not to communicate in any way. She remembered saying that she intended to start a new life.

She returned to Pebble Beach and accepted Grandmother Clara's offer to help start a business. Rita was able to purchase a gazebo type building within the circle of shops around the Retreat, and after some alterations, it became The Old Booktique, purveyor of rare, antique, and out of print books. Shortly after the shop opened, she became reacquainted with the newly widowed Mike Minetti and they fell in love. Clara made it clear that she wanted them to marry while she was still living. She wanted to enjoy the event. Mike and Rita found it easy to comply with her wishes, and Carmelita was born before Clara died. Rita was contented and happy with her life. Only the recent burglary had disheartened her. Now, she intended to bring to life the story of her family in California. This was the life she had always wanted to live.

When Mike arrived home that evening Rita said, "I have had all sorts of funny happenings at the shop today."

"That's good because I had a very boring day at the office," he answered.

When Carmelita had been tucked into bed, they went into Rita's office and sat on the small sofa. The diaries and notebooks laid on the coffee table in front of them.

"Before getting into Isabel's notebooks, tell me what happened at your shop today." Mike asked.

"Captain Lewis dropped by. He didn't start with his usual round of questions. He just started talking about Tessa."

"You mean he's really pursuing his investigation of Tessa?"

"No, he's pursuing Tessa. He says he has closed the burglary case. He's going down to Scottsdale this weekend to see her, and he wanted some input from me about Tessa."

"Wow, and all the time I thought he was intrigued by you.'

"One of the funny parts about this whole thing is his concept of himself. He thinks he is a sophisticated sort of guy because Pebble Beach is his district. He told me that he grew up in a small town in Idaho and married his high school sweetheart. I don't think he's dated since she died five years ago. He asked me to put in a good word for him with Tessa."

"Oh my God. That is a turn. What do you think? We know that Tessa calls him "Deputy Dog.""

"I think she's probably calling him Tim by now. Tessa was quite shaken by Charlie's return to Missy. She needs a little ego boosting. Since he hasn't dated in a while, I bet that before the weekend is over, he'll be in love with her."

"That's a riot. I really didn't think this would happen? What next?'

"Then I called Mel about our meeting with them, and he wanted us to come down near the end of the next week. I told him early March, after Carmelita's birthday party. I think that will work out best. Dolores will be back, and you said you could take off some time."

"Sure. I'm finishing up the paper work on the Roja purchase. It is all going through, and they want to move in right away. It's a good time for me to get away.

"Mel told me that Dave has given up his plans to do something with the Carmelo story. He and Maggie are getting married quietly and soon. He made the big announcement of it at the last Friar's Club roast. He's going to be her full time manager and give her all his attention."

"Love is in the air," Mike laughed and started to hum a little tune.

"Dolores will be back next week and is going to manage the store, so we can go south." Rita paused. "One more surprise. Today at the shop I was interrupted by an unexpected visit from someone I knew in Europe. Then, Mother stopped by. She wanted me have lunch with her. She put me in an awkward spot by asking the friend to come along. She suggested the Shore Club Grill, so I could get back to the shop right after lunch."

"That was pretty considerate of her. Don't forget she's lonely."

"She really took over the conversation."

"As always."

"And I would almost say she was flirting with him."

"So this was an old boy friend. Was your friend by any chance your friend, the Senator?"

"The very same. And believe me, the visit took me by surprise. Anita remembered seeing him on Larry King Live, so she loved every minute of it," Rita paused. "Now guess who told him to drop by The Old Booktique to see me?"

"Not Charlie?"

"The one and only. It seems as if he saw him at a wine convention, and he blithely told him to look me up at my Pebble Beach shop."

"Did Charlie tell him you were married?"

"Of course not. I told him."

"And he was surprised?"

"He seemed to be."

"It's a good thing I snapped you up," Mike said emphatically.

"I had never been inspired to marry because of the marriage of my parents. You are the only one who changed my mind," she said as she reached over and kissed him.

"I thought it was Aunt Clara."

"It was my choice, and you didn't have to ask me twice, did you?" she teased happily.

"Do you think I would have asked you twice?"

"I didn't stop to think. I just pounced on you. I think that all the time, I had been waiting for you to come into my life," she paused. "It had nothing to do with Grandmother. The only thing I did for Grandmother was to have a child right away. I am so glad she was able to attend her christening. That was the most important event for all of us."

"You mean there will be no others?"

"Who knows?" she smiled and squeezed his hand. Then she opened a small blue satin book and began to read while he listened.

CHAPTER 41

▼

These are excerpts from Isabel's blued satin notebooks.

"It is March 22, 1890, and *Mamacita* is seventy-eight years old today.

We celebrated quietly by going to church and having our cook prepare her a special noon meal. She asked for tender baked chicken and green vegetables. She always likes something made with chocolate for her dessert. In the evening while we were sitting in the upstairs parlor, she said she wanted to tell me things about her life that she had never told me before. It was a stormy evening with water rushing down the street toward the Battery. My husband, Mr. Shaw, was away on a business visit to Los Angeles, or 'The City of the Angels', as he likes to call it. I ordered Elaine, my upstairs maid, to bring us hot chocolate, and I offered *Mamacita* a little glass of Cognac to ease the pains she endures during this kind of weather. I made preparations for us to have a comfortable evening of conversation after Nanny brought the children for a kiss and their recital of evening prayers. Edward does not attend our church, but he has agreed that the children be brought up in our faith. *Mamacita* has always been devout and insists on prayers for all of us at the children's bedtime. We also attend mass together.

"After she sipped her Cognac, *Mamacita* quietly started talking about the past. She told me what happened after my mother, my Aunt Anita, and Great-Aunt Felicia left Monterey. She told me more about my grandfather, Will O'Farrell.

"'My life has had many sudden changes. When I was ten years old, I saw the strange red, white and green flag of Mexico pulled to the top of the *Presidio* near the house of the governor. We were told that we were no longer Spanish. I did not understand this, because my father always said we were Spanish. When I was growing up, I went to mass at the Mission San Cárlos, and the courtyard was filled with brown neophyte Indians. Later when I was grown, the mission was closed by orders from Mexico City. The neophytes left, the buildings fell into ruins, and now there is a group of citizens making an appeal for funds to rebuild the church.

"'My personal life changed when I was first married and went to live at the ranch of my husband who was a stranger. After he died, I spent many happy years married to your grandfather. The next great change occurred after the wedding of your aunt Rosita and Uncle Enrique Alonso. Our family stayed at the García ranch for a week. Suddenly, Ramón arrived and told us that all the buildings of Rancho Carmelo had burned down to the ground. This included our house with all the furniture. Esperanza was killed.

"'Will and I, Patricia and Anita went to live in Monterey. We were there in July of the year of 1846 when Commodore Sloat sailed into Monterey Bay. Señor Larkin rowed out to the ship to talk to him. In a few days, the Commodore landed on the wharf, marched his men to the Customs House, and informed the citizens, in Spanish and English, that the United States was taking possession of Monterey. It was official. Soon there were American soldiers in the town. Although no one was injured, there was always fear that the soldiers would hurt us. Your grandfather kept his gun in his holster at all times. If Will needed to go anywhere, we had trusted *vaqueros* take turns watching our house. They slept in our courtyard. During that time, Will worked for Señor Larkin. Don Tomás was a man who was respected by both the Americans and the *Californios*. He advised us to apply for a deed to our ranch lands as soon as the war was officially over.

"'When California formally became part of the United States, we were promised possession and inheritance of our property. It was even written into the new California constitution that was signed by our delegates. Don Tomás advised Will to save money so we could hire lawyers. Don Tomás said we would need to prove our rights of ownership. Already, Will found a few men and a woman living on a part of the ranch land near the river. They had built wooden huts, and the first lawyer who talked to us said that they had rights to the land, since we had no buildings. We objected and were told that we needed the official United States government maps and measurements to describe the property.

"'Your grandfather's ranch in the hills, Rancho Segundo, was much smaller, and his *vaqueros* continued to live in the bunkhouses there. Will had papers proving his American citizenship, so that we believed that Rancho Segundo was safe. I was fully occupied with our home in Monterey since I had only two maids to help me. I continued to teach your mother and Anita, to read and write both English and Spanish. Felicia lived with us and taught the children of the Coopers and the Gutiérrez family who came to our house for lessons. I taught all the children their social duties, dancing, and customs that were necessary for the education of young people in Monterey.

"'Although the American Flag had been raised, and we were under military rule, the social life of Monterey had not yet changed. We entertained often. The christenings and wedding parties lasted for three days and nights, and there were large family dinners. When there were *fandangos* in Monterey, all the American officers were invited. Most of the officers attended, and they marveled at our enjoyment in dancing at such a time. It gave us an opportunity to dress in our clothes of silk and velvets. I saw very little of Consuelo as she did not like Americans, and she always called them *Yanquis*. She did not need to have anxiety about a romance between Timoteo and Felicia, as my little sister had begged to be allowed to join a religious teaching order as soon as one was organized.'

"'I spent many hours with Rachel Larkin during the war. Rachel was alone, because Mr. Larkin was a prisoner of the Americans for two months. Rachel did not enjoy talking in Spanish, and I was now fluent in English. We learned even more about each other. The youngest Larkin child was born in 1847; a month after the last battle of the war was fought in a pass called Cahuenga near the *pueblo* of Los Angeles. When the war was over, and Don Tomás returned to Monterey, he became much more interested in purchasing land in the North. He bought land in Yerba Buena and near to the area where Don Mariano lived. They wanted to make a new town on the north end of San Francisco Bay. Don Tomás continued to tell us to secure new titles to our land.'"

"*Mamacita* stopped talking and opened a little leather bag that she had in her lap. She shook it and handed me a gold nugget about the size of a walnut. 'This is for you, dear child. You listen to my stories. Next time I will tell you about the Gold Rush,' she said as she put the gift into my hand.

"The next morning it was still raining, and I canceled my social visits by carriage. *Mamacita* asked me to listen to more of her story. 'I may repeat myself,' she commented. 'So please humor me.' I drew up a chair and gave her a footstool and she continued.

"'It was 1848, and Captain Sutter decided he would build a mill on the river near his fort. There were no flourmills in California, and knew that Americans did not eat tortillas. They would want wheat flour to make their bread He employed a man, James Marshall, to build the mill. There was much rain that January, and Mr. Marshall was inspecting the storm damage to the new mill, when he saw something bright below the surface of the water. Because he thought it was gold, he quickly rode back to Sutter's Fort and told the Captain about it. They could not keep it a secret because Mr. Marshall had already talked about finding gold to the men in his work party. The news spread quickly. I will not tell you about all the changes that happened to Monterey and to California at this time, because you asked me to tell you my story.

"'After Rancho Carmelo was burned, we lived in Monterey. We needed money for lumber to make small buildings on Rancho Segundo and to feed our *vaqueros*. We used all the money Will earned from Mr. Larkin. The discovery of gold excited Will, and he wanted to go to the gold fields with his own *vaqueros*. Will had been to Sutter's Fort many times for Mr. Larkin, and he knew the country. The first time he traveled to Coloma, he was able to find some small nuggets, and he brought them back to show Mr. Larkin. They decided to have the nuggets verified. Will had found something called placer gold. He could pick it up from the dirt. When it was loosened from the rocks with picks, or if it was found in the water, this placer gold could be sifted out of the dirt. When Will learned it was truly gold, he was very eager. So was everyone else. By the time a newspaper in the Central Valley printed an article about the gold at Sutter's Mill, everyone in the territory began talking about it.

"'What a strange time. Because of the war, there was not yet a true government in California. We were still under Army rule. Any one who could get the tools together wanted to go to find gold. However, no one knew if they really had a claim. This worried me, and especially because I knew Will would be away for long periods of time. He assured me this was the answer to our prayers. If he found gold, we would have enough money to pay for the best lawyers, and we could build a big house and live on our Rancho Carmelo again. Will was not a city man. He never wanted anything more than the ranch life he knew. He said if we could secure all the land he had described in our Mexican deeds, we would have more than enough for ourselves and all our grandchildren.

"'Will decided to go with supplies and ten of his most trusted men. They would make a camp just as they did when they went out on the range. They came back with astounding results. There were many men from California going to the gold fields, and other men began to arrive from as far away as the Sandwich Islands, Sonora, Mexico, and even Chile. Will and his *vaqueros* were especially successful, as they had all worked outdoors much of their lives. By the time it rained in late autumn, Will had carried back enough gold to satisfy our needs. He also brought stories of friendship and good will among miners, and it seemed like an impossible dream come true.

"'Mr. Larkin warned us that this feeling of friendship in the camps would not last long. He told Will what he had heard from men in other parts of the country. Men were coming in boats and wagons from the East, and even the Americans stationed in the Army were deserting so they could try their luck in the goldfields. He asked Will to work for him full time. Mr. Larkin had decided that selling supplies to the miners was the best and easiest way to make a fortune. He was right. By 1849, gold was no longer easy to find. Men from everywhere were arriving at San Francisco Bay by boat. We were told that the boats were abandoned, and that a man could walk from boat to boat and see no one. The boats were deserted. Don Tomás was now interested in buying more land in Yerba Buena, which was now renamed the city of San Francisco. He was a prosperous man, and he wanted to be an extremely wealthy man. He asked Will to be one of the agents who would look after his interests in the countryside from Monterey to San Jose. I was quietly hoping that Will would not want to return to the gold country, and I urged him to do whatever Don Tomás asked. Will told me what Don Tomás wanted him to do was for the benefit of Don Tomás. He knew that Don Tomás had even decided to leave Monterey and to move his family to San Francisco. We talked about it and decided to do the next best thing, which was to rebuild our house at Rancho Carmelo.

"'It was the summer of 1849. True to what had been foretold, the gold fields were overrun with prospectors. Some of our *vaqueros* stayed in the goldfields. They wanted a fortune for themselves. When they occasionally came back, they told us tales of murder and theft. Some gambled and drank whisky and did other sinful things when the gold was not so easy to find. Mr. Larkin had been correct. Some men were setting up stores and selling everything from soap to eggs and they were the ones making the money. The newspapers all over the world were printing more and more stories about the gold in all of California. Men were coming from all directions. At least Will was working nearby at our ranch. He had the Indians making adobe bricks and he built more bunkhouses for both ranches. He did much of the work himself with only the help of Ramon and his relatives. In the fall when the *rodeo* was finished Will was content to live in town with us.

"'The town of Monterey was prosperous with miners spending money and there was excitement as the town made preparations for a gathering of the most important men of California. They were needed to write the new constitution. Delegates were elected from all over the territory, and the place for the meeting was to be in a schoolhouse near the edge of Monterey. It was a large two-story building already named Colton Hall. As there were no real hotels yet in

Monterey, everyone who lived in town was expected to offer rooms to the delegates. There were many Americans coming to the gathering. Since we spoke English, we were asked to let two of the American delegates reside at our house. Who came to Monterey? Governor Riley was present, and Mariano Guadalupe Vallejo from Petaluma looked handsome in the beautiful clothes of a *Californio* grandee. Captain John Sutter was easy to recognize in his dress uniform. Pablo de la Guerra and José Antonio Carrillo, who are descendants of Spanish, families were among the delegates from the south. Captain Frémont, now a Colonel, was not a delegate, and yet he was seen everywhere in Monterey with the delegates. His wife, Jessie, had managed to arrive in California to be with him. She traveled across the strip of land called Panama to the Pacific Ocean with their little daughter and I thought she was a brave woman. I have always been puzzled by the behavior of John Frémont; however, I admire Jessie for the courage and devotion she has shown her husband through the years. Don Tomás was a delegate and you can imagine the lavish entertaining at their house. The delegates had important questions to decide. The first one up for debate was the question of the admission of California as a state in the lands of the *Yanquis*."

Isabel inserts that her grandmother became emotional and sometimes paused as she told the story.

"Mamacita continued. 'I knew little about how the people lived in other parts of America. I did not know about the differences of the people who lived in Boston and the people who lived father to the South. As you know, later in the years that followed this, the Americans fought a terrible war with each other because of slavery. When the *Yanquis* annexed California, it was expected that California would become a state against slavery. For that reason, there was a group of American slave owners who voted against the admission of California. There were also some California delegates who wanted to make two states out of the territory. The south part would be called a slave state, while the north would be called a free state.

"'The delegates met for many days until they voted on all the laws we needed. There was even a law against dueling with weapons. Copies were made of the constitution, and these were carried around to every place that was inhabited. New government officials were elected. At the end there was a wonderful ball that everyone wanted to attend. Even Consuelo and Miguel came into town. Their daughter, Rosita, and husband Enrique Alonso came with Fernando Alonso, who had been recently widowed. We decided that Patricia, who was thirteen, should attend this historic event. She wore a dress that was made especially for her. Patricia had hair the color of amber honey and a fair skin that blushed easily. Her gown was made of a blue silk and her abundant hair was held in place by a black ebony Spanish comb. Beautiful women of many nationalities danced at the *fandango*, but our Patricia was an exceptional beauty with her simplicity and natural charm. Fernando, your papa, was a widower at that time. General Riley enjoyed himself at the grand ball. He stayed in Monterey until the summer of 1850. We wished that all our governors could be so understanding as General Riley. In those days we looked forward to a better future for all of us.

"'For months we knew that the Larkins were going to New York for a long visit. Oliver and Frederick were in school in that land and the boys had never even seen their baby brother, Alfred. Don Tomás asked some of his business agents to keep him informed of properties for sale in San Francisco and lands by the bay. In the spring of 1850 the Larkin family left San Francisco on a new steam ship. Captain Cooper accompanied them.

"'Will continued to work full time to rebuild our *hacienda* at Rancho Carmelo, while we lived in our Monterey adobe. Will told us he hoped to find enough men to help him, and then we could live in our new house in the autumn. He always returned to us on Saturday. After Sunday mass, I served a bountiful dinner. I often asked Encarnacion Cooper and members of her family to come and have dinner with us. The sons of Ramon stayed in Monterey to help me and be protection for the family.'"

Rita stopped and showed Mike a place in the book where Isabel made a notation.

"*Mamacita* stopped and wiped her eyes with a handkerchief and then folded her small hands in her lap. She looked like she was wearing a halo. Her white hair was wrapped in a roll and there was light shining from a window behind her"*Mamacita* asked if she should finish this part of her story before we went to church, and I told her it was best not to go out in the storm. *Mamacita* replied, "Very well then," and she continued where she left the story last night.

"'A little more than a year passed. In the autumn of 1851, Will went to Rancho Carmelo alone one early morning. The adobe bricks had dried well in the summer sun, and he had instructed some of Ramon's family, who lived up the valley, to build the outside walls of the courtyard. These men had already built the large room in the center of our new house.' *Mamacita* stopped at this point and asked for a sip of Cognac, which I gave to her.

"'I do not know if I ever knew the true story of what happened that day, but it must have happened very early before the workers arrived. One of our *vaqueros* said they heard two shots and the sound of horses galloping away. When they reached, Will, he was lying on the ground, and blood running from his chest. One of the men went to find Ramon, who lifted his body onto a horse, and brought him to Monterey.

"'Ramon knew that Will was dead and did not come to our house. He went to the buildings where the governor used to live. The surgeon of the soldiers lived near there and confirmed that Will must have died instantly. When Ramon came to tell me, he said Will had been shot by some bandits who were roaming the hills to the south of Monterey. The surgeon asked me if I needed to take medicine salts. I told him I would not faint. Then I remember telling Ramon to take the children to the home of Encarnacion Cooper. I wanted to go to the surgeon and be with my husband.

"'When we entered the barracks, I saw Will, and I kissed him and had him lifted to a bed. I told someone to take him to the San Cárlos Chapel. I asked for the resident *padre*. I arranged for a rosary and mass and decided that he should be buried near my parents and our infant son. After bathing his wounds, I stayed beside Will for some time until I could gather the courage to tell the children. I rode with Ramon at my side, and two other *vaqueros* rode beside us to the house of the Coopers. I had to tell the children. I told them we would not return to Rancho Carmelo. I told them that their Papa would be with them in spirit. *Por siempre jamás.*'"

Rita looked up. "When Isabel concluded her little book, she made a notation. The Spanish words mean' forever and a day.'"

"And did Isabel write more books?" Mike asked

"Yes. There are two small books about *Mamacita's* years in San Francisco. Isabel wrote that her grandmother never talked about the death of Will again. *Mamacita* lived in the present and enjoyed the company of her great-grandchildren, Edward Junior and Sara Isabel, whom they called 'Belle.' *Mamacita* always spoke English with a soft Spanish accent, and sometimes she used a favorite Spanish word to convey her thoughts."

"If you'll have a glass of merlot with me, I'll let you read another book to me," Mike cajoled.

"Let's just sip what we have left, and I'll tell you a little about what I know."

"Aunt Clara told me there was no record of Will's death in any official archives. Is that true? Mike asked.

"Clarita always believed that Don Diego ordered those *vaqueros* to the murder Will. After the American Conquest, he lived the rest of his life in Sonora, Mexico. No one was held responsible for the death of Will. There was no way to prove anything."

"And that was all there was to it? There was no pursuit of justice?"

Rita sighed. "The new state of California had very little law enforcement at that time. The Anglos said the murder was the work of the dreaded bandit, Joaquin Murrieta. Thomas Larkin was in the East, and when he inquired, he was informed that the death was reported as another murder by a band of outlaws. He advised Clarita to take her small family and move to San Francisco quickly. He also advised Clarita to sell her rights to their ranches for whatever price she could and use the money for living. Will had no money, and she needed money for the move. Through one of his agents, Mr. Larkin made it possible for her to live in one of his houses in the district near the Mission Dolores. It is in the oldest area of San Francisco and situated near the church of the Mission Dolores where Clarita and family could attend mass."

"How old was she then?" Mike said.

"Thirty-Eight. She lived fifty more years in San Francisco."

"I think you'd better wait to tell me the rest of the story. I'm getting sleepy."

"Me, too. We have another week before we finalize this with the Sterns."

CHAPTER 42

▼

Early Sunday morning, Anita called Rita. "Charles and Missy have decided to go on their trip at the end of next week, and I am going up to Napa to stay with the girls. I will fly to San Francisco on Wednesday. I hope Charles will pick me up."

"Isn't that sooner than they planned?"

"Charles said it is best for him to go now. The seasons are different than ours, and it is harvest time in Australia. He needs to be back in Napa by April for important business. The acquisition of all his new vineyards is really quite complicated."

"Is there anything we can do for you?" Rita asked.

"Just take me to the airport in Monterey, and of course look in on Roberto and Alma at Stonecrest. Roberto is going to oversee the repair of our circular driveway, and Alma is going to clean all the silver in the house. How about going to a movie with me, this afternoon?"

"Oh, Mother, I promised Carmelita a good Sunday playtime."

"I think you're being rather selfish. You're always doing what you want to do. Some day you'll know what it is like to be alone like I am. Charles says I should forgive Rex. He says I should ask him to come back and live at Stonecrest with me. Charles thinks your father is tired of Bebe. Rex always enjoyed playing golf around here, and I still belong to the Forest Country Club. Charles says all I have to do is look the other way when Rex has a little fling on the side. What do you think?"

"It is something to consider," Rita answered cautiously.

"Rex and I aren't getting any younger. He can't go on running after other women forever, and I know he'd like to live here in this lovely house." Anita paused just long enough to change the subject. "I think it is so wonderful that Charles and Missy are back together. Charles says they are going to sign all the papers for the new winery when they come back from their trip."

"Do you want us to come see today, dear?" Rita answered.

"Oh, I don't know. I have no business going to the movies when I should be packing. Yes, come over in the afternoon. Just you and Carmelita. Then I'll have the little tea party I promised her. Oh dear, I'll miss her birthday party next week. Well, the little tea party will make up for it. Does she like orange juice or apple juice?"

"We'll come after her nap time. She loves apple juice."

Anita phoned again. "I'm pressed for time. I just can't have you two over today. I still have so much to pack," she explained.

Rita continued to read Isabel's satin notebooks. During Carmelita's naptime, she and Mike talked about the family.

"Did Charlie tell you he's forming a corporation for his new appellation?

"He wasn't that specific." Mike said,

"At some point in the conversation during their party, he told me he wants to go public with his corporation. He even offered to let me buy some shares early. I most certainly do not want to do that." Mike said with emphasis.

"Nor I. We have enough to think about with our own businesses." Rita said firmly.

"Amen," he echoed. "Let's forget the family the rest of the day."

The next morning, Rita went to work early at The Old Booktique. The shop was back to normal with books in proper categories and the shelves in order. Near nine o'clock, Dolores entered the shop. "I had a wonderful vacation, and I even missed being here with you," she said as she greeted Rita with a smile. "Anything new?"

"Not much. I'm getting started on inventory, and that's pretty boring. I think I'll plan a literary tea and have you tell about one particular book. We'll advertise a little and have it as soon as I come back from L.A. When's a good time for you?"

"After the first few weeks of March. What do you want me to do today?"

"The display tables need some refurbishing. Can you start with that before the customers arrive?"

The telephone rang, and Rita answered. "Rita, I just had to call you and tell you the good news. I am going to have a new love life." Said Tessa.

"That's great," Rita said with genuine relief. "I guess Captain Lewis visited you."

"His name is Tim. He doesn't want me to call him Captain anymore. And he's really not the way we thought he was when he first started asking questions."

"Is the investigation over?"

"Yes. Right out of the blue he told me that and we didn't talk anymore about it. He said he liked me from the minute he first saw me taking off my muddy boots at the shop. He said it wouldn't have been professional to let me know then."

"I can understand that. Does he want you to move back? You can still have your job even though I have Dolores."

"I like it here. It gives me a chance to see Mother in Sedona. We're on better terms you know. And Tim can come see me here. I have such a great apartment, I think he likes the adventure of coming to see me."

"Then it's serious?"

"Pretty intense. He's a real lover boy. Believe me. Before I forget it, I don't want you to say anything to Tim about Charles and me. That might ruin it."

"It would ruin a lot of things."

"I might as well tell you I had one more fling with Charles a week ago. He called it a corporate meeting. At the time I thought it was cute? The sex was great. I was just about to get all crazy over him again, when he told me his plan for the new winery was going to take a little more time than he first thought. He told me he and Missy were leaving for Australia at the end of the next week. Something just snapped inside of me. Then and there, I decided I needed another lover, but I don't want Charles to know about it yet. I've learned it doesn't pay to upstage Charles. He can get mean. We parted on good terms, because he thinks my mother might put money in his new business venture."

"The Captain came at the right time," Rita put in.

"I first thought I might get involved with an eager guy who comes into the boutique here. He always flirts with me. Then Tim came to see me last weekend, and I really fell for him."

"I didn't think he was your type."

"You never know. I thought we'd have a couple of dates. That was before I found that he's really starved for sex. He hasn't dated since his wife died. Rita. He's so eager to please me, and he's kind of naïve. Charles can be so callous. He's always full of sarcastic remarks. I bet Tim even believes in Valentine's Day and Santa Claus. It's refreshing because he's sweet."

"Mike's a sweet man, but he's not naïve."

"Mike's more worldly. I don't think Tim's really had sex with anyone, but the girl he married. They probably had sex when they were in high school and never thought about changing their routine. But that's not what I called you about," Tessa rambled on. "I called to tell you that I think the burglary case is really closed. The lost diaries will never be found, and nobody's going to think it's your fault."

"How can you be so sure?"

"Trust me, you can."

"But are you sure." Rita started to say something else, and then she said, "Is Tim going to be in Scottsdale again?"

"Next weekend."

"He might ask me what you said about him."

"I know he will. Just tell him I think he's great. Make it big, and for God's sake don't tell him anything else."

"Don't you think you might be leading him on?"

"No. It's too early to tell where it will all lead, but it's so great. We're both free. There's no hiding and telling lies. I like it this way. We can sit and hold hands, and we don't have to worry about anybody else."

"It sounds mutual."

"Oh yes. I have another piece of news for you. I found out you were right about one thing concerning Charles. He has been trying to pay you back for something you did to him."

Rita was interested in the turn of the conversation "What do you mean?"

"When I saw him last week, he boasted that he had really played a joke on you. He contacted your Senator Lover Boy and told him you still cared for him. Charles said he met him at a wine auction recently. Charles told him you'd like to see him again."

"And Mr. Bates came into the shop last Friday."

"Too bad I didn't warn you. What was he like?"

"He was unaware that I was married and had a child."

"And?"

"He wanted me to go to lunch with him. I definitely didn't want to do that."

"Why?"

"Tessa, You and I are different. I really didn't want to start anything, no matter how innocent. While he was at the shop, Mother came along and insisted we all go for a quick lunch at the Shore Club Grill. It worked out to be O.K., and we all went to lunch. I left them while they were finishing dessert and coffee. I understand she invited him to Stonecrest afterwards. I told Mike about the whole thing last Friday night."

"Yeah, but I bet you had a flutter when you first saw him after all this time."

"Not really," Rita said with emphasis.

"Charles told me that he just wanted to play a little trick on you. I thought it was kind of funny, but now I think he really does hold a grudge. He can be rather heartless."

"A little trick?"

"He's selfish, Rita, and he always wants his own way. Maybe we're lucky that he wants to make a big name for himself with this wine thing. He wants to get the best of his Torelli cousins. He plans to go to the top of the connoisseur wine business. I know that's why he is going back to Missy. Really. Rita, he was going to marry me. Honestly. We had a date for it, and we had the place all picked out, but he kept changing the date."

"What do you mean a trick on me?"

"It's so wonderful to have someone like Tim that can be all mine. Charles really used me, Rita."

"Then you're wise to him now."

"I really am. Rita. I might as well go on and tell you. Remember when he was at the Retreat for that last wine convention. Charles and I were with each other every night. It was the time he told me I could help him play little trick on you. He was separated from Missy then, and we were serious about getting married. I was ready to do anything I could to prove I was indispensable to him."

"What are you referring to?" Rita asked with a premonition of what was about to be said.

"Rita, It's hard to come right out and tell you. I didn't mean for it to happen. It started when he said it would be fun to make love in your little office and then trash the place. He said we'd do it just to freak you out."

"Oh God." Rita had been standing while she was talking on the phone. Now she quickly pulled up a chair and sat down.

"You are a neat freak, you know, Tessa went on. "Anyway I'd had a little bit to drink, and I thought it would be fun to make love at the shop so I opened the shop so I worked the alarm and we both went in. We didn't turn on any lights. We made love right away and then we found a great bottle of wine to drink. After we each had a glass or two, we were really mellow. We did it again in the little powder room. After we were through, he said we couldn't be seen together, so he told me to leave and go back to my cottage. He said for me to buy something at a little market nearby. And he said to be sure to have a conversation with the checkout clerk. I did what he said, and he called me in about an hour to see if I was safe. I thought that was so sweet of him. And so help me God, that's all I know about that night. I just went to sleep at my own place. Now I know it was a set up."

"It all makes sense to me," Rita said slowly.

"After the police started asking me questions, Charlie told me to go to Scottsdale, get a job. He said something went wrong with his joke and he didn't want me involved. I really thought he wanted to protect me. I didn't know he was going back to Napa and make up with Missy. Now I think he wanted me in Scottsdale just to get me out of the way."

"Tessa are you sure you haven't told Captain Lewis even the tiniest thing about this?"

"I haven't, really. It embarrasses me to tell you all this. I have been very careful not to say anything about Charles to Tim."

"Um," Rita murmured. "A trick sounds like something Charles would do. I had a feeling that Charlie had come into my upstairs office and rearranged my sentimental toys on the morning of the burglary."

"Did you tell that to the police?"

"No. It was such a trivial thing. Did Charlie tell you why he wanted to get even with me?"

"He said you were a spoiled kid and always got the best of everything from Grandmother Clara. It was Charles that made sure she knew you were playing around with the Senator when you lived in Europe. Then when you came home and met Mike and your grandmother was so happy about it all, he was really furious. Charles said Clara favored you even more when you two got married and, and especially when Carmelita came along. Charles really thinks that he's entitled to the biggest share of the family inheritance because he's Anita's son."

"I'm glad you told me all this"

"Rita, it just came out. I really called to tell you that I'm in love with Tim, and I wanted to put your mind at ease. The burglary case has ended."

"That's good news. I don't know about the other information. I would like Captain Lewis o tell me that the case is closed. Then I would be sure."

"It's time for me to go to work at the shop here. I sell mostly perfume and stuff like that."

"I need to go, too," Rita said as she looked toward several customers.

"I'll call if I hear anything more," were Tessa's last words.

Dolores came up to Rita with a tall middle-aged lady who was wearing thick glasses. She carefully held up a copy of *Fool's Gold,* which was a biography about

Captain John Sutter. "Mrs. Ames has a collection of books about the life of John Sutter." Dolores said.

"How did you get interested in Captain Sutter?" Rita asked

"I had a classmate at Stanford who had some connection to the Sutter family. Her last name was Sutter, although she didn't claim to be very closely related."

"I can arrange to get a copy of Captain Swasey's *California in '45-'46*. Or maybe you already have it. Captain Swasey supplied important notes for Sutter's own *New Helvetia Diary*," Rita said.

"Do you have any other books about Sutter that you could show me now?" Mrs. Ames said after looking at a piece of paper she extracted from her cavernous leather purse.

"What about Volume V of Bancroft's *History of California*?" Rita asked as she escorted Mrs. Ames to a chair.

"I already have the whole series. I'm looking for material that includes anecdotes. Perhaps it could be a book that covers the Constitutional Convention in Monterey. You see I'm writing a play. I remember my friend told me how Captain Sutter liked European-style pancakes. It seems it was hard for him to find wheat in California. Everyone ate tortillas that were made with hand ground corn. I think he purchased wheat from Thomas Larkin who also sold him butter that had come from the Sandwich Islands The missionaries there came from New England and ate American style food."

"I understand what you're looking for. I'll inquire around." Rita promised.

"Where do you purchase your books?" Mrs. Ames questioned.

"I have good sources in San Francisco and Reno as well as a list of private estates that have good collections of books about the nineteenth century in Northern California. And also, there are some stores in Sacramento. Have you gone to the State House Library there? They have a wonderful newspaper index."

"I'm going to be staying in Pebble Beach with my family for about a month. Would you compile a bibliography for me and write which books or publications are for sale and available?"

When Rita started to hesitate, Mrs. Ames said, "Naturally, I expect to pay you by the hour. I realize that Captain Sutter lived in California a long time. There are many bits and pieces of information that can be discovered and collected. Frankly I'm not interested in just a fictionalized biography."

"My associate here," said Rita motioning her head towards Dolores, "is particularly good at that sort of thing. Would you like her to start as soon as possible?"

"I wouldn't be here if I just wanted to talk about it," Mrs. Ames said.

Soon, Dolores was sitting at the table and taking notes concerning the project, and Rita was attending to the wants of other customers. After hearing from Tessa, she was not surprised to see Captain Lewis.

"Hi," he said in a relaxed manner. "Has Tessa talked to you?"

"She called this morning,"

"I'm going to see her on Friday afternoon. I want to hear what she said about me."

"She told me she had a great weekend with you. I'd like to talk to you, but I have customers right now, and Dolores is tied up with someone who has a research project for her."

"I'll come back at noon. Do you take time out for lunch?"

"Probably not today. Tell me, are you really through with my burglary case? Can I file an insurance claim?"

"Yes, file it if you want to. Most of your stolen books have been found. They will be returned. It is just the diaries that are missing. Are you sure you really want to file a claim?"

"That's what I have insurance for," Rita came back.

"Then we'll talk about it when I come back," he said and left quickly.

After what Tessa had said in their last conversation, Rita was sure Charles was responsible for the burglary. She was not sure if she really wanted to go digging into the case again. She had asked Captain Lewis about the insurance to learn whether the case was really closed. It seemed to depend on the Captain's feelings for Tessa? From her first sight of The Old Booktiques after the burglary, she had the feeling she was looking for missing pieces in a jigsaw puzzle. Tessa's last phone call added some clues. "I'll be at my desk, if I am needed." she told Dolores

Customers continued to arrive all morning and afternoon. Rita finished all her phone calls about back orders. Captain Lewis arrived again at two o'clock. He gave Rita something rolled up in a napkin. "I bet you didn't eat lunch, and you look like the type who eats sprouts and cream cheese with a little salsa wrapped into a flour tortilla. Am I right?"

"Thank you. I love to eat a wrap, although it's a little messy for my kind of business."

"You'll eat it like a lady. Tessa told me you're a 'neat freak'."

"Just here in the shop. I don't let anyone eat in The Old Booktique and that includes me."

"Then come on out and sit with me on that bench over there," he said. "I can't wait any longer to tell you I think Tessa really likes me." A blush came easily to his pale complexion. "In fact, she was more than cordial. She asked me to stay at her place this coming weekend. She said it was crazy for me to take a hotel room when I wasn't going to use it."

"I told you she likes you," Rita said looking at him until he lowered his eyes.

"Did she tell you how much?"

"Plenty. I don't think you need to worry about her affections. I think it's great. I'm happy for the both of you."

"Is she always so ready to have a good time?" he stopped. "Well, you know what I mean."

Rita knew he really wanted to tell her he had already made love with Tessa. She figured he was unaccustomed to talking about sex even it he wanted to boast about it.

"I might as well tell you. Tessa told me you spent the night with her last weekend," Rita said.

This time he really blushed. "She's quite a gal. I wish it were Friday right now. By the way, call me Tim," he said.

"Tessa says and does what she feels like at the moment. Are you shocked?" Rita said.

"Yes, a little and I like it. That's what I wanted to talk to you about."

"Have a good time, Tim," Rita smiled. "I need to get back to work. And thanks for the lunch."

"You've been a good friend to us both," he said and walked off.

When Rita saw Mike after dinner that night she told him about Tessa and Captain Lewis. "I think I know some answers now," she added.

"What do you mean?"

"I'll tell you more after I'm sure that the burglary case is closed."

"Has Captain Lewis solved it? That is interesting."

"Now that he's dating Tessa, he'll probably put the case in a file somewhere."

"Is that what you want?"

"I think so. At least, for now."

"You sound mysterious. That's not fair to me," he laughed.

"Right now it is. We can talk it over thoroughly tomorrow."

"And Dolores is going to help you out?"

"She's going to stay on for as long as I want her."

"Then it's on to the Sterns with your California Saga. I finished the Roja deal today."

CHAPTER 43

▼

During the next few days, Rita continued working on the "Carmelo Project." She organized her notes, stories, and information from the assorted diaries. She wrote the last chapters about Clarita's life after she left Monterey. This is the story Clarita told Isabel, who preserved these recollections in her blue satin books. Rita shared it with Mike.

"My husband, Will, died in 1851. As soon as he was buried, I went to the local *alcalde* in Monterey to report what had happened. I was told to go to the courthouse, where I learned there was no way to seek the justice I wanted. Since the Gold Rush, the few courts of law in the state were years behind with cases against bandits who roamed the countryside.

"'I had no one in Monterey to advise me, since the Larkins now lived in New York. I sold some of my necklaces to the American ladies in Monterey. Then I sewed the rest of my jewelry in the underneath folds of my skirts. I sold our furniture. Mr. Larkin had learned of Will's death and advised one of his agents to assist us. He arranged for us to live in a small empty house he owned in San Francisco. It was located in a district near the Mission Dolores, where the first *Californios* had started a community.

"'Before we departed from Monterey, I sent a letter with Ramon to the ranch of Consuelo and Miguel. I told them we were departing from Monterey. I asked for no help. Mr. Larkin's agent arranged to have a stagecoach take our family to the home of the Buelo family, who lived near the *pueblo* of San José. This first stop was for Felicia, who hoped to become a teaching sister in the new school for women housed in a building adjacent to the Mission Santa Clara. While in the pueblo of San José, I sold my hand painted China dishes I had purchased only two months before Will's death. This paid for a stagecoach ride to San Francisco. I took one maid, Lupe, an orphan who had lived with our family for many years.

"'I had never been to Yerba Buena. It became a city during the Gold Rush, and the name changed to San Francisco. As we approached from the south, we saw large hills of sand dunes. Patricia and Anita peered out of the carriage in amazement. When we reached the top of a hill, we saw a large town of tents and wooden sidewalks. We also saw empty spaces where a recent fire had burned many buildings. It was the autumn of 1851, and the weather was warm, so the streets were filled with people. When we descended the hill we rode through dusty streets. There, we saw venders pushing carts and wooden stands where men yelled about the things they were selling. We saw fruit stands, fishmongers, and peddlers with household goods. Especially Anita was frightened by the clamor. I had already paid the coachman to take us to the Mission Dolores, but when he found our destination was several blocks from the Mission, he would take us no further. I coaxed him to complete our journey, and finally he conceded when I gave him a valuable beaded purse. For a few more coins, he was willing to carry the trunks and boxes to the front door. When the stage departed, I was left with fewer possessions and many doubts about our future.'"

Rita marveled at the bravery of Clarita. As she read further, she realized that Isabel must have asked her many questions about this time in her life. The narration continues.

"It was so long ago, and I do not remember what I did at first. I do know we attended mass regularly. It was there that I met Madame LaRue. She often attended mass in early morning as we did. Soon she addressed me in Spanish and complimented the manners of my daughters. Everyone at mass seemed to know one another, and yet Madame LaRue spoke only to me. When she introduced herself, she spoke with an accent that was not like any I had heard in California. I wondered where she was born. She wore skirts of reds, greens and yellows, and always I could hear her beads and bracelets as they jangled merrily when she knelt or walked to the altar. She always spoke to me and was a cheerful person. I was lonely and was glad to talk to someone. As for food, although we ate sparingly, our supplies were getting low and food was expensive in San Francisco. In fact, we ate beans for most of our meals. Lupe cooked the beans with onions in a big pot that we hung in our fireplace.

"'I often wore a pearl ring and sometimes a pair of dangling silver earrings. Madame LaRue admired the ring. One day after mass, Madame LaRue and I walked to a little park near the church. I asked her if she liked jewelry, and when she gave an enthusiastic answer, I found the courage to tell her that I was low on funds and had several rings I wished to sell. I invited her to visit us after mass the next Sunday. When she came to our little house, we served chocolate in silver cups, and she looked at the rings Don Felipe had given me. She told me that many of the men from the gold fields had money and wanted to buy jewelry for their ladies. She said she could sell the rings and all the other jewelry I could bring her. This gave me hope for the future.

"'After a few months, she told me that I must find some other way to take care of my family when the jewelry was gone. When I said I could teach children to read and write Spanish and English, she suddenly embraced me and told me that God had answered her prayers. She said several young ladies boarded at her house. They needed to learn to speak English. She asked me to teach them and offered to pay me well.

"'It may seem strange, but I did not know that the young ladies were the ones who sold themselves to men for an hour at a time. Madame La Rue told her they were orphans and had to work for their board and room. She gave me her address, and she invited me to her house for tea the next day. It was a long walk up many hills and was situated in the American district where the men were rich and lived in fine houses. Madame LaRue took her carriage to the Mission Dolores in order to attend Catholic mass.

"'When I entered the elegant mansion of Madame La Rue on Bush Street, I was ushered to a place called, the front room. Here, there was an abundance of furniture, large chairs, upholstered in velvet, and many silk pillows displayed on the settees. There were tables on long legs with potted ferns and fancy vases filled with dried flowers. I had never seen such a room. It was too much for my eyes to see.

"'After we were served tea and little cakes, Madame La Rue introduced me to a beautiful young lady who was dressed for a fancy party. Madame said this girl wanted to work for Americans, and needed to know how to speak some of their language. She said the girls did not have time for many lessons, and they would need a special vocabulary Then Madame brought in another young lady to meet me. When I looked at this young girl, I noticed her cheeks were the color of the stain of berries. I finally realized that she was like a person Rachel had described to me. She was being paid to give her body to rich Americans. Madame LaRue must have seen that I was embarrassed. She quickly told me I would have the use of a private parlor to teach the girls. I was to teach them six lessons. She said her girls did not stay for more than a few months, and I would have many pupils. She told me again that these girls where orphans, and she assured me that it was better for them to live at this house than to live on the streets. I was sad that the girls lived this way, but I wanted to teach them.'"

Isabel makes a notation here that Mamacita explained how hardship began to change her from the person who lived with Will on their ranch by the River Carmelo. She left Monterey to escape from the Vargas family. However, in the new American city of San Francisco, she had very little protection. She and her girls lived quietly and did not attract attention. Lupe was able to keep the house clean as it had only two rooms. On the days she did not teach, Mamacita took her daughters on long walks in every direction.

"The experiences at the house of Madame LaRue changed my life. The young girls were new to what they were doing. Some of them had been beaten or had been kept like slaves before they found their way to Madame LaRue. Many of them had mothers, who died when they were young, and they did not know their fathers. They had never had a home and were grateful for a place to live. Not one of them attended mass.

"'Madame told me most of the young girls hoped to find a man who would be their husband. She said this was often possible if one of the girls met someone who liked her. San Francisco was a city where there were many more men than women, and a marriage was often quickly arranged.'"

"'My former life was over. Never again did I see the pine covered mountains of Santa Lucia or the dark forms of the cattle grazing in the nearby pastures of our ranch. A new life was ahead of us.'"

Grandmother Clara rarely included the story about Clarita's first difficult year in San Francisco. Grandmother Clara loved to tell about Clarita's life when it was exciting and prosperous She merely said that Clarita took care of her small family. Isabel's book continues.

"'I often saw very well dressed men at the house of Madame LaRue. One day a certain Mr. Herman Hirsch had been invited to tea. He was hoping to find a special lady who would come to live with him. He mistook me for a candidate. When I was introduced to him, I saw a man of medium height. He had a round face, ruddy cheeks and a trim goatee. His eyes twinkled, and he chuckled and talked with a strange accent. His manners were simple and polite. He seemed shy, so I started the conversation. When I asked him what particular words he wanted me to teach the young lady he desired, he looked at me with puzzlement. When I told him Madame La Rue had employed me as a teacher to her girls, he laughed out loud. He told me he assumed I was the special lady that Madame had chosen for him.

"'I laughed at this misunderstanding, and it was the first time I had laughed since Will died. I could feel my face growing warm, so I quickly told him about teaching English to the young ladies of this household. He seemed interested to know all about it. I explained I taught the girls special English words and also manners in how to eat and dress. He asked if I taught the young ladies any secrets of the bedroom. I was embarrassed until I saw a twinkle in his eyes. We both laughed again.

"'I asked him if he had been a miner, and he told me he knew how to make beer and he sold beer in the gold fields during '49 and '50. He said he came from a kingdom called Bavaria, and he grew up speaking the German language. He believed in the new ideas of government where men were free from the demands of kings and queens. He was once a student at the University in Leipzig, but he ran away to America when many of the students were killed in their fight for political freedom. That was in 1848. He landed in New York, and hearing about the California Gold Rush, he came west to make his fortune. I told him about the de Segovia family, who came to California from Spain and also about Rancho Carmelo and the community of Monterey. I was careful to tell very little about my private life, although I said my husband was an American and was now dead. He asked me where we lived, and when I told him the location, he insisted that he take me there in his carriage.

"'When Patricia and Anita saw me step out of the horse and buggy that arrived at our little house, they ran outside and greet me. They wanted to pet the horses, but they did not ask until I introduced them to Mr. Hirsch, and he gave them permission. After that day, the carriages of Herman Hirsch often transported me from Madame's house to the adobe where we lived. On rainy days, he sent his closed carriage for my transportation. At first, we rarely saw him, except on an occasional weekend. He was occupied with the building of his brewery. Although he had been raised in the Catholic faith, he had not attended church since his rebel days at the university. Later, on Sundays after mass, he would arrive at the church and take us for an outing in his carriage. I knew that my arrival home by carriage several days a week was a topic of conversation for my neighbors. They were women of the former small Mexican community of Yerba Buena. I knew their gossip with each other was just *madrina* talk. My friendship with Madame LaRue, did not lead to much socializing with the families who lived near by. No one from the community came to call on me. I did not need these friendships, because I was occupied with my teaching and my daughters. Later, Mr. Hirsch arranged for Patricia to attend a school for young ladies. It was located not far from his mansion, and we often had dinner with Mr. Hirsch.

"'I communicated with the Thomas Larkin family through his agent. I worried that sometime he would want to sell the San Francisco adobe where we lived. Then Mr. Larkin wrote me a letter saying he told his California agent to arrange for the change of title of this San Francisco property to my name. He said that my husband, Will, had given him honest service, and this house was a gift to me in memory of Will. He wrote me a letter to explain that all California land titles were tied up with legalities, and the newly appointed U.S. Land Commission had settled nothing. In the interim, he told me to live in our little adobe house without the worry of ownership. I occasionally received a personal letter from Rachel Larkin. She wrote she was pleased with her life in the East, but that Mr. Larkin missed California and his friends whom he called "*los paisanos.*" She wrote that Mr. Larkin retained his business ties with California and was always looking for real estate in San Francisco, which he affectionately called the "City." She thought her husband really wanted their family to return to California."

Isabel began a second silk book in 1852. She described Clarita and told about her daily life in San Francisco during that year. It includes information about Isabel's parents, Patricia and Fernando Alonso.

"The friendship of Herman and Clarita grew progressively. There was a mutual attraction from the beginning. Although not a young woman, I think *Mamacita* must have been beautiful. To this day she has soft creamy skin, flashing eyes, aristocratic features and abundant dark hair. Herman was a wealthy man and was of pleasing appearance. He had a compact frame, soft hazel eyes, small regular features and abundant wavy brown hair. *Mamacita* and Herman exchanged stories about their different childhoods. Herman came from a land of strong established traditions. His parents were strict. He was well educated for the times and had studied for at least two years at a university. However, he was a practical German and looked upon business as a way to become wealthy in California. He took his modest fortune from his two years at Mokelumne Hill in the Gold Country and expanded it to the business of building, owning and operating a brewery. He prospered with the growth of San Francisco.

"*Mamacita* said she told Herman about her life as Doña Clarita. He listened to her with astonishment, as she described a world and a people, who were quite different than those in Bavaria. He had always lived a city life. *Mamacita* had lived in a smaller world. Although Will was an American, he lived as a *Californio,* and the center of his world was the cattle ranch. He was accustomed to use barter instead of money, and the hierarchy of a ranch family was the strongest social institution he knew. There was a great contrast in these two ways of living. Cut off from their own past, both Herman and Clarita needed friendship. They were strangers in the crude, energetic, changeable world of burgeoning San Francisco, and they grew to depend on one another for affection and understanding.

"In 1853 Madame LaRue rather suddenly announced that she was going to Europe to live. She sold her house and said she would place her young ladies in other homes where they could live as they would in a boardinghouse. *Mamacita* spoke Spanish with an educated Castilian accent, and she accepted a teaching position at the school that her daughters attended. Herman asked *Mamacita* and her girls to come to live in a wing of his mansion, and when they moved, *Mamacita* rented the adobe in the Mission district to one of Mr. Larkin's agents.

"During the summer, she took her daughters to San José, and they visited Felicia at the convent at nearby Santa Clara. After *Mamacita* was satisfied that Felicia was contented, they accepted the hospitality of Consuelo and Miguel. The Garcías hosted a traditional fiesta in honor of Clarita's visit. Rosita and husband Enrique Alonso arrived at the *fiesta* with his brother Fernando. His wife had died during the first year of their marriage, and Fernando had never forgotten the lovely young Patricia who danced with him at the wedding of Rosita and his brother. Patricia and Fernando became acquainted under the watchful eyes of a widow in the Alonso family and in a little more than a week, Fernando asked *Mamacita* for Patricia's hand in marriage. He told them the engagement would follow a proper courtship. He said he was not a rancher and planned to go in business with an American friend in San Francisco. My mother, who was seventeen, was delighted with the prospects of a marriage to Fernando Alonso.

"When *Mamacita* and her family returned to San Francisco, she told Herman of the engagement of Patricia and Fernando Alonso. He heartily approved and at that moment he asked *Mamacita* to marry him. He told her he wanted a simple wedding and promised they would make a grand tour of Europe after Patricia married and Anita joined Felicia at the convent at Santa Clara.

"*Mamacita* knew she loved Herman. She told me when she looked into his eyes, she saw a man who was gentle and caring. *Mamacita* told him that she would be proud to be his wife. Her only request was that they marry as Roman Catholics at the little church near the Mission Dolores. Herman told her he had left the church for important personal reasons, but to honor her devotion to the church, he told her he would talk to the *Padre* at the Mission Santa Clara to see what could be arranged. Herman was a generous man, and he made it possible for a special chapel to be built at the new convent school of the Sisters of Notre Dame. To everyone's satisfaction, it was decided Patricia and Fernando would be married in early summer of 1856 at the new chapel. In this way, both Anita and Felicia could attend the wedding. A dispensation was made for Herman to wed *Mamacita* in the fall of 1855 at the church of the Mission Dolores."

When Rita read this to Mike, he asked, "Are you finished with the story now?"

"I'm not finished, because Clarita lived many years in San Francisco."

"Then tomorrow, it will be about San Francisco." Mike finished.

CHAPTER 44

▼

February 18, 2000

Rita took her mother to the Monterey airport at an early hour. Since Carmelita was involved with her Friday playgroup, Rita returned home to finish her narrative about the life of Clarita. She continued to read from Isabel's satin books.

"*Mamacita* told me the Larkins returned to California in 1853. They settled in San Francisco and were soon building a mansion on Stockton Street, between Jackson and Pacific. It was made of brick and had eighteen rooms with three stories on one side of the hill and five stories at the back. *Mamacita* continued to enjoy her friendship with Rachel. Although Mr. Larkin concentrated on buying land around San Francisco Bay, he was nostalgic about his former life in Monterey. He decided to start an association of men who were early pioneers in California.

"The Larkins were pleased about the marriage of *Mamacita* to Herman Hirsch, and they hosted a reception for them at a large private room in a German restaurant on Pacific Street. Mr. Larkin approved of Fernando's decision to enter the banking business in San Francisco and after they were married the Larkins invited many important people to a special ball in their honor.

"I have a daguerreotype of *Mamacita* and Grandpa Hirsch on their wedding day. In the picture, *Mamacita* is sitting on a carved, formal straight chair, so I can only describe her from the waist up. She told me that the skirt was made of gray taffeta with yards and yards of material. Many ladies of that era wore skirts with a hoop, but Mamacita did not think this was a comfortable style. The top of the dress was dignified with a long sleeved velvet jacket. Underneath, could be seen a blouse with a maze of rows of handmade lace that wrapped around her neck like a collar. The modesty was befitting a wedding where she knelt at the center altar of the church. Herman wore a formal black wool suit with a stiff white collar that almost encompassed his throat. He wore a square white bow tie. He had neat side burns and looked more distinguished than I had ever seen him."

Rita liked this description of the wedding picture. She had always wondered whether Grandmother Clara embellished some of the episodes of Clarita's life in San Francisco. After reading Isabel's satin book, Rita decided Clara had exaggerated a little. Although *Mamacita* worked to support herself and her household, she never flaunted any social customs. It was true that she was more adaptable than many of the other women of Spanish descent who had been born at the same time in Monterey. She made the best of the frightening, sad, and desperate events in her earlier life. She quietly practiced her religion and had great faith in God and the saints to whom she prayed. She found contentment in her life with Herman. She was at ease as the competent doyenne of the Hirsch Mansion while Herman was the master of his brewery. She toured Europe with Herman, and they arranged to meet her brother, Estéban, who was now Father Juan Cárlos and served as a secretary to the Archbishop in Madrid. Herman admired his wife and enjoyed buying clothes for her. He insisted she have a dress made in Paris that would be appropriate for an inaugural ball. Although they never attended such a party, she wore the garnet taffeta gown with the portrait neckline to many a small dance in San Francisco.

Isabel tells more about Clarita's later life.

"I asked *Mamacita* about her friendship with the Larkins, and she said it was like a family friendship rather than social one. The Larkins moved in the upper class circles of San Francisco society. Mr. Larkin had always been generous with his entertaining, and their parties were affairs of great opulence in their new mansion. *Mamacita* said she and Herman lived modestly and did not entertain with such magnificence. They enjoyed reading books in English, Spanish and German, and they regularly attended many musical events. They always hosted numerous family gatherings.

"*Mamacita* visited Felicia and Anita whenever it was possible, and she was present at all the christenings and special events of our family. She enjoyed using her own carriage, and on designated days, she visited those of her Monterey friends, who now lived in San Francisco. *Mamacita* visited Rachel most of all.

Mr. Larkin had many properties all over California, and was often away from San Francisco. He was constantly involved with the legalities of titles to lands that were acquired through Mexican grants. The proving of deeds and titles was not easy due to informalities in the original descriptions of properties. Exorbitant legal fees denied most of the *Californios* of their property rights. It was well that *Mamacita* sold the original Rancho del Rio Carmelo. As was his intention, Thomas Larkin started the Society of California Pioneers. He was President of this society in 1856–1857. Mr. Larkin went on a trip to visit his Sacramento River properties and became ill with a fever, which was probably typhoid fever. He died October 27, 1858, leaving many of his projects and political aspirations unfinished.

"During the years of *Mamacita's* marriage to Herman, San Francisco went through many changes. First, there was the rise and fall of fortunes made from gold mining. The Comstock Load, a vein of silver in Nevada, was discovered in 1859. Although it was not of the same proportion as the California Gold Rush, the wealth it generated for the next fifteen years changed San Francisco to a truly opulent city with powerful banks, office buildings, theaters and a hotel so large and so grand it truly deserved the name of the Palace Hotel. It opened in 1875, ten years after I was born.

"*Mamacita* and Grandfather Herman built another home, farther up the hill, near Powell and Sacramento streets. It was the house I knew while I was growing up. Rachel Larkin died in 1873 and left a void in the life of *Mamacita*. There was no one in San Francisco who remembered Will or knew of Rancho Carmelo. Because of this, she renewed some of her friendships of earlier times. Herman and *Mamacita* made visits to see Mariano and Francisca Vallejo at their ranch in Petaluma, which is north of San Francisco. Mariano had financial and legal problems that were never resolved; nevertheless, the Vallejos always entertained lavishly, and our families enjoyed seeing each other. Herman, a genial man, easily made friends with the *Californios*. The Hirsch family was generous with their hospitality and invited many members of the Vallejo family to be houseguests at their San Francisco mansion. I met some of the Vallejo grandchildren. We sometimes danced with them and always sat through long dinners together. Our grandparents always talked about the olden times in Monterey.

"The *Californios* of *Mamacita's* generation lost their lands, their homes, and the ranch way of life. Perhaps, that is why they clung to their old customs and their pride of heritage. I talked to Grandfather Herman about their customs, and he said he understood their feelings. He was born thousands of miles from California. His homeland was in the hills near the Danube River.

"*Mamacita* had an ancient box with rope handles. She kept it by her bedside altar. Once, she opened it to show me various pieces of jewelry wrapped in pieces of silk. Then she showed me scrolls of paper, which were letters that she had received from Cousin Consuelo. She had other letters she had written Consuelo. I think Rosita Alonso gave these letters to her. She also kept letters from Padre Antonio, the church name given to Ardo, her first-born child. He was assigned to a church archival library in Mexico City, and has become a widely recognized authority on the native peoples of ancient Mexico. There is a reliable postal service by boat from San Francisco to Mexico City, and *Mamacita* received mail from him several times a year."

One letter from Clarita's, son, Ardo, was in the collection of letters and diaries that Rita inherited. It was a simple letter in which he told of his duties and research. The letter was written in a clear and elegant style of penmanship.

In the evening, Rita showed all the letters to Mike before she settled down to finish Clarita's story. Mike looked them over without reading them, as they were in Spanish. He most enjoyed looking at the photographs Rita had given him.

"Is there a picture of Isabel? She seems to be a very pivotal person in this chronology."

"Here's an old tintype." Rita handed Mike the picture. "I have only one picture of her that was taken after she was married and had children. When she was young, she was considered a beauty. It is said that she had bright, blue-green eyes, refined features, and her curly hair was reddish gold. You can hardly see anything of her face in the picture because of that mound of hair piled on top of her head."

"Yes, that's a real hair do," Mike commented.

"Isabel was Clara's grandmother. Clara loved to tell about her extravagant courtship. When she was of marriageable age, San Francisco was in the midst of another boom, and she attracted the attentions of more than the usual amount of beaus. Edward Butler Shaw, who came from the East Coast with a modest family fortune, had a good head for investments and shipping. He was almost as wealthy as the men of the famous' Big Four.'"

"You mean, Crocker, Hopkins, Huntington, and Stanford?"

"That's what Clara said. He was at least ten years older than Isabel, and determined to win her hand. He succeeded by perseverance and an elaborate courtship. She was of an easygoing temperament and enjoyed all of his attentions. Isabel had been tutored at home in languages and the arts, and that meant she was properly educated for a high social position. They were married in 1885.

"Although Edward was uninterested in the Spanish heritage of his wife, he honored her attachment to her family, and when Isabel asked to have her grandmother live with them, he readily agreed. Their late Victorian house on California Street had extra rooms for every whim, and *Mamacita* was given a separate wing, which even included a small bedroom for her personal maid. She sometimes made lace as a parlor pastime She always attended mass and gave gifts to the Mission Dolores. *Mamacita* kept her mind sharp by reading Shakespeare in English and Cervantes in Spanish. In her last year, she was crippled by arthritis and stayed in her bedroom where she could look down on the streets below. She loved to watch the activities of the neighborhood. It was in this room, while Isabel was reading to her, *Mamacita* asked for her rosary beads and died quietly in the first month of the twentieth century.

Mike was thumbing through an album of family photographs while Rita finished reading him Clarita's story. Occasionally Mike lingered over a photograph, and he showed Rita one where workmen were planting trees in Golden Gate Park. "When was that?"

"I think around 1870. The park became a popular place for strolling, carriage rides, and exhibitions," Mike admired a picture of Isabel in the park with her two small children, Belle and Edward Junior. Young Belle was dressed in what looked like a starched white linen small replica of her mother's costume. Belle posed with a large rolling hoop."

Mike looked at the photo with interest. "Now tell me about Belle," he said.

"That's next," Rita laughed. "She was my great-grandmother. Belle was a family nickname as she was christened, Sara Isabel Shaw. I don't know much about her when she young, except I know she was educated by tutors in French, German, piano and drawing. When she was thirteen, she traveled with her parents on what was then known as 'the grand tour of Europe.' Soon after they returned, she caught the eye of Augustus Gustavus Schaeffer, the silver tycoon, whose wife had recently died. He arranged to be introduced to Belle at a small reception at the Collis Huntington mansion on California and Taylor Street. During the next winter social season, Gustavus immediately courted her. They went to operas, balls, and music receptions. When they became engaged, he gave her lavish gifts of jewelry. Isabel and Edward provided her with an elegant wardrobe of pastel silk and satin gowns that emphasized her tiny waist and her regal posture. She was truly a Belle."

"I didn't realize your family was at the pinnacle of San Francisco society. It's no wonder Clara was the way she was." Mike commented. "She was Belle Schaeffer's daughter."

"Her only daughter. However, they were not of the same temperament. Belle was conventional, and it seems she did everything her husband asked of her. Gustavus had great social aspirations, and she cooperated by entertaining and presiding as the highborn hostess. Look here at a photograph I found. Clara gave it to me. It showed young Belle in a portrait, painted by Gutherie Hugo, a student of John Singer Sargent."

Mike looked at the picture of a languid young woman with a dignified half-smile. Her eyes were a bright blue, and her hair, piled high, was a light chestnut brown. The white gown was flowing and diaphanous and made of wispy material. There was a painterly draping of her clothing. "When was the portrait painted?"

"1904 and the year of their wedding. They had a private wedding with only immediate members of the family present. Afterwards, there was a reception matching the splendor of a royal coronation. It mirrored the extravagance of a city bidding to host the Panama Pacific International Exposition. Edward Shaw died of a heart attack shortly after Belle's wedding."

"Where did the newlyweds live in San Francisco? Mike asked.

"Nob Hill, the coveted pinnacle. Belle moved into a Queen Anne style mansion located on California Street. They did not live there for long, as it was destroyed in the great San Francisco earthquake of April 18, 1906. The Schaeffers were not in residence at the time. They were enjoying a holiday at their horse farm near Menlo Park on the San Francisco Peninsula. Clara had not yet been born. However, she remembered her parents saying that the earthquake was a disaster and did terrible damage, even to the San Francisco peninsula."

"After the Schaeffers experienced the first tremor, they sent their servants to bring them information. Soon one of their liverymen told them that the campus of the new Stanford University had been severely damaged. The spire of the Memorial Church had fallen, the façade had collapsed, and other university buildings were in shambles. Gustavus immediately wanted to return to San Francisco. No trains were running, and the telephone and telegraph wires were down. The only way he could go was to have his liveryman fetch the surrey and drive him there. When he returned, he told his family he saw a sight he would never forget. To him, it looked as if all of San Francisco was in flames. He was determined to go to the City Hall, and when his surrey arrived there, he found the building partially destroyed. Armed sentries stopped the surrey, and Gustavus could go no farther. He returned to his family quickly and continued to conduct business at his country home. Nine months later, Clara Isabel was born."

"Where did you get your information?" Mike asked.

"Mostly from Grandmother Clara. I think she was pretty accurate about that sort of thing. She remembers the country house, because she stayed there almost every summer. She told me that after the earthquake, the family lived at the horse farm for two years while a new home was being built for them in San Francisco. She said after the earthquake, the former mansion on Nob Hill was in total ruins. Isabel Shaw, now a widow, although unharmed, was devastated in spirit. Her beautiful home was a pile of rubble. As soon as it was possible, Gustavus arranged for Isabel to be brought to the country to live with them. Then he sent a crew of workmen to clear the rubble and clean up her property. He hired guards to patrol the remains of both houses, and then he, like the rest of San Francisco, made plans for rebuilding the place they called 'The City.'

"What was he really like? Clara knew him."

"Gustavus was a purposeful, direct, autocratic man with relentless drive to gain money and power. Belle was contentedly submissive, and she thoroughly enjoyed being enormously wealthy. She participated by entertaining, planning luncheons, and attending balls. Since Gustavus was of a generous nature, they made large donations to civic and church projects. Their name is carved on many a marble slab in the foyer of buildings of San Francisco.

"They had only one son, August Gustavus Junior, who was sanguine and placid, a delight for Belle but a disappointment to his father. Clara was headstrong, rebellious, manipulative, and quick to understand her father's personality and interests. She was an excellent horsewoman. When she was thirteen, she spent a year of study at Santa Margarita School in Sonoma County. The Mother Superior advised Gustavus to arrange for her to be taught by the family's tutors. She prescribed a rigorous education in Latin, Spanish, and French with History and Chemistry in preparation for attendance at Dominican College near San Rafael. Thus she was tutored until she talked her father into allowing her attend Stanford University. She much preferred the climate of that area, and it was near to their horse farm. She entered when she was sixteen, majored in Spanish and was planning to go to graduate school. Then she met Gianni Leonardo Torelli in a chemistry class. When she brought him to meet her parents, they were not enthusiastic about the friendship. He came from an Italian family who owned vineyards in the Napa Valley, and all the wineries were experiencing hard times during the years of prohibition of liquor in the United States. Leo went to Stanford on a scholarship and waited tables on campus. They both graduated in 1927. Leo asked Clara to marry him, and when Clara told her parents, Augustus explained to Leo their intentions to take Clara with them to Europe for the summer. They forbid Clara to be engaged. Clara was forbidden to marry anyone until after she had made her formal debut into San Francisco society. Belle was not in favor of Italians unless they were of nobility. Gustavus took Leo aside and explained the life he had envisioned for Clara. He then added the concession that if Leo wanted to marry Clara, he should become a lawyer and qualify for a secure position with a prestigious law firm in San Francisco."

"I have never heard the whole story," said Mike, who was now more interested.

"One of Leo's uncles gave him a Model T Ford for graduation. Late in the evening after an elaborate party for Clara at the Schaeffer estate, Clara met Leo near the garage area, and they drove to Santa Clara where they stayed with her Alonso cousins until morning. Then, they were married at the church of the Mission Santa Clara, located on the campus of The Santa Clara University. Leo had arranged it all with Clara's enthusiastic approval. After the marriage, they sent Clara's parents a telegram informing them of the marriage. Clara and Leo went to Napa, where they lived in a small cottage in the midst of the family vineyards. Leo worked for his uncle, who owned a successful grocery business. At the same time, he went to law school at night. The Torelli family thought it would be useful to have a lawyer in the family. Clara and Leo did not receive the Schaeffer family blessing until after their first child, Pauli Augustus, was born. Years later, it was discovered that one of Leo's uncles was successful in bootlegging liquor off the northern coast of California near Mendocino. This uncle helped the Torellis keep their vineyards during the lean years. He made it possible for the Torelli Brothers to enter the wine industry soon after the repeal of prohibition and the passing of the eighteenth amendment in 1933. Leo became the legal and business manager of Torelli Brothers, and soon he became the chief executive of the entire operation."

"When was Anita born?"

"1934 in San Francisco."

"Maybe that's where your story should end." Mike said.

"That's what I hoped you would say."

CHAPTER 45

▼

February 23, 2000

Mike and Rita were relaxing in the den after dinner. "Since you're about finished with the Carmelo Story, Babe, I think we should plan our trip to Los Angeles. By the way, has Captain Lewis been around?" Mike asked.

"Not since he and Tessa started seeing each other every weekend."

"Then the case is really closed?"

"I guess so. The last time I talked with him, he only talked about Tessa. That was after he spent the night with her."

"Are you going to do anything about the lost diaries?"

"Not at the present."

"But you're pretty sure you know what happened to them."

"Tessa turned over the last card in the game."

"I'm not fond of subterfuge. You promised to tell me all about it."

"It made sense to me when Tessa said she was with Charles the night before the burglary. It was she that made it possible for him to enter the shop and not have the alarm go off. After a little kinky lovemaking, he suggested she should go back to her cottage in Carmel. She wasn't aware of the part she was playing in a burglary.

"I can't believe Tessa would do that to you," Mike said with amazement.

"Tessa didn't expect Charles would commit a burglary. This is what I think happened. When he had the store to himself, he was able to search for whatever he wanted to find. However, he couldn't find the *Carmelo Diaries*. He went back to look for them very early the next morning. He thought he knew how to open the wall safe, but he tripped the alarm because he is an amateur at that sort of thing. I'm also sure he came into our house that morning when we first were summoned by the sheriff. He knew we would be occupied at The Old Booktique, so he messed up things in my office. He thought he deserved pay back time for some imagined wrong."

"Why wouldn't you tell about all this?

"For a long time I didn't know what part Tessa played, and then I didn't know if you'd understand how Tessa felt about Charlie."

"I think I understand Tessa, but women still surprise me with their ability to love the wrong guy."

"When I found that my little wooden bear was missing, I had a déja vu feeling that Charlie was involved in the burglary. Charlie was the one who gave me that little bear that has been missing."

"So now that we know who took *The Carmelo Diaries* are you going to do something about it?"

"We can't prove it. I don't need them for research, but I want them back. They are a valuable source of California's history. They are irreplaceable and would bring a good price or I could give them to an institution."

"Why do you think Charles wanted *The Diaries?*

"He probably thought he would use them to make a deal with Dave Goldman."

"What do you think he'll do now?"

"Maybe he found working with Dave was too complicated. He still needs money for his new vineyard, and he found it was easier to make up with Missy. That way he'll have the assets he needs. He probably still has *The Diaries*, but he can't do much with them. I don't want to press charges. I think Tessa will keep the captain satisfied, and I'm betting that the original diaries will never be found."

"I don't like that. Why should your brother get away with taking the diaries?"

"That doesn't bother me. If I made charges against him, it would be hard to prove. Mother would be upset, and Charles would think he's the winner."

"From what you've told me, I don't think you can change his ways. He'll always want to be the top dog."

"Maybe, he thinks I'll succumb to him. But I won't," she said and quickly added. "I never want to be chummy with him."

"That's OK by me. I'm not about to say, 'let's get together with Charlie.' Besides I have my own issue to settle with him. His insertion of your past romance into our lives was malicious. I didn't like it at all."

"This really didn't accomplish what he wanted. Let's give it a rest. If he hadn't stolen the diaries, I wouldn't have pursued the whole story with such perseverance. It's going to be a great docudrama."

"Then we'll go for that," Mike said, but with some personal reluctance. The next day Mike called Mel, and they made arrangements for the business meetings needed for the future production of The Carmelo Saga. The Minetti family planned to go to Los Angeles after Carmelita's birthday party.

Anita called every day from Holly Ridge, where she was staying with her granddaughters. The first day, she said, "Darcy is taking fencing lessons in Napa on Saturdays, and Angela has to be at ballet class three times a week, so I hired a driver to help me. What do think, Rita?" Rita agreed quickly and the phone call was over.

The next day, Anita called and said, "Charles and Missy are in Melbourne. They just love it. They've already met Lord mayor in his chambers at a special reception. Isn't that wonderful"

On Saturday, Anita called to inform them, "Charles and Missy are touring the Barossa Valley today. It is the best wine region in Australia, you know."

On the morning of Carmelita's birthday, Anita called to advise Rita, "Be sure that Carmelita wears the jumper I gave her. It is so colorful, and it will look good in all the pictures. Mike will take pictures, won't he?"

The last day Anita asked, "When will be the best time to call you? Next week when you are in The Southland?"

Rita was patient with Anita and glad the time was nearing for them to go to Southern California.

Carmelita's birthday was the ninth of March. Although sunny, it was cold, and a little snow could be seen on the distant hills. The party was held in the den. There were ten children, ages three to four. Miss Blakely had sprained her ankle the previous week, so she sat on the sofa while Rita directed the action. Two ice cream cones dropped on the rug, at least eight cookies were crushed underfoot, one three year old boy cried because he thought the Peter Rabbit puppet would get caught by Mr. McGregor, and the other nine children played with the hand puppets after the show.

Carmelita was dressed in the stripped yellow and orange wool jumper that Anita had given her. She enjoyed the role of hostess. Her cheeks were rosy with excitement, and her brown eyes shone even brighter. She carefully passed the plate of cookies and did not spill any. Mike discovered he purchased the wrong tape for the video camera and made a quick trip to the local video store to buy a different kind. He really enjoyed taking the pictures and watching the children's reactions to the puppets. At 4:30 when the last child had left, Mike and Rita sank down on the sofa in exhaustion while Carmelita played beside them with her new toys.

The telephone rang. It was Mel. "How's the birthday girl?"

"She's having a ball with the presents, and she loves the Little Red Riding Hood puppet you sent her. Thank you so much." She handed the phone to Mike.

Mike and Mel talked about next week's agenda. They agreed on two days of conferencing and added a day for socializing. The next day, Mike made an appointment with a Los Angeles lawyer who was a friend from his college days at the University of San Francisco.

The trip to Southern California was a big success. Although the weather can be capriciously chilly in March, the climate in Beverly Hills was warm and balmy. Ellen had much to contribute to the discussion about the photographic possibilities of the Monterey Peninsula. The terms of the contract were compatible. They were all enthusiastic about telling a California saga beginning with the *Carmelo Diaries*. They met Dave and Maggie for a dinner at Spagos. The Minettis spent a few extra days in Santa Barbara, and then returned home ready to resume their lives.

CHAPTER 46

▼

Charles and Missy arrived in Napa County soon after the Minettis returned from Southern California, and Charles volunteered to drive Anita from Napa to Pebble Beach. When the phone rang, Rita was expecting to hear her mother's voice. It was Charles, instead. "I left Mother at her favorite beauty shop. She said she couldn't wait another minute for a hair cut. I'm going to drop off some special Australian wine at your house. Will you be there?"

I'm due at The Old Booktique pretty soon, but I'll stay home until you come," Rita answered.

"I'm on the car phone, so I'll be there right away," he said and hung up.

Charles arrived soon after the call and brought four bottles of different vintages of Australian Shiraz. "This is the prize one," he said putting it on the hall table. "Vintage 1990 from the South Australia Grange. Take it from me, it will challenge the best wines in the world as soon as the word gets around."

"Mother said you went to the Barossa Valley."

"The great Australian wines are found there. The vines are seventy-five years old, and the small yields encourage their quest for quality. Keep the 1990 until you try the young ones. Then you and Mike will really appreciate it."

"Mike loves red wine. It'll be a treat. Thank you, Charlie. And I'm glad you and Missy are home safely and had such a good time."

"Yes, it was a profitable trip. The Australians have been quietly making some great wines for a long time. Since I am here, I'll tell you my ideas for our new wine venture."

"Would you like a cup of coffee?"

"If you make it fresh."

"Come to the kitchen and tell me your ideas."

Charles sat down in the breakfast nook, and while Rita ground the coffee beans and proceeded to make the coffee, he carefully looked around the room. "It's great to be here with you. I have a lot on my mind that I want to tell you."

"Do you take cream or sugar? I forgot," Rita said as she brought two yellow and blue porcelain coffee mugs to the table.

"A spot of cream, if you have some, Sis. I really like being here in your kitchen. We did grow up together, you know, and since we both heard Grandmother Clara's stories, I always thought we would share *The Carmelo Diaries*."

"In what way?" said Rita as she put down a small pitcher of cream and handed him a spoon.

"I have an idea about that. When we were flying home…" He paused. "It's a very long flight, you know," he began as if telling a story. "I decided to create something for all of us. I've already talked it over with Missy. Here it is. It is my idea to form an Atherton Family Trust and also The Atherton Corporation. This would include all our enterprises, and I want to count you in."

Rita was just about to say, "No way." Instead, she said. "What is the objective?"

"Oh, it would be a way to put all the family assets and businesses under one roof. We could all save money on taxes, accountants, lawyer, and financial management fees."

"Does this have to do with sharing *The Carmelo Diaries*?"

"It could. We would form a trust, and all of us would put in money. There would also be shares from The Atherton Corporation to which we all would have contributed. Then, whenever we have a project that needs money, we would vote on it. If the project is approved, money could be drawn from the corporation. We would have a board of directors, regular meetings, and budgets. Everything would be legal. The Atherton Family Trust would also have a trustee and co-trustee. It will take a while to set it up. I think we need to think of our children's future, don't you?"

"Who would be included in the family trust?"

"You and me, of course. It could also include Missy and Mike, Mother and Dad, and our children would be the beneficiaries, and the inheritance would go directly to them."

"Who would be the trustee?"

"Well, it's only logical I would be the trustee. Dad doesn't like that sort of thing. He's not a business man."

"Mike's a business man."

"Yes, but not the kind we need, and besides, he's not an Atherton or a direct heir of Clara's fortune. He will have votes because of the assets he would contribute, and Missy would be in that category. There would be a provision where anyone could cash out, in case anything happens to the marriage. We need to be careful and protect Anita, you and me, above all."

"I like to be independent. Besides, our businesses are so different." Rita said.

"Independence is a luxury you can't afford in today's world. It's time to put aside our differences and stick together."

"I think it would be hard to agree on many decisions when our money is all tied up together."

"We should be able to get along because our lives are more alike now. You have a family, and you are interested in doing something with *The Carmelo Diaries*."

"So this has something to do with *The Carmelo Diaries*. Didn't you know? Regarding *The Diaries*, I've gone in another direction."

"You make good coffee, Sis. I think I'll have a splash more, please," Charles said, and as Rita poured, he continued. "Also, I've talked to Mother, and she says she thinks there are some claims to parcels of land south of the Carmel River. They aren't good building sites, but she says the parcels are something that Clara bought a long time ago, because they were probably a part of the original Rancho Carmelo. Mother said that you might not know about it, because she thinks the land was in a separate trust. That means it didn't go through probate with the rest of the estate. I thought we could put those parcels in The Atherton Family Trust. Wouldn't you like to own some of the original Rancho del Rio Carmelo? It was a Spanish land grant."

"Charlie, the formation of a trust is a lifetime decision. I couldn't give you a quick answer. As for the so-called Spanish land grant, I happen to know that Clara intended to give that land to the Big Sur Trust. She was even on their board of trustees for a while. She approved of the idea of preserving wide open spaces, especially California ranch land."

"I never knew she was involved in anything like that. Why doesn't Mother know?"

"She probably knows and forgot about it. Anyway, I think those parcels of land are getting pretty far from the subject of us pooling our assets."

"Sis, the family doesn't think you should go your own way too much. You are not the carefree woman of the world you used to be. I realize you need to talk to Mike about it. Take your time."

Rita felt she was collecting jabs and put-downs. She wanted to discourage a discussion of something she knew she was not going to do. "By all means, I will talk to Mike about it," she said emphatically.

"Then I'll throw in an incentive. You and I can share *The Carmelo Diaries*. Clara promised them to the both of us. We have equal claim to them, and you can borrow them from me. I think you might need them, right now,"

"Are you telling me that you positively have them?"

"Tessy says you know about it. Hell, I dropped enough hints for you. The whole trick thing grew out of proportion because of the police investigation. Last month, I told Tessy I just wanted to borrow *The Diaries*. She understood. Now, I hear that the case has been dropped. I knew you wouldn't want to drag your best friend into it, and besides it might look like you had something to do with it yourself."

"Charlie, you're talking about something you don't' really know much about. And your solutions are just for yourself. That burglary upset our lives. I didn't like any of it and neither did Mike. And I certainly didn't appreciate your telling Monty Bates to look me up at The Old Booktique."

"Oh, Sis, you take everything so seriously. All my life, I've enjoyed playing tricks on you. Wise up. Maybe, we should leave you out. The rest of us can form a corporation and a trust. We have far more assets than you have. Mother is delighted that I can manage her property. She and Dad are going to have a fling at living together at Stonecrest. It will be during the U.S. Open Tournament and maybe for the rest of the summer. I think it'll be good for both of them. They are even going to give a big party on the final day of The Open. They'll invite lots of friends for a buffet on the lawn at Stonecrest. Mother has asked Missy to help her organize it. Missy is good at that."

"I'm sure she is, and it will be a beautiful party. And you're right. You can form a trust without me. If you really want us to get along, we can leave things just as they are now."

"I still think you should talk this over with Mike tonight. I believe he really loves you, and you can't make family decisions without consulting him."

"You've said enough, Charlie."

"And you are not even interested in *The Diaries?*"

"I think they are lost."

"Good. That's something we can agree on." Charles said quickly, His cell phone rang., "Yes, Mother, I'll be right along. I'll come into the shop for you. Just wait there" He paused. "Yes, I'll ask her."

"Charles pocketed the cell phone. "She asked if you would like to come and have lunch with us, right now."

"No, I'm long overdue at the shop. Give my regards to Missy and thanks to both of you for the wine."

As soon as Charles drove away, Rita left for The Old Booktique. Late morning was a good time to talk to Dolores. "Shall we make plans for a vintage book seminar? We could even send out invitations," said Dolores.

"I've developed a special interest in Thomas O. Larkin, after reading about Clarita's friendship with his wife, Rachel, "Rita told her. "We have added more books about Thomas O.Larkin. Some are reprints and some are originals, such as the one by Alfred Robinson."

"That would be *Life in California: 1846.*" said Dolores.

"I also found the William Heath Davis book, *Seventy-five years in California*, but it is only a reprint," Rita went on.

"We could make up a bibliography of the printed primary sources about the lives of prominent citizens of old Monterey. It would be a good handout,' Dolores suggested, and they continued planning until another wave of customers arrived.

Just before it was time to close, Rita found Dolores putting away some books lying on the table. "Dolores, I am the luckiest lady around here. At first, I thought I needed you for a little while. You know, we're going to be going down to Southern California quite often. I find my life is more complicated than I expected. I really need you to manage the shop for several months. Is that at all possible?" Rita paused. "Please think about it." "It's been a long day for both of us, so let's talk about it tomorrow. Don't worry Rita. It will all work out." Dolores put her arm around Rita.

Rita and Mike drove into the driveway at the same time. Mike looked carefully at Rita. "You've had a long day, hon. Are you O.K.?" he asked after kissing her.

She nodded, and he carried in the sacks of groceries. Carmelita stopped playing and taking their hands, she tugged them along with her. "Come see our puppet show. Marquita said we could have it right here in this room," and she led them into the downstairs bathroom. Marquita had taken Carmelita's new puppets and put on a show for her. She pretended the bathtub was a stage, she opened and closed the shower curtain between the scenes.

"Just draw up a stool, and we'll give you a show." Said Marquita. "We've been doing this ever since Carmelita got up from her nap."

"You've had a long day, too," Mike said to Marquita. "Can you stay for dinner with us? I think Rita has some steaks in that sack of groceries."

"I would like that," Marquita agreed, and after Mike and Rita watched the skit about Little Red Riding Hood, they all ate dinner in the kitchen. Mike and Rita didn't have time to talk much until later when Carmelita was asleep.

"Mike, I asked Dolores to manage the shop at least for six months. Maybe a year."

"You know your business. That's up to you. Sounds like a good idea with the Carmelo project coming up."

"By the way, Charlie drove Anita down from Napa and stopped by to give us some bottles of Australian Shiraz. They go from vintage 1999 down to a 1990. He said to save the 1990 until your palate was educated.

"That was that nice of him. Was that all he said?"

"He said a lot more. In fact, I don't know where to start. He kept telling me to talk it over with you. He even told me that I was too independent in our marriage. He really doesn't know what kind of a couple we are does he?"

"He always says too much. What does he have up his sleeve?"

"I'll get to the point. He wants to form an Atherton Family Trust and The Atherton Family Corporation."

"And he wants you to talk to me about it?" Mike said with a sarcastic laugh.

"He wants me to be part of the trust. In fact, he wants you to be part of the trust too. We're supposed to put our money into the trust. Then, he'll be the trustee and manage it."

"You've just said a mouthful. You didn't take him up on it, did you?"

"Absolutely not. However, at one point I brought up *The* Carmelo *Diaries*."

"Good for you. And what did he say."

"He offered to share *The Diaries* with me."

"He actually said that?"

"He said Clara had promised *The Diaries* to both of us, and he told me that I could borrow them. Oh, there was a lot of other stuff, and I finally told him 'to shove it' or words to that effect."

"You did?"

"Well, not quite, but I told him I wasn't interested in being a part of the Atherton Trust or The Atherton Corporation, and that's when he insisted that I talk it over with you. Oh, yes, and he tried to pass over the burglary as if it were a big prank. I think that's when I told him that we didn't like anything about that whole mess."

"So how did it end?"

"He said Mother was delighted he could manage her property. He said Mother and Rex were going to try to live together. At least from May until the end of summer."

"That doesn't surprise me. But how did the conversation end?"

"He told me to consult you again and he mentioned *The Diaries*."

"And?"

"I said, 'I think they are lost.'"

"And that's it?"

"That's all I could think of, on the spot. He said he could agree to that. His cell phone rang, and he left to pick up Mother. Oh yes, Mother must have asked him if I would have lunch with them, because he tossed out her invitation to me. I declined and thanked him for the wine. I immediately went to the store and worked all afternoon,"

"What next?"

"He just returned from a long trip. I hope he'll be totally involved with his new wine venture. But I know he'll bring it up again, if he gets a chance."

"Do you want me to talk to him?"

"No, but if you two talk, and he asks, be sure to tell him we are not interested. Period. Saying any more to Charlie would just bring more dialogue. We have more important things to do with the rest of our year," and Rita smiled at him.

"Then it's settled for me." Mike finished.

CHAPTER 47

▼

The first weeks of June 2000 on the Monterey peninsula were monopolized and dominated by the One Hundredth U.S. Open Golf Championship. It was to be played on the Pebble Beach Golf Links from June 12–18. Even cynics, non-golfers, and local residents, who distained the publicity, understood the historical significance of this millennium event. The staging and hosting of the tournament was of foremost interest. It was hyped as the biggest event in golf history. Crowds of golfers, journalists, sports fans, and local residents became spectators.

In the midst of the pandemonium, an elite field of professional golfers vied for the prize and honor of winning the pinnacle of championships. Tiger Woods, the young golf hero, had the best odds for winning. He had already shattered previous records on the course. The event had been planned for several years, and all classes of tickets had been sold out weeks ago. Except for the residents of Del Monte Forest and those with special badges on their automobiles, no one was allowed through the gates to the Seventeen Mile Drive without a ticket or credential. During the weeks of preparations, all the areas around The Retreat, The Shore Club, the condominiums, and private residences were over populated. Tents and tent parties were everywhere to be seen on the periphery of the course. It looked like a vast carnival.

The Old Booktique stayed open during the practice rounds. It was closed during the actual competition. Rita spent some of each day walking on the designated paths that outlined the fairways, and she accompanied Mike to many of the tented social events. Anita called Rita every morning. "How are you, dear? What are you going to wear today? Did you see any celebrities?" she asked in rapid succession.

"I really don't plan to walk very much. It's just too crowded. What party are you attending today, Mother?" Rita answered.

"Oh, I am going to a lovely luncheon at the Miltons. It is all the bridge group ladies Betsey knows. I think I'll wear my favorite pink Chanel suit. I've had it for ages, and it is always just right for our cool June weather. Do you know that your father bought a new suit for our big party? He said he gave up wearing suits in Hawaii, I must say he has been very cooperative with all the plans."

After the first day of competition, Andres and Petra Duncan invited Rex and Anita for a ride in their airplane. Terry, the youngest of the Duncans, found a professional photographer to take aerial pictures "You should have been there, dear," Anita told Rita. "We could see all of the private mansions surrounding the golf course, and we recognized Shore Club in the center of it all."

"That was a great idea of the Duncans. Did you see Stonecrest?" Asked Rita.

"I was just coming to that. Andres didn't know where to look, but I could see our lovely landscaping. I saw our tall Italian pine trees, the low rock fence, and our border of bright red geraniums, blue lobelia, and white alyssum. I am using an American theme for the Atherton U.S. Open party. You will come early, won't you?"

"Mike has someone from the office to drive us in, so we'll be there in plenty of time."

"I want you to come early, because members of our family will be there early to make a toast to your father's return to Stonecrest. Missy has arranged it all. I am very happy about the way it has turned out. Rex was very enthusiastic when I agreed to let him come home to Stonecrest."

"I'm glad you told me that. We'll be there at whatever time you say," Rita said, feeling a relief from responsibility for her mother

As soon as she could, Rita told Mike, "Anita wants us to come early on Sunday. Some of the Torellis and other family members will be there to welcome my father to Stonecrest."

"Then it's important to be early," he assured her.

June 18, 2000 Sunday was a rare day in June on the coast of central California. The weather was picture perfect. The breeze was warmish, the air was clear, the sky an intense blue and the ocean even more azure. It was the last day of the championship.

From the air above, one could see the golf course as a playing field surrounded by a moving crowd of people. Beyond the course, and yet within the general milieu, was the stately mansion of Stonecrest. It was situated across a small cove on the ocean side of the golf course. The hyperbolic press put out extra editions of *The Peninsula Sentinel*. The private Stonecrest party was written up as a social event. They named the hosts, Mr. And Mrs. Rexford Charles Atherton II, and the article gave a short history of the family. It said Mrs. Atherton's mother and father built Stonecrest as a country home, which included seven acres and a small dock for sailboats. The article included information about Gustavus Schaeffer, Mrs. Atherton's grandfather, who attended the 1919 opening of the Pebble Beach Golf Links. He thought the area would be a perfect place for his family to relax. The article called the event the "Party of the Season," and they referred to the guests as "the beautiful people."

When Mike read *The Sentinel*, he laughed and commented, "That beautiful people business is a always an exaggeration."

After the Torelli and Atherton family gathering an hour earlier, the invited guests began to arrive. Rita and Mike walked down to the edge of the property toward a small stone porch that faced the cove and Pebble Beach. Rita gestured to Mike. "This is my favorite place at Stonecrest. Ever since I was a little girl. It's far from the madding crowd."

"Do you know every one at the party?" Mike asked her.

"Almost. Although Missy was in charge of party planning, I helped Mother make out the list of guests. As always, there were a few more people added. Some even asked to be included."

"Anita is enjoying her part as the Grande Dame of the manor, "Mike commented.

"Particularly with Rex at her side," Rita agreed. "She told me he agreed to come here for the summer. He told her he'd like to see the Open and then play some golf afterwards. She still loves him, and he seems to have settled into his role of a husband quite easily."

"Do you think he'll stay on?"

"I think so. She wants him to be here."

"How do you feel about it?"

"It's totally her choice."

"OK. Next question. Tessa and Captain Lewis are here. Did you ever think they'd get married and so soon?" Mike changed the subject.

"With Tessa you never know. The big question is about Captain Lewis. Did he suspect Tessa was a partner in the burglary?"

"Maybe he knows and just doesn't care. I think he's really in love."

"They both act like teenagers just starting to go steady. Tessa keeps telling me to call him Tim," Rita replied.

"If they live here, will she work at the shop?"

"They're still on their honeymoon. Dolores is in charge of the shop now. She might need an extra hand, sometimes. I don't know. I'll talk it over with her before I say anything to Tessa."

"I don't see Dolores anywhere."

"She wanted to be as far away from here as possible. She went to a writer's conference in Santa Barbara."

"I think the Sterns are really enjoying the tournament, don't you?"

"They told me they might use some footage Ellen took yesterday. The U.S. Open would make a good ending for the documentary. The Sterns are planning to do some photographing in Monterey next week because Ellen wants to take pictures of the historic adobes."

"And I never thought Dave and Maggie would come today. Did you?" Mike added

"Maggie loves Monterey. She comes up for the Monterey Jazz festival every September. I think she's the most beautiful woman here," said Rita with enthusiasm.

Mike looked at the stone stairway that led to the house. "Look, Charles and Missy are talking to your parents. I bet they are envisioning themselves as owners of Stonecrest someday."

"They really look proprietary. Missy told me they couldn't come in sports clothes, because they're on their way to attend a wedding reception in Hillsborough."

"I wish we could have brought Carmelita this afternoon. She loves parties, but she'll have more fun at the park with Marquita."

"You spoil her, you know," Rita laughed."

"That's because I am older and wiser than you," he answered. "I try to let you do all the correcting."

"Will it always be that way? When can I be the one who gets to spoil her?"

"By the way, we can't keep our secret much longer. After the party, would be a good time to tell your parents about the coming baby."

"Maybe, since everyone's in a good mood." Rita took the binoculars. She saw several of her mother's bridge friends. The ladies were dressed in flowery long summer dresses, suitable for a lawn party.

"What time's the buffet?" Mike asked. "I'm hungry."

"At four, when the tournament is over. It's a good time. Nobody wants to leave here in the traffic."

Earlier and before the guests arrived, Rita had helped her mother with the place cards and seating arrangements for the small garden tables. She saw the name, Belmont Bates, written on one of the cards.

"I was surprised that Monty wanted to come," Rita commented to Anita.

"Of course, he wanted to come," answered Anita enthusiastically. He told me he's thinking of running for the Senate again. There will be a vacant seat in his state. He might even be considered for a vice presidential candidate. He's quite a celebrity. I think he is a good addition to the party."

Rita caught a glimpse of Monty coming down the stairs to the lower terrace of lawn.

"Isn't that your friend, Monty, with Christy Turnbull?" Mike said as he scanned the garden through the binoculars.

"Let me look," Rita said reaching for the glasses. "Yes, it's Monty with Christy. She's wearing a green leather pantsuit and looks as informal as she knows how to be." She's a San Francisco lady, and she likes to dress up."

"Her husband's one of the new partners of Pebble Beach Golf World. The Turnbulls want to lease a place in Pebble Beach before they buy another home."

"I hear they own an apartment in Washington D.C."

"You heard right. Bud told me he likes to live in Washington. He says that's where the big game is being played. He wants to be appointed to a commission from time to time."

Rita started to say something and grew silent. Mike continued. "What's up Babe? We'd better go up there and mingle some more? You can make sure Mel and Ellen have been introduced around. Maybe, I'll schmooze a little with Dave and Maggie."

"Particularly Maggie," she laughed. "Oh Mike, I'm glad you're such a good looking man. Maybe you should go and thrill some of Mother's bridge friends who didn't bring escorts."

"No, I'd rather talk to Maggie."

"We'll see them in L.A. in a few weeks."

As they walked slowly up the incline toward the upper level, Rita felt relaxed and wanted to talk more to Mike. "I feel good about what we've done with the Carmelo Story."

"Bringing it to life. That's what you've wanted."

"The production's in good hands, and that's important with our new baby on the way."

"Do you think Anita will be glad about the baby?"

"I never know about Mother. She's still busy complimenting Charlie."

"Speaking of Charles, I think he committed a criminal act when he stole *The Carmelo Diaries*."

"Mike, let's stop a minute. I want to tell you how I feel about Charlie. "Rita replied.

"Does it have to be right now?"

"Yes, and after that, I don't want to talk about Charlie for quite a while. With luck he'll leave us alone for a couple of years. His new ventures will involve more time than he anticipated. If he's successful, he'll have the starring role he likes."

"I don't believe he'll ever be satisfied," Mike shot back.

Mike and Rita arrived at the upper patio where café style tables were being arranged for the buffet guests. Just then, Anita rushed forward to meet Rita and Mike. She had Monty and Christy in tow. Anita looked at Monty and said to the group. "I'm trying to convince Mr. Bates to stand for senate again. He has more experience than all the other candidates who are running in the primaries."

Christy turned to Mike. "We're staying until next week. We want to take a look at a few Pebble Beach houses. Can I call you for an appointment tomorrow?"

Monty looked at Rita and said, "Since I am definitely going to head the new federal commission for interstate shipping regulations, I don't think I will have the time to run a winning campaign. I want to be on the commission, because I know quite a bit about the national problems of several industries. And that includes the California wine industry. I can be impartial, because I don't come from a state with a wine industry."

"Sounds as if you have many plans for your future," Rita said being noncommittal. She glanced over at Anita deep in conversation with Christy and Mike.

Monty continued on. "Rita, I am telling you about the commission, because it means I can help or thwart your brother, Charles. Frankly, I realized your brother lied to me about several things influencing me to come to see you last February. I have a few IOUs to collect from people I know in D.C., and I investigated his business. I was surprised to find a government agency that already had a file three inches thick on your brother and one almost that size on his wife."

"This news comes at a time when I thought I could forget about Charlie," Rita said with a grimace.

"I think it would be very wrong to trust him with anything concerning your family, and this includes the recent burglary which occurred at The Old Booktique. I have real reservations about his best intentions towards you and anyone in your private life."

"Maybe I've been too naïve. I'm quite sure Charlie was responsible for the burglary at my shop. Mike and I were having a talk about it, a minute ago." Rita said, and she looked thoughtful.

"Rita, I've put the files about your brother and his wife on compact discs." Monty put his hand in his breast pocket and handed her an envelope containing two compact discs, copies of the files on Missy and Charles.

After opening a large white leather purse, Rita calmly deposited the envelope and zipped the top of the bag. "Thank you, Monty. You have been a true friend."

"You can discuss this with Mike, or I'll talk about it with both of you. You decide. I particularly wanted to come to your Mother's party today, so I could give you the information. I included a card with my private cell phone number. I am only a phone call away."

Anita glanced to where Rita and Monty were earnestly talking and began to be nervous. Then, she heard the sound of a laugh. Monty was telling Rita a joke. Anita beckoned to Rita and turned to Christy, "There are so many of my Pebble Beach friends I want you to meet. We can't let Rita and Mike monopolize you all afternoon."

Monty and Rita joined the others, and Rita put her arm around her mother's waist and said, "It's a great party, Mother."

Monty said, "Mrs. Atherton, you have been a most gracious hostess, and I enjoyed meeting your husband, Rex. As much as I wish to partake in a feast of California delicacies, I have a plane to catch, and I need to leave now before there's too much traffic. Thank you so much for inviting me. Since I will be living in D.C. again, I hope you can be my guest for lunch anytime you are in town there."

Anita was beaming and appreciated Monty's warm response. "It was a good idea to have this party," she whispered to Rita. "And your father said he was prepared to live at Stonecrest for a long while. I told him I would like that very much."

"Mother, That's good news. Your life will be complete," Rita said softly. Mike and Monty exchanged a few words, and soon they were joking about the skywriting above them.

"That hubby of mine will be finding all the lovely young fillies who are flouncing around in their high heels and short dresses. Anita. I think I better wend my way up the path to be at his side," Christy said coquettishly as she left quickly.

Mike and Monty shook hands, and Monty accompanied Christy up the last few steps.

Mike, Rita and Anita walked slowly as they gave greetings to the guests who were descending toward the lower gardens.

"Oh, I see Rex," Anita announced, and she lightly patted her hair. She was smiling as she walked up the last steps to where Rex was talking to Charles and Missy.

Rita stopped. "Mike, let me just catch my breath a minute before we go up to join the party." She looked a little tired and then said, "I remember, we were talking about my brother, and you cautioned me about Charles."

"If you don't want to talk about now, that's OK, Babe. But I strongly believe we need to make some mutual decisions about his interference in our lives. We need to lay down some boundaries."

"I fully agree, and I need to tell you a few more things," Rita said as she took his hand.

"By the way, Monty looked as if he had something rather serious to tell you. He was cordial to me, so I gathered what he had to say was about his political plans."

"Monty had something to tell me about Charles and Missy. He has evidence that some of their land deals might not be legal. Although I was hoping we could just forget about Charlie for a while, I realize we need to be ever watchful. I've been so elated about our Carmelo production with the Sterns. I haven't cared about the loss of the original *Carmelo Diaries.*"

Tessa and Tim Lewis walked toward Mike and Rita, who were standing near the upper parterre. Tessa was dressed in a bright raspberry flounced silk dress. Her face had an unusually rosy glow and her eyes twinkled. Tim was dressed in casual gray wool slacks with a well-tailored dark blue cashmere jacket. He looked relaxed and satisfied.

"I can't wait to tell you, Rita. We've just found out I am pregnant. Isn't that wonderful," she gushed.

Rita and Tessa hugged, and Rita stepped back to look at her as if she were a work of cherished art "Tess, it is wonderful," she said with emphasis. "You look positively radiant. I'm a bit envious. I don't look quite as dazzling as you do. In fact, today, I'm a little lethargic."

"Oh, you've just been so busy running back and forth to L.A." Tessa said until she carefully looked at Rita, and then she started laughing. "Rita, you are you going to have another baby? We'll both be pregnant together. What fun."

Rita nodded, and they both hugged again.

Mike and Tim were talking nearby and approached their wives. "So you've heard the news. We're going to continue to live right here, for now," Tim said and smiled broadly. "I've always wanted to be a Dad. We also have something else to tell you two." He turned to Rita, "Tessy has told me everything about her long relationship with your brother. As you can imagine, I was pretty ticked off, especially because she told me just before our marriage. Then I thought it over, and it made me love her even more. It took guts for her to tell me about the burglary because she could see how it might affect my feelings and our lives."

"Tim, you don't need to tell us all about it. We are aware of the truth," Mike offered.

"Mike, I want to say something important, so it might as well be now. It is true that the burglary case is closed, but it can be opened again any time in the next five years. We're glad you and Rita are teamed up with the Sterns, but that doesn't change certain facts for me."

"So what do you propose?" Mike asked.

"Nothing, right now. Tessy is so happy about having a baby, and her happiness means everything to me. However, I'm going to be watchful for even the slightest intrusion of Charles Atherton into our life. Seriously, I advise you to do the same thing. I don't think the case is over quite yet, and if it is reopened, I can assure you that Charles and Missy will take a fall."

"That's pretty strong language, Tim. I really appreciate your frankness." Mike paused and indicated he had more to say. "You have every right to pursue the matter of the burglary, if your feel it is necessary. I'm glad you're going to live around here and be part of the community. Our wives have been friends for a long time."

Tim seemed genuinely relieved, and he pumped Mike's hand with enthusiasm. Tessa continued to chatter with Rita. "I still haven't come off cloud nine, but I can tell you that being pregnant is the best thing that has happened to me," she said with a wide grin "Tim is just the greatest."

Rita put her arms around Tessa again. "Your news is the best yet."

"And I want you to know this too, pal. Your friendship means everything to me," Tessa continued.

Tim and Mike joined Rita and Tessa. "I think I heard Tessa say something about you being a mother again? Way to go, Rita!" Tim said with animation. "After we have a bite, I think Tessy and I will go home. Tomorrow's a work day for me." He took Tessa's hand, and they walked to the buffet table.

Mike took Rita aside near the stone steps. "Rita, we've just had another 'wake up call,'" he said in somewhat hushed tones. "Tim just informed me that Tessa told him of her part in the burglary. At this point, he hasn't done anything about it, but he wanted me to have the information. He told me the case could be opened at anytime, and especially if your brother interfered in their life, in any way."

"I didn't know this would be a day of days, did you?" Rita asked Mike.

"It's really all for the best. Now we're ready to move on." He said with relief. Mike pulled her toward him and gave her a quick intense kiss. "You and I are together, and that's all that matters" In the distance, they saw Anita approaching them. She was by herself.

"Isn't the weather lovely? Rita you look perfect in that summery print silk dress. Has Charles had a chance to talk to you about the Atherton Trust?"

"Yes, he did." Rita answered. "He said you should be relieved of all your many duties concerning finances."

"There are so many demands on my time." Anita sighed.

"As trustee, Charles will be the one to approve of your requests to buy clothes and have parties. He will also approve of Dad's expensive golfing trips with various lady friends. I declined to take part of the Atherton Trust because Mike and I can manage our own affairs for sometime yet."

Anita looked disappointed and said, "I'm sure Mike knows what's best for you."

Pauli Torelli arrived and after greeting Mike and Rita said, "Anita, you gave a perfect party. Clara would be proud of you. We're on our way to San Francisco to spend a few days, so we're leaving now." He gave her a brotherly kiss.

As he was leaving, Charles, Missy, and Rex reached the group.

Charles addressed Mike first. "I'm sure Rita discussed the Atherton Trust with you. We all think it's a good idea."

"We discussed it thoroughly, and we decided it's just not for us." Mike said and he looked confident.

"Too bad. It's your choice." Charles quickly replied.

Anita was standing quietly at the edge of the group. She looked at all of them as if she was seeing them for the first time. "I am not sure whether I want to give up control over my own life yet. I have a good financial consultant, and I like my assets to be separate from other members of the family."

"Mother, I think you are tired. Don't be hasty about changing your mind," Charles said with a comforting tone of voice.

Rita looked at her mother in amazement as she was looking fiercely at Charles.

"At this point, I can still do what I want to do. I feel competent to take care of my assets."

Charles looked startled. Before he said anything, Missy took his arm and announced, "Dear, we must leave for Hillsborough. We don't know what the traffic will be like." She turned and started up the steps to the next terrace. Rex and Anita accompanied her.

Mike was talking to another Torelli relative now. Rita was alone. Charles turned around and came to where Rita was standing. "Sis, I've been thinking. It seems strange that someone would steal those old diaries. I bet they are just misplaced. They are probably somewhere in your bookshop. Maybe they're on a shelf under a table in the back of the store."

"Anything is possible," she said, "He didn't answer. He was already gone.

Rita beckoned to Mike, and they talked to Anita and Rex briefly before Mario Torelli said, "Mike, we'll take you and Rita home."

"No thanks, we brought our car."

As soon as Rita put on the seat belt and settled in the car, she said, "Mike I want to stop by the shop. Charlie said something very strange when he said goodbye to me."

"What did he say?"

"Just take me to my shop and you'll see."

"You are mysterious again. OK, lady."

The crowds had quickly dispersed, and it was easy to park near The Old Booktique. Both Mike and Rita entered the shop, and Rita went quickly to the back of the stop. Kneeling down to a shelf under an old table, she saw a familiar box. Could it be *The Carmelo Diaries?*

"So Charlie returned them," she said as she held up the box. She opened it, and they saw three dissimilar small books bound in leather, *The Carmelo Diaries.*

He whistled and said, "That closes the case for sure, and Charles has slipped away untouched, this time."

"Mike, you're right." Rita said. "Should he try to interfere in our lives again, Monty and Tim have given us enough information to stop him before he even gets started."

Mike took Rita's hand and said,"Let's go watch the sun go down on Carmel Bay."

The sunset was spectacular.

Glossary

adiós, a greeting such as hello or goodbye

adiós y hasta luego, so long (in taking leave)

aguardiente, name for common alcoholic liquors used in Spain

alcalde, mayor of town or village, justice of peace

alcoba, bedroom

Alta California, Upper California, a name used before 1846

Amapola, poppy, a flower. a name of endearment

amorosa, loving, pleasing, gentle

baile, a dance or a private ball in early California.

Bostoñeros, people from Boston

brasado, a measurement, length of an arm

bueñas días, good day, morning

carreta, a four wheel cart drawn by oxen

carta, a letter, a government document

casa, a house, a dwelling

casita, small house

chaparreras, leather covering over pants

comandante, a commander, leader

comisario, a delegate

comisionado, an agent, proxy, attorney

concedes, in early California meant crown gifts from king of Spain

contracto matrimonial, wedding contract

cuarto, a room, a chamber, a hall

diputado, a deputy, representative, delegate

diputación, a delegation

Don, a title for a gentleman

Doña, a title for a lady

Dueña, a married lady, landlady, a lady in authority, chaperone

duendo/a, gentle

enamorado/a, lover, sweetheart

encantadora, name of endearment or enchanting

encanto, charm, fascination, delight, enchantment

estero, estuary

fandango, a Spanish dance, also a municipal dance

fiesta, a holiday, a saint's day or celebration

frijoles, beans, a dish usually cooked with beans and some meat

Gavalán, a small mountain range that is east of Monterey

Hacienda, a plantation, farm or ranch house

hacendado/a, a landed, owner of real estate, a planter

hijos del país, sons of the country, native sons

huevos rancheros, eggs poached in a hot mixture of beans and sauce

jefe politico, political chief

junta, council, conference, union

Las Posadas, the journey of the Holy Family in search of lodging.
   A traditional way of celebrating the Christmas season.

Los Pastores, A festival at Christmas time when the nativity is enacted.

madrina, godmother

mamacita, little mother, also an endearing term

mantilla, head covering for ladies worn on the street or in church

merienda, a light meal, luncheon, picnic

Natividad, nativity, Christmas

negocios, business, transactions, commerce

noticia, news in a general sense, information

novio/a, a betrothed person or a bridegroom/bride

Nuestra Señora de Belen, Our Lady of Bethlehem

otoño. autumn

paisanos, countrymen

paloma, a dove and term of endearment

patio, a courtyard, enclosed area

Padre Prefecto, Father Prefect, religious title

politico, political, politician

presidio, garrison of soldiers; fortress; citadel

Punta de los Lobos, Point Lobos today is a California State Reserve.

querido/a, lover, also dearest

rancho, cattle ranch

ranchero, in Mexico means a rancher

ranchería, a cluster of huts-hamlet-Indian village

reata larga, rope to tie horses, any rope. In early California, made of cow hide

rebozo, a woman's shawl in Mexico and early California

rodeo, cattle round up, enclosure for cattle, a winding road

reredo, altar decoration

rincón, a corner

rúbrica, a mark, a flourish added to one's signature

sala, drawing room, parlor, large room

Sardana, a special dance from Catalonia, Spain

sentimiento, a feeling, sorrow, sentiment

serape, used in Mexico, a blanket used as a cape or saddle blanket

Señor, a title that means mister, lord, owner

Señora, a lady, owner of a place

Señorita, a young lady, miss

siesta, afternoon nap

simpático/a, special as in congenial, sympathetic,

sombrero, hat

tortilla, a type of corn flat bread, shaped like a pancake

teclado, musical instrument

testamento, a will

vaquero, a cattle herdsman, cowboy

visitador general, visitor, inspector general

Zacatecano/a, a person from Zacatecas, Mexico

0-595-29062-0